TOO CLOSE FOR COMFORT

Easing back on the throttle, Amanda walked her *Bush-wacker* down to an easy limp and then to a complete stop. A gauss rifle slug caught her left arm as she turned to face her enemy. The shot snapped the 'Mech's limb back and wrenched through the shoulder socket. A particle cannon's shot glanced off her right flank, sending a cascade of melted armor onto the street.

She stood still, her wide-shouldered 'Mech squared off against the approaching *Falconer*. Her crosshairs pinned the enemy machine dead center, framing the gyro casing suspended from the main body. The reticle burned the hard golden color of a good sensor reading, the whistling tone alerting her to a solid missle lock.

Still, she couldn't fire.

What kind of damage could one missed shot cause? And what would a reactor overload do in the middle of a city? Amanda had run her course, given her people a chance to escape. Now she settled back into her seat, hands falling away from the control sticks as she waited for the end. A dark shadow crossed over her as a cloud hid the sun. The *Falconer* came to a full stop, preparing to fire. It was over. . . .

D1513441

BATTLETECH®

FLASHPOINT

Loren L. Coleman

A ROC BOOK

ROC
Published by New American Library, a division of
Penguin Putnam Inc., 375 Hudson Street,
New York, New York 10014, U.S.A.
Penguin Books Ltd, 27 Wrights Lane,
London W8 5TZ, England
Penguin Books Australia Ltd, Ringwood,
Victoria, Australia
Penguin Books Canada Ltd, 10 Alcorn Avenue,
Toronto, Ontario, Canada M4V 3B2
Penguin Books (N.Z.) Ltd, 182–190 Wairau Road,
Auckland 10, New Zealand

Penguin Books Ltd, Registered Offices:
Harmondsworth, Middlesex, England

First published by Roc, an imprint of New American Library,
a division of Penguin Putnam Inc.

First Printing, April 2001
10 9 8 7 6 5 4 3 2

Series Editor: Donna Ippolito
Designer: Ray Lundgren
Cover art by Ed Cox
Mechanical Drawings: Duane Loose and the FASA art department

 REGISTERED TRADEMARK—MARCA REGISTRADA

Printed in the United States of America

PUBLISHER'S NOTE
This is a work of fiction. Names, characters, places, and incidents either are
the products of the author's imagination or are used fictitiously, and any
resemblance to actual persons, living or dead, business establishments, events,
or locales is entirely coincidental.

To Allen and Amy Mattila,
for the many nights of movies
and wine and talk.

All it takes is pressure and time. That and the help of some very good people. I hope the following people know how important they were to this project.

Mike Stackpole, for the brainstorming and constant assistance. Dean Wesley Smith and Kristine Kathryn Rusch, who I haven't seen for far too long, though they always remain close by my career.

Jim LeMonds, to whom I am very grateful for that first push. My agent, Don Maass, for the recent nudges and signposts.

Bryan Nystul and Randall Bills, keepers of all things BattleTechy. Donna Ippolito, Annalise Raziq, and Wyn Hilty; for their various turns in helping this book see print. Jordan Weisman, Mort Weisman, Ross Babcock: the FASA trinity.

My parents, LaRon and Dawn Coleman, most recently for their help in reducing the stress of nonrelated topics.

Russell Loveday, Keith Mick, Allen and Amy Mattila, Vince Foley, Matt Dillahunty, Tim Tousely, Raymond Sainz, and Tim Huffer, for taking turns in "the gaming group that refuses to die." The Battleforce IRC community, for their continued pestering. Group W for the diversions they provide at GenCon. Doug Vernon, ditto that and add in a late morning the next day.

Laurie and Robin Olson, who helped out with extra child-watch duties.

My wife, Heather Joy, who bore up well with my multiple deadlines. My two sons, Talon LaRon and Conner Rhys-Monroe, and my lovely daughter, Alexia Joy, who gave up time with me that I plan to repay with interest now.

And the cats are still here—Chaos, Rumor, and Ranger—who get far too comfortable in my chair when I'm not looking.

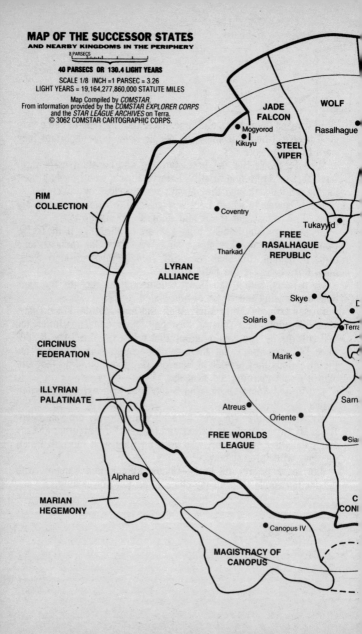

MAP OF THE SUCCESSOR STATES
AND NEARBY KINGDOMS IN THE PERIPHERY

8 PARSECS

40 PARSECS OR 130.4 LIGHT YEARS

SCALE 1/8 INCH =1 PARSEC = 3.26
LIGHT YEARS = 19,164,277,860,000 STATUTE MILES

Map Compiled by *COMSTAR*.
From information provided by the *COMSTAR EXPLORER CORPS*
and the *STAR LEAGUE ARCHIVES* on Terra.
© 3062 COMSTAR CARTOGRAPHIC CORPS.

JADE FALCON

WOLF

Mogyorod

Kikuyu

Rasalhague

STEEL VIPER

RIM COLLECTION

Coventry

Tukayyid

FREE RASALHAGUE REPUBLIC

Tharkad

LYRAN ALLIANCE

Skye

D

Solaris

Terra

CIRCINUS FEDERATION

Marik

ILLYRIAN PALATINATE

Sarn

Atreus

Oriente

FREE WORLDS LEAGUE

Sia

Alphard

C CONI

MARIAN HEGEMONY

Canopus IV

MAGISTRACY OF CANOPUS

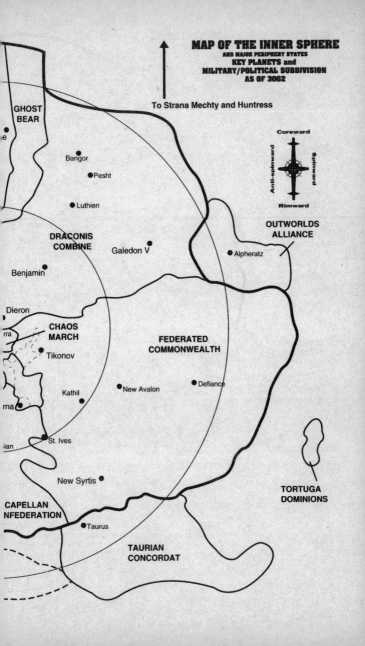

Legacy

(Two years before)

Huntress
Kerensky Cluster, Clan Space
28 March 3060

It would be the Uhlans' last stand. The hunters had driven their quarry to bay, all right. Only to have the Jaguars fall back on them with a vengeance they could never hope to match.

An early morning mist persisted into a noon fog, filling the shallow valleys of the Dhuan Swamp, roiling over sward-covered knolls that stood as small islands, barely discernible from one another. Thick and gray, the fog gave rise to shifting light and shadow that had the pursuing MechWarriors jumping at phantasms. It was as if Huntress herself favored the Clan defenders, would give them every last advantage they needed to drive away the invading armies.

The haze swirled about trees and boulders, tangled among the legs of the Uhlan BattleMechs, clinging to their upper bodies like a shroud of dingy, damp gauze. Kommandant David McCarthy, commander of the First Kathil Uhlans' Second Battalion, forced himself to look away from the ferroglass shield that protected his *Devastator*'s wraparound cockpit. Nine meters above the ground, swaying under the lumbering stride of the giant war machine, the sensation of flying through the fog was almost hypnotic.

He gave himself a mental shake. He couldn't sit here dreaming. He should be studying the sensor images fed back by his targeting and tracking suite. He shifted in his seat to ease muscles cramped from several long days of hard fighting in the cockpit of his 'Mech. If only the Smoke Jaguars would just leave off, let his unit fall back with the others.

David checked his unit's formation on the heads up display, a 360-degree sensor sweep compressed down to the 120-degree arc of his two-dimensional tactical screen. He'd positioned the unit in a loose arrowhead, with himself only one row back from point. They were down to sixteen BattleMechs—two abbreviated companies left of his original battalion—and every warrior surely as battered and exhausted as David himself. The rest were dead or scattered in the face of the Smoke Jaguar counterattack.

He hoped that at least a few had managed to fall back into the Dhuan Swamp to rendezvous with Leftenant-General Redburn's unit while David led this rearguard feint. The responsibility sat heavily on him. Even his neurohelmet, pressing down against the padded shoulders of his cooling vest, seemed heavier today. But he was still here, and still able to fight. How many of his men could no longer say that?

Too many.

His hundred-ton *Devastator* stood more than a head taller than most 'Mechs, not counting the *Berserker*, which was the only other assault-weight machine left to him. What happened next might have been due to that extra meter or two of height, his position near the front, or simply the fact that he happened to be concentrating on the sensor-image feed. Whatever the reason, David was the first to call out a sighting of the Smoke Jaguars. The enemy 'Mech icons spilled onto his HUD, the red shapes brightening the display's eastern edge like some kind of angry artificial dawn.

"Contact!" he called out, throttling his *Devastator* into a side-stepping walk that brought it to the top of a wide knoll. His throat tightened with the familiar surge of adrenaline. "Eight-zero through one-oh-five," he called over his neurohelmet mic.

A trio of enemy OmniMechs crowned a nearby rise to

the east, a collection of vague shadows in the mist. Four . . . five, a full Star. Then two Stars—ten Clan Omni-Mechs spread over the hillocks in a hunting line. Mostly heavies and assaults. David shivered and tried to blame it on the coolant surging through his vest. This was it, then. He and his men would buy General Redburn's retreat with their lives. He toggled for active targeting.

Its feet planted firmly in the loamy ground, the *Devastator* became a fixed weapons platform towering some ten meters over the hillock where it stood. David thrust forward the two gauss rifle barrels that served his humanoid 'Mech for arms. His targeting crosshairs burned from red to gold as they dropped over the computer-imaged silhouette of a *Mad Cat*, only to be jogged aside as the *Devastator* took a hard-hitting flank strike from a Jaguar warrior farther down the line. Energy cored into his 'Mech's left leg and armor melted off the side, splattering molten fire against the dark earth. David tied his particle projection cannon into his main trigger, fighting to reacquire target lock, and then jerking into a hasty shot. One gauss slug streaked toward the enemy 'Mech, the rail-propelled device smashing armor into impotent shards and opening a wound that his PPCs could exploit as their man-made lightning whipped across the *Mad Cat* like some god's scourge.

The bulk of the two forces were not far behind, the exchange of weapons staggering into a full-fledged storm. The air between the two lines opened up with a wash of violent energies as lasers and particle cannon fire lashed back and forth. A lethal rain of bullets hammered away and missiles arched up, over, and into each line, tearing up the ground, shattering trees and pounding armor into scrap. A common soldier wouldn't have lasted more than a few seconds trapped on such a hellish battlefield, except in the fog-shrouded valley that separated the two armies.

Even that would have become impossible as David ordered his lighter 'Mechs—a *Scarabus* and a pair of *Stealth*s—into the lower no-man's-land. With shorter-range weaponry, they needed to close distance to be effective. But they were protected only by light armor that could never hold up against the Clan assault. Speed allowed them a slight edge, but hardly enough against the Clans' superior targeting ability.

"We're taking heavy fire on the right," called Hauptmann Kennedy, David's one surviving company commander. Despite the grave news, her voice was calm. *"Gladiator, Thor, Cauldron-Born,"* she said, naming the more dangerous 'Mechs confronting her.

Brevet-Hauptmann Polsan was less composed. *"Gladiator, Kingfisher, Masakari, Daishi!"* he called—assault-class OmniMechs all. "We need help fast or we're done for!"

He'd barely spoken when a barrage of ruby and emerald laser fire pounded in against Corporal Denning's *Scarabus*. The pulses of coherent light gouged into its armor, slicing through molten-edged wounds and piercing the thirty-tonner's wedge-shaped chest. Golden fire blossomed inside the deep rents torn through the 'Mech's metal skin. The fusion reactor, freed from its magnetic shielding, quickly devoured the small BattleMech as it faltered midstride.

Escape panels blew away from the top of its head as the pilot's command couch ejected on a tongue of argent fire that chased it into the gloomy sky, and caught the pilot before a canopy could spread and glide him to safety. The flames consumed the ejection seat and pilot both in a silent, short-lived flare that arced briefly over the battlefield. No calls for rescue or mercy.

"Blake's blood!" Polsan said.

David McCarthy bit down hard on his lower lip to keep from making a similar outburst that would only serve to demoralize his own troops. Their job was to give their comrades the chance to fall back. Some of his people would simply not make it.

With slow, deliberate steps, David moved his *Devastator* forward while keeping up his pressure on the *Mad Cat*. Off his right shoulder, the gray silhouette of Kennedy's ax-wielding *Berserker* did the same. David nodded silent recognition to his senior company commander. Their two assault 'Mechs could stand up to the Clan machines better than anything else the Second Battalion fielded. Moments, he decided, triggering another salvo. It might buy them moments.

Heat washed through the *Devastator* cockpit with each

exchange of weapons fire drawing enough power to spike the fusion reactor. Heat bled upwards past the physical shielding to bake David in his cockpit. Sweat poured off his face and stung at his eyes. The cooling vest he wore kept his body temperature down enough to prevent heat stroke—though just barely—and special heat-sink technology labored to keep the rising temperatures under control. But the heat sinks couldn't keep that up indefinitely. He was risking reactor shutdown.

Damn the heat curve, he told himself, and tied his medium lasers into the main trigger as well. He pulled into another exchange, slapping at the shutdown override when it blared for attention.

The Clan *Mad Cat* was not holding up well. A dangerous heavy-class design, with weapon loads more suitable for an assault machine, David had chosen it as his early target for its vulnerability to hard-hitting weapons such as the gauss rifles he wielded. It limped along the far rise, attempting to hide its savaged right side from David's reach. A pair of gauss slugs slammed into its left leg, snapping the endosteel femur in half, even as two of his *Devastator*'s lasers reached past the leg to dig slender, sapphire fingers through the ruined armor of its right flank. The claws of brilliant energy ruptured its missile bin, lighting off solid propellant and detonating warheads.

Toppling toward the ground, the ammunition explosion gutted what remained of the *Mad Cat*'s torso cavity. One arm spun away and smashed into the side of a *Thor*, crushing its autocannon into twisted wreckage. Razor-sharp shrapnel sprayed a nearby *Vulture*, pitting and gouging otherwise pristine armor.

One finger crooked over his main trigger, David told himself to hold back. The loss of the *Mad Cat* wouldn't stop the Clanners. He knew that. This was no simple grievance to be settled easily. The Uhlans were here to help drive the Smoke Jaguar military into extinction, repayment for the decade of savage war that the Clan had visited upon the Inner Sphere. The Jaguars were fighting for survival, with a blind rage that the Uhlans couldn't match. David didn't plan to make it any easier for them. He would give his heat a chance to recover.

But that was a chance the Smoke Jaguars wanted to

deny him. Through the fog, David could see their line wavering along the far rise as several OmniMechs plunged down into the shallow valley that separated the two forces. Laser flashes appeared through the soup of fog that filled the valley, and David knew, sick at heart, that his light 'Mechs could not have survived the exchange.

"Here they come." Hauptmann Kennedy sounded as if she were reporting on the arrival of unwelcome neighbors, not a deadly military force.

The *Devastator* rocked back on its heels, a cascade of brilliant light washing over it as a *Masakari* leading the Jaguar charge trained its four energy cannon on David. Alarms blared their warnings as armor sloughed away to the ground, burned and smashed to oblivion. He hung in his seat thanks to a restraining harness, working control sticks and pedals to keep the one-hundred-ton BattleMech upright. The neurohelmet fed David's own sense of balance down into the *Devastator*'s stabilizing gyro, preventing him from losing his fight with gravity. Violent tremors continued their attempts to unseat him as he fought to hold the line, and his finger clenched over the trigger as he fired again . . . and again.

And again . . .

Indictment by Persuasion

═══ 1 ═══

DropShip Korpsbruder
Near Orbit, Kathil
Capellan March, Federated Commonwealth
8 October 3062

David McCarthy hooked his toes under the low ledge surrounding the DropShip's observation deck to keep from drifting off bodily in the null gravity. A career infantry sergeant had done just that earlier, stranding himself ten centimeters off the decking and just out of reach of the bulkhead. Tumbling and grasping for a handhold, he'd turned the air blue with invective that would have had raw cadets shaking in their boots but merely amused the ship's crew, who finally pulled him back to safety. The sergeant kept close to the handrails and foot anchors after that, the knuckles of his leathery hands white with his tight grip on the posts. Apparently, even a chestful of ribbons wasn't enough to keep your feet on the deck.

David had adjusted much more quickly than the space-green sergeant, having pulled much more time in space than most MechWarriors, thanks to his stint with Task Force Serpent. The Serpent fleet had spent ten long months secretly journeying to the Clan homeworlds, and then another eight returning to the Inner Sphere once they'd achieved their goal of destroying one whole Clan and ending the invasion for good. After an odyssey like that, David found the last three months of hopping star systems from Tukayyid to his homeworld of Kathil, in the Capellan March of the Federated Commonwealth, almost commonplace. Thinking of Huntress called up images of the final desperate battle in the Dhuan Swamp, but his mind quickly flinched away. It was easier to focus on the physical predicaments of zero gee, no matter how distressing. Nausea was a constant companion as his stomach protested the lack of gravity, and bile burned at the back of his throat.

It had been easier when the *Korpsbruder* remained under constant thrust, first accelerating away from the JumpShip that had delivered them to the Kathil system, and then decelerating as the *Leopard*-class DropShip finally fell in-system toward the planet. On most journeys, a DropShip stopped decelerating only after touchdown, letting passengers pretend they had almost never left terra firma.

On this trip, however, the *Korpsbruder* had to rendezvous in high orbit with the McKenna Shipyards to take on personnel rotating back to their ground facilities. The McKenna Shipyards were possibly the Capellan March's most important industry, one of the few shipyards in all of the Inner Sphere capable of reproducing the barely understood technology of Kearny-Fuchida drives. Sitting at the heart of every JumpShip, the engines were even more valuable in WarShips, making possible almost instantaneous travel between stars and connecting the various interstellar empires.

David only wished they'd hurry, as the DropShip had been drifting at the shipyard's loading dock for several hours, with only an occasional maneuvering thruster supplying any semblance of artificial gravity. Movement in zero-G felt awkward, uncontrolled. David might have felt more secure strapped down in his shipboard bunk, but after a few agonizing minutes, he couldn't stay put. The protective straps reminded him too much of a BattleMech's restraining harness—and that was exactly what he had come back to Kathil to forget.

Besides, he wanted to see the Federated Commonwealth's newest WarShip. The impressive new *Avalon*-class cruiser boasted advanced levels of automation and remote-station controls. The entire war fleet of the Federated Commonwealth consisted of less than fifteen of the vessels, and David knew such opportunities were not to be taken lightly.

In any event, it made for a good excuse to leave his room.

The *Robert Davion* hung in its construction gantry against a starscape of black sackcloth punctured by brilliant, diamond-edged flares. David always found the sky so much crisper, so much crueler, outside a planet's atmosphere. Specially placed mirrors collected and reflected back sunlight to bathe even the ship's eclipsed side in its harsh glare. The broad-hulled WarShip massed some 770,000 metric tons, and word was that it would begin its shakedown trials in six months. Still, at two kilometers away—an extremely close distance in spacefaring terms—the missile cruiser looked small and fragile despite the web of steel framework wrapped around its eight-hundred-meter length. Having seen other WarShips at a lot closer range, David decided he vastly preferred them at a distance. It made them seem more . . .

"Unimposing," he muttered to himself. That was the word.

"The hell you say."

David turned at the sound of the gravelly voice. So absorbed in observing the WarShip, he'd failed to note that someone had come up alongside him. The other man stood gazing fixedly at the distant ship through the ferroglass that shielded the entire exterior bulkhead of the observation deck. He was a short gamecock of a man in the uniform of a Lyran Alliance naval officer; his fiery red hair and the thrust of his sharp chin promised a fractious temper.

"She's an incredible piece of work," the man said. "A real hunter, that one."

David would have recognized him as naval personnel even without the black "spacer's stripe" running down the outside of his service-green dress slacks. It was obvious in his casual stance, the way he held himself in place with only the lightest touch of his fingers on the handrail, and in how close his face was to the transparent shield. The shield's ten centimeters of ferroglass made it stronger than the DropShip's armored bulkheads, but only some-one on the most familiar terms with space travel could be comfortable so close to that deadly, alien environment.

"I only meant from a distance," David said evenly, hop-ing to head off an argument with a superior officer. The two broad bands and a single narrow band on the spacer's epaulets made him a leftenant general—a rear admiral in the naval ranks.

"From a distance is where she can hurt you the most, *Hauptmann*." The spacer stressed the rank difference be-tween them as if that automatically won him the day. "The *Robert Davion* could blast us into component atoms with her lasers from only two klicks' distance. From two hundred klicks, those AR-10 missile launchers would break the *Korpsbruder*'s spine, and we would probably never know what hit us."

The man finally turned toward David with little more than a slight adjustment of his hand on the rail. He read David's uniform with a practiced eye, no doubt noting the differences that marked David as a solider of the Feder-ated Commonwealth, and a MechWarrior. He smiled thinly. "From orbit she could obliterate a 'Mech regiment without breaking a sweat. Impressive."

Impersonal, David translated. A WarShip could not hold territory or protect a city, except by laying waste to every-thing around it. The *Robert Davion*, for all its technological achievement and massive firepower, could not land on a planet, pick out the enemy and liberate the civilian sectors with minimal harm. BattleMechs could. David himself had done so in the past.

But the admiral was not really interested in a debate. David had no idea what he'd done to attract the admiral's ire. The guy was obviously spoiling for a fight. David shifted one foot free of the anchor while gripping the rail with his right hand so he could turn to face the admiral. He felt his ears burn from the rebuke. "I stand cor-rected, sir."

The admiral's eyes caught and held David's. Pale green surrounded by the brightest whites David had ever seen, they stared up at him, hardly blinking. They were eyes used to gazing into the vast reaches of space, and their distant focus made David feel like a mere pinpoint of light among thousands of others—until the admiral let his gaze drop to David's campaign ribbons. His focus narrowed like a laser, targeting on the black-gray-black ribbon at the end of a very short row. For all of the admiral's own "salad" of ribbons, this was one he would never earn.

"Serpent?" The admiral's voice was razor sharp, both jealous and accusing. "You fought on Huntress?"

"Yes, sir. Hauptmann David McCarthy, lately of the First Kathil Uhlans."

Suspicion flitted through the man's pale green eyes. "I thought the surviving Uhlans were forming up a new regiment in the Star League Defense Force."

David nodded. The Uhlans were—had been—a famous regiment, one of the most elite forces in the Federated Commonwealth. He wasn't surprised the admiral had heard and remembered the news. "I decided not to join," he said. "I'm returning to Kathil for assignment with the forming Capellan March Militia."

"Hrrm." The sound seemed to convey an impending verdict.

David was starting to understand how he had attracted so much hostility. He was a native of Kathil and the old Federated Suns, while the admiral obviously owed his allegiance to the Lyran state. Until recently, the two nations had been allied to form the Federated Commonwealth, ruled by Prince Victor Steiner-Davion. Five years back his sister, Katherine, seceded the Lyran half of the union to reestablish an independent Lyran Alliance, with herself as Archon. Then, while Victor's loyal armies were off fighting the Clans on Huntress and Strana Mechty, Katherine stole Victor's throne in the Federated Suns half of the Commonwealth as well. The injustice had raised hackles across the Commonwealth and even angered some in the Lyran Alliance, sparking bloody riots on Solaris VII not two months prior, as the violence of Solaris' arena games bled into the streets. Those riots were being held in check now only through Lyran force of arms.

Now the original Federated Commonwealth, with the Lyran Alliance already seceded, was a nation more divided than ever. Half of its inhabitants were swearing allegiance to the Archon-Princess, and half still hoping that Victor, recently named Precentor Martial of the Star

League Defense Force, would return to claim his rightful throne.

Katherine's insult to Victor had almost been enough to drive David into exile with Victor, taking permanent post with the surviving Uhlans' new SLDF regiment. Except that Prince Victor himself had urged his warriors to return home, hopefully to a peaceful service, and David's memories of Huntress haunted him. Eighty percent casualties among Task Force Serpent regiments. David's command shattered—David himself among the few survivors. The Kathil Uhlans disbanded. Taking into account the growing unrest on many Commonwealth worlds, accepting a post with his homeworld's militia had seemed the better choice.

"Admiral Jonathan Kerr," the other man finally said, deciding that the Task Force Serpent ribbon demanded at least a minimal acknowledgment. Kerr refused to offer his hand, however, and a salute was not required of David in such an informal meeting. The admiral thrust his chin toward the ferroglass shield and the WarShip beyond. "She's mine."

And he was welcome to her, David decided, also turning back to the transparent shield. He had no desire to get into a pissing contest with the Lyran officer—no matter how much the older man seemed to be trying to provoke one. The depth of Kerr's hostility had surprised him—he had no idea how close to the surface the Katherine/Victor tensions had risen in the FedCom. He stared back out into the darkness, his thoughts equally dark. An *Octopus* DropShip tug had moved in toward the front of the space-dock gantry, latching on to one of the portable factory complexes that had been attached to the framework. With the DropShip to provide scale—its spheroid hull dwarfed by the *Robert Davion*—David marveled at the size of such an engineering project.

"Tell me what it was like," Kerr said, startling David after a long minute's silence. "The fighting on Huntress." It carried the weight of a direct order—no doubt intentional.

And David was suddenly back in the harsh, gem-hued light, the dark plains lit by the fires of that final battle before the Uhlans retreated into the Dhuan Swamp—before he sacrificed his men to the ferocity of the Clan warriors, to save the others as they fell back. The shattered hulks of BattleMechs littering the ground like giant corpses left to rot where they fell. The treacherous footing as his *Devastator* trod over severed 'Mech limbs . . . the violent shaking of the cockpit . . . missile-lock warnings and reactor shutdown alarms and all the while the inexorable, relentless advance of the Clan Smoke Jaguar OmniMechs . . .

He squeezed his eyes shut, driving away the ghosts for a little while. "Hard," he said, knowing he could never explain that battle, especially to a naval officer. "Costly. But we won."

That was enough for most people of the Inner Sphere, who really didn't want to hear what their victory had cost in lives and materiel. All anyone really cared about was that the Inner Sphere had won. They had destroyed the Smoke Jaguar military on Huntress and then moved on to Strana Mechty, where Prince Victor put an end to the Clan invasion. And now Victor Steiner-Davion was living in exile, deposed by his treacherous sister, and the Uhlans were no more.

Kerr did not look satisfied with the simple answer, apparently suspicious that a native of the original Federated Suns might be holding back. Whatever grudge the man had with the Commonwealth, it ran deep. David decided to change the subject. "You're going to—"

Three harsh tones blared over the *Korpsbruder*'s address system, interrupting David and distracting Kerr: a warning that gravity would be shifting again as the DropShip engaged its main fusion drives. The deck thrummed with released power, and everyone settled back to the decking at one-half standard gravity—enough that David's nausea retreated and he could finally swallow away the acidic taste at the back of his throat. The DropShip powered up above the plane of the space-borne construction yard, the WarShip and its docking array falling from sight below the edge of the transparent shield. Beyond the titanic gantry, David could now see some of the assault-class DropShips sitting guard duty over the nearly completed WarShip.

"You're going to captain the *Robert Davion*?" David

asked once the alarms gave way to the fusion drive's distant rumble. He knew enough about naval protocol to understand that the term "captain" was a sign of respect for any officer in charge of a vessel.

Kerr continued to scowl daggers at David, apparently unmollified. "No. Executive officer." He leaned into the shield, getting one last glimpse of the WarShip before it disappeared off the aft beam. "But I know every centimeter of her, every system. She'll be mine someday." He grinned, but there was no humor in it. "Someday, when you're lucky enough to command a few hundred tons of war machines, I'll have the *Davion*."

The man sighed then, a moment of unexpected frustration that he likely did not notice he'd revealed, especially to someone he viewed as being on the opposing side of a growing conflict. "Two months," he said. "Two months before the official ceremony and my investiture aboard." He tapped impatient fingers against the railing and glared into space as if reading the positions of the stars. "All right, we're over the dock. Now we begin the roll toward Kathil."

David tried to hold the *Korpsbruder*, the *Robert Davion*, and Kathil in his mind all at once, picturing the three-dimensional model Kerr grasped instinctively. There was something he was missing. "Kathil is to the DropShip's rear, isn't it?" He caught Kerr's flash of annoyance, but plunged ahead. "I was trying to figure out why we needed to move above the WarShip's construction dock at all."

The admiral's smile was not kind. "Just try to cross between any construction dock or orbital factory of the McKenna Yards, and see if you even live to regret it."

After eight years in the military, David's first thought was for patrols. The *Robert Davion* would be protected by several assault vessels and an array of aerospace fighters, of course—each precious WarShip was an appreciable chunk of the military budget, after all. But factories? Why would the military condemn the *Korpsbruder* for cutting across a factory's line to the planet . . .

A piece of history floated up to the surface of his memory. "The microwave uplinks," he said.

Kerr nodded curtly. "Kathil has one of the most severe

approach paths of all planets in the Inner Sphere. As far as I know, only Outreach applies more stringent regulations."

David should have remembered about the microwave-power generation facilities. Weren't they a part of his Uhlans history? Several geothermic power plants situated around the world beamed power to the orbiting factories and construction yards in the form of tight-beam microwave transmissions. Most orbital facilities held geosynchronous positions and so received continuous power from one particular station. Others, such as the construction yard, which was situated at the LaGrange point between Kathil and its one small moon, had to switch between stations.

"I forgot about the power stations," he admitted, feeling all the more foolish for being lectured by a Lyran admiral about his homeworld.

Capitalizing on his advantage, Kerr took up a lecturing, almost condescending tone. "The Capellan Confederation tried to destroy some of those back in '29. Sent in the Death Commandos and Tau Ceti Rangers near the end of the Fourth Succession War. One of the microwave beams was redirected—smashed a full company right out of the atmosphere. No survivors."

David nodded and replied without thinking. "That was Morgan Hasek-Davion. He formed the Uhlans from Redburn's Delta Company, some veterans from the Fifth Fusiliers, and the local militia. We stopped the ones that landed."

He'd meant *we* in the collective sense that the Uhlans had done it, a regiment he'd been part of for eight years. But it sounded again like he might be trying to one-up the Lyran. And the reference to Morgan didn't help. Morgan Hasek-Davion had been assassinated while on Task Force Serpent, giving him a martyr's status over and above his position as a hero of the Fourth Succession War and Marshal of the Federated Commonwealth armies. It was no secret that his family supported Victor.

As hereditary March Lords, the Hasek family name carried no small amount of weight. George Hasek, Morgan's son and current Field Marshal of the Capellan March, was an outspoken critic of Katherine Steiner-Davion. If David could have picked a worse story to remind Kerr of their differences, he wasn't certain what it might be.

There was little doubt that the admiral was indeed thinking along those lines. He stared pale green lasers through David, silent for several long heartbeats. It was hard to guess what he might have done or said next. But David would never find out because the *Korpsbruder* rolled over and the world of Kathil appeared off the starboard observation deck, allowing him to snub the younger officer for his first view of the planet.

Turning back to the ferroglass shield and its view of the world, David was just as glad for the distraction. Blue waters framed yellow-green continents, the washed-out vegetation a result of chlorophyll-poor plant life that was used to the system's bright F-type star. Muran's mountain-wrinkled landscape was full beneath them, and the island continent of Thespia had just peeked its shorelines over the eastern horizon. As usual, the clouds piled up against Muran's western coast, drowning it in rain, while the interior remained an arid plain that ran all the way to the temperate and moderate eastern seaboard.

Yes, David knew this world. Kathil. Home.

And when you were running from your past, home was always the best place to go.

2

David's *Devastator* stood at the fore of the Kathil Militia's
'Mech bay. Feet planted wide, it fronted a company of
twelve BattleMechs frozen in review formation, three columns across by four rows deep. As the only assault-class
machine, the *Devastator* stood a full meter over the next-
tallest 'Mech and towered two meters over the thirty-five-
ton *Garm* that led the next lance. The *Devastator*'s broad
shoulders were a match for anything but the squat *Bushwacker* racked in directly behind it.

David stood on the floor of the bay, his head barely
reaching the 'Mech's giant ankle, and stared up at his war
machine. Stared up at it and felt a violent shiver run up
his spine.

No one noticed. Two astechs working from a lift were
touching up the 'Mech's new colors, a scheme of dark
green with red highlights. They wore breathing gear, a
necessary precaution with the industrial-grade paint. The
heavy aerosol had already driven David back eight or ten
steps, burning his sinuses and threatening to suffocate him
even in the well-ventilated space. A third astech had just
finished stenciling the words "Duty, Honor, Loyalty" over

the Capellan March insignia—a torch set against a red shield—on the *Devastator*'s left chest.

That was fine with him—as long as no one was asking for bravery. That had died on Huntress, along with most of his men. He just wished he didn't have such a strong feeling that the *Devastator* might be required—and soon.

"An impressive machine, sir."

David turned at the voice, a husky contralto belonging to an officer with leftenant epaulets on her uniform. Her honey-gold hair was pulled back in a severe knot that seemed only to set off her heart-shaped face and soft, chocolate brown eyes. She spoke with the manner of a veteran, though the lack of ribbons on her uniform told David she couldn't be more than two years in the military. He wondered if she was a member of his unit.

Both the leftenant and her enlisted escort, a corporal, managed to draw themselves up into some semblance of attention and an official salute, which David returned. The corporal immediately reverted into a relaxed slouch.

"Leftenant Tara Michaels, Corporal Richard Smith," she said. David recognized the names from the list he'd picked up from personnel; both were MechWarriors assigned to Second Company, his new command. Tara Michaels offered her hand and frowned slightly when David was a touch slow in taking it. "The old man sent us to find you, Captain. One of the techs pointed you out to us."

Old man? Captain? "The old man being . . . ?" he asked dryly. Leftenant Michaels had an unwarranted attitude for someone who likely had very little military experience. He was starting to realize the problems he might be facing with his new command.

"Major General Donald Sampreis. I think the LC—that would be Leftenant Colonel Damien Zibler, our battalion commander—is waiting with him."

David gave his *Devastator* one final glance, then nodded toward the tall hangar doors that opened onto the Kathil Militia's Radcliffe staging grounds. "Let's not keep them waiting, then," he said.

Corporal Smith trailed a few steps behind David and Tara as they went. She nodded regally to the technicians they passed along the way, obviously enjoying her status as a MechWarrior and an officer. "Word is that you fought on Huntress with the Uhlans," she said, stealing a side-long glance at his Task Force Serpent ribbon. "As a major."

David didn't show his surprise. "Major" was the old Federated Suns rank for the post he'd held. It was the second time Tara had defaulted to the old system, and David wondered whether that was by personal choice or command policy. "As a kommandant, yes," he said.

Tara's eyes narrowed only briefly at being corrected. "Was it as rough as they say?"

David didn't speak for a moment. "Yes," he said finally. He knew she wanted to hear his war stories, but Huntress still had too many painful memories attached to it for him to want to stir them up.

When they stepped outside, he felt refreshed by the late spring air, all the sweeter for displacing the paint fumes. He spat dryly, trying to clear the oily taste of paint that coated his mouth. He savored the pleasant weather after so many months in the artificial environments of space.

Tara indicated a nearby utility jeep, and the three piled in. She drove, with Smith lounging in the back. No one spoke, and the silence stretched out so long that David decided he wouldn't give Tara another chance to bring up the subject of Huntress.

"Does he ever speak?" he asked, loud enough for Smith to overhear.

"Only when I want to get in trouble," Smith said, his tone lightly sporting. "Besides, I'd rather listen to the lef-tenant talk."

David turned slightly to look at him. "Is that why you're a corporal now? You got in trouble?" One of a MecWarrior's privileges was usually automatic promotion to sergeant.

"No," Smith said, suppressing a smile, "but it didn't help."

"Corporals Smith and Barnes came up through the mili-tia's rural recruitment program on the continent of Thes-pia," Tara explained. "It's a probationary rank. We expect Barnes to make promotion on his yearly review, no problems."

David considered the implications of her comment and filed it away for future review. Another drawn-out silence followed, interrupted only by the artificial rush of wind created by the truck's speed. The base was large, containing several hundred 'Mechs and armored vehicles, as well as providing billeting for half of the thousand-man infantry regiment.

Radcliffe had formerly been the eastern seaboard's primary base, but newer facilities had been constructed in the planetary capital of District City while David was away. He was surprised to learn those facilities were currently under the control of another unit.

Traffic had picked up, both vehicular and pedestrian. David also sensed more tension in the air than one would normally expect on a peacetime base. It was as though something hovered, thick and heavy, over the hurrying men and women.

"I had hoped to speak with my staff sergeant this morning. Any idea where she might be?" he asked Smith over his shoulder, knowing that the enlisted ranks tended to band together.

As they rounded the corner of a supply warehouse, it was Tara who answered while maneuvering down a road between long rows of administration buildings. "She's in the sims today. When you didn't show at muster, she called for a training exercise."

If Tara had hoped to head off Smith's response, she was unsuccessful. "Yeah," the corporal drawled from the back seat. "She said it was time to give Pachenko's Pack another good drubbing. Tara's Terrors had their turn last week."

Tara blushed furiously, avoiding David's gaze. She braked the jeep to an abrupt and rocking halt and pointed out some nearby buildings. "You'll find the upper brass in there, Captain. Anything else we can do for you?"

David nodded curtly. "Find Sergeant Major Black and tell her training is suspended for the day. Have the whole company report for a meeting in two hours, back in the 'Mech bay." Then he caught himself. The 'Mech bay was the last place he wanted to be. "Wait. Let's make that something more suitable for introductions. You know the base, Leftenant. Find us a room and send Corporal Smith to get me." He glanced back at Smith. "You can drive?"

Smith opened his mouth to say something, hesitated, then shrugged. "Yeah, I can drive."

Sliding out of the jeep, David began considering what he was getting into with the Kathil edition of the Capellan March Militia. Sloppy attitudes. Overconfidence. Familiarity with superiors—and that one ran from the lowest enlisted position at least up through Leftenant Michaels. Borderline insubordination from Smith, though David couldn't be certain if the man was deliberately insolent or merely unschooled in proper discipline. Not to mention a staff sergeant setting herself up in competition with his lance commanders, both of whom had taken on airs—along with prideful lance names.

Those thoughts kept him preoccupied all the way through the front doors of the command center and past the wards of two secretaries, until he finally reached the working office of Major General Sampreis. The "old man" greeted David personally at the door, then led him into a room smelling of cigar smoke and paperwork. David pondered briefly how those two scents seemed to be typical of offices of regimental commanders throughout the Inner Sphere. A light haze drifted near the ceiling, evidence of a cigar only recently extinguished.

Sampreis actually looked fairly young for his rank; David guessed the man was in his early forties. Of course, the large holograph on his desk of Sampreis shaking hands with Field Marshal George Hasek, duke as well as military commander of the Capellan March, might have something to do with that. In fact, David spotted at least three other pictures on the wall that had been taken with more than a few friends in high places. One of them, a holopic of Morgan Hasek-Davion, caught his eye, and he felt a sudden lump in his throat.

"I'm a friend to his son," Sampreis explained, following David's gaze. David took that to mean the general was squarely in Victor Davion's camp. George Hasek was one of the strongest supporters of the former Prince of the Federated Commonwealth.

Sampreis adjusted the formal cape of his uniform, then moved behind the kidney-shaped desk. "We all looked up to Morgan. His loss was tragic."

David waited for the inevitable questions about Task

Force Serpent, but none came. That surprised him enough that he almost missed the fact that Sampreis used the old Federated Suns rank when introducing David to Leftenant Colonel Damien Zibler, David's superior officer. He accepted a seat next to Zibler.

The man was recruiting-poster material: an impressive build strapped over a 180-centimeter frame, reddish-blond hair, sparkling blue eyes, and a proud nose. His grip was firm. He wore the old Federated Suns dress uniform, sans the formal cape, the same as David.

"Welcome home," Zibler offered as they all retook their seats. "Captain McCarthy is a Kathil native," he explained to the general. "We met several years ago when he was still serving in the Uhlans."

Sampreis pursed his lips. "Local family?"

"Further inland," David said, then spent the next few minutes answering inquiries concerning his background and pedigree. Sampreis seemed genuinely interested, but then family ties must have meant a lot to the general on his way up the chain of command.

"Most of them are near Vorhaven," David said. "About a dozen managed to make it to District City for a quick reunion after I landed. Hardly enough to catch up, but it made my arrival a partial homecoming." He paused. There was a fine line between making polite conversation and boring your new CO.

"Apologies for my tardiness today, General," he said, giving Sampreis an opening to change the subject. "I didn't find out until this morning that I was to report down here in Radcliffe and not to the District City base."

Sampreis glanced at Zibler. "Well, now, that's a touchy subject," he said. "We've got orders to occupy District City. Field Marshal Hasek officially activated the Kathil CMM last month, and he ordered the Eighth Regimental Combat Team to turn garrison of the planet over to us. Their orders were to relocate to the world of Lee, but the Eighth has refused to budge, despite efforts by Duke VanLees to pry them out."

David frowned. "Koster VanLees is putting up with that? I remember the Duke being made of sterner stuff." Then he remembered that Duke Koster must be in his seventies now.

"Not the father," Sampreis said, "the son. Duke Petyr VanLees. He's got his father's fortitude, but the Eighth RCT has a regiment of 'Mechs and eight supporting regiments that say they're staying."

"Why are they so determined not to leave Kathil?" David asked, genuinely puzzled. It was true that the shipyards made Kathil an important industrial planet, but Lee was near enough the border with the Capellan Confederation that a posting there could promise significant military action. The RCT would not lose any prestige in the move.

"The Eighth was appointed as Kathil's garrison force last year, by Katherine Steiner-Davion," Zibler said, notably omitting her title of Archon-Princess. Zibler was also following the Federated Suns refusal to acknowledge her change to the name Katrina, a rallying point for many Lyran citizens.

"Kathil is an important world, but there's no significant danger of attack from the Capellan Confederation. The real reason the Eighth is here is to guarantee that Katherine retains control of the shipyards—and, more importantly, the WarShip fleet. Lieutenant General Weintraub, commander of the Eighth RCT, has recently announced that his orders came personally from Katherine Steiner-Davion, and until she tells him otherwise, he will not leave Kathil to 'unproven defenders.' "

"That would be us," David said, realizing that the situation on Kathil was more tense than he'd suspected. Admiral Kerr's hostility aboard the DropShip was beginning to make some sense, as was the fact that a Lyran officer was being "loaned" to a FedCom WarShip. If the political situation had degenerated to the point that a Regimental Combat Team was defying a Field Marshal's orders, then the conflict between Katherine and Victor's supporters would soon boil over—just as it had on Solaris.

"To his credit, Mitchell Weintraub has a point." Sampreis seemed able to see both sides, if not more, of any issue, another sign that his position was as much a political appointment as a military one. Unfortunately, in David's experience, politicians were better at starting conflicts than at avoiding them. Cool heads were required now—for Kathil's sake.

"We're still having problems activating the CMM on

Kathil," Sampreis continued, "though I hope that with a strong officer corps we can handle the transition smoothly. Meanwhile, we have to trust George Hasek to pry the Eighth RCT off Kathil. Cooler heads will prevail, Captain."

"Yes, sir." David could read the dismissal in the general's voice. "With your permission, then, I should get to know my new command."

Sampreis nodded. "Dismissed."

Zibler offered his hand again, and David extended his as well. The colonel met his eyes as they shook hands, and something in the other man's eyes made David linger in the hall outside Sampreis' reception area. He sampled warm water from a nearby fountain, read the posted "Orders of the Day," and straightened his uniform in the reflection of an encased model of a Union-class DropShip.

His gray-blue eyes looked dark in the ghostly image reflected by the thin glass. Lifeless. Deeper in the glass, caught somewhere between his reflection and his past, a lone *Scarabus* ran across fogged ground, its paired medium lasers darting ruby arrows into an unseen enemy line. The mirrored hall lights blurred into the colored streaks of laser fire, converging on the hapless light 'Mech, ripping it apart.

A voice whispered in his mind: *And here they come.*

"Thanks for waiting." Zibler's voice brought David back to the present. He laid one hand lightly on David's shoulder, a gesture of camaraderie. Zibler was just that kind of officer.

"It's good to see you again, sir," David said sincerely. He had always regretted not getting to know Zibler better when they'd first met several years ago; perhaps now they would have an opportunity to make up for lost time.

"I'd like to speak with you at length, later, but I thought a word or two on our way out now . . . ?" He trailed off.

David nodded. "Of course."

"I usually don't pry into my officer's reasons for taking assignment with me, but your case is a little different." Zibler lowered his voice. "For instance, how does a hero from Task Force Serpent get demoted en route to his next assignment?"

David shifted uneasily under the title of "hero." "There

wasn't much left of my personal command," he said, "and our new Marshal of the Armies decided to disband the Uhlans." It was hard to keep the bitterness out of his voice when referring to Nondi Steiner as Marshal of the Federated Commonwealth armies. She was a blue-born Steiner who would forever place the Lyran Alliance ahead of the Commonwealth.

"When I declined to follow the rest of my regiment into the Star League Defense Force, I was officially discharged from service. The only way to get my commission reinstated was to return to active duty from retirement. The open position in the Kathil CMM called for a hauptmann, so my rank was reduced accordingly."

"If you haven't already noticed, Captain McCarthy, you'll find that many regiments have reverted to the old rank system. A silent protest that we don't appreciate being overrun by Lyran prejudice." There was no rancor in Zibler's explanation—only the calm statement of fact. "So was it a bureaucratic snafu?"

David shook his head. "No. It was intentional. Several veterans fell through the cracks that way, and we've heard rumors of returning veterans getting shoved into assignments along the Periphery or in other high-danger areas. There was a lot of pressure on us simply to retire."

"Katherine is worried about having her brother's supporters in her army. She should be." Zibler's words were angrier now, which David figured had to do with the way Katherine had betrayed her brother. "General Sampreis is too trusting of George Hasek. The Field Marshal is a good man, and loyal to the Capellan March, but he's not here. He doesn't know just how bad it could get. If you've seen vids of the Solaris VII riots . . ."

David nodded. "The latest news reports say that the gaming stables split on nationalist lines," David elaborated. "Mainly Steiner and Davion." The family names, historically governing the Lyran Alliance and the Federated Suns, respectively. "The footage says the rest. 'Mechs fighting in the streets instead of in the arenas. The Game World is being held in a state of martial law, but just barely."

"Then you know what I mean when I say that I can see

it happening here," Zibler said solemnly. "There's trouble coming."

David knew the feeling only too well. It had haunted him ever since his run-in with Admiral Kerr. He shuddered inwardly to think of a slaughter like that on Solaris happening on his homeworld, maybe even to his family. But it was hard to decide how much of that was a soldier's instinct, and how much was the residue from his time on Huntress.

"How bad is it?" he asked, knowing Zibler wouldn't pull punches.

"You wouldn't believe some of the things Weintraub is saying." Zibler's blue eyes blazed angrily. "It doesn't seem to matter to him that Field Marshal Hasek has the indisputable right to move troops in the March as he sees fit. In fact, he's openly calling Field Marshal Hasek and Duke VanLees traitors, claiming that they want to subvert the rightful government and turn everything over to Victor."

"So much for calmer heads prevailing," David said, but he had a hollow feeling inside. "Is there any hope of reprieve?"

Zibler smiled grimly. "Certainly. But only if Katherine Steiner-Davion recognizes George Hasek's authority and supports his orders that the Eighth RCT transfer to Lee, where Field Marshal Hasek ordered them."

That was an outcome David wanted to believe in but couldn't.

David thought that sending the Eighth to the border world of Lee made good strategic sense, what with the Capellan Confederation in the grip of their militaristic Xin Sheng fervor. If the sabre-rattling got out of hand, the fighting in the St. Ives Compact could easily bleed over into FedCom space, and Lee would need the Eighth's protection. As he and Zibler stepped from the building out into Kathil's bright sunlight, the day didn't seem as warm, and what had been a refreshing breeze now gave him a chill. "Don't take this the wrong way, sir . . . but are we ready for a fight?"

If Zibler was shocked, he didn't show it. David wondered how long his commanding officer, and others, had been asking themselves that same question; how long since they'd begun to sense dark storm clouds piling up just over the horizon. Ever since Katherine stole Victor's throne two years ago? Maybe. Ever since the outbreak of violence on Solaris VII? That seemed more likely.

"Candidly?" Zibler asked. "No. I'm still hoping it won't come to that. Marshal Hasek might find a diplomatic solution yet. Or he could withdraw his orders to transfer the Eighth RCT."

"You mean knuckle under." From what David had known of Morgan Hasek-Davion, founder of the Uhlans, he couldn't see that happening. Not if George Hasek was indeed his father's son.

"Compromise," Zibler corrected. "Kathil is as important as any March capital world because of the shipyards— maybe more so. That gives the nobles room to maneuver. And it would give us the time we need to polish up the militia."

David ran his fingers across his closely shorn dark hair. "Right now I'll be happy just knocking off some of their rough edges."

"You've met your people?"

"A few, and I've already heard and seen enough to know I've got my work cut out for me."

Zibler continued down the walk at a leisurely pace, looking like a man trying to put an unpleasant subject in the best light. "I can't say you're wrong," he said finally. "Bottom to top, the CMM has no sense of 'self,' not as a unit. Those who think they do are generally under the misconception that we're the heirs to the Uhlan traditions and reputation, and that's a very dangerous conceit for inexperienced soldiers. They're liable to bite off more than they can chew, and that will get warriors killed." He grimaced. "I'm sorry to say that your company might be the worst off, especially given your ties to the Uhlans."

"If I can disavow them of that, I will," David said. "Hopefully I can use my past to influence them in a positive way."

"Can't hurt," Zibler agreed. "Soldiers generally respect the word of a veteran—especially a war hero." He caught David's sour look. "It's true, and you know it. You'll be something of a celebrity for a while. Especially after the presentation."

David glanced sharply at Zibler. "What presentation?"

Zibler smiled, this time with the promise of what he undoubtedly thought was good news. "The word arrived ahead of you. Andrew Redburn nominated you for the Star League Medal of Valor for your rearguard action on Huntress, and First Lord Theodore Kurita conferred it. I guess it goes on your previous service record, but since you're not SLDF, you don't get the automatic promotion. Still, the medal is yours."

His. Bought with the lives and limbs of his soldiers. Denning. Whidbey. Kennedy. Damn it, too many! "Can we hold off on that?" he asked, straining to sound casual. "Give me time to make a dent in them before we haul out the flags and banners and tell them what a great and glorious thing it is we do?"

Zibler looked narrowly at him, but nodded. "At your discretion, of course. Sampreis won't care for it—I know he's looking forward to making a ceremony out of the presentation. But I can probably buy you some time."

David exhaled sharply, his relief palpable. "I appreciate that."

"I know you do." Zibler stopped and looked directly at David. "I've seen the battlerom footage they've released. Watched them one battle at a time. But I still can't imagine what it must have been like to live through the entire campaign on Huntress."

For the first time, David was tempted to talk about it with someone who hadn't been there. Maybe it was the respect and liking he had for Zibler, or maybe it was because Zibler hadn't tried to pry. Neither had Sampreis, of course, but David thought that was because the general didn't much care. "Ask me about it sometime," David said slowly. "Later, though. I'd like to meet my people today. But . . . ask."

"I may," Zibler said. "Good luck with your new command, David."

David nodded absently and walked on alone, remembering the screams, the explosions, the flames, and the oven-like temperature of his cockpit. The questions about Huntress were always the same. What was it like? How bad was it?

Bad enough that David believed with all his heart that

he should have died on Huntress. Bad enough that he woke every day with a feeling of impending doom, as if the danger he'd barely escaped was racing to catch up with him.

Bad enough that David wasn't sure he could pilot a BattleMech into battle ever again.

3

Hall of Nobles
District City, Kathil
Capellan March, Federated Commonwealth
20 October 3062

The Hall of Nobles, situated in District City, was Kathil's most impressive structure and the gem of the planetary capital. No expense had been spared in its design and construction, as if some long-forgotten duke had wanted to impress visitors already overawed by the spacefaring docks and shipyards in orbit around his world. Grand arches stretched even the simplest corridors into titanic proportions, easily large enough for the biggest assault 'Mech to stroll along. Marble columns held lintels of thick, polished hardwood over every doorway, and higher up, balconies opened along the walls.

Even the janitor's closets, Kommandant Eván Greene suspected, would have vaulted ceilings trimmed in gilt.

Greene was part of General Weintraub's military entourage, along with the Eighth RCT's other two 'Mech battalion commanders. At 190 centimeters, a great deal of that leg, Eván stood of a height with General Weintraub and easily matched his commanding officer's long gait. The other four officers had to quicken their stride to keep up. Eván felt a touch of amused pity for the short attendant,

Duke VanLees' man, who almost had to sprint in order to guide them.

This was his first venture into the Hall of Nobles, though not his first in attendance at a battle between Weintraub and VanLees. There had been two other, similar meetings between the general and the duke in the past week, each less productive than the last, each getting no closer to breaking the stalemate. What would it be today? Subtle threats? Not-so-subtle incentives—bribes, really—to encourage the general to obey George Hasek's commands to leave Kathil? Shouting?

At least the Kathil Militia had seen fit to stay out of the conflict thus far—probably realizing that their soldiers were too raw, too new to combat to be of any use in a military confrontation. As far as the militia was concerned, the longer the stalemate went on, the longer they had for training—a fact Eván hoped General Weintraub was keeping firmly in mind.

Eván smoothed his salt-and-pepper hair back from a receding forehead, a habit he'd recently acquired. He consoled himself with the fact that his mustache was still raven black, helping to soften his hatchet-faced features. He fastidiously straightened the gold braids falling down his right arm and smoothed flat the Nagelring Academy sash that circled his slender waist, then hung in a loop down his left leg. But with each long stride, the blue and red sash billowed out proudly, rendering his efforts immediately useless. He desisted from a second attempt, and then noticed the other battalion commanders picking even more nervously at their dress uniforms. The Hall of Nobles apparently had that effect on people.

But not Eván. The lavish expense spent in maintaining the monument might intimidate his fellow MechWarriors, but he had long believed he belonged in a place like this. This was his due. Not that he could claim a rung on the social ladder with any noble, even a common lord. Not yet. But this was a monument erected for the pretentious—for those with ambitions.

And Eván had his ambitions. That was the reason he wrangled himself into every meeting he could, looking for those rare chances to stand out, to be noticed. He did not intend to stay a MechWarrior forever. He was impatient to advance in the ranks. What he needed was a grand gesture, one heroic stroke in battle that would gain him the recognition he craved.

After the excesses of the grandiose Hall, their final destination came as something of a surprise. Eván was third through the door after General Weintraub and Leftenant General Karen Fallon, edging out the other two battalion commanders and even Leftenant General Detton, who commanded the Eighth's three armor regiments.

The room they entered was fairly spartan, at least by the opulent standards of the Hall of Nobles. No lavish artwork decorated the walls; no overstuffed chairs occupied the floor. Flanked by a pair of advisers, Duke Petyr VanLees was already seated at a crescent-shaped table at the far end of the room. The group of nobles awaited the cadre of officers like some tribunal about to pronounce judgment. VanLees had obviously put a lot of thought into the psychological effect he wanted to create—to make the general look like a criminal come to be judged.

Very likely what was about to happen.

"General Weintraub," the duke said coldly in greeting. He did not rise or make other pretense toward civility. He had chosen a paramilitary uniform today, including a purple cape cut along the lines of classic Federated Suns military dress. "If you and your officers would take a seat?"

"Very kind of you, Duke VanLees." Weintraub's tone was equally frosty. "Though I doubt we'll be staying long enough to get comfortable."

Petyr VanLees smiled, flashing white teeth that looked all the brighter against his olive-toned skin. He stroked his square-trimmed beard with one hand. "I have thought the same thing for several weeks now, General. Yet still the Eighth remains on Kathil, against all orders to the contrary. Please. If you insist on staying, for now, have a seat."

Eván recognized at once why the general did not want to sit down. If the RCT officers attempted to sit inside the short arc of the curved table, they would be pressed for elbow space and unable to look at one another without having to twist about in the hard-backed chairs. However, to remain standing would cede a strong tactical advantage to the nobles, who remained sitting in relative comfort.

Karen Fallon solved the problem by walking forward and pulling three seats away from the table, angling them in toward Duke VanLees and ignoring the junior nobles. The three senior officers sat, and the three battalion officers, including Eván, took up standing positions behind them, creating an impressive backdrop.

While Petyr VanLees led a quick round of introductions—no doubt trying to reinvest his snubbed companions with some measure of authority—Eván quickly analyzed the room. It was a cold space, with marble tile floors and bare walls of dark-stained hardwood that reflected their voices with a sharp echo. The only windows were narrow and set too high for a view. Buzzing fluorescents cast down harsh light. There was little compromise in this place—it was a severe room, meant for discussing hard matters.

Duke VanLees had not even brought in a scribe. What happened behind doors such as these remained off the record. And there was no compromise in the way the nobles were sitting: leaning forward, braced for combat.

Eván readied himself for a shouting match.

"I speak not only for myself," the duke said by way of coming to the point, his voice taking on a haughtiness that spoke of practice in royal court, "but also for the Duke of New Syrtis and the Lord of the Capellan March, Field Marshal George Hasek. We are distressed by the unwillingness of the Federated Commonwealth's Eighth Regimental Combat Team to recognize proper and lawful orders delivered by us; to wit, demanding your relocation to the planet Lee." The formal language felt out of place in this room—which Eván felt sure was intentional.

Weintraub merely crossed his big arms over his barrel-like chest and repeated the same explanation he had delivered the month before. "Kathil is an important world," he said smoothly. "I cannot in good faith leave it in the hands of an untested militia."

A junior noble sitting to VanLees' right shuffled some papers together, set a small electronic notepad atop them, and offered them to Weintraub. "I have here reports on the material readiness and skills assessment regarding the

Kathil Capellan March Militia," she stated. "These reports have been verified by Duke Hasek to be—"

"The general has seen those reports," Karen Fallon said.

"—to be adequate in all events save a full military invasion," the countess continued as if there had been no interruption. "Is the general privileged to military information that suggests this is a possibility?"

Eván forced a short bark of laughter, drawing the eyes of every noble seated opposite. His mouth was dry, but he plunged ahead. "How could General Weintraub answer that if your own March Lord has not deigned to inform you of any such possibility?" he said pointedly.

It was a calculated risk, speaking out of turn. But Eván knew the best way to trivialize the noble's argument was to have it answered from the lower ranks. His companion kommandants shifted uneasily at his ploy, but Karen Fallon glanced momentarily back at him, a look of interest mingled with the beginnings of admiration. Recognition. The first step toward delegation, and then further promotion. Eván had handled it just right—neither admitting nor denying any such information, but attacking instead the countess' logic.

The gambit stalled, Duke VanLees took up the flag. "Regardless, the point stands that the Kathil CMM has a full 'Mech command and four supporting regiments—more than adequate for protecting the planet. You will leave."

"My Katzbalger has eight regiments." Weintraub's voice was low and dangerous as he called the Eighth RCT by its common name—German for an undisciplined, close-quarters combat. His use of the nickname just then could not have been accidental. "Three armor and five infantry, all with more experience than your militia. That says we are staying."

VanLees' manner dropped from chilly to glacial in a split second. "Was that a threat, general?"

Eván held his breath, realizing that this time the general might have gone too far. Claiming to take orders only from the Archon-Princess was a defensible, if controversial, position. Suggesting that the Eighth would use force against its own ostensible allies was a line neither the general nor the duke was willing to cross. Yet.

Fortunately, the general knew when to sidestep. "Not

at all, Duke VanLees," he lied, and everyone knew it. "Merely a comparison."

A local baron leaned into the conversation, hands splayed flat on the table's dark wood. "We also have the Second NAIS cadre on planet."

"Children," Weintraub scoffed, secure in his own strength. "Though they can at least claim the credit of a decent academy."

"The Second is the most skilled training cadre in the Commonwealth," the baron protested. "A valuable addition—"

The general's thick black eyebrows drew together in a frown, as he cut off the baron in mid-sentence. The man was the very picture of stubborn determination. "I was ordered to Kathil by the Archon-Princess personally," he rumbled. "Those orders have not been countermanded to my satisfaction."

The duke looked down his thin nose at the general. "And can you sketch out for me this chain of command that bypasses four of your own superior officers and at least three nobles with sovereign rights to order you off their worlds during peacetime? I would very much like to see this, Mitchell, and to have the armed forces Administrative Department verify a line of authority from Katherine Steiner-Davion directly to you."

"I am here to protect the Archon's interests on Kathil," Weintraub retorted. "I was not ordered here by George Hasek, and I will not allow him—or you, *Petyr*—to remove me in defiance of the Archon's wishes. Or does George Hasek no longer recognize Katrina Steiner-Davion as his Archon-Princess?"

"You pretentious, low-browed, son of Amaris!" Van-Lees shouted, leaning forward across the table, trembling with rage. "No true noble of the Federated Suns could ever—" The countess' hand on VanLees' arm warned him to say no more, and the duke subsided into an angry glare.

No true noble of the Federated Suns could ever call Katrina their Princess? Eván had no doubt that was Van-Lees' meaning. Katrina had, after all, deposed Victor Steiner-Davion's regent, their sister Yvonne, and taken his throne. And she was manifestly preferential to the Lyran

Alliance over Federated Suns worlds such as Kathil. To Eván, it didn't much matter which member of the family sat on New Avalon. To a staunch Davionist, though, someone who had never erased that line that separated the Lyran Alliance from the Federated Suns, Katrina no doubt looked like the evil usurper.

But regardless of the truth of the matter, at this moment speaking it aloud would constitute high treason. Every RCT officer except Eván and the general himself had leaned forward in anticipation of hearing it.

Eván smiled thinly. *Almost, VanLees. Almost.*

The duke quivered with pent fury. His skin had flushed even darker, and his eyes cut like lasers. But when he spoke, his cultured voice had regained its studied calm. "I will not forget this conversation, General. And I will no longer tolerate insubordinate troops in my capital."

Weintraub spread his hands wide and shook his head, as if confused by the duke's words. His reply, however, promised that he understood the other man perfectly. "Your pardon, Duke VanLees, but what can you do about it?"

If there was a more blatant declaration of war that could be made between the two men, Eván could not think of it. The duke had made a mistake coming down to Weintraub's level. The general had the power of the Eighth RCT backing him up and a lifetime's experience with posturing, threats, and the proper use of force.

But regardless of whatever psychological victory the general could claim, the meeting had accomplished nothing. These arguments had been made, by both sides, countless times in the past few weeks. For all the pomp of the Hall of Nobles and the pretension of VanLees' seating arrangements, the confrontation had produced no better results than any other. They were at a stalemate.

Petyr VanLees rose, fishing a sealed folder from a nearby stack of papers. He tapped it into one open palm, as if weighing its importance. Eván did not like the look on his face; the duke clearly had one card he hadn't yet revealed.

"As I understand it, General, your primary objection has always been the lack of proven troops on Kathil," the duke said, his tone suddenly deceptively mild. Eván frowned in suspicion, and he imagined Weintraub must be doing the same. "I thought, however, that you might not be aware of my family's ties to the First Capellan Dragoons."

Evan was sure that wasn't true. Everyone knew that the First Capellan Dragoons had once been the fealty-bound troops of the Duke of Kathil. They'd been sold, however, to the regular armed forces of the Federated Suns years ago by then Duke Michael Hasek-Davion. Duke Michael's long power struggle against the ruling Davion line left him chronically short of cash and he'd been forced to part with the unit. The Dragoons were known to be hard men, with a resounding loyalty to the Capellan March.

"Your father sold them off back when George Hasek's traitorous grandfather tried to steal Hanse Davion's throne," the general said.

This time, the slur rolled off Petyr VanLees easily, like small-arms fire bouncing off BattleMech armor. "Here"— he brandished the envelope—"are written orders from Field Marshal Hasek, ordering your forces to relocate to the world of Lee. It is the last polite response you are likely to get." He tossed the envelope to the table in front of Weintraub, who picked it up as he rose slowly to his own feet.

"Attached to those orders," VanLees went on, "you will find an official notice that the First Capellan Dragoons are en route to Kathil for the purpose of increasing our garrison forces. I have purchased back my family's regiment from the Field Marshal, General." The duke's mouth was a thin, hard line, just the aggressive side of a smile.

"In a few short weeks, the Capellan Dragoons will be home," he said. "Then we will see whether or not you leave my world."

4

"She's going to give you trouble," Damien Zibler said.

David nodded, rubbing one hand along his smooth-shaven jaw. He brushed the hard, thin line of knotty scar tissue hidden just beneath the jawline—another souvenir of Huntress. Most of the time he forgot about it, remembering only when he shaved. The five-centimeter gouge had missed the right carotid artery, though it had bled freely enough. He remembered his throat slick with warm blood, and those first few seconds of panic.

"Sergeant Major Black has given me little but trouble for the past week and a half," he said. "Why should today be any different?"

"Give her time. She's one of the best we have—the problem is that she knows it. She'll be slow coming around, but she will eventually. You just have to have patience."

The two men stood in one hall of the Radcliffe Base's primary training facility, just opposite a large window that looked into a ready room filled with David's company. Half of the MechWarriors were ignoring them, while the other half pretended they weren't watching their senior officers in return. David crossed his arms over his chest, leaned against the wall, and gave off the same studied lack of interest. He noticed that the tiled floor was already losing its daily battle with scuff marks from black-soled military boots.

"They're all slow in coming around," he said. "Except Tara—Leftenant Michaels. She's trying hard to understand what I'm doing, and why. The rest don't take well to the new regs." David glanced at his superior. "Am I pushing too hard?"

Zibler smiled with warm humor. "They're MechWarriors, David. If they can't take a good shove, they're in the wrong profession." His light tone darkened a few shades. "Though I have received two requests for transfer."

"Black," David guessed, though he was surprised to discover that the thought actually hurt him. Despite her prickly attitude, he thought well of Amanda. "And Smith." The irrepressible corporal chafed more than anyone else under David's tightened command. Well, perhaps not more—just louder.

"Actually, no." Zibler tugged his left sleeve straight and made a pretense of studying the cuff. "Though if you really want to know . . ." He trailed off, leaving David the opening.

"No, it's better if I don't." David said. In the Uhlans, the men had trusted each other with their lives. The least he could do was trust his company with training. "How did you leave it with them?"

"I haven't. I thought I should at least mention it to you first, see how you wanted to handle it."

David frowned, trying to make up his mind. If he knew who it was, he might tailor a response. But he couldn't spend all his time catering to eleven wounded egos. "Turn a deaf ear toward them for a while," he said finally. "Once a few of them start responding to the tighter discipline, most of the problems should vanish. When I loosen things up again, I think we'll have a unit to be proud of, and one with more requests to transfer in than we can handle."

Zibler nodded his approval. "I believe you're right. And I intend to adopt a few of your new regs in my other companies. That should help your people adjust." He smiled thinly. "You do know how to pick a target that will hurt, though, hitting them in the ego like this. That's almost drill instructor tactics. You've trained recruits before?"

"Singly. Pairs, sometimes. You know the routine, sir, getting replacements to fill holes in the Uhlans' TO&E. But never like this, so many all at once." Eleven individuals. Hardly comparable to the team he'd inherited and then commanded for several years—the team that had disintegrated on Huntress.

"But those new recruits, you pushed them just as hard?"

"No."

Zibler turned from the window. "Then why now, with them?"

Because lately, all he could think about was the feeling of impending danger racing to catch up with him. But he couldn't very well say that to his superior officer—even one he considered a friend. "I just don't know how much time we have left," he said. "This stalemate with the Eighth can't go on indefinitely. The Dragoons should arrive in a month and that should help resolve matters, but we can't depend on them for all our military support. We need to get our troops into shape as quickly as possible, in case . . ." David trailed off. "Just in case," he finished quietly.

"How long have you been thinking that? Since the Eighth's latest refusal to relocate?"

David hesitated to answer, but he trusted Zibler, and that helped. Something about the man reminded David of Morgan Hasek-Davion—a steadfastness that automatically inspired high morale. "Since Huntress," he said finally.

Zibler regarded David with his bright blue eyes for a moment, but his expression was unreadable. "I may just have to take you up on your offer to tell me about Task Force Serpent. But next week, after you get back from your family reunion and after the presentation. We'll have time enough then." He look back toward the warriors waiting for David in the ready room. "Go on. Turn them into a company."

David nodded, borrowing from the other man's strength as he moved toward the door. "But she's still going to give me trouble," he said, his thoughts returning to Sergeant Major Black.

"Count on it," the colonel promised.

The ready room was alive with conversation and the nervous energy that preceded battle. This wouldn't be a real battle, of course—just simulator pods—but that was still enough to charge up the company, especially as they would be performing under their captain's eye.

Sergeant Major Amanda Black wasn't immune to the excitement, but right now she was more interested in Captain McCarthy, who'd apparently finished his corridor conference with Zibler and was now headed for the ready room door.

Though pretending to be fascinated, she listened with only half an ear as Leftenant Dylan Pachenko reported the latest news on the Capellan invasion of the nearby St. Ives Compact. Pachenko had more interest than some because of his Asian heritage, and he'd taken it upon himself to become the local expert on all matters Capellan. There wasn't much to tell, though. The Capellans were pounding the Compact into submission, and Kathil was too far away from the border to worry about the fighting spilling over anywhere close to home.

Amanda surreptitiously studied David McCarthy, who she still had not figured out.

The company's new CO had come in and torn down the unit she and the two leftenants had worked so hard to build. Strict adherence to the titles of rank, a regulation to which only he, apparently, was immune. No nicknaming lances. He rode Corporal Smith pretty hard, though of course Richard took it in stride. And the training schedule . . .

McCarthy had all but pulled her off the schedule, where before she'd fought in every simulator exercise. She'd lost her position as top MechWarrior because of someone who only got his command because he had fought with Task Force Serpent. And he wouldn't even talk about Huntress! She was damned if she'd make it easy on him, then. Amanda wasn't bowing to a man who had yet to sim with the company—or to that fawning Tara Michaels either.

She knew that wasn't really fair. Tara wasn't fawning

over their new commander, and McCarthy certainly hadn't betrayed any interest in the leftenant. Was there a girl back home? McCarthy was a Kathil native, so that was certainly possible. He might be trying to rekindle a relationship he'd left behind eight years before—some civilian, no doubt.

The room quieted as the captain entered and took a chair near the front of the room. Amanda threw a quick glance toward the window, confirming that Colonel Zibler had gone.

She turned back as McCarthy cleared his throat meaningfully. "All right. I assume you've all heard the news by now of the DCMS Alshain Avengers striking at Clan Ghost Bear. I can confirm it, but I know nothing that wasn't printed in yesterday's *Kathil Korroborator*."

Yes, yes, yes. Of course Amanda had heard. Three regiments of the Draconis Combine's army had gone rogue, striking back at Clan Ghost Bear in an attempt to liberate their old homeworld of Alshain. "A bit off topic, wouldn't you say, Captain?" she asked. "This is the Capellan March, not the Draconis." Amanda had even less interest in that skirmish than in the Xin Sheng conflict.

"Indeed," McCarthy said neutrally. "So, other than that, anyone have grievances they would like to air this morning?"

He looked faintly surprised when no one, not even Corporal Smith, volunteered. Having the LC stop by had cowed many of them. Not Amanda, though. She was saving her energy for fights she could win. Like today's simulator battle, with any luck. She swept brown locks from her temples and imagined the tight weight of a neurohelmet against her forehead.

"No? Okay, then I'll get to today's business. Mister Pachenko, I traded away your *Garm* to Leftenant Colonel Zibler's third company."

Dismay flared in Pachenko's normally impassive brown eyes. He had been very proud of the *Garm*, a BattleMech built on New Syrtis. "The *Garm* was a brand-new design," Pachenko protested, belatedly adding, "sir." Recovering, he fell back on solid military bearing, standing stiffbacked. "May I ask why, Captain" he asked in a low, though not particularly respectful, voice.

"Yes, Dylan, you may question me when we're in a training environment or with permission when in private," McCarthy said. "The answer is that I didn't like the *Garm*. I don't believe it fit the profile of your urban scout lance."

Amanda frowned. "Sir, it's a thirty-five-tonner," she said. Pachenko nodded enthusiastically. The militia requirements only demanded that scout lances stay within a thirty-five-ton average weight.

McCarthy shrugged slightly, accepting the fact and dismissing it all at once. "Leftenant Michaels, I had you profile Mister Pachenko's lance. Tell him what you told me." He glanced back at Pachenko. "And don't worry, Mister. You'll get your chance to review her command as well."

Tara Michaels had looked eager to begin—until she heard that Pachenko would get his crack at her lance. Her bright smile dimmed by a few watts. "The *Garm* was the only 'Mech of Mister Pachenko's lance to suffer from ammunition depletion," she said gamely. "It was also fifteen percent slower and almost thirty percent under-armored when compared to the pair of *Firestarters*."

"Thank you, Tara," McCarthy said. "Also, one of your two weapons suffered difficulties in close-range engagements, which is probable in a cityscape. And it had no good scout features, forcing you to rely too much on the *Firestarters*. Sergeant Moriad's *Wolfhound* is there for fire support. I want you up front and with the speed to reinforce any member of your lance who gets in trouble. I prevailed on General Motors' local factories and bargained for a *Stealth*. It should suit your needs much better. You'll begin training with it in sims today."

Put that way, the exchange certainly made sense to Amanda, and she could see Dylan being persuaded by the argument. Still, she also saw value in allowing a MechWarrior to pilot the 'Mech he or she wanted. She wouldn't give up her *Bushwacker* as easily as Dylan had given up his *Garm*. "Are you training with us today, sir?" The question came out a bit sharper than Amanda would have liked. Almost a challenge.

"I wasn't planning on it, *Sergeant*," McCarthy said, placing a deliberate emphasis on the shortened form of her rank.

And in doing so, he gave Amanda some insight into the reason behind at least one of his regulations. By enforcing strict adherence that the company members refer to each other by their rank titles, he could use them to reward or chastise a MechWarrior without belaboring the point: first names to signify a job well done, shortened ranks for displeasure.

Not that her understanding of the situation calmed her rising anger. If the captain wasn't simming, odds were better than even that she wouldn't either. Even when he did send her into the simulator pods, he often kept her on a short leash, reining her back from showing off all that she was capable of. What was he afraid of?

The realization hit Amanda hard, almost as a physical blow. In the same way she read enemy weaknesses on the field and exploited them, she suddenly knew that Captain McCarthy was worried about his performance. He was a Task Force Serpent veteran, but what did they really know about his combat record? He wouldn't talk about it. There was a mess-hall rumor going around about McCarthy winning some kind of decoration. But if that was so, why hadn't it been announced? Why wouldn't a warrior display his awards proudly? He must have something to hide—and she knew how to find out what it was.

"Your company would really like to see you in action, sir," she said innocently. She glanced at a few of the nearby soldiers, garnering a few nods from her fellow warriors and one "you betcha" from Smith. "How long has it been since you've sat in a simulator, Captain? You do know that militia training policies require at least one combat sim every three months." As senior enlisted, Amanda had to oversee training schedules—for enlisted and officers alike. If she found no other way, Amanda would force him into it.

McCarthy pushed right back. "I'm certain I can get dispensation from Leftenant Colonel Zibler if I happen to wander outside the guidelines."

Feigning disappointment, Amanda shrugged while rocking her chair back on two legs. "I'm sure that's true, sir, but I'm sure we'd all like to observe your techniques on the field." She let her chair legs fall back on the floor and sat up, as if struck by a sudden thought. "Well, then, if we're not going to have the privilege of simming with you, might I recommend that we take part of today's training time to hear about your last military engagement? Wasn't it on Huntress?"

The captain's haunted—almost hunted—look told her she'd scored with that salvo. He exhaled sharply and shook his head, though never once breaking eye contact with Amanda. "So this is what it's going to take, is it?" he asked softly.

"That's just my recommendation, sir," she replied blandly. "We'd like to hear about you fighting in your *Devastator*. We'd love to see it even more. Maybe against one of us?"

"Maybe against your *Bushwacker*?" he asked dryly, gray-blue eyes taking on a harder glint. "Hardly a sporting match."

Victory! Amanda smiled and rubbed her hands together briskly to bleed off the nervous energy finally coursing unbridled through her. "It would be my pleasure to cede you an advantage, Captain."

McCarthy rose suddenly, turned from the gathered company and walked to the window. For several long minutes he gazed down the empty hall as though at something no one could see but him. Finally he turned back, eyes alight with a firm resolve that made her suddenly question calling him to task. Those eyes had seen too much.

"All right, Amanda," he said flatly. "Let's get this over with."

5

CMM Staging Grounds
Radcliffe, Kathil
Capellan March, Federated Commonwealth
24 October 3062

Memories of Huntress stalked David McCarthy all the way to the simulator rooms, dampening his underarms and forehead with a clammy sweat. The bulk of his company trailed along as he and Amanda led the way at an even pace. Twelve MechWarriors. There had been sixteen, then.

He'd lost Denning first, the corporal's *Scarabus* spread in pieces across the battlefield, the burning pilot's chair lost on one of the distant, fog-shrouded hillocks. The remaining light 'Mechs scattered before the Clan advance—David wheeled them off to the left in an effort to bring them back behind the Smoke Jaguar line. Myer and Riccols fell next, fronting the ridge held by the Uhlans. Then Whidbey traded his *Nightsky* to help Brevet-Hauptmann Polsan finish off a *Gladiator*.

The damp ground was burning in several spots, flash-dried and set afire by intense energies gone astray. Through smoke and remaining wisps of fog, the ninety-five-ton *Gladiator* closed rapidly on the Uhlan warriors. Engaging its MASC system, the Clan OmniMech effectively "supercharged" its myomer musculature, barreling forward at an impressive eighty-five kilometers per hour. The *Nightsky*'s pulse lasers stabbed a swarm of emerald stingers into the larger 'Mech's chest and head before being literally torn limb from limb by the *Gladiator*'s gauss rifle and paired large lasers. Polsan's *Caesar* paused in battle only long enough to pick up the *Nightsky*'s severed right arm, the one with the titanium hatchet molded onto the wrist. He brandished it like a club while continuing to deliver his own gauss slugs with telling effect, following each impact with hellish streams of particle energy and the more refined cutting power of the *Caesar*'s lasers.

David almost thought of it as poetic justice when Polsan caved in the *Gladiator*'s head with the *Nightsky*'s arm, crushing the Smoke Jaguar MechWarrior inside. But there was little poetic about this battle. Justice alone would have to serve.

Another heat wave slammed through the *Devastator*'s cockpit with almost physical force, driving the air from David's lungs and replacing it with burning coals. He gasped for breath and shook his head to clear the burning sweat from his eyes, splattering damp drops on the inside of his neurohelmet's face shield. Through streaked vision he watched the approach of a *Masakari*, trying to force a lock-out of a targeting system addled by the high temperatures in his 'Mech.

The lethal *Masakari* stabbed out with paired large lasers guided by the Clan's superior targeting computer, the intense energy sloughing away armor from David's left leg. Autocannon fire chipped away at his *Devastator*'s fusion-powered heart and walked up to the left shoulder, while a brace of fifteen long-range missiles corkscrewed in on gray contrails to hammer at his right arm and head. The stunning impact threw David against his restraining harness, the straps digging deep at his shoulders. Pain flared at his chin, and he could feel the desperate warmth of blood running down his throat.

One missile had slammed into the side shield protecting David's wrap-around cockpit, and the shield exploded inward, raining razored shards into his right arm and chest. One piece had snicked up beneath the neurohelmet's protective guard, slicing deep into his jawline.

David swiped at the blood and then returned both

hands to the controls in an effort to bring the *Masakari* down with him. He had simply accepted that he and his battalion were already dead, and that seemed to set him free.

Stabbing down on his triggers, David carved molten furrows along the *Masakari*'s right side with his PPCs. The edges of the wounds glowed orange and then a dull red as they quickly cooled—not enough to bring down his enemy. He toggled for his gauss rifles, worried about ammunition but in no position to be choosy. One slug skipped off the OmniMech's left arm, carrying away shards of armor. Another smashed deep into the right hip, exploiting earlier damage and lodging in the joint.

The *Masakari* stumbled on its next step, overbalanced by loss of armor and the bound hip joint, and toppled clumsily to the ground. The barrels of its large lasers dug into the moist earth, twisting the machine sideways. But a *Black Hawk* immediately moved in to shield its fallen comrade until the *Masakari* could regain its feet. It bought David time, nothing more.

Buying time.

David was nearly shaking with pent-up energy as he and Amanda entered the auxiliary sim complex, the task at hand driving the legacy of Huntress back into the depths of memory. He had realized in the ready room that even if he somehow avoided the neat trap Amanda Black had laid for him, a delay would be all he could hope for. If she didn't win the argument today, she would be back with a renewed offensive another time. It was a persistence David had to reluctantly admire, and it would eventually mold her into a solid leader—if she didn't push it too far.

Better to have done with it. He would have to face his demons sooner or later.

Today's demon was a thick, black clamshell set on its end, one side raised on upper-mounted hinges to reveal a replica of a 'Mech cockpit. The simulator pod's interior combined the general features of most BattleMechs and the specifics of none. Pilot's couch, control sticks and throttle, foot pedals—everything you needed to control one of the humanoid battle machines. There were only two pods in the auxiliary room; no need to take up the large sim complex for a simple head-to-head match.

He paused only for a moment to let Pachenko and Michaels know which simulation they would run, which 'Mechs would be piloted, and how he wanted the sim results scored, and then approached the simulator with a wary eye on the replica cockpit. He felt a sinking sensation in his stomach, which felt like lead. But this wasn't a real 'Mech or a real battle. Only a sim. David used to jump right into a simpler version back in his teenage years. Then it was a game!

True, but not compelling enough. David stopped just short of ducking under the pod door and stood, shifting his weight from one foot to the other, until he noticed Sergeant Black looking sidelong at him from beneath the door of the next sim pod. Steeling himself against any further hesitation, David ducked under the door and into the pilot's seat.

And the door slid down on a silent motor, sealing him into the darkness.

Settled into the darkness, waiting for her screens to come alive, Amanda Black fastened herself into the chair by feel. She snugged the harness against her shoulders and hips and clipped the buckles into the four-point release system. Loosing the mechanical brakes, she adjusted the seat for her height and reach. The neurohelmet rode loose on her head—a size too large, but it would serve for a simulation. She had just finished tightening the chin strap when the screens lit up, bathing her in the amber glow of cautionary lights and the backwash of her tactical display.

These pods were not the best model—the ones that swayed with the correct gait for whichever 'Mech you selected and could actually roll as far as ninety degrees to simulate falls. Those were an incredible ride, but these were only one step down. A tremble seat physically simmed damage by shaking and jumping, and vents located over each shoulder would dump heated air into the pod in accordance with her virtual heat levels. Video screens replaced the usual ferroglass shields, and a master computer controlling her sensors and other displays completed the illusion of a 'Mech in battle.

The view did not surprise her, given the captain's earlier mention of a cityscape environment. McCarthy's company, after all, was designated an urban-warfare command. Dark gray buildings flanked a wide street that stretched into the distance, and the cockpit of Amanda's fifty-five-ton *Bushwacker* was level with the third-story windows. A few vehicles rolled along on programmed paths, and rudimentary people shuffled by aimlessly, as if the sudden appearance of a computer-generated 'Mech was no cause for alarm. It soon would be.

She throttled into a walk, beginning the hunt.

Her first warning of McCarthy's whereabouts came from the magres scanner, which detected a large source of ferrous material on the move—always a giveaway. If the *Devastator* stood still, her computer would not be able tell the difference between the 'Mech and any building with steel frame construction. McCarthy could have parked his assault 'Mech inside a building and waited in ambush—the best way to fight an assault machine in a city, in her opinion.

But apparently, McCarthy didn't want an ambush; he was out to settle a score. Amanda could appreciate that. She hadn't found a real challenge in some time.

And that was what McCarthy was giving her. Intermittent readings made it impossible for her to acquire even the most basic target lock, McCarthy always on the edge of the sensor display as he drew her deeper into the city. The uncertain contact worried at her confidence. McCarthy moved with a speed that almost rivaled her own, disappearing around another corner every time she got a bead on him. The *Bushwacker*'s feet slipped and skidded at each corner, fighting for a grip on the smooth ferrocrete road as she pivoted into harder and harder turns, trying to catch him.

Hoping to pin him down, Amanda dumped a few flights of Thunder munitions into important intersections. The missile-delivered minefields scattered charges over a wide area, creating a navigation hazard for any 'Mech or large vehicle. Case in point: a civilian truck rolled into one intersection and was blown into a poor graphic representation of a burning shell. Just one reason why Thunders were frowned upon in urban environments.

But then, this wasn't a real battlefield—an assumption her commander put to the lie almost immediately.

Warning sensors blared for attention as McCarthy came sailing over the top of a nearby building, riding trailers of burning plasma that flared from the jump jets in his back. Amanda read the BattleMech's designation from her heads up display a split second before she caught a confirming glimpse through her ferroglass shields. A *Stealth*! McCarthy wasn't here in his *Devastator*; but had chosen a medium-weight 'Mech that gave him an edge in mobility. She barely had time for that realization. A hard jostling immediately followed missile-lock warning alarms, the forty-five-ton *Stealth* peppering her with short-ranged missiles while still in midair. The hard rain of SRMs gouged and pitted her armor all along her 'Mech's right side.

The lighter machine came down atop a large building behind and to Amanda's right, lasers stabbing sapphire beams into her arm and leg. Twisting back as far as the *Bushwacker* could reach, the sergeant just managed to bring her left-arm LRM launcher into play. If McCarthy thought all she had were Thunders, he was in for a surprise. Amanda had modified her *Bushwacker*, yanking out the machine guns in favor of two extra tons of ammunition stored in the left-torso magazine. Her flight stung at the *Stealth*, giving back at least some insult for the injury she'd taken.

But as easily as it arrived, the *Stealth* lifted off on its jump jets again and leaped across the intersection where Amanda was parked. She tried to turn the wide, squat *Bushwacker* but could not quite make it before another salvo of missiles and lasers slammed into her back and shoved her forward against the harness. Amanda clamped her teeth together in frustration while flicking a practiced eye over her wire-frame damage schematic. The weaker armor had help up, preventing any serious damage, but that wouldn't last. There wasn't much of the ferro-fibrous composite left.

If McCarthy kept to the rooftops, eventually one of the buildings would collapse beneath the weight and spill his *Stealth* to the street. But could she last that long? And did she really want to hinge her victory on that event? Right now he owned this fight.

Knowing better than to push a losing position, Amanda throttled into a run that aimed her *Bushwacker* at a nearby building. Thrusting the 'Mech's right arm forward, she shoved its autocannon barrel into the wall, creating a breach through which she wrestled the wide-shouldered *Bushwacker*. The simulation was not quite good enough to rain bricks and girders around her; instead, the wall collapsed in large polygonal chunks that quickly disappeared.

"Round one to you, Captain," Amanda yelled as her 'Mech broke free of the building's far side, kicking through drifts of debris.

Amanda knew that a good shout would carry between pods, and she'd hoped to sound sporting, taking the initial exchange in good stride. But she heard the edge in her voice and knew others would as well. Amanda was angry, and everyone knew it. She had let McCarthy surprise her in the *Stealth*—an opportunity she wouldn't give him again.

Backing her way down the new street, floating her targeting crosshairs over the nearby intersection, Amanda awaited for the captain to chase after her while quickly comparing the two machines in her mind. She held an edge in firepower and armor; the captain had better maneuverability. An even contest. Though, of course, it looked better that McCarthy had thrown away the forty-five-ton advantage he'd have kept in his *Devastator*.

As she'd guessed, the *Stealth* finally came down off the rooftops and sped across the intersection she was covering. It paused to trade salvos, lasers cutting away at Amanda's chest and left leg while another spread of SRMs pockmarked the upper half of the *Bushwacker*. One rang off the machine's forward-thrusting head, and the tremble seat whipped hard to one side. A sharp pain lanced through Amanda's neck.

She rode into the rocking motion, determined to pay back the damage with interest. An emerald beam speared out from her torso-mounted large laser, catching the *Stealth* in the left flank and carving away half its armored protection. Unable to achieve a solid lock for her autocannon, Amanda twisted toward the far side of the wide intersection and cut loose with a stream of hard-biting, eighty-millimeter slugs as the *Stealth* throttled back into a run. The heavy-caliber tripwire caught McCarthy's *Stealth* at the left ankle, chewing away more of his protection before the 'Mech disappeared behind the corner of a new building. Walking the fire after him, she chewed deep into the building before letting up on the trigger.

Fade back, hit, advance, and circle was the game they played through the streets of the virtual city, trading weapons fire at irregular intervals. Amanda laid out Thunders whenever she had a few seconds to plan and smashed her way through a new building whenever McCarthy's *Stealth* took to the air in an attempt to flank her. The vehicles and simulated civilians still didn't react to the battling titans, even though simmed people occasionally disappeared beneath the *Bushwacker*'s step and every so often Amanda came across the wreckage of another car or truck that had wandered into one of her minefields. Stupid computer.

Her mining of the major intersections had forced McCarthy to keep to side streets and rooftops; this time the *Stealth* darted out of a narrow alleyway that Amanda's wide-shouldered *Bushwacker* could never have fit into, stepping right into her shadow. At point-blank range Amanda's long-range missile racks were all but useless, only her large laser and the roaring burst from her autocannon answering his full barrage. Several of the *Stealth*'s short-range missiles exploited breaches in her armor to blast away deep in the *Bushwacker*'s chest. The explosive force warped the housing to the BattleMech's massive gyroscopic stabilizer and cracked the physical shielding that helped bottle up heat bleeding from the fusion reactor.

Trailing fire-orange globules of melted armor-composite from its side, the *Stealth* dodged around the *Bushwacker* and ducked into another alleyway, leaving Amanda's machine reeling drunkenly as she fought with gravity for possession of her 'Mech. This time she won, the signals processed by the neurohelmet able to compensate for the damaged gyro.

But the toll of battle was mounting. Amanda sweated freely as the vents dumped hot air on her neck—simulating the critical damage she'd taken to her engine shielding. The heat quickly turned the cramped pod cock-

pit into a sauna, scorched air shortening each breath into
a gasp for oxygen. Her neck pinched where the strained
muscles continued to ache. Each step with the *Bushwacker*'s off-kilter gyro jogged the tremble seat, lancing fresh
pain along her spine. She limped into the next intersection,
fighting her 'Mech into a right-side twist to guard the
direction in which the *Stealth* had disappeared.

McCarthy appeared on the edge of her forward screen,
rounding a far corner and pounding into a full run. Half
a dozen steps later, a glowing nimbus outlined the back
of the *Stealth* as its jump jets once again routed plasma
from the fusion engine into streams of focused downward
thrust. The forty-five-ton machine leapt at her, skimming
along twenty meters above the street, lasers stabbing jeweled brilliance and missiles streaking out in short arcs.
Sucking in a long, steadying breath of the acrid air and
ignoring the tight bands clamped around her chest,
Amanda leaned into her trigger while gliding her crosshairs up and across the street. This was it; she knew that
neither 'Mech could stand up to much more of a beating.
One of them would fall now!

The *Stealth*'s medium lasers punched holes deep into
her left arm, coring the missile launcher and ruining it.
Missiles pocked and gouged her damage-racked frame,
shaking the *Bushwacker* but not enough to spoil her return
fire. Autocannon and laser walked a swath of destruction
from nearby buildings up into the air and across the
Stealth's line of flight. The energy beam connected first,
sloughing away the last of the composite protecting the
other 'Mech's right leg. A stream of depleted-uranium
slugs smashed in to exploit that damage, chipping and
carving at the titanium femur until finally the supporting
skeleton buckled and the leg twisted off to fall to the
ground behind the jumping *Stealth*. The crippled machine
fell toward earth.

But not soon enough.

Already on target for collision with the *Bushwacker*, a
maneuver known in MechWarrior parlance as death from
above, the *Stealth* fell into the impact off-balance but with
a force no less damaging. Its remaining foot drove into
the *Bushwacker*'s left shoulder, telescoping its own leg up
into the torso cavity but not before crushing Amanda's

left side into ruin. The ammunition magazine built into the *Bushwacker's* left torso caved in, crushing the missiles, rupturing fuel cells and impacting warheads. One spark caught the spilled propellant, and the resulting fire set off the warheads in a cascade of destructive force that ripped both 'Mechs to pieces.

In simulation, there was no mind-numbing shock feeding back through the neurocircuitry to cripple a warrior. No fireball to scorch flesh or roast the soldiers alive. Amanda's forward screen was a chaotic display of fire and polygonal debris . . .

And then nothing. Darkness, warm and moist from her soaked jumpsuit, smelling of exertion and clean sweat. A light cracked at the floor, quickly spilling in as the clam-shell door rose to the sound of scattered, polite applause. The rest of the company had watched on auxiliary monitors and congratulated both MechWarriors on an impressive battle. Only Leftenants Michaels and Pachenko held back as Amanda and Captain McCarthy worked out of their harnesses.

McCarthy was drenched, his dark hair plastered to his head. Sweat runneled down his brow, streaking his face. Amanda could well imagine why: the jumping *Stealth* had been running a critically high heat curve right from the start. But the quick look of relief he threw back toward the sim pod hinted to Amanda that there might be more to it than just the temperature. Whatever his problem, McCarthy had proved he was no tired hand at the controls of a 'Mech. She'd take the draw against him—at least for today.

"Good fight, Captain." Amanda offered McCarthy her hand, which he accepted.

However, there was nothing amiable in those gray-blue eyes. "An even match, yes. But a little out of control in there, weren't you, Sergeant Major?"

"Sir?" Indignation welled up in Amanda's chest.

McCarthy nodded to Tara Michaels. The young leftenant shifted nervously as she gave her report. "Estimated property damage in excess of fifteen million C-bills. Estimated cost in civilian lives, two hundred and eighty-five."

Amanda began to retort, only to be silenced by the captain's raised hand. "Wait," he told her. "Dylan?"

"Your estimated damage was less than half a million in C-bills, Captain." Pachenko glanced at Amanda with uncertain brown eyes, possibly remembering how often her force had decimated his lance in sims. "Lives lost, five. Four of those resulted from the combined explosions of your two 'Mechs there at the end. The other was a stray shot that hit a pedestrian."

"Damn," McCarthy swore. He seemed genuinely upset by his losses. "All right, everyone to the main simulator room. Leftenant Michaels, divide them up and run a standard city defense drill. Sergeant Black," he said as the others filed slowly from the room, "you will please remain."

She waited until they were alone, unsure how to react to his implied reprimand. He couldn't be serious. Amanda shook her head in annoyance. He certainly looked serious. "It was a simulation."

"Simulation," McCarthy said, as if repeating a definition from memory, "a process intended to demonstrate, resemble, or otherwise emulate a live combat environment. Your strong-arm tactics . . . if I saw a soldier under my command intentionally cause that much damage inside a real city, that soldier would be up on charges, Sergeant." His voice dropped to a near-whisper. "Even on Huntress, Amanda, we spared civilian sectors that kind of violence."

Her ears burning from the rebuke, Amanda stiffened to a formal military bearing. Worse than being lectured was the fact that the entire company was likely discussing the estimated casualty cost. It turned her draw into a loss, and that kind of defeat did not sit well with her. "I'll certainly treat simulations more seriously, Captain. I assumed—wrongly—that our battle was simply a test of skill." She paused. "Permission to speak freely, sir?"

When he nodded, Amanda chose her words carefully. "You could have made your point in private, or at least with only the other officers present."

"Maybe the others needed to hear the lesson as well." McCarthy's expression hardened. "Do you object to being the subject of one of my lessons?"

"I believe it might undermine my authority, yes. Most of them could do far worse than to follow the example I try to set. Without meaning to sound conceited, Captain, and excluding yourself, I'm the best MechWarrior you've got."

McCarthy's expression softened, but reflected more pity than true understanding. When he spoke, he sounded disappointed. "And what makes you believe, Amanda, that is enough?"

6

Vorhaven, Kathil
Capellan March, Federated Commonwealth
2 November 3062

The McCarthy home was large, a two-story edifice sprawling over five hundred square meters of sitting rooms, library, banquet kitchen, and six large bedrooms now in use as guest suites. A covered porch wrapped around three sides of the home, gazing out over the hundreds of acres of cultivated farmland David's parents owned and managed. AgroMechs and more conventional farming vehicles operated on distant fields, never close enough to disturb the third day of David's homecoming. The house felt almost cozy despite its grand size, filled with playing children and the mouth-watering aromas of the approaching Sunday dinner.

David's arrival two days prior, after nearly three weeks of grueling training with his company, had attracted more relatives than he'd even known existed. The grand party had filled up the ballroom in one of Vorhaven's finest hotels, beginning after the children's Halloween celebrations and lasting well into the early hours of the following day. A thoroughly bedraggled David had suffered welcome-home hugs and handshakes and well-wishes enough to last several years. He enjoyed every minute. Mostly.

There were the expected questions about Huntress, all the more insistent now that news of his decoration had been announced by General Sampreis. The Star League Medal of Valor was an impressive feat for a "local boy," a title David couldn't duck even though he had been gone for better than eight years. The ceremony was scheduled to take place in nine days, and he wasn't looking forward to the experience.

David was toasted for several hours, but the novelty finally wore off, and he switched to a fruit punch in order to clear his head. Soon toasts were raised to the Uhlans, in memory of Morgan Hasek-Davion and to Morgan's son, Field Marshal George Hasek, and finally to Prince Victor Steiner-Davion. Many of these were flung out with a peculiar defiance, daring anyone to disagree. Were people trying to provoke arguments, David wondered, or simply reaffirming their own loyalties?

Similar events were happening all over Kathil, and supposedly the entire Capellan March. People were waving the old Federated Suns flag and calling openly for Victor to return from exile. Whether he liked it or not, Victor was the champion of House Davion—the Federated Suns. That was only to be expected, since Katherine Steiner-Davion had pushed so hard to identify herself with the Lyran state and her Steiner heritage. David was worried that the lines of battle were being drawn so clearly. The Haseks were clearly in Victor's camp; if it came down to a fight, there was no doubt who they would support. But Katherine had her own supporters—the Eighth RCT's defiance of George Hasek's orders was proof enough of that.

Such thoughts had persisted into the following day, as the celebration quickly dwindled to intimate family— brother and sisters, a few close cousins, and their children—and moved to the country home of his parents, who could not get enough time with their long-absent son. Especially his father, who kept at him for news of Prince Victor and the Star League Defense Force.

"Surely you've heard something of the Prince's plans," Jason McCarthy said now, cornering David where he stood surveying the family land from the front porch. "He can't seriously intend to leave Katherine on the throne." The elderly man was still fit for his age; the lifetime he had spent working a large and successful farm was apparent. A thick fringe of iron-gray hair circled a sun-tanned pate, and his storm-blue eyes were as intense as his son's. His hands were large, fit for the oversized controls of an AgroMech, and they clenched the railing as if he wished for something a bit more military in his grasp.

"Victor Steiner-Davion has accepted the post as Precentor-Martial of ComStar and also commands the SLDF," David reminded his father, sipping a cup of the strong local coffee. "He can't use that position to further his own goals."

"That hasn't stopped his sister," the elder McCarthy groused, retreating only slightly. "You haven't heard half of what we have, son—especially if you're relying on the InterStellar News network or even the Federated News Services. I've never seen so much pro-Steiner propaganda, not even when the marriage of Hanse Davion and Melissa Steiner was a hot item. The *Korraborator* does what it can, but there seems to be a determined effort offworld not to give local networks much to feed on. Still, we hear things."

"Such as?" David asked, as always paying his father mindful respect. Jason McCarthy was no man's fool, and this was information David wasn't likely to get from military sources. Rumors had a life of their own within a command, but the military grapevine rarely stretched between worlds.

"Well, the explosion on Solaris VII was hard to keep quiet, but that's a Lyran world anyway," he said bleakly. "We've heard worse about New Aragon, where demonstrators were labeled as subversives and 'detained for investigation.' And there's Kentares, of course. News was suddenly blacked out, but a few merchant ships brought word that Katherine's supporters are keeping the planet in check with BattleMech forces. The local duke—Duke Sharpe, I think his name is—supposedly his stronghold was torn down to its foundations and his family imprisoned, or worse."

"I heard that 'Mechs leveled a city there." Pauline, one of David's four sisters, joined them in time to hear mention of Kentares. "Five thousand people dead or injured."

The idea of BattleMechs loose in a city reminded David

of Amanda Black's sim battle the previous week. It was so easy, he knew, for a MechWarrior to begin thinking of himself as invulnerable and grow careless with the firepower at his command. The results of battle could be brutal enough even when moderated. David had seen that on Huntress. And now, apparently, that brutality had come to the Federated Commonwealth. Looking out at the fields bathed in warm sunshine, it was hard to imagine 'Mechs rampaging across the land, but he had a bad feeling in his gut that it could very well come to pass. This standoff with the Eighth couldn't last forever, especially with the Dragoons on the way to reinforce the militia. They would just have to wait and see whether General Weintraub would acquiesce and take his force to Lee, or whether he would choose to make a stand. Wait, and in the meantime, prepare to fight.

"I think Katherine is too smart to do anything so drastic," David said aloud. Pauline worked in Vorhaven as an insurance agent—her big news would be a combination of local rumor and scandal vids. "Especially on Kentares. Repeating the Kentares Massacre would demand a reaction from several sources." He turned to his father for support, but the elder McCarthy hesitated.

"I'm not so sure. Katherine would know better, I agree. But that doesn't mean the people she put on the planet would listen to reason. Look at Kathil. Our new Archon-Princess hasn't directly challenged George Hasek or even Duke VanLees. But we still have the Eighth RCT minding the store for her, don't we?"

It was hard to argue with that, considering the Eighth still occupied the planet's main military base while the Kathil Militia was squeezed into the older quarters at Radcliffe.

"Old Koster VanLees would have turned this General Weintraub out on his ear," Pauline said with a nostalgic tone David remembered hearing in his parents' voices as a child. The "good old days" syndrome, he had called it.

"Don't be too certain," David said. "Duke Koster wasn't as independent as we like to remember. He did sell his Capellan Dragoons into Davion service rather than get pulled into the struggle between Hanse Davion and Michael Hasek." And now the Dragoons were returning. So what did that say for Duke Petyr and his intentions? Would he fight harder for his planet and his people than his father had?

Pauline dismissed her brother's point with a wave of her hand. David's war-hero status had not noticeably increased her respect for him. "That's because Michael Hasek was wrong, David. Anyway, I've heard that Duke VanLees has purchased back the Dragoons from Duke Hasek. You think that might be a sign that Duke Petyr is getting tough, or maybe that George Hasek is reinforcing his authority in the Capellan March?"

"Could be," David admitted. "If it's true."

"*Is* it true?" his sister asked.

David shrugged, and the subsequent silence lasted long enough that his sister gave up on getting a straight answer and went back to chasing after her four children. Pauline had never been much for waiting.

Jason McCarthy, however, was made of much sterner stuff. "Is it true?" he repeated.

There would be no outwaiting his father—the man had a natural obstinate streak. David nodded, and the two stood quietly for a while, thinking about the implications of that.

The sounds of children happily playing and the adults' insincere scolding were enough to momentarily drive away his feelings of impending disaster. Nephews, nieces and a few second cousins continued to run around in their Halloween costumes, unable to give them up after only one night. He'd noticed quite a few MechWarriors—the usual representatives from Wolf's Dragoons, the Kell Hounds and the Davion Heavy Guard, but most displayed the colors and crest of the Uhlans, as an homage to their suddenly famous relative.

David returned the salutes of a trio of MechWarrior children that paused briefly in front of the porch before being chased away by a five-year-old Immortal Warrior character armed with nothing more dangerous than a fresh-baked roll snatched from the kitchen. He would never get used to seeing children taking so early to the icons of warfare. The next generation's warriors. It dampened his mood considerably. David relieved the television hero of the roll, sending his niece on her way with a friendly pat on the bottom.

The roll was warm, reminding David of his mother, who was still working on the evening's feast. "What does Mom think of all this?" he asked, tearing off a piece of the sweet bread and popping it into his mouth.

The elder McCarthy shook his head. "She worries. Especially with your younger sister, Grace, using that magazine she edits to take pot shots at Katherine. I tell your mother it'll all work out, though. I mean, this is George Hasek's world. We can still count on some freedoms here."

Except that Field Marshal Hasek wasn't here. What rights was Kathil assured of that Kentares wasn't also supposed to have? And look what had happened on Kentares. "I'll have a talk with Grace," David said. "Right now is not the time to be drawing attention."

"You think we're ready for a fight?"

That was the same question David had asked Damien Zibler. David wished Zibler was here now to answer it instead of him. "We're all still expecting to avoid that," he said with more confidence than he felt. "At some point, the nobles have to reason things out with each other. I mean, this is the Capellan March, not the Capellan Confederation. Right?"

"The Confederation has its ruling nobles, too—it didn't do them much good," his father said darkly before pushing off from the porch railing and turning to go inside. David followed him into the main living area, past a half-dozen adults watching a holovid. The two men declined to join them for another episode of *The ComStar Files*, an older suspense show grown popular again now that the once-secret organization had actually admitted to some of the paranoid precepts on which the series had been based.

Once out of the room, his father sighed heavily, and for an instant his broad shoulders sagged. "When war comes, David—and it will come—I hope it doesn't find you officers with your heads buried in the dirt. That works with some vegetables and most politicians, but not with soldiers."

David smiled thinly. "We know better than that, Dad. If war comes, we'll be ready. But we also have hope.

Every now and then, peace threatens to break out and make a lasting try at things."

"I hope you're right. It's only about four centuries overdue, after all."

Groans and complaints arose from the living room, and for a moment David thought his relations in the next room had overheard them. Then he smiled as he heard his brother, Adam, complaining about the broadcast being interrupted.

That smile didn't last long, as a frightening silence suddenly gripped the living room, broken only by the distant sounds of the children playing outside and the muffled sounds of a news broadcast.

"David!" Adam's voice was deep, made for reaching the other side of the farm. Inside, it almost rattled the windows. "David, get in here. Dad!"

That he had called David before their father must mean the news was military. The hairs on the back of his neck already standing up, David made it back to the living room one step ahead of Jason McCarthy. Six somber adults sat there, their eyes glued to the tri-video set. It showed the angular design of Clan OmniMechs dispensing a deadly barrage of laserfire. The camera pulled back to show at least two Trinaries blazing away at unseen defenders—an unsettlingly familiar sight to David.

An announcer's voice drowned out the sounds of battle, relegating explosions and the burning, crackling passage of a PPC to the background. "Once again, we have confirmed reports that Clan Ghost Bear yesterday launched a major offensive into the Draconis Combine, apparently in reprisal for recent attacks by the Alshain Avengers. A dozen worlds have been attacked, but House Kurita is reportedly bearing up under the assault. This does not, we repeat, does not appear to be a resumption of all-out invasion, and neither the Federated Commonwealth nor the Lyran Alliance appears threatened at this time. No other Clan has made any indication of moving into the Inner Sphere. The main objectives by Clan Ghost Bear, at this time, are thought to be punishment and warning."

Punishment and warning. On a scale that would cost billions in C-bills and who could tell how many lives.

The announcer's voice was once again lost as the

sounds of battle took over the report. The thundering tread of BattleMechs on the move could barely be heard behind the spitting lightning of particle cannon and the throaty roars of autocannon fire. Missile impacts threw dirt at the camera and shook the picture. This was not gun-cam footage, shot by a Combine MechWarrior. Someone had a video unit on the ground out there—hopefully on remote.

David looked somberly at his father, both of them remembering their conversation of a few minutes ago. David swallowed in a suddenly dry mouth, now unsettled by the distant sounds of the Immortal Warrior continuing her pursuit of the older, laughing MechWarriors.

His father, as usual, had the right of it. The question was never if war would come.

It was always a question of when.

7

**District Military Compound
District City, Kathil
Capellan March, Federated Commonwealth
11 November 3062**

"I know some of you don't have a lot of time this morning, so let's keep this on-topic and brief," Hauptmann General Weintraub was saying even before Eván Greene had found his assigned seat. Something had happened—Eván could feel it in the room's charged atmosphere. Now the question was, what was it, and how could he take advantage of it?

He eyed his superior officer, trying to second-guess him. The general's aide, Leftenant General Karen Fallon, was seated next to him, wearing full dress uniform. Eván guessed that she would be representing the Eighth RCT at the Radcliffe ceremony later this morning, where the militia would award the SLDF medal to their local hero. Weintraub had declined to attend, preferring not to place himself in the militia's grasp, which spoke volumes about the relations between the two military forces.

Those relations had been deteriorating steadily over the past couple of weeks—ever since Duke VanLees had made his announcement about the arrival of the Dragoons. The militia was keeping its head down for the most part, but Greene had heard rumors that they were preparing for war, and a number of RCT troops had begun muttering loudly about the militia's chances against them. Some were positively spoiling for a fight.

This command-level meeting of the Eighth RCT filled the District Military Compound's executive briefing room almost to overflowing. Senior officers sat at the head of a long table, followed by battalion commanders and then BattleMech company leaders. Supporting companies and 'Mech lances were represented by officers who stood against three walls, a human fence that, to Eván's admittedly biased eye, radiated strength. The air was close, warm from the press of so many bodies and thick with morning aftershave and cologne. One of the auditoriums on the base might have allowed more breathing room, but then there was always something to be said for a display of raw solidarity.

Mitchell Weintraub remained standing at the very head of the room, his back to a wall of darkened glass and his thick hands clasped behind him in the semblance of a parade rest position. The general's posture belied any sense of rest, though: his spine ramrod straight, barrel chest thrust out, and shoulders back in the military's classic wind-cutting profile. Even the military creases in his uniform looked razor-sharp this morning.

Expressions in the briefing room ran the gamut from tension to indifference to the general's hawk-like pride. Eván hoped his face displayed a neutrality that masked his actual wariness. He noted that Fallon betrayed a slight nervousness as her brilliant blue gaze flickered from one officer to the next as if gauging attitudes and weighing loyalties. The only other face that drew his attention was that of Leftenant Xander Barajas, one of his own junior officers, who stood against the opposite wall watching the general with a look that bordered on hunger.

Xander was as eager as Eván for advancement, but he lacked Eván's patience. That would cost the man someday. His service record also indicated a penchant for savage fighting, as demonstrated when he'd served against the Liao-Marik invasion of '57. Stationed with the RCT since then, he chafed in garrison duty and agitated for combat assignment. The problem was he had a tendency to go after the enemy without a thought for his safety, and often to the detriment of his unit.

Putting your goals ahead of the needs of your unit was something Eván understood, of course. Unlike General Weintraub, who held a strong and very real loyalty to Katrina Steiner-Davion, Eván was in it for his own gain. He could smell opportunity in the RCT's resistance to George Hasek. If they succeeded in holding Kathil for the Archon-Princess, all of their careers would be made. But Eván had no particular ties to the Steiners—if he'd served in the Uhlans, like the militia's local hero, he probably would have wound up on the other side, and probably been just as content. So long as he could advance in rank—and quickly.

Fallon had picked up Weintraub's train of thought. "You've all heard about the imminent arrival of the First Capellan Dragoons regiment," she announced. "They have officially been relieved of their duties and are en route to Kathil. We expect them to make planetfall in a few weeks, depending on the JumpShip route they take and the availability of recharge stations. We're still debating whether we will allow them to take post on Kathil, but further discussion on this should wait until other matters are cleared up."

"We have received a response from Archon Katrina," Weintraub informed the assembly, causing a great deal of uneasy shifting and the buzz of muted conversation. If Katrina was ordering them offplanet, it would reinforce George Hasek's claim of authority over the Eighth RCT and greatly damage the unit's reputation. Weintraub allowed the quick surge of conversation to die away and said, "I'll let you judge her words for yourselves."

He stepped to the side, and the glass wall he'd been standing in front of lit up with a three-dimensional crest of the Federated Commonwealth. The holographic display faded to a scene of the New Avalon throne room. Archon-Princess Katrina Steiner-Davion sat on the immense throne with the ease of one born to rule. Though slender, there was an iron cast to her presence that was at once regal and commanding. Everyone in the room, even Xander and Eván, sat straighter in the virtual presence of their ruler, as if feeling her cool blue eyes boring into them.

"Leutnant-General Weintraub," she began, greeting the general by his equivalent Lyran rank. There was little accommodation in her tone. "I have received your numerous requests for clarification and am distressed by your need to question orders. Kathil is an important world to the Federated Commonwealth, as should be apparent by the commotion you have caused. Carry out your orders." One slow, regal nod, and the image dissolved back to the FedCom crest of a gauntleted fist over a sunburst. The room burst into a confused clamor.

That was it? Eván had expected a great deal more, whether or not her ruling would be for or against the Eighth's current course of action. His mind shifted into overdrive, but then he smiled as he realized that the Archon had left her orders intentionally open to interpretation.

"So, people, what do we make of this?" the general asked the assembly.

"We stay," Eván called out quickly. His answer drew nods from most of the assembled officers and a long, considering look from General Fallon. "General, the Archon knew what she was doing in leaving her reply noncommittal. Your stance is well-documented, and her message invests in you ultimate authority."

"And ultimate responsibility," pointed out Leftenant General Price of the Eleventh FedCom Mechanized Infantry. "In short, we've become a deniable asset. Don't forget how the Blackwind Lancers were sacrificed in those early months of the Confederation's war on the St. Ives Compact: broken and disbanded, their colors stricken. If Hasek manages to take Kathil away from us, the Archon-Princess will sacrifice us just as quickly."

"A bit of an alarmist viewpoint, Charles," Fallon said, with a touch of condescension. "You talk as if Hasek has the superior position, militarily or politically. Do you really think he can unseat the Princess?"

"Of course not," Price said hastily. No one was willing to go near that touchy subject. While some in the room certainly preferred Katrina to her brother Victor, and vice versa, the majority were behind her out of respect for the sanctity of a legal chain of command. Katrina sat on the throne, so she ruled. "But he might be able to force us off the planet. There's no question we can stand against the militia—for the most part, they're ill-trained, ill-equipped rabble. But once the Dragoons get here . . ."

Eván could see nods of agreement around the room. The First Capellan Dragoons were unquestionably a formidable force, and if they reached Kathil and sided with the militia—as they certainly would—the RCT would stand little chance against them. Eván hoped Weintraub and Fallon were taking that into account as they laid their plans.

He was sure, however, that the Eighth would be staying. Weintraub and General Fallon were simply playing out the scene to rededicate the junior officers—which meant they had to shut down this line of thought fast, or the meeting might go in the opposite direction than they intended.

General Weintraub moved back to the head of the table, and stood resting his hands on the back of his seat. His rough voice took on an even sharper edge. "Rest assured we will be prepared to deal with the Dragoons when the time comes," he said firmly. "George Hasek might think he can countermand the Archon's orders, but I will not capitulate to that traitor in noble's clothing."

"What about Duke VanLees?" asked Yoshitomi Tendo, commander of the RCT's jump infantry and coordinator for infantry training maneuvers. "He's still trying to force us from Kathil using diplomatic means, but that will last only as long as the Dragoons are en route. And it's damned inconvenient. We've had to suspend training exercises due to lack of munitions."

Fallon nodded. "It's going beyond military supplies now, too. Today we received word that because of shortages, part of our food shipment was rerouted to the 'needs of the CMM, Kathil's primary defenders.' We'll be down to military rations next week. I doubt VanLees is stupid enough to actually try and starve us off-world, but he'll make it uncomfortable." She smiled without humor. "I would expect power outages in the coming days."

Eván swallowed dryly, the thought of living off military

rations enough to remind him of their sawdust taste. That alone might swing any Victor-supporters back into the neutral camp. Thank you, Petyr VanLees. It also opened a window of opportunity, and Eván Greene didn't intend to pass it up. "Don't food shortages often lead to riots?" he asked.

"Real shortages?" Fallon asked. "Not these conveniently arranged ones? Of course. But the public is not going without food." Her blue eyes brightened with cruel interest as she seemed to catch Eván's meaning. "Duke VanLees will never admit that he's only shorting *us* on provisions, and he's made it sound as if it's a general problem."

Eván nodded. "Then as the garrison force in District City, aren't we responsible for maintaining order and curbing any unrest that might rise up due to this unfortunate shortage?" Eván played it straight, as if the food problems were real enough. And they were, if he was going to be eating army rations. "So where would such protests—possibly violent protests—likely occur?"

Now he had Weintraub's attention as well. "The Hall of Nobles," the general said slowly. "And those spear-carrying ornaments they refer to as guards would be of little use, in my opinion." His grin was predatory. "Charles, can you spare a few men to help safeguard the nobility?"

Leftenant General Price hesitated, considering, then nodded. "Only a few battalions," he warned—better than five hundred men. "I'll have to pull out of the rotation here at the District Military Compound."

Mitchell Weintraub waved that away. "I'm upgrading the DMC patrols to include 'Mechs forces as of now."

A solid trade, Eván decided. Even one 'Mech was worth hundreds of regular infantry, VanLees had given them a reason, albeit a thin one, to occupy his seat of government—but a thin excuse was all they needed. Perhaps it would lead to a compromise—hopefully before the Dragoons arrived, but if not, the Eighth's possession of the Duke might stall any plans the Dragoons had for evicting the RCT.

Leftenant Barajas stepped forward, coming to strict attention. "Permission to head that detail, General? I'll have my lance on the fence line in thirty minutes."

Damn Xander Barajas! If the general agreed, Eván was likely to lose a full company or even his entire battalion to a rotation that kept them pinned to security detail at the DMC. He'd much prefer to send his forces to the Hall of Nobles.

But Barajas was thinking ahead of his kommandant. General Weintraub nodded permission. "See to it, mister. And work up a rotation among other lances to take six-hour shifts patrolling the three gates." Weintraub paused. "Pushing the situation this hard will get a reaction out of VanLees. I'm sure of it. But he'll most likely want to stall until the Dragoons arrive. If not . . ." He glanced back at Leftenant Barajas. "The use of force is authorized in the unlikely event that Duke VanLees or the Kathil CMM attempt any early action against us."

Eván mentally saluted his junior. The general was correct—the base was more likely to see actual military action than the Hall of Nobles. Their forces there would be protected by the thin diplomatic fiction that they were bound to "protect" the city—any strike there by the CMM could turn public opinion against them and bolster the Eighth's position on Kathil. Xander was no doubt banking on that, hoping to be at the front of any fighting. And now the young leftenant had caught the general's attention. Well, Eván could still garner accolades for "overseeing" his man.

And Karen Fallon, at least, had not forgotten Eván's contribution today. "Kommandant Greene," she said, "you will accompany me to the ceremony in Radcliffe." She glanced at Weintraub. "If things are beginning to escalate, I'd like one or two officers backing me down there."

"My pleasure, General Fallon," Eván responded. It would give him a chance to recommend himself further to Fallon, and he wouldn't mind meeting the soldier all Kathil wanted to celebrate as a hero.

"Good," General Weintraub said, settling the matter. "Full military dress and my compliments to General Sampreis. Put our best foot forward for their ceremony." His penetrating gaze swept from Eván back to Fallon. "And when that's over, you can let Duke VanLees know the good news.

"Don't step on his toes too hard," the general said, "but make one thing very clear to them, Karen. The Eighth RCT is on Kathil to stay."

8

Clouds were building to the east of Radcliffe, piling into dark thunderheads that promised an early afternoon storm. This late into Kathil's spring season, you could almost set your watch by the "two o'clock showers" that washed across the southeastern seaboard for ninety or so minutes and then swept off, leaving behind fresh-scoured skies and a pleasant evening. For the late-morning ceremony, however, there was little fear of rain. Kathil's bright yellow sun still tracked steadily across a blue sky of liquid sapphire, with only a few rogue clouds to cast intermittent shade over the militia command assembled on the Radcliffe parade grounds.

Onstage before a crowd of several thousand soldiers, his own family, and several news agencies, David McCarthy stood at strict attention, bearing up under the weight as Major General Sampreis heaped praise on his head. Courage under fire. Leadership in the face of difficult duty. Composure and conduct exceeding even the normally high demands placed on a soldier in Task Force Serpent—a polite way of saying that David didn't fall apart and lose his warriors in a less-than-useless manner.

More than that, though, the general was taking every opportunity to confer on the Kathil militia, through David, the legacy of the now-disbanded Uhlans. David could almost hear spines stretching taller as their commanding officer built them up, promising them the mantle of "protecting Kathil as well as safeguarding the throne of New Avalon." With every word, Sampreis was emphasizing the militia's new responsibility for the planet, and aiming some not-so-subtle jabs at the Eighth RCT—a few of whose officers David had spotted in the crowd. Sampreis' pointed references to Victor Steiner-Davion were not lost on the crowd, either, and a few shifted uncomfortably at the slights to the Archon-Princess. But Sampreis was a politician as well as an officer, and he was careful not to issue any challenges that could not be withdrawn.

This, of course, was the real reason for the ceremony. It wasn't so much to honor a local boy, but to make it clear to everyone—the Eighth, Duke VanLees, George Hasek, even the distant Archon-Princess—who held military authority on Kathil. David was more than a little uncomfortable about being burdened with so much political symbolism, but Sampreis had made it quite clear that his patience with David's reluctance was at an end. Mercifully, the mandatory reading of the citation was almost complete.

"And for the meritorious bravery with which he led the Uhlans' rearguard action," General Sampreis intoned, "placing his life, his command, between harm and the survivors of his regiment, Commanding General Victor Steiner-Davion hereby commends David McCarthy for his heroism and extreme proof of valor. May it serve the Capellan March Militia as well."

Duke Petyr VanLees, as the ranking noble on Kathil, stepped to the podium General Sampreis vacated. The general had offered him the final act of this presentation in a show of support—a political windfall for the duke. The public address system carried his normally moderate voice over the crowd. "First Lord Theodore Kurita, acting as elected representative of the Star League, hereby confers upon David McCarthy, captain in the Kathil Capellan March Militia, the Star League Medal of Valor. It is my great honor to present this award to Captain McCarthy, on behalf of the Star League, and to also extend Marshal George Hasek's personal accolades. The Marshal is proud to recognize a new hero of the March. Captain McCarthy."

David stepped forward smartly, the blue cape of his formal dress uniform billowing behind him in a sudden gust of wind. The duke, flanked by Sampreis and Leftenant Colonel Zibler, turned to him with the medal, a Cameron star worked out of brilliant metals, descending from a ribbon of silver and black. Very much like the Task Force Serpent ribbon, David noted. Duke VanLees pinned it on his chest and pumped David's hand vigorously. David saluted the duke and then turned and rendered the same honors to Sampreis and Zibler, who returned the salutes proudly.

The duke led a long moment of thunderous applause, the acclamation rolling over the grounds like the afternoon storm come early. David swallowed his emotions. He had something to say to the assembled command—something that would be difficult for him, but at the same time a relief.

An expectant hush fell over the assemblage as he stepped to the podium, which he gripped with both hands. "Thank you," he said. "Your support means a great deal to me. Truly.

"When I learned of this award," he continued, his voice gaining strength as he went on, "I wasn't certain how I felt about it. Part of me still feels that I do not deserve it. Yes, I did give my all on Huntress. But so did many others. And like most military decorations, this one was purchased with blood. My comrades in arms fell in the fighting both before and during that final rearguard action. My friends. My military family. So it is with great reverence that I accept this decoration as much in their name as my own: Sergeant Dennings, Leftenant Okhapkin, Hauptmann Jess, Kommandant Terrace, Marshal Morgan Hasek-Davion. These, and all the others who fell along the way."

The light breeze had died down, now barely strong enough to carry away the heat that rose off the parade ground tarmac. The resulting silence was unnerving, as thousands hung on his every word. Right up front, in a place of honor, David spied his current command. They looked proud of their commander, and of themselves by association. Well, they had a right to be. Many of them had come a long way in a very short time. The discipline and drilling was paying off, and they were starting to come altogether as a unit. A new military family.

"Replacing that family is what led me back to Kathil, birthplace of the Uhlans. It was a chance to rebuild what was lost, while many more of my comrades entered service with the Star League Defense Force in an effort to keep alive the honor and traditions that once bound us together. I . . . they . . . we all are heir to the Uhlans' proud traditions. May we continue to be worthy. Thank you."

This applause was not as frantic or as enthusiastic as the demanding ovation he'd received earlier. But it was, David hoped, more sincere. His company of MechWarriors now looked thoughtful—many of them were finally becoming aware of the weight of responsibility they bore. Now he was giving them something back, confirming their claim to a portion of the Uhlans' legacy. Sergeant Black and perhaps a few others might still consider it only their due, but David knew he'd reached most of them. And he wasn't about to stop trying with the rest. It was important they understand.

All too soon, he feared, they would have to start earning it.

With the bulk of the command dismissed by General Sampreis, the militia MechWarriors, officer and senior enlisted of all supporting regiments, and any guests adjourned to one of the base's halls, where a luncheon had been laid out in honor of the celebration. His relatives tried to stick close to David, clinging to the only familiar face in this world of uniforms and weapons, but all too often he was efficiently cut out of their tight knot to receive congratulatory praise by another commander or noble.

His company did a slightly better job of shepherding him, Sergeant Black forming the enlisted ranks into an impromptu honor guard. Though they weren't about to deny colonels and generals, counts and marquises, access to David, they at least streamlined the process and prevented him from being swarmed. Corporal Smith took perhaps too much pleasure in thwarting senior officers, but David was of no mind to reprimand him today.

"We'd like to congratulate Captain . . . Excuse me!"

"Sorry, ma'am." Smith didn't sound particularly apologetic—his "sorry" came out more cheerful than contrite.

Trying to disengage from chitchat with a local baron, David glanced back to see that the corporal had intercepted a pair of unfamiliar officers in uniforms of the Eighth RCT. One was a kommandant and the other a general, favoring her left foot. David sipped at his watered-down drink, steeling himself for what would probably be an unpleasant encounter.

Then he choked as Richard said with smooth insincerity, "Didn't mean to step on your toes, General Fallon. I'm sure they're sore enough from Duke VanLees."

David set his glass down fast, trying not to cough as the cocktail burned his sinuses. Smith was taking cheap shots at a senior officer in the Eighth RCT!

Fallon's tone was cold enough to cause frostbite. "That's quite all right, Corporal. Stomping around blindly is certainly not the sole privilege of Duke VanLees."

If she thought her weight of rank would be enough to flatten Smith, Fallon was sorely misinformed. "That's great to hear," Smith purred as David was in mid-turn, on his way to intercept the Eighth RCT officers. "I'd hate for anyone to think I'd usurped his position."

That remark left the general open-mouthed with rage, and David had to suppress a smile of amusement. "General Fallon," he said hastily, interposing himself between Smith and Fallon before someone got killed. "It was very kind of the Eighth RCT to send representatives to the ceremony."

"Indeed." Fallon looked ready to pursue the matter with Smith, but as Sergeant Major Black stepped up to back her man, Fallon shrugged it aside with a visible effort. "Yes, well, General Weintraub would have liked to come himself, but . . ."

But he wasn't about to put himself at the mercy of the Kathil CMM, who just might decide to take him into custody and "escort" him off Kathil. The thought had crossed a few minds in the past week, David knew. "Very kind," David repeated again. Amanda silenced Corporal Smith with a glare, and David made a mental note to thank her later.

An awkward silence stretched among the five soldiers. Finally, Fallon nodded. "Congratulations on your decoration, Hauptmann McCarthy." She stressed David's equivalent FedCom rank. "Now I should speak with Duke VanLees." She moved off, but had to edge around groups of militia warriors who recognized her as an officer with the Eighth RCT and innocently pretended not to notice her attempts to pass.

Smith opened his mouth for a parting retort, but David stepped gently on his foot in warning, and Smith obediently closed his mouth again. Sergeant Black pulled him back to a satellite position. David considered once again the idea of firmer discipline with Smith, then dismissed it as a useless effort. The corporal was not insubordinate, not really. But he did approach the military with an eye for the absurd and a penchant for pointing it out. Company clown, or the company conscience? Even David had to admit that Richard Smith had aided morale a great deal in the past month, helping the company not take itself quite so seriously. He was even beginning to dent Amanda Black's elitist attitude. Perhaps that was worth a few stubbed toes.

"One of your men?" The kommandant had not followed after Fallon, and he stared after Smith with something akin to fascination. "Not afraid to speak his mind, is he?"

At first glance, David had thought the other officer much older—the receding hairline and salt-and-pepper hair tricked him. Reading the ribbons on the other officer's uniform, though, the kommandant could not have been in the armed forces for more than ten years: he did not wear the ribbon allowed anyone who'd served during the Clan invasion, up to 3052.

"No," David admitted. "And unfortunately I've yet to make him understand the benefits of tact." David offered his hand. "Captain David McCarthy."

The kommandant's pleasant expression vanished with David's use of the old Federated Suns rank, replaced by a new wariness in his hard brown eyes. "Kommandant

Eván Greene. Tell me, Captain, is your entire command so indifferent to correct military protocol?"

Reading the meaning underlying the other officer's guarded words, David knew he was being tested. But for what, he couldn't be certain. "Pretty much," he said, keeping his tone light. "We're building up slowly toward the idea of directly defying our legitimate orders."

The kommandant's hatchet-faced features darkened but cleared almost instantly. This was a man accustomed to hiding his thoughts, David decided. He brushed at his mustache with his fingertips, considering. "Against my better judgment, Captain McCarthy, I think I like you," he said at length. He finally turned to follow in General Fallon's wake, his manner inviting David to walk with him. "And of course, there is no denying I feel a measure of envy. That was quite the opportunity you found on Huntress." He nodded abruptly at the medal David wore.

David's jaw tightened at the insulting choice of words. "I've never seen a better place to lose good men and women," he said, his tone still mild.

"That was too bad," Greene agreed. "But look at what you accomplished. What you gained."

David shook his head. "It came at too high a price, Kommandant Greene."

"Someday, I hope to judge that for myself." Greene glanced ahead to where Fallon was talking to Duke Van-Lees. "Sooner than later, perhaps."

"On Lee?" David asked, deliberately bringing up the world to which Marshal Hasek had ordered the Eighth.

"Perhaps," Greene said again. "Perhaps even sooner than that."

David glanced sharply at the other man, but Greene's face was bland. Impossible to tell if he had meant what David suspected. But he was fairly certain he'd just acquired a rival.

"You *what*?" the duke exploded suddenly. They were close enough now to see the incredulous expression that had settled over Petyr VanLees' face, his olive skin flushing several shades darker as he shouted at General Karen Fallon.

"This ought to be good." Green nodded his farewell to David and quickened his pace for the last several meters.

David caught the satisfaction that briefly flickered across General Fallon's hard gaze and knew that she was deliberately goading Duke VanLees. General Sampreis was moving toward the confrontation, as were several senior officers of the militia and what were certainly two more from the Eighth RCT. The familiar hollow sensation began to build in David's stomach. There were no calm heads to prevail here—and this was the kind of situation that could turn very ugly very fast. Across the hall, Damien Zibler had made his excuses and was working his way toward the budding confrontation. He would not be in time to help, though.

David gathered Smith and Amanda Black to him with his eyes and signaled to them that he needed a safety net. He trusted Amanda's discipline, and for once he could use Smith's usual disregard for protocol. That the corporal would enjoy himself was beside the point. The pair moved off, passing the word along and quietly forming up a solid cadre of soldiers a short distance from the center of the conflict.

David arrived a few steps behind Major General Sampreis, just in time to see Duke VanLees round on his chief military supporter. "Weintraub has ordered the occupation of the Hall of Nobles," he said, omitting any title or gesture of respect for the Eighth's commander. "You will do something about this at once!"

A new wave of tension rippled through the room as the duke's announcement made the rounds. A few insubordinate shouts from the back, directed at Fallon, made the militia's attitude fairly clear. Officers began crowding in closer, obviously expecting some kind of confrontation and ready—eager—to get involved. All the tensions of the past several weeks were building to a head, and the slightest flare could touch off a catastrophe.

Karen Fallon was the picture of studied innocence. "Food shortages often lead to demonstrations and riots," she said blandly. "Hauptmann General Weintraub is merely acting in your best interests, Duke VanLees, to keep order."

"By placing a military presence among the nobility?" VanLees demanded.

Eván Greene turned to Fallon. "Well, we do have the

option of placing District City itself under full military control, if the duke would prefer," he said, ostensibly addressing his senior officer. "We could communicate this desire to General Weintraub immediately." If he noticed the deadly glares directed at him by some nearby militia warriors, he ignored them.

"You won't be communicating with anyone," Van Lees promised Greene, his hands balled into impotent fists. "Not any time soon."

If anyone doubted that Petyr VanLees was about to demand that the RCT officers be placed under arrest, it could only be the few civilians present, who were not exactly privy to the full array of tensions that had been building between the units. David stepped up quickly, one hand falling on Greene's shoulder. "What Duke VanLees means is that you will certainly be too busy protecting the Hall of Nobles." He looked to General Sampreis, fishing for help, and missed Eván's ferocious glare at him for stealing the initiative in the conversation.

Not quite as offended as the duke was by the idea of troops holding the Hall of Nobles hostage, Sampreis had apparently caught on to the difficulty fairly quickly. Arresting Weintraub's exec and a few minor officers would almost certainly lead to open hostilities between the militia and the RCT—something most were still hoping to avoid. And having the Eighth confine their tactics to the Hall of Nobles was infinitely preferable to having them spread out over the entire capital. "Of course," he said. "And I'll send a regiment of infantry to D.C. at once, to support your actions."

"Thank you, General Sampreis, but I'm certain the Eighth can handle things adequately, for now," Fallon said quickly. "Moving more troops into the capital will only cause further difficulties." She clearly knew better than to allow the Kathil CMM an opportunity to move troops that close to the RCT's base.

Sampreis visibly weighed the political situation, and once again took the road of compromise. "I will hear from you if there is any trouble?"

"I think that is very safe to say, General." There was no doubt that Fallon's promise was more of a threat. A heavy silence descended over the room, each side waiting

for the other to say just the wrong thing. And one of them
would, if given much more time.

As the confrontation played itself out, David had noted
Amanda gathering soldiers to her side. Word spread
throughout the banquet hall as infantry called to each
other with whispers and hand signals, moving into position. Corporal Smith caught his eye and nodded, restraining a grin with difficulty. Amanda quietly moved
up behind David, with Lieutenants Michaels and Pachenko and two full squads in tow.

"Since everyone seems agreed," David said, breaking
the spell, "we shouldn't keep General Weintraub's aide
and officers away from him for something as insignificant
as a luncheon. I'm sure they'll be needed to help maintain
order in the city." Fallon turned a withering expression
on David, but Greene noticed the organized warriors and
looked at him with resentful admiration.

Zibler had finally arrived at the center of the brewing
storm, saw what David had planned, and immediately
insinuated himself between Fallon and Duke VanLees. He
eased the reluctant duke aside, striking up an obviously
inane conversation. Sampreis sketched an informal salute
to Karen Fallon and joined the retreating pair. The waiting
infantry sergeants and not a few junior officers moved in
to bracket the Eighth RCT's officers, who quickly found
themselves isolated.

Amanda Black stepped up smartly, saluted, and said,
"If you would follow me, ma'am and sirs." Tara Michaels
and Dylan Pachenko slid in behind the group, ready to
follow them out.

Twin lines now stretched across the hall, leaving open
a wide channel that led toward the door. Corporal Smith
was near the end of that line, arranging the final dozen
meters and then ushering the RCT cadre forward with a
sweep of his arm and a wide smile. No one in the line
spoke, staring silently as they put quiet pressure on the
Eighth's officers to simply leave.

"Thank you for your attendance, General Fallon,"
David said in polite dismissal. He nodded at Greene.
"Kommandant."

"Captain," Greene returned. As David had guessed he
would, Greene led the Eighth's retreat, partially saving

his commander's dignity. The channel of militia soldiers collapsed in their wake, forming a solid wall against any thought of returning.

A furious conference had developed among Duke Van-Lees, several generals and a few colonels. No one below the rank of major, in fact, until Leftenant Colonel Zibler motioned David over to the impromptu planning session.

"This is an outrage," VanLees said, his fury barely held in check. "Kathil's Hall of Nobles has never been held hostage before, and I won't allow it now. General Sampreis, I must insist that you answer this challenge."

It was easy enough for the politicians to call for action—they weren't the ones who would have to live—or die—with the consequences on the battlefield. David watched Zibler and Sampreis for some sign of which way they were leaning.

Sampreis frowned at VanLees—he was obviously wavering. "What would you have me do? Arrest a few officers? That would only bring protests from Weintraub and perhaps Katherine Steiner-Davion herself."

"No," VanLees agreed reluctantly. "Your man here saved us from that problem well enough. But I want to know if you're ready to finally act."

No one wanted to answer the duke—no one wanted to put what they were all thinking into words. Once that happened, it would be impossible to go back. David cleared his throat cautiously and proceeded only when Zibler and Sampreis both indicated their approval. "Begging your pardon, sir," he said, diffidently, "but that's not the question."

The noble might not have much of a grasp on military tactics, but he did not suffer from ego, either. He had already recognized that David had prevented him from making one mistake. He ran rawboned fingers through tight, dark hair and simply asked, "Then what is, Captain?"

Zibler knew. It was the same question David had asked of him on arriving. The same one that had followed them as they worked hard to build the Kathil CMM into a solid military unit. "Are we ready to fight?" he said simply. Nothing else mattered if they weren't ready to back up action with force.

David noticed Sampreis conducting a straw poll of his officers in immediate attendance, saw the various men and women nod their willingness. Zibler hesitated, looking at David, who smiled grimly and nodded on behalf of his company. They were ready. Two weeks ago—even one—and his answer would have been no. But the unit was finally coming together, and if a battle loomed they were as ready as they were likely to get. He didn't want to fight, but if they had to they would.

"Hopefully, it won't come to that," Sampreis said, echoing David's thoughts. "We still have options short of full-scale armed conflict. Taking Fallon and a few minor officers into protective custody might not have accomplished much, but if we can corral a good portion of their officer corps . . ."

"Sever the head from the body," Colonel Dwight Mancuso nodded. "Quick and painless." He glanced at the nearby militia infantry commander. "I have two companies of security specialists that could handle that job. Just say the word."

"It won't be easy," Zibler said, folding his arms over his chest. "Mitchell Weintraub is no fool. He'll be expecting some kind of reprisal."

"So," Sampreis said, "we give them a few days to relax. By the week's end, their soldiers will have settled down into a new routine. And in the meantime, we can make our preparations."

One week. So much could happen in a week. So much had already happened since David's arrival on Kathil. Events seemed to be spinning far out of control—he felt himself caught up in a deadly current, where the best he might hope for was to hang on to some kind of stable float and ride it out. And hopefully, this time, bring the majority of his people safely through. One week. "And then what?" he asked aloud.

Sampreis polled his officers once more and then nodded his promise to Duke Petyr VanLees. "Then we strike the head from the Eighth RCT."

9

District Military Compound
District City, Kathil
Capellan March, Federated Commonwealth
16 November 3062

Leftenant Xander Barajas pounded his FLC-8R *Falconer* along the fenceline of the District Military Compound, walking at a leisurely pace of thirty-five kilometers per hour as he patrolled the five klicks between the DMC's northern and southwest guardposts. A cleared path four hundred meters wide followed the fence on both sides, separating the industrial areas of D.C. from the rows of infantry barracks built in long-house design. The seventy-five-ton 'Mech moved with a rolling gait, a result of steep-canted legs that fastened to hip joints mounted far behind the machine's center of gravity. It was a design Xander was comfortable with, and it gave him an incredible range of motion when twisting toward the side and rear—a good advantage if he ever managed to see combat on this stinking world.

He had been on guard duty for five days now, and his boredom was increasing exponentially with every hour that passed. The militia was only a couple hundred kilometers away in Radcliffe—a few hours' travel for a 'Mech. What was taking them so long?

But for five days, there had been nothing—no response,

not even a verbal protest, from General Sampreis over the RCT's seizure of the Hall of Nobles. And the longer the silence stretched, the more suspicious Xander became. They had to be planning some kind of reprisal—and when it came, he would be ready.

He just wished it would hurry up and get here.

Just for amusement's sake, he planted the *Falconer's* broad-splayed left foot hard against the ground and twisted back to his right, bringing weapons up to track Sergeant Case's camouflage-painted *Caesar*. The tremor of his hard step joggled the cockpit, jumping the targeting crosshairs but not enough to spoil the imagined shot. Framed perfectly under the darkened reticle was the wedge-shaped torso of his lancemate's *Caesar*. The Katzbalger insignia of a 'Mech silhouette spitted by a broadsword, set right over the *Caesar's* fusion-powered heart, made for an ideal target. The leftenant selected for active targeting, lighting the *Caesar* up and no doubt ringing several alarms in his lancemate's ear.

Xander laughed, low and harsh. "Bang—you're dead," he said, not loud enough for the comm system to pick it up.

"Damn it, Xander! I wish you wouldn't do that," Case said into Xander's ear; his voice did not sound amused.

The neurohelmets each man wore served multiple functions. Not only did they help balance so many tons of upright, walking metal, but comm systems built into the helmet itself also made for hands-free communication. This time Xander spoke loud enough for the voice-activated mic to transmit his words. "You should keep on your toes, Brian. One of these days I might actually pull the trigger." Xander flicked off his active targeting, laughing again.

Brian Case did not. Xander did not doubt that his lancemate believed him. He knew there were whispered rumors about him, about what he had done in the ferocity of combat, and he knew that deep down, many of his fellow warriors feared him. he preferred it that way.

Or maybe Case had just been distracted by sensor readings. "Contact," he called out suddenly, voice tight with concern. "Three neutrals crowding the southwest gate."

Xander's gaze flicked expertly over his sensors, coming

to rest on the heads-up display of symbols and brief designation tags. The gate stood out as a friendly blue bar, tagged as a static fortification, though there really wasn't much fortified about a watchpost set in the gap of a chain-link fence. A single blue triangle represented the Hetzer wheeled assault gun each guard post relied on for military backup.

But it was the trio of green triangles, piled into an overlapping cluster, that had drawn Sergeant Case's attention. Even before punching up a zoomed feed on his forward camera, Xander read their designations and frowned. The video confirmed that they were all unarmed military vehicles: two open-bed transports with extended cabs and a military-use sedan. No real threat, except the symbols were not Katzbalger icons, which tagged the vehicles as Kathil CMM. That, and the suspicious fact that the gate had not radioed out their arrival.

This could be it.

"At a hard walk, Brian," Xander ordered.

He throttled up to the *Falconer*'s best cruising speed of fifty-seven kilometers per hour—if they ran any faster, they might tip off the potential hostiles at the gate. The cockpit swayed and shimmied for a few seconds before settling down into its new gait with that same firm, rocking motion. As the watchpost loomed nearer, a prickly sensation crawled over Xander's shoulders and neck, his hackles rising. He reached out to toggle his active targeting back on.

The sedan and one truck had just passed through the gate when the BattleMechs came into view. The sedan continued on, but the truck braked to a rapid halt, as if the driver was worried. Now Xander knew something was wrong. The sedan rolled to a halt immediately thereafter, as if waiting for the trucks. One arm waved lazily through an open window—too friendly by far.

Xander toggled for the watchpost frequency, putting his private channel to Brian on "listen-only" status. "Southwest gate, this is Alpha patrol." The leftenant knew he should try for a light touch, but his voice sounded hard despite his best efforts. "Who are your new friends?"

"They're Kathil militia," a voice crackled back through very light static. Nothing too suspicious, but enough to make the voice unidentifiable—meaning the transmission could be faked. "They have orders to move some old equipment down to Radcliffe that is in storage on the DMC. We were just now passing them through, but we can hold them. Is there a problem, Alpha patrol?"

Close enough now to switch from video monitors to the cockpit's ferroglass shield, Xander saw a man step from the gatehouse and motion for the sedan and truck to remain where they were. Another pair of guards moved toward the Hetzer. Though not as intimidating as a BattleMech, the Hetzer's twelve-centimeter autocannon gave pause even to most MechWarriors. The depleted uranium slugs it spat out could amputate limbs or crack a BattleMech's torso in seconds.

They were halfway to the wheeled assault gun when Xander altered his course slightly and slowed to an easy walk. He was now far enough from the gate that the guards—if they were militia impostors—would not be worried about an up-close inspection blowing their cover, but not so far that the gate was out of reach of his weaponry. "Have you informed Leftenant Barajas of their arrival?" he asked, suddenly all charm and easy manners.

"Not yet, Alpha. But we'll do so at once. Thanks for the reminder."

Xander smiled with feral satisfaction, lips skinning back from barred teeth. Now he had them. He twisted the *Falconer* to his right, dropping darkened crosshairs over the first truck and pulling into the trigger for his particle projection cannon even as the crosshairs burned the gold of target acquisition.

Hellish lightning streamed out of the barrel that served as the BattleMech's left arm, a cerulean cascade that slammed into the transport's cab at the front cornerpost. Under that intense burst of raw energy, the metal and safety glass simply folded back in on itself, torn and melted. The cab filled with harsh, blue-white light, catching at least a half-dozen bodies in the arcing flash. Glass shattered and side doors plumped outward. Then the hood jumped up as the engine compartment belched out a roiling fireball. The gas tank went next in a ground-shaking explosion that tossed the large vehicle over onto its side. The main guard leapt back into the shack, where no doubt the Eighth's regular security detail was being held—bound, unconscious or dead. The two men near the Hetzer hit the ground as hot shrapnel from the explosion cut the air overhead.

"Good God," Case breathed over the intercom, shocked at Xander's sudden attack. Not trusting Brian to hold his end, Xander shuffled the *Falconer* around and split his arms wide to focus on two targets at once. His PPC covered the sedan, targeting crosshairs pinning it in place. The gauss rifle that made up his BattleMech's left arm was pointed loosely at the Hetzer—close enough to deter anyone from a wild run for the weapon. No one outside a 'Mech could move now without getting several more people killed.

"I want everyone out there on the ground," he said, voice deceptively warm now that he had established control of the situation. "Faces in the dirt and hands behind your heads. Any trouble—anyone tries to run or we detect even one transmission to your friends in Radcliffe—and your team in the sedan joins your friends crisping in the truck."

Belatedly, Case's *Caesar* moved up to cover the sedan. "You'd better be right," Case said in a harsh whisper. "If you just fired on our own men, or on civilians . . ."

Xander could have laughed again at the man's timidity. Authorized to use force, that was what the general had said. It had taken longer than he'd thought, but the militia had finally tried something. Duke VanLees and General Sampreis would regret their actions today. Weintraub would not take kindly to the enemy trying to infiltrate his base. And that was what the militia was, now, Xander thought, swiveling his *Falconer* on its hip joints just far enough that he could admire the burning wreckage of the transport truck. Leftenant Barajas had seen to that.

"Bang," he whispered. "You're dead."

Trial of Wills

These are the times that try men's souls.
—Thomas Paine, 1776, The American Crisis

10

District Military Compound
District City, Kathil
Capellan March, Federated Commonwealth
16 November 3062

Tightening the side cinch on his well-padded cooling vest, Eván paced Leftenant General Fallon as they broke from a corridor and trekked across the 'Mech bay's wide, open expanse. The spring chill raised gooseflesh on his exposed arms and legs—traditional MechWarrior garb wasn't designed for cool weather. Once he was in combat and running up his BattleMech's heat curve, though, Eván knew he would appreciate the effect.

"That man is out of control," he said, his voice snapping with displeasure. He had to make it clear that he had not ordered Barajas' assault, which had taken place barely an hour ago. Since then, the base had resembled an overturned anthill, with RCT members scurrying every which way. Eván himself had barely had time to yank on his combat uniform before Fallon had dragged him out to the 'Mech bay. "Hauptmann General Weintraub authorized force, yes, but not excessive force. Especially not against the Kathil militia."

"It's a fine line," Fallon answered easily, which startled Eván. He had not expected her to defend a borderline psychopath like Xander Barajas. "If those two men had taken control of the Hetzer and destroyed our 'Mechs, do you think the general would be less displeased right now?"

Eván frowned. There was a chance the Hetzer might have destroyed one 'Mech—possible, though slim. But taking out both—that hovered on the edge of improbability. "It's hard to argue hypotheticals," he said.

Her blue eyes pinned Eván with steady resolve. "My point exactly. Leftenant Barajas acted as he saw necessary to protect his command and obey the general."

Cautiously, Eván nodded. Ever since Fallon had taken him under her wing after McCarthy's award ceremony, he had been kept busy trying to figure her out. It seemed she was a bit more aggressive than he'd given her credit for. "If you were to say so to General Weintraub, that might go a long way toward vindicating Xander's actions," he ventured.

"And it would cover your back rather well, too," she said dryly, seeing through to his real concern. "Don't worry, Eván. Your man will take some heat, but I'll safeguard him. And I'll firewall any attempts to roll the blame uphill toward you."

Eván knew how much the direct support of Karen Fallon could mean for his career, and wasn't about to play the role of the undeserving soldier. His silence spoke well for him, apparently, as Fallon looked pleased with his lack of response.

When he finally spoke again, Eván softened his tone to a more conversational level. "All right. Regardless of the might-have-beens, that security detail was on site to take our officer corps into 'protective custody?' "

Fallon nodded. "If they had gotten close to our operations building, they might have caught Mitchell and me and a number of our key tactical staff in a morning meeting and snatched us before anyone had a chance to raise the alarm. Leftenant General Price would have been the highest-ranking officer left free, and he wouldn't have known how to coordinate our various forces." She smiled slightly. "A simple plan, but it would have gutted our strength very efficiently if it had succeeded."

"And our response?"

"The general intends to use their actions to justify

breaking the Kathil CMM into smaller, city-based militia. If we can split their forces, we can make it much harder for them to oppose us—and that much harder for them to coordinate with the Dragoons when they finally arrive. We're sending 'Mech and armor assets to Radcliffe in hopes of taking quick control of their administrative complex and catching their leadership unawares. If we're going to move at all, it has to be now."

"Because if we don't, the militia might take Barajas' assault public, and use it as grounds to forcibly evict us from Kathil," Eván said, uneasy at the thought. "If the militia had public opinion on its side, we'd have to leave, or risk a massacre like the one on Kentares. I don't think that would sit well with the Archon-Princess—she's having enough problems keeping things quiet as it is."

"I think you have the situation scoped out and locked in," Fallon said approvingly. "We plan to scatter them into impotent pieces all across the world—with their senior officers in custody, the troops will have no choice but to comply. It's a sound plan—providing they aren't already set to move against us with full force, that is. We have to get this situation under control fast, before it escalates."

It already has, was Eván's first thought. Barajas' impulsive actions at the gate had crossed a very definite line: a military officer had fired on soldiers who were theoretically their allies. It was the first step toward a word no one wanted to think yet, let alone say out loud: war. But if the Eighth launched a preemptive strike, and carved the militia into ineffectual units, they could prevent things from getting any worse, and in the process strengthen their claim that the Eighth was the only military force on planet strong enough to protect Kathil.

And if they were going to do it, it had to be done before the Dragoons arrived in a little more than two weeks. Weintraub was of the opinion that VanLees' reluctant "cooperation" with the Eighth would ensure the Dragoons came out on the right side of the conflict, or a least keep them neutral. Eván wasn't so sure. These were the Dragoons, after all—they had no particular love for Katrina. And if they hitched up with the militia, Weintraub would have a real problem on his hands.

They had to strike now—and, if truth be told, Evàn was kind of hoping for a shot at David McCarthy. Evàn had to admit that the man was likeable enough, but his envy of McCarthy's accomplishments colored his feelings. What made McCarthy any more deserving of admiration? Just because he'd happened to be in the right place at the right time, he was suddenly a hero. If Evàn had the chance, he'd see how well the other warrior's "heroism and extreme proof of valor" stood up under a pair of gauss rifles. Then they'd see who was hailed as the "hero of Kathil."

They had arrived at the feet of Evàn's *Cerberus*, an assault 'Mech he had come to love. Named for the mythological beast that guarded the gates to the infernal reaches, his *Cerberus* would not have looked out of place among either gods or monsters. The ninety-five-ton machine rested in a wide-legged stance on its unique, paw-styled feet, a lowered center of gravity giving it superior balance, in addition to better-than-average speed. It lacked the articulated hands of many other BattleMechs, trading them for two of the heaviest weapons a war machine could carry onto the battlefield. Evàn stood directly beneath the lowered right arm, staring up into the wide, dark bore of the arm-mounted gauss rifle. Those cannon could throw out nickel-ferrous slugs at better than supersonic velocity. And Evàn had two of them.

A personnel gantry had been wheeled over to the machine, its ladder leading up to the *Cerberus'* cockpit. "Orders?" he asked Fallon, hoping for an assignment that would put him at the front of the offensive, where he might have a chance to shine.

"You'll be backing up Jim Wendt's command," she said instead. "He's already en route, hoping to take the militia by surprise and occupy their base before news of the botched attack on our gate gets back to them. Your personal company was the next full 'Mech command we could pull together on a moment's notice, though we have a full armor regiment preparing to roll out, and our alert-ready aerospace wing is already in the air." Fallon braced him with one hand on each shoulder, her brilliant blue eyes boring into his like energy cannon. "We're talking minutes here, so get moving. Another battalion will be powered up and on the move within the hour. Soon, we'll either be the undisputed force on Kathil, or we'll be in for a real fight."

Eván nodded and cracked a slanted smile. "I think you'll find they're deployed and ready for us," he said. "Sampreis might have laid his bets on a security team, but Zibler and McCarthy didn't strike me as men who leave themselves open to unnecessary risk."

"You're likely right," she admitted. "But we won't know until that first shot—make that the second shot now—is fired. Now button up and head out." She held up one hand to forestall his next question. "And to make it official, General Weintraub has authorized the immediate use of force if you encounter patrols from the Kathil CMM."

Frowning, Eván paused with one foot on the gantry's lower ladder rung. "What about the second NAIS Cadre?" The academy training unit had forces in the area. If they had hooked up with Sampreis' militia, Eván wanted to know how far he was authorized to go.

Fallon shook off the question with a dismissive air. "The trainees haven't taken sides so far, and there's no indication that they might take a stand against us. I expect they'll fold into our lines as soon as word reaches them." Her smile did not touch her eyes. "Anyway, most of their cadre remains on extended training maneuvers on the west coast. But if they're out there, and you witness any hostile act or have proof positive that they're working with the CMM, you may consider the general's orders to apply."

"I report directly to General Weintraub?"

This time Fallon shook her head, smiling thinly at his barely disguised ambition. "No, you report to me. I report to Mitchell. You made that bed when you jumped onto my side against Countess Reichart."

"Fair enough. And it's always a good thing to know whose bed you're sleeping in." He scaled the ladder then without another glance back, allowing Fallon to ignore the flirtatious comment. Besides, he had already scored enough points off her. It was a rare thing to get the last word with a general.

The *Cerberus'* cockpit design was unique, buried beneath thick-plated shoulders and an overhead turret that

housed the antimissile defense system. All that protection
left no easy access hatch to open or canopy to be levered
away. Instead, the entire face of the BattleMech extended
out on a hydraulic system, as if partially removing a mask.
The gantry Eván climbed deposited him on a small platform, just one step off an extended bridge wedged in between the unhinged face and the humanoid machine's
"collar line."

He stepped across, climbing up and back into the cockpit and squirming into the slightly reclined pilot's couch.
A five-point harness snugged him in, the quick-release
buckle pressing into the padded cooling vest at his abdomen. From an overhead shelf, he brought down the BattleMech's neurohelmet and tugged it on, resting the lower
edges against the reinforced shoulders of his cooling vest
for added support and securing it via a thick chin strap.
A bundle of cables snaked down from the helmet's extended chin and puddled in his lap. The four thinner cables he attached to biosensor pads secured from an
underseat compartment and quickly taped to his upper
arms and inner thighs. The thicker, longer lead he plugged
into the 'Mech's computer port.

Throwing toggles and making a series of control adjust-
ments in response to assorted cautionary lights, Eván
quickly brought the 'Mech's fusion engine to life. Its pow-
erful growl warmed the *Cerberus'* heart and shook the machine with restrained power. The computer blinked on
with a green phosphorescent glow, detailing status checks
on the various subsystems and then shunting in the voice
synthesizer to echo the last few examinations.

"Fusion-engine startup sequence completed," he announced aloud. "All systems operational. Initiate security
system check."

With each BattleMech worth tens of millions of C-bills,
security was never taken light. Two separate stages confirmed a MechWarrior's authority to control the battlefield
juggernauts. The first, a simple identity check, would
match Eván's voiceprint with the recorded pattern saved
to memory.

"Kommandant Eván Greene," he identified himself,
"Eighth Federated Commonwealth Regimental Combat
Team, Second 'Mech Battalion."

"Voiceprint match obtained. Please verify with personal identification key."

Given the ability to simply record and play back some-one's spoken voice, the PIK was a code known only to the MechWarrior. It could be as simple as a few spoken words or as elaborate as a series of nonsense syllables; most MechWarriors chose a phrase easy enough for them to remember but personal enough to make it difficult for anyone else to guess.

"Opportunity knocks," he said evenly.

Eván smiled to himself as the computer released control of the myomer musculature, the *Cerberus* flexing at the knees to a deeper stance. A flick of another toggle, and the extended face of the BattleMech slid back in to lock down into an airtight seal. He opened the throttle for an easy walk, his touch light on the control sticks as the ninety-five-ton war machine began to move out of the bay.

Opportunity was knocking, all right. And it was time to kick open the door.

11

Howell River Valley
Daytin, Kathil
Capellan March, Federated Commonwealth
16 November 3062

Halfway between Radcliffe and District City, the Howell River left the highway and turned west, the silver ribbon running back inland and then south for several hundred kilometers before making its final and direct stab toward the distant ocean. The resort community of Daytin spread itself along this stretch of the river. Large private estates claimed the western bank, while the eastern was given over to vacation spots, recreation areas, and local businesses. Thick forests and pale meadows had dominated the river valley.

Now the soft, yellow-green sward detailed the path of the running battle where the ground had been torn apart by heavy 'Mech tread and missile detonations—a rough and fire-scorched path that stretched into the distance. Errant laser fire had set several small fires among groves of white maple and pale elms. Luckily, the spring-green wood was not spreading flames quickly. One venerable elm wrenched free of the ground as a pair of BattleMechs shouldered past, pushing aside the stately trees that could never compete with several hundred tons of dedicated metal.

The first 'Mech, a *Rakshasa*, reached out with both arms and speared shafts of coherent ruby light at David McCarthy's *Devastator*. David ducked to one side, the neurohelmet's circuitry translating his motion into a shoulder-dipping crouch that pulled the hundred-ton BattleMech out of the line of fire. The twin laser beams sliced the air over his left shoulder, allowing David to concentrate for the moment on a pair of encroaching Manticore heavy tanks. Though 'Mechs were the undisputed masters of the modern battlefield, the Manticore's pulse-laser technology and good armor made them just as dangerous at close ranges. Allowing them to crawl in and set up a strongpoint would be a major tactical mistake.

David couldn't afford any mistakes. General Sampreis' raid on the Eighth's base was one mistake too many. Judging by the size of the Eighth's counterassault, the raid had failed, and now David and his soldiers had to face the consequences. Leftenant Colonel Zibler had originally placed the company on patrol to make contact with the returning security team; that was the most backup General Sampreis would allow, for fear a heavy 'Mech movement could alert District City and the Eighth RCT to their sneak attack. But then the Eighth pulled off their own surprise attack, a full battalion stomping down from Kathil's capital toward the militia's base at Radcliffe. Sampreis, on orders from Duke VanLees, had overridden Zibler, ordering David to fall back toward Daytin and hold a defensive line while the rest of the CMM mobilized.

He had no time to wonder whether the fighting had spread far enough inland to threaten his family at Vorhaven. His company was fighting below their abilities. They'd been emotionally unprepared to face off against another Commonwealth unit, even if they knew it was a possibility if the D.C. raid went sour. But the militia's reluctance to center crosshairs on the gauntlet-and-sunburst symbol of the Commonwealth did not appear to be reciprocated by the Katzbalger forces.

David took this into account as he orchestrated the militia's defensive posture. He'd straddled the river at a spot fairly well-removed from the local population, placing Pachenko's lance on the far side while he and Tara held the eastern bank. Nearby estates had been given advance warning, and hopefully their inhabitants had abandoned them by now. It gave his people more freedom to move about, safeguarding the area.

But why they'd been ordered to make their stand here, David couldn't say. The maneuver made no sense to him, but then he wasn't a general—or a politician. Besides, any order that might put off combat for even a few minutes had seemed a godsend. Simming with his company had been hard enough. Now that he was facing live fire again, he was about ready to jump out of his skin.

The reprieve he'd hoped for—a chance for calmer heads to prevail and end the crisis peacefully—now seemed impossible. Kathil was in the grip of a firestorm. The best he could hope for was to fall back and regroup, and then come back at them from the rear when Zibler set his remaining two companies in the RCT's path. If they acted swiftly enough, they could end the escalating conflict almost before it started.

Except that the Katzbalger battalion split off two lances to pursue David's company and delay their retreat. Already down two 'Mechs, the Katzbalger forces continued to press forward. The RCT forces were not strong enough to deal a crippling assault, but they efficiently pinned David's company in place while the bulk of the battalion pressed on toward Radcliffe.

The lead Manticore crawled forward into the shade of a white maple, its swinging turret scoring a large gouge into the immense bole. David floated his targeting crosshairs over it, squeezing into the shot and scouring the front of the tank with twin particle projection cannon. The blue-white energy snaked out, crackling and spitting, to punch in just below the turret—not enough to penetrate the armor. He resigned himself to another salvo when suddenly a sapphire beam rode in behind his damage to cut the wound deeper. A stream of autocannon slugs pounded in after that, filling the interior of the Manitcore with lethal metal. The turret swung around, and around, locked into its rotation with no live hand to arrest its turn.

"You're welcome," Amanda Black called out over the commline, backpedaling her *Bushwacker* into the relative safety of a small copse on David's left.

Even further back, Tara Michaels' *Enforcer* and two of

her lancemates plowed forward to stop a *Maelstrom* attempting to flank the company. "Welcome for what?" she asked, that husky voice instantly recognizable. "Everything holding there, sir?"

As well as it could, David decided, when your own planet was tearing itself apart. But he had no time for conversation, even though he and Amanda had managed to temporarily stall the enemy advance. The second Manticore threw itself into reverse, unwilling to follow its comrade into death. David hauled on the control sticks, reaching for the *Rakshasa* as it and its companion *Nightsky* paired off against him. The *Nightsky* rose on jets of plasma, arcing toward David's position and pulling back its arm-mounted titanium hatchet. Sapphire darts spat out of its large pulse laser, stinging into the *Devastator*'s hip and left leg. Missiles launched by the *Rakshasa* cut in front of the *Nightsky*'s flight, bursting over the *Devastator*'s upper torso.

The assault machine rocked back under the attack, but it was not about to be overturned. David held the 'Mech on its feet in a wide stance, flinching away from the threatening *Nightsky* as he tried to concentrate on the first 'Mech. When the reticle burned the golden hue of a hard lock, he toggled for all weapons, ignoring his still-high heat curve, hoping to put the *Rakshasa* down hard and fast.

Gauss rifles threw out a pair of high-velocity slugs, a flash of silver their only telltale sign before smashing into and through the *Rakshasa*'s left arm. PPCs scourged the machine's entire left side, melting and blasting away its protective armor plating and opening up large, molten-tinged rents. Three medium-class lasers stabbed emerald knives in afterward, digging into the *Rakshasa*'s critical internal structure.

David didn't know if it was one of the energy cannon streams or the lasers, but his salvo ruptured the *Rakshasa*'s left-side missile bin. Solid propellant touched off by the intense energy began a chain reaction as warheads detonated in sympathetic explosions. The *Rakshasa* was thrown back into the toppled elm, its remaining limbs tangling in the timber. Fire belched upward, running from the reddish-orange of the erupting ammunition to the golden fire of a fusion-engine overload.

The violent explosion trembled the ground and threw a shock wave into the air that tumbled the airborne *Nightsky* off course. Fifty tons of upright metal flies about as well as one might expect, but it still constituted a danger even when out of control. David throttled into a backward walk, trying to gain a few critical meters as the unbalanced behemoth rushed toward him at better than fifty kilometers an hour, arms flailing and turning its left shoulder toward the ground to muffle what was certain to be a devastating landing. As it crossed David's line of sight, he triggered off a second barrage out of reflex, hoping to somehow deflect it from a collision.

A wave of scorching heat washed through the cockpit as the *Devastator*'s fusion reactor spiked hard to accommodate the power drain. David gasped for breath, pulling hot coals down into his lungs and then tensing against the coming impact. The gauss slugs had both flown wide, flashing off into a nearby stand of maple, but amazingly the *Devastator*'s intense cascade of energy weapons caught the *Nightsky* in right profile. Armor sloughed away, trailing a molten rain over the ground and adding to the jumping 'Mech's misfortune.

But it would never be enough to counter the *Nightsky*'s momentum.

The fifty-ton machine plowed into the ground only ten meters short of the *Devastator*, digging in at the shoulder and cartwheeling its legs back over its head. It came back down on its hip, tearing a furrow into the soft earth as it slid and finally hitting David's BattleMech full against the left leg. Its leg wrenched back against its hip joint, the *Devastator* lost any hope of maintaining its balance and tumbled forward, falling onto the *Nightsky* and rolling off the back side to bounce several times against the ground. The impact threw David repeatedly against his harness, the straps digging in and bruising his legs and shoulders. His vision swam, and pain lanced through his neck from the whiplash effect. Then a sharper pain stabbed deep into his brain, and the world went black.

And he was suddenly back on Huntress.

*   *   *

A chill gripped David as he watched the eighty-five-ton *Masakari* struggle to its feet behind the *Black Hawk*. It had nothing to do with his heat scale, which was edging into the red band; it was the loss of blood. He wasn't certain how gravely he'd been hurt. The neck wound didn't bleed with the intensity of a sliced artery, but it bled freely enough to concern him.

Only seven 'Mechs left of his battered company. The clan warriors were fresher, better armed and armored, and they fought with the ferocity of a wounded and trapped animal. That the Jaguars were down four of their own people was nothing short of a miracle, or an indication of the desperation of the Uhlans' rearguard. No one here expected to leave this battlefield alive.

And that included David. Ignoring the *Black Hawk*'s incredible array of twelve medium-class lasers, knowing that such an energy salvo could burn away the last of his armor and leave him a walking skeleton—if it left him walking at all—David sidestepped for an angle on the wounded *Masakari*. One less assault Omni might spell the difference for an Uhlan on this field.

One gauss slug missed wide, his targeting thrown off by heat-addled sensors. The other, his last shot from that ammunition bin, creased the assault machine's right arm and smashed one PPC to ruin. His own energy cannon dug along the *Masakari*'s right side, one pouring megajoules of energy into the wounded hip area and slicing through the ferrotitanium femur. Shaken by the onslaught, the Omni lost its balance and collapsed again to the ground. Its mutilated right leg was left trailing behind on a few thick strands of myomer, still flexing at the ankle and knee but lost as any form of support. Although not out of the fight, the *Masakari* would be easy prey for any follow-up attacks.

Though not by him. Charging forward at better than eighty kilometers per hour, the *Black Hawk* challenged David at point-blank range in an effort to bring down the *Devastator*. Ruby-tinged beams of light stabbed out from its arm-mounted lasers, splashing damage across the *Devastator*'s broad chest and sending rivers of molten armor to the ground. Warning alarms signaled damage to the internal skeleton, to actuators and the assault machine's myomer muscles, to one of his medium lasers, and to the physical shielding of his fusion engine. David stumbled from the loss of three tons of protective Durallex plating, staying on his feet by sheer force of will.

But will could not withstand the violent impact as the *Black Hawk* slammed full-front into his *Devastator*. The collision caught David off-guard and already reeling from the blistering laser attack. Clan warriors rarely resorted to physical assaults in combat. But again, these were desperate times. David surrendered to the hard fall, knowing it was unlikely he'd ever rise again.

The jostling and bone-shaking impacts. The sizzling of shorted circuitry and the ozone scent of burnt wiring. Alarms rang loudly in his ears, complaining about the abuse his 'Mech had just taken.

And then there was the barrage.

"Stupid, Archon-loving, son-of-a-Liao! Can't fly . . . wanna play rough . . . don't think you're gonna get back up . . . just try it!"

The world swam around him disjointedly, all flashing lights and smoke. David couldn't see his sergeant major, though he certainly heard her over the comm system. Dizzy, he followed her voice back toward some semblance of alertness and found himself suspended over the control panels of his *Devastator*, which lay face-down against the ground. The smell of fried circuitry assailed him, its acrid scent stabbing into his sinuses as he struggled to breathe the scorched air. Shaking hands found his control sticks, wrapped onto them with white-knuckled strength, and quickly raised the *Devastator* on extended arms.

"Don't know when you're not wanted . . . think you run our planet . . . use that chicken-chopper on my friend . . ."

"Inbounds are closing the gap," Leftenant Pachenko warned, cutting through Amanda's tirade. "Someone mind that last Manticore!"

For an instant, staring through his forward shield, David thought he was still back on Huntress, staring up at the *Black Hawk*, its foot poised to smash in his cockpit and end his life—and then the intense wash of light and explosions as three of his MechWarriors concentrated devastating firepower on the Clan OmniMech.

Sergeant Vahn had paid for that rescue, the redirected fire giving the wounded *Masakari* time to eviscerate Vahn's *Bushwacker* while David pulled himself back to his feet. If he'd been faster . . . But he hadn't been. And he was not about to let that happen again.

He shook away the illusion, spotting Amanda Black's *Bushwacker* and Corporal Smith's customized *Cestus* standing over the fallen *Nightsky*, pounding down on the struggling 'Mech with every weapon at their disposal. As a testament to the survival power of the design, or of the MechWarrior inside, the *Nightsky* had raised itself on extended arms and was attempting to get a foot beneath it to stand again. Then Dylan Pachenko jetted in just short of the trio, his *Stealth* hammering short-range missiles into the back of the *Nightsky* even before he landed.

It was too much against one BattleMech. The *Nightsky* lost its footing and fell back to the ground, flailing its arms a few times, and then lay still. When the three 'Mechs turned away from it, it looked nothing like a sophisticated war machine. The brute tactics had pounded it into unrecognizable scrap.

Amanda's *Bushwacker* kicked it a few more times for good measure, her tirade finally trailing off, and then her 'Mech twisted around on its lower torso to hammer at the retreating Manticore tank. The rest of Pachenko's lance, denied any chance at the *Nightsky*, fell on the armored vehicle with a vengeance and tore it apart.

"I'm alive and well," David said over the comm to the rest of the company. He winced as the effort of speaking sparked a new headache. "Alive, anyway. But thanks for asking."

The three nearby 'Mechs froze in exaggerated surprise as David worked his machine back to its feet, noting that one shoulder joint was damaged and that one of his gauss rifles was off-line due to ruptured capacitors. No wonder he felt like hell. An unregulated capacitor discharge often caused intense feedback through the neurohelmet's circuitry. Surprising that he hadn't lost consciousness.

Or had he? Sergeant Nichols' *Dervish* lay nearby, armor plates over the gyro housing crushed by a blow that would just about fit the *Nightsky*'s hatchet. Nichols hadn't even been close before. And a glance at his heads up display showed a radical shift in the positions of his company and the enemy—including another downed machine. Sergeant Moriad's *Wolfhound*.

"How long was I out?" he asked.

"Several minutes, Captain." Sergeant Major Black reported, beating Pachenko by a split second. Her voice was tinged with something akin to relief. "We thought . . ." She trailed off, not needing to say what the unit had thought.

A cluster of red icons on the HUD, farther east than he would have expected, tempted David toward optimism. "We have them on the run?" he asked, and then realized that there were too many enemy icons.

More than they'd started this fight against.

"Not exactly," Leftenant Pachenko said. "Tara pushed the remnants we were fighting off to the north, and she's holding our flank there, but we have a new company inbound. Fresh from District City."

Transmission robbed a person's voice of some emotional content. Nonetheless, David sensed a hesitancy in Dylan Pachenko—that he had left something important unsaid. "What is it, Dylan?"

"Sir," Pachenko began, and then faltered for a moment before regaining enough control to deliver a solid report. "Captain, Tara and I picked up a warning over our command frequencies. Leftenant Colonel Zibler is down, and the rest of the battalion is in disarray near Radcliffe. Apparently he fought the Eighth to a standstill, but he overloaded his reactor doing so."

By "down," Pachenko meant dead. Damien Zibler was lost, and that left Sampreis picking up the pieces near Radcliffe. The loss stunned David, leaving him cold and empty—that such a man should meet his end under the guns of the Federated Commonwealth was a double tragedy. "Any word from the general?" he forced himself to ask

"No, sir. But we haven't had much time for comm traffic."

Tara jumped in on the tail of Pachenko's report. "Sir, I think the time has come to ask: just how important is this area?"

That was always a hard question, and unfortunately,

there was no easy answer. In battle, there rarely was. David cycled up his air-reclamation system in an attempt to clear the smoke from his cockpit and began a more thorough review of his *Devastator*'s status.

"Important enough that we weren't pulled back to Radcliffe," he responded. "Now I want a skirmish line set at the river with whatever we have left. I hold the center. Dylan, relieve Tara on flank. In the meantime, I'll keep trying to contact the general and find out what his plans are.

"Whatever we're defending out here, let's hope it's worth the price we're going to pay."

12

Howell River Valley
Daytin, Kathil
Capellan March, Federated Commonwealth
16 November 3062

Even Kathil's bright sun could not compete with the energies being released in the Howell River Valley, paling by comparison as jeweled light carved into hardened armor and man-made lightning struck out again and again. Missiles rose on brief, gray contrails, arcing in to hammer away at opposing BattleMechs and, occasionally, scattering missile-deployed minefields into the path of some unlucky MechWarrior.

Eván Greene was one of those, but his *Cerberus* stood up well to the ground-based explosions, rocking with the force but only surrendering about a ton of armor off his left leg. More worrisome were the enemy gauss rifles. One had already lodged a nickel-ferrous slug into his right shoulder, binding up the joint and throwing off his aim. Another two meters to the left and that slug would have punched through the *Cerberus'* face to smash the cockpit into ruin.

Toggling for his medium pulse lasers, Eván left off his own gauss rifles and sniped at a *Firestarter* dodging among nearby trees. Two of the four shots scored, drawing carbon-scorched lines along the BattleMech's right flank. Then it broke cover, racing for the safety of the CMM line, and the gauss rifles, held in reserve for a clean shot, sparked their telltale blue flashes and sent twin slugs streaking toward the *Firestarter's* back. One missed low, plowing into the ground and throwing up a spray of loamy earth. The other took the enemy 'Mech at the right elbow, snapping the arm off at midpoint and destroying roughly half of its firepower.

The *Firestarter* jumped for the treeline again, disappearing into thicker stands and leaving Eván free to turn his attention back toward the *Devastator* that held the center of the enemy line.

"All right, McCarthy," he whispered to himself, "just what are you up to out here?"

Eván had almost bypassed this fight, eager to catch up to Jim Wendt's command in time to join the final push into Radcliffe. Except Wendt had reported to District City that he now doubted they would ever reach the militia staging area—they had encountered strong resistance from the CMM Second 'Mech Battalion. And he had had to divert two heavy lances to delay a militia company led by a *Devastator*.

Eván was willing to bet that was McCarthy—the *Devastator* was not a 'Mech common to the Capellan March. Eván had lost no time tracking them back toward Daytin, coming on them just as McCarthy's command broke the last three 'Mechs left to Wendt's lances and sent them fleeing north.

He had expected that his fresh company would be more than a match for McCarthy's already-battered machines. But, irritatingly enough, the militia's line still held at the Howell River. Beyond them, on the western bank, some very plush estates stood as a serene backdrop to the pitched fight. Eván soon stopped wondering what David McCarthy was defending, and instead began to wonder who.

Then word came that Kommandant Wendt had been killed while dueling with the enemy commander near Radcliffe, and the rest of his command had shifted to a fighting retreat. Suddenly this battle became strategically vital. The Eighth RCT needed a victory. If the militia pushed them back into D.C., it might give them the impetus they needed to push the Katzbalger out of D.C. and take over the capital themselves. It was up to Eván to produce that victory, no matter the cost.

"Stalker Lance, ready to move forward," Leftenant Barajas called out, for the third time in almost as many minutes.

"Negative," Eván snapped loud enough for his voice-activated mic to pick up his command and broadcast. "Hold position and keep their southern flank pinned down." Barajas was too impatient to advance. This fight would come off the way Eván wanted it, not Barajas' way.

A missile-lock warning wailed at him, and the *Cerberus* trembled as its head-mounted anti-missile system put out a hail of bullets to intercept the incoming missiles. He counted at least a half-dozen intercepts, the warheads detonating impotently in the air, but still a good dozen or more rained down on him, blasting new pockmarks into his shoulders and chest. He answered with a new pair of gauss slugs, donated to the militia's *Rakshasa*, which ducked one and took the other on its right side.

The *Rakshasa* and *Bushwacker* were concentrating their missile fire on him, forcing Eván to eat heavily into his ammunition reserve. If he allowed it to continue, he'd have no protection from the deadlier short-range missiles once the final push came. Eván slapped at the override switch, cutting out the AMS and conserving the last of his ammunition.

A new voice crackled over his comm system. "Bussard Flight, inbound. Five . . . four . . ."

At last. Eván's strategy called for dislodging McCarthy's light scouting lance from the river and forcing a breach into the enemy lines. The scout lance would be the easiest to push aside. Two . . . One . . . "Pack Lance, Hunt Lance, advance now!" he commanded.

The pair of Cavalry attack copters fell down on their strafing run from 3,000 feet, raining down inferno-warhead missiles on the enemy line. The gelatinous mixture burst into flame upon contact with air, raising a wall of flame along the river bank, or, when they struck a 'Mech, spiking heat scales deep into the red. Most MechWarriors feared inferno rounds—the possibility of being burned alive inside their cockpits was very real.

Now Eván's light lance could push back McCarthy's, while the Eighth's assault 'Mechs tied up the center of the CMM line. Barajas would keep the *Bushwacker* and the rest of McCarthy's medium-weight machines tied up, and they would finally break the enemy line.

It was a solid plan, until it made contact with the CMM company.

A *Cestus*, not nearly as intimidated by the inferno spread as most MechWarriors would be, actually leapt up into the strafing run on plasma jets. Burning gel from the inferno barrage spread over the *Cestus* in a hellish aura, the 'Mech shielding its comrades from the attack copters. Then its paired large lasers struck out, emerald lances spearing into one Cavalry and neatly slicing away the rotor from the attack craft's body. The copter belly-flopped into an elm grove, raising a huge fireball that did little to advance Eván's plans. The second Cavalry broke away, ending its run prematurely, before it could lay down a good screen of infernos between the *Devastator* and the *Cerberus*.

With his lighter machines already committed, Eván could do little but attempt to force the breach he needed anyway. His targeting reticle drifted over the *Devastator*'s wide-shouldered outline, burning from red to gold as he traded salvos with McCarthy. Gauss rifles punched at each other, smashing armor into shards that rained to the ground, glinting in the afternoon sunlight.

One of those hard-hitting slugs glanced off the *Cerberus*' right shoulder, smashing into ruin one of Eván's rear-facing machine gun turrets. Not a critical loss, until McCarthy followed up the assault with his particle cannons, one of the azure whips digging farther into the ruined right shoulder and severing myomer bundles. His right arm fell down to hang impotently at his side, his effective firepower halved.

A critical loss, except that one of his slugs had taken the *Devastator* in the left leg, knocking it out from under McCarthy and toppling the assault machine to the ground.

"Forward, everyone!" he snapped. "Split their lines and drive them back."

Eván was picturing what a Medal of Valor would look like welded to the left shoulder of his *Cerberus*, right where he painted traditional kill markers for every 'Mech he brought down. The idea thrilled him. Then his *Cerberus* rocked back in its tracks, nearly toppling over as an *Enforcer* shifted to cover the fallen *Devastator*, and punching Eván square in the chest with both a large laser and an eighty-mill autocannon.

And that wasn't the only sudden setback. The *Cestus* that had ruined his Cavalry copter run jumped again, still covered in flames, pushing an incredible heat reserve as it landed among his advancing light 'Mechs. Its large lasers drilled emerald lances into the guts of one *Battle Hawk*, cutting at the supports to the massive gyroscope needed to keep the thirty-ton 'Mech on its feet. The *Hawk* stumbled but kept to its feet—though without a doubt it was hurt. It might have made its escape, then, except for two *Firestarter*s setting on it and pumping fusion-powered flame sources deep into its interior. The plasma-induced flames scorched out the last of the gyro housing. The *Battle Hawk*'s cockpit blew away on special charges, and the pilot's couch rocketed out and up on thrusters designed to lift a MechWarrior clear of a battlefield.

Why hadn't the *Cestus* used its gauss rifle and saved the heat build-up? Eván had barely asked himself the question when the immolated 'Mech turned toward him and fired off a gauss slug that thundered into the *Cerberus'* right leg. And the *Devastator* might be down, but it certainly was not out of the battle. Holding itself up by the arms, it stabbed out with a pair of PPCs to worry away more of the *Cerberus'* protective armor. Eván shifted to a wider stance, his drive stalled for the moment.

"We're through!"

Xander Barajas' call trumpeted over the common frequency, drawing Eván's attention away from his thwarted charge. On the southern flank Barajas had driven his *Falconer* into the midst of the CMM line, exploiting a small break left behind the *Enforcer'*s shift in position. He fought with unparalleled savagery, firing his extended-range PPC point-blank into the militia BattleMechs and following it up with a flurry of medium-class lasers and his gauss rifle. One gauss slug took the head clean off a BJ-2 *Blackjack*, caving in the cockpit and adding one more KIA to the militia rolls.

Eván had almost forgotten he'd ordered everyone forward, and now the leftenant was exploiting those orders with the widest possible interpretation. Stepping over the armored corpse of the *Blackjack*, he left room for one of his lancemates to join him in the gap, and then another. But the militia company was beginning to react to his presence, curling back in to trap the small command.

Stabbing at a preset frequency, Eván opened a private channel to his lance leader. "Xander, get out of there," he ordered. "We're not in position to support you."

It could never be said that Barajas did not follow orders. Immediately his *Falconer* rose into the air on twin jets of superheated plasma. Except that he did not retreat, which had been Eván's implied meaning. Instead, he rocketed over the river, coming down on the western bank and immediately turning about to hammer energy bolts and gauss slugs back at the far shore. Not to be left behind, the *Lynx* and paired *Quickdraws*—jumping 'Mechs all—followed, leaving Xander's Stalker Lance in possession of the western side of the Howell.

It might not have proceeded according to his plans, but Eván knew better than to argue with a success, no matter who handed it to him. "Swing south," he ordered, switching back to the unit's common frequency. "Everyone pull south." McCarthy was too preoccupied with pulling his own unit together to plan any on-the-spot counteroffensive. "Bridge the river with Stalker Lance. Xander, any militia 'Mech that crosses the Howell is yours to deal with as you please."

And if that wasn't a dangerous order, Eván wasn't sure what was. Turning Xander loose was like playing with a rabid dog, but he wasn't about to lose this precarious foothold. At any cost, he had promised himself. He would bring General Fallon back a Katzbalger victory even if he had to share the credit with Xander Barajas.

The *Cerberus* moved quickly for an assault 'Mech, able to reach a running speed of better than sixty kilometers per hour. Now, where seconds counted, that speed helped secure the Katzbalger's advantage by plugging the gap between Xander's lance and Eván's scout lance. Along with a *Penetrator*, Eván's next strongest design, he held the line as McCarthy quickly tried to swing the *Enforcer* and a *Hatchetman* back toward the trouble spot.

But even with the nearby *Cestus*, it would not be enough to stop Eván. Especially as the *Cestus'* sluggish movements showed that it had finally run its heat curve beyond safe limits. The 'Mechs of his own Pack Lance were now regrouping, swinging wide of the militia's center line and, on Eván's orders, fording the river by jump jets or wading in to reinforce the western bank.

It wasn't the decisive victory he had wanted, but Eván had the satisfaction of knowing he had beaten McCarthy's unit. And as the militia captain finally began to pull his people back, dragging along their wounded 'Mechs when possible, Eván smiled fully for the first time since the battle had begun.

"You lose, McCarthy," he said. "Whatever you were defending out here, we'll find it.

"The hero of Kathil," he mused—but this time he was trying the title on for size himself.

13

CMM Staging Grounds
Radcliffe, Kathil
Capellan March, Federated Commonwealth
19 November 3062

Newly promoted and once again wearing the insignia of a major within the Federated Commonwealth, David McCarthy entered the briefing room with a crisp military stride and steel-spine bearing, despite his fatigue. He knew his people were equally tired—exhausted from three days of sporadic combat assignments and still feeling the loss of Leftenant Colonel Zibler. He couldn't blame them—Damien Zibler had been a natural leader of soldiers. To lose him so early in the fight . . . it was difficult to accept.

David had reviewed the battleroms a dozen times already. Damien Zibler had been pushing his *Victor* to the limits, running an incredibly high heat curve as he squared off against the opposing commander. He'd fired again and again, always pushing forward, drawing fire away from his unit. It reminded David eerily of Huntress—no quarter asked, and none given. And then came the devastating explosion of Zibler's reactor breach, and, only ten seconds later, the aerospace strafing runs that forced the Eighth RCT to retreat.

He'd never even talked to Zibler about Huntress, damn it all.

Two companies of MechWarriors now looked to him for leadership: ten warriors of his original company and the full company plus two were all that was left of Zibler's command. Several of the company's officers had moved up a notch in rank to fill the hole that Zibler's death had created. And Zibler wasn't the only loss. That first day's fighting had cost Second Battalion almost a full dozen MechWarriors dead or injured. One more had been lost in a skirmish the next day, a pair of broken legs adding Sergeant Deveroux to the list of wounded.

Fortunately, after their initial confrontation, the Eighth had seemed content to remain in District City and consolidate its holdings, sending out only occasional scouting parties in limited engagements. David's company had inadvertently made that easier for them by retreating from Daytin—a mistake David did not intend to repeat.

"All right," David began, reaching the front of the room and taking a place behind a small podium, "let's start with the good news. As you may have heard through the grapevine, Major General Sampreis has received a reply to his request for orders from Marshal Hasek. It will be broadcast on local trivid stations later today and will hopefully repair some of the damage caused by Duke VanLees' desertion."

Leftenant Eric LaSaber, one of the officers David had inherited from Zibler, leaned forward in the front row. "Did he brand VanLees a traitor?" By his tone, LaSaber couldn't decide whether he wanted such a proclamation.

David left the podium and moved around to slowly pace across the front of the room. "Now look. We know that VanLees is not a traitor," he said firmly. "The Eighth RCT has his family held hostage to ensure his cooperation."

And that was a situation that sat in David's stomach like a lead weight. It was only after withdrawing from the Daytin area that he'd learned that his company had been guarding Duke Petyr VanLees' personal river estate. It was a double tragedy—that they had been unable to defend it, and that his command had been out there at all. If they had fallen back toward Radcliffe, they wouldn't

have led the Eighth RCT right to the VanLees' doorstep.
And if Damien Zibler had had David's help to defend the
base here, he might still be alive.

"Duke Petyr had no choice but to side with the Eighth
and brand us rebels. Does anyone here really believe he
prefers Katherine Steiner-Davion to George Hasek?" No
one looked even remotely convinced, despite the broadcast VanLees had made two days before claiming just that.
"Good. And neither does our Field Marshal Hasek. He
excuses VanLees' compliance for exactly what it is—duress. He also calls for the world of Kathil to support the
militia's efforts to restore order, invites the Eighth RCT to
relocate to Lee until the 'accident' here can be properly
investigated, and requests of the Archon-Princess that she
formally acknowledge his own right to order the Katzbalger off Kathil."

Tara Michaels whistled tunelessly. "That's quite a lot,"
she said.

"What are the chances that any of that will happen?"
Corporal Smith asked, his tone casting one clear vote in
the "unlikely" column.

"Well, I think Kathil's loyalty is secure," David replied.
"Not even VanLees' repeated broadcasts have really hurt
us in popular support. As for the rest—wishful thinking
at best. We haven't heard anything from either District
City or New Avalon on the other points, and I doubt we
will. The longer they ignore Marshal Hasek, they force
him to greater, more desperate lengths to restore peace."

Tara caught on. "So he either capitulates, and the
Archon-Usurper uses the incident to gut Hasek's power
base, or he escalates the conflict, and Katherine portrays
him as the instigator of . . ." She exhaled a long, drawn-
out sigh, unable to say it.

"Civil war." Amanda Black crossed her arms over her
chest defiantly as she said what they all were thinking.
"Katherine is pushing Hasek into a corner. She wants to
cut him down. She knows that until she does, he'll always
be a threat to her rule."

David couldn't disagree. "Unless we retake and hold
Kathil in spite of the Eighth RCT's assault," he added.
"We—General Sampreis and the command staff—believe
that George Hasek may be able to scale things back then.

But the longer this drags out, the worse it will be for everyone."

LaSaber nodded. "Any chance he can send us more help? Mercenaries?" He jerked his head at Pachenko. "Dylan and I were talking about what's been happening with the war in the St. Ives Compact. Group W and the Arcadians have been released from their subcontract with the Duchess Candance. They're closer to us than—"

"We've already batted that one around," David interrupted. "The mercenaries *have* been recalled, but both are technically still under direct contract with the Lyran Alliance. No matter how they lean politically—and Group W, at least, has shown respect for Prince Victor in the past—mercenaries of their standing will honor a contract to its final clause." He regretted that fact, since the mercenaries' involvement might have helped end things quickly and as painlessly as possible. "The best we can hope for is that they'll refuse an auxiliary contract to aid and assist the Katzbalger position"—which would spell immediate ruin for the militia.

"Anyone else?" Amanda asked, her green eyes clouded with doubt. Something was troubling her. "There must be other units nearby."

"Marshal Hasek can't afford to pull garrisons from other worlds. Not without the possibility of sparking similar unrest elsewhere. With reports of new riots on Solaris VII and a few 'incidents' on worlds such as Kentares IV and now Robinson, I'd say we're on our own."

That news hung heavy in the room for several minutes as David returned to the podium, trying to collect his thoughts.

"Any news about the Second NAIS cadre, or the arrival of the First Capellan Dragoons?" Dylan Pachenko asked. Several officers nodded their support for his question. "Either one could tip the balance heavily in our favor."

David shook his head and exhaled noisily, summing up his own frustration. General Sampreis certainly knew something about one or both units, but he wasn't saying anything as yet. "You know what I know. The NAIS cadre is apparently worried about committing to the fight on either side. The Dragoons will be with us, when and if they get here. General Weintraub has to be coming up with plans to intercept them. Let's hope Field Marshal Hasek has planned ahead for that contingency.

"That's it for now, except that we're off the patrol rotation for today. Services for Leftenant Colonel Zibler will be held this afternoon at three. I hope to see you all there."

David walked over to the window and stood there at modified parade-rest stance, with hands clasped behind his back but with a more relaxed bend to his knees. He stared out the second-floor window as his people filed quietly out of the room. A pair of *Centurions* lumbered by, heading for the parade grounds that had been turned into a secondary staging area. Then the BattleMechs were gone, and he was left looking at a mostly empty street.

Thrust into greater authority by Zibler's death, David had stood up to the burden rather well. The demands placed on him had even helped quiet the demons from Huntress. Piloting a 'Mech into battle still worried him— that feeling of impending danger like some weight held over his head—but he fought past it every time because he must. That was part of the responsibilities he had agreed to take on, not just with his promotion to major but his initial acceptance of a new combat post here on Kathil. Perhaps he should have retired instead. David wished he'd had a chance to have that talk with Zibler.

"What would you have done, Damien?" he whispered.

He jumped when a voice behind him replied, "Whatever it was, I doubt it would be accomplished through talking to himself. Sir."

His ears burning, David turned to face Amanda Black. His sergeant major had remained behind when the others left, sitting still and quiet in her chair. She was chewing on her lower lip, looking unsure about how to proceed. Her barbed comment hadn't helped get things off to a good start.

"You have something you wish to discuss with me, Sergeant?" he asked.

Amanda nodded and spoke slowly, as if choosing her words carefully. "I was hoping to apologize for my performance at Daytin. In fact, for the last few days. I've been waiting for you to say something . . ."

David walked closer and stood over his senior enlisted.

"Your performance has been exemplary," he said, perplexed. "I don't see why you would be expecting a reprimand of any sort."

"Major, I failed to hold the line against the Eighth RCT. I should have—I could have. That *Falconer* ran up on us so fast, and I had shifted to help Tara cover the *Cerberus'* approach." Her eyes sought David's. "I should have seen them coming sooner. And Sergeant Franklin paid for my mistake when his *Blackjack* took that gauss slug to the head."

Now he was beginning to understand. "And we haven't been able to turn the battle since. Amanda, what exactly do you think I expect of you?"

She shook her head. "I'm not explaining this right." She thought for a moment, the silence broken only by the humming of a wall-mounted clock as its hand swept in lazy revolutions. "I guess it's more what I've been expecting of myself, Major McCarthy. How I've acted. I thought before that skill was everything. And I hated you after our little simulator skirmish, making my performance look cheap. I thought—I knew—you were wrong. I've been trying so hard to prove that."

Amanda hunched back into her chair, folding in on herself. "Then yesterday, on patrol, I walked past what was left of Daytin. We left it in the hands of the Eighth RCT, but thanks to your efforts it was still standing. The next day, though . . ." She winced. "I found out that the Eighth's armored cavalry and our own armor brigade had both rolled through there. Major, the eastern half of the town . . . it's gone."

News of the ruined resort community had bothered David as well. Amanda's faith had been shaken—just like his own illusions about warfare had been permanently smashed by Task Force Serpent. "The military life teaches us hard lessons, Amanda," he said. "Being good, even being the best, is no guarantee against failure. And what's even more frustrating, perhaps, is when it seems like we're just marking time. But there's a big difference between doing and actually accomplishing something, isn't there?"

Amanda nodded and looked hard at him. "Did you learn that early in your career?"

David shook his head with a sad smile. "I was invincible in the early years of my career. But then I was a Uhlan, and we'd never known a real defeat. It took Huntress to prove that a lie."

Amanda frowned, confused. "But you won on Huntress."

"Did we?" David paused, swallowed hard. Damn it anyway. He hooked a chair around with his foot and settled onto it backward, with his arms folded over the backrest and his eyes on a level with Amanda's. "We hit Huntress with some of the most elite regiments the Inner Sphere has ever produced. The Uhlans. Eridani Light Horse. Northwind Highlanders. The Knights of the Inner Sphere. Warrior for warrior, we were every bit as good as—if not better than—anything the Smoke Jaguars fielded. And we came very close to losing. As it was, the cost ran high. The Uhlans disbanded, Amanda. We were a broken command, as much because of the fighting as the loss of Morgan Hasek-Davion."

She softened momentarily, almost looked ready to sympathize. Then her features set in a hard line, guarding against any show of weakness. "Is that why you're still afraid? Because you never got to finish that fight?" The questions weren't cruel. Not quite.

His command instincts warned David away from that question. Officers were never afraid. Or, at least, they didn't admit to it easily. But there was that nebulous feeling still, haunting him as it stalked the shadowed recesses of his mind, and he had never had a chance to talk to Zibler about it. "Maybe," he finally admitted to his senior sergeant. "Maybe I'm afraid it will happen again here. I don't know. I think what frightens me most—what frightens anyone the most—is the not knowing. But you find a way to live with it, to keep it from interfering, because that's part of your responsibilities."

David stood then, unable to discuss the problem further. It was as good a place as any to end their conversation. Movement . . . action . . . that was what he needed now. Maybe he could get a meeting with Sampreis before Damien Zibler's memorial service and find out exactly what the general had planned to make sure the Dragoons arrived.

"Major," Amanda said as he neared the door, that look of vulnerability back on her face. "How do we stop this?"

Her face was searching, open to ideas she possibly had never entertained before. David hated to be the one to disappoint her now, but he had no good answers for her. "We don't," he admitted. "We can't. Not you or me, not General Sampreis. We just can't end this fight easily. Until one side or the other gains the upper hand and holds it long enough, or until outside forces decide to intervene, we simply ride it through."

"And hope the fighting burns itself out?"

"And hope the fighting doesn't burn us out," he answered, and then slipped from the room.

14

Multiple missile-lock warnings screamed for attention, silenced only when the shower of missiles slammed home on either side of Amanda's *Bushwacker*. The squat, broad-shouldered machine weathered the assault well, trembling only slightly as it traded precious armor for time, while Amanda fought her controls to return fire.

Targeting crosshairs flashed irregularly over the screen as damaged sensors tried to keep a hard lock and failed. Taking her best guess, the sergeant sent out a brace of shots, spearing out with the sapphire lance of her large laser before tying in missiles and autocannon for the follow-up salvo. The missiles all fell short, splashing earth, rock, and pieces of petrified wood over the legs of the enemy *Salamander*. Her laser had scored an angry red weal down the left leg of the eighty-ton assault, but her autocannon failed to exploit the wound as it hammered depleted-uranium slugs into the *Salamander*'s chest instead. Better than she'd expected, really, but less than she'd hoped.

All things considered, far less than she'd hoped.

Battle had loomed nearly every day for the militia for

the past week, on one front or the other. Lances sparred and danced along the border between RCT-controlled territory and the militia's sphere, while major clashes occurred over possession of cities and towns in an ongoing tug-of-war. Radcliffe enjoyed strong support in most of the small rural towns, but the Eighth maintained a firm grip on District City's environs. Refugees—those rendered homeless or orphaned after such fighting—flooded Radcliffe after each battle with the certainty of the tides. It underscored the need for a rapid conclusion to the fighting. Units were cycled into a rest and refit period every three days now, though volunteering for extra duty was accepted if not encouraged.

Running a lance out on long-range recon, Amanda had been looking for some time away from the Radcliffe base to sort out her own feelings concerning the hard-pitched fighting turning her homeworld upside down. Instead she'd found a battle tearing through the Winstan Ridge National Park, one of Kathil's best-loved primitive areas. Not that the "Keep to the Trails" signs had stopped elements of the Eighth RCT from attempting to decimate two companies of the CMM's Third 'Mech Battalion.

She wasted no time committing her small force to the aid of the Third, the timely arrival of a fresh heavy lance turning the tide of battle from a rout toward a stalemate. This far inland, neither side held a true advantage. Neither had static defenses or familiarity with the terrain—not even air superiority. A few *Corsairs* tangled with a lance of *Lucifer*s high above, one side or the other breaking away periodically for a quick strafing run but by and large keeping to their own battlefield. At this side of the ground-based battle, the Eighth worked light hovertanks with assault 'Mechs, a difficult combination to employ but—when done correctly—harder to fight. Assault-weight BattleMechs could deal out a lot of hurt in a short time, but if they made the mistake of ignoring the Plainsmen hovercraft, the very mobile missile platforms wound up parked in their six, hammering away at a BattleMech's weaker rear armor.

The *Salamander* threw a new cloud of missiles into the air, arcing three-score warheads toward Amanda's position. The sergeant kicked her *Bushwacker* into a run, turning into the spread and running beneath the umbrella so that the majority detonated behind her. The maneuver also brought her in close to the enemy line, however; a move not unnoticed by a nearby *Gunslinger*, which acquired a quick lock and shot two gauss slugs in her direction. One slug skipped off a rare column of standing petrified wood, knocking off the top two meters and raining brown and gold splinters over the ground. The other caught her square in the chest, punching through the last of her centerline armor to crack the physical shield around her fusion engine. The temperature in her cockpit jumped another few degrees as the additional heat burden overwhelmed her already-struggling heat sinks.

"What you're doing is called charging a superior force," Corporal Smith informed her over the comm system, his tone at once concerned and irreverent. His *Cestus* moved up from the backfield to support her, though the other half of her lance remained dedicated to holding the Third's southern flank.

And it was a good thing they did, Amanda decided. If the assault 'Mechs forced a breach here, there would be no closing it again. "Forget the tactical analysis," she said, panting as she fought for oxygen, "and target that *Gunslinger*!"

Amanda might wince at the damage this battle was doing to the once-beautiful Winstan Ridge area, but damned if she would allow that to keep her from her duty. The one thing she still knew as how to win battles. Right now her combat instincts were all triggering off the *Gunslinger*. With its twin gauss rifles, the eighty-five-ton assault machine posed the greatest threat the Eighth could offer, able to put down any 'Mech with two well-placed nickel-ferrous slugs. It also anchored the middle of the Katzbalger line and stood ready to spearhead any drive forward. The *Salamander* that had challenged her earlier was dangerous only at a distance, dependent on long-range missiles, and since moving up she had crowded in beneath its optimum range.

Smith had exhausted his limited gauss ammunition earlier, but he lent Amanda a pair of large lasers that cut deep along the *Gunslinger*'s left side. Molten armor runnelled to the ground, splashing fiery slag onto the once-pristine trails. Amanda's own laser scoured the last armor from the head of the *Gunslinger*—enough to warm things up in the cockpit, she hoped—while her autocannon hammered new gouges into and through its right arm. The gauss coils built into the arm ruptured with a flash of arcing blue light, dancing brief tangles of lightning up the arm and shoulder.

The assault 'Mech stumbled as its gyro fought against the loss of so much armor. Adding to the enemy Mech-Warrior's troubles, Amanda knew, would be the brain-aching feedback usually caused by unregulated discharge of the gauss coils. She cycled her weapons quickly, risking the power spike such an energy draw would demand of her fusion reactor. The *Bushwacker* traded another one-two combination of autocannon and laser against the *Gunslinger*'s hasty—and only—gauss shot, the hypersonic slug smashing her right flank protection into ruin as she worried away more of the *Gunslinger*'s heavier armor.

Richard had devoted his two large lasers to skewering an advancing *Plainsman*, gouging through armor to eviscerate drive fans hidden beneath the protective cowling. Having lost his immediate support, Amanda steeled herself for another trade of weapons fire with the *Gunslinger*. Then a silver blur streaked in against the assault 'Mech's already damaged left side, a ferrous slug punching through the last of its armor to lodge deep in the *Gunslinger*'s guts. Myomer muscles snapped under the impact, and the foamed-titanium bones of its chassis-skeleton warped and cracked. One support ripped away from the gauss ammunition bin built into the *Gunslinger*'s left side, tearing a gaping hole through it. Gauss slugs tumbled free of the wound like an improbable jet of silver blood, the *Gunslinger* trailing its ammunition behind it as it hastily turned back toward the safety of its lines.

While not threatened with destruction, the assault machine had lost its usefulness with the crippling of its two major weapons. The *Salamander* and a *Rakshasa* moved up to cover its retreat and began a steady but slow withdrawal, tempting Amanda to press her newly won advantage.

Instead Amanda walked her *Bushwacker* in reverse, trading sniping shots as the distance opened up between them. She knew better than to chase too deeply into the enemy line, as much as it galled her to allow the *Gunslinger* to retire from the fight.

Assault 'Mechs be damned anyway, she cursed as the *Salamander* belched three flights of missiles into the air. She ducked behind a small hill covered with brilliantly colored petrified wood, wincing as most of the missiles impacted against it, saving her limited armor but costing Kathil even more. A half-dozen warheads chewed at her left shoulder, opening up fresh wounds but not deep enough to cause any serious damage. Yet.

Corporal Smith had also sought temporary refuge behind the hillock, ducking his taller *Cestus* down into a crouch and waddling backward.

"Damn—I thought we had them there," he said.

Amanda shook her head, answering the empty cockpit before transmitting. "We hurt them, but this isn't over by a long shot. And I thought you were out of gauss slugs," she accused him.

"What do you know? I happened to find one more."

If Smith was hoarding his last few pieces of gauss ammo, at least he'd spent them wisely. And Amanda had no time to argue the point. They were about to emerge from the hill's protective shadow. "Fall back toward our line, Corporal. Use your lasers on any *Plainsman* that gets too close. I'll keep on the *Salamander*."

"There's not going to be much left of Winstan Ridge if we don't put them down or push 'em back soon." A hint of frustration showed through Smith's normally lackadaisical front.

Though it was hardly a tactical concern, Amanda couldn't help agreeing with the junior enlisted man. It was one thing, as a member of the Kathil Militia, to accept that they might someday have to fight on Kathil's soil. It was quite another to participate in destroying a national treasure. The enemy certainly knew how to hurt them—except that this time the enemy wasn't Capellan invaders, or House Marik, or even the Clans.

They were a Federated Commonwealth unit, destroying her world for no reason that she could see except for the political ambitions of a woman hundreds of light-years distant and the ego of a general who thought himself greater than the chain of command.

Breaking cover, they stepped up their pace to gain the safety of their line. The *Salamander* immediately targeted them for a full spread of sixty LRMS, throwing an umbrella of destruction over the field as a new pair of *Plainsmen* tried to skate in for a quick pass. One of the hovercraft drifted in too close to a standing formation of petrified wood, the same one the *Gunslinger* had broken the top off earlier, the sideswipe finally unbalancing the natural structure and toppling it, where it smashed into a million fragments against the ground. Amanda gripped her control sticks with a strength born of anger as better than two dozen missiles hammered in on her location, shaking the *Bushwacker* with violent tremors.

"No one's going to push them back any time soon," she whispered, careful not to speak loud enough for her voice-activated mic to pick up the words for rebroadcast. "We keep on them until one side or the other dominates or picks up reinforcements."

Amanda realized suddenly that she was parroting Major McCarthy, and agreeing with him as easily as if she'd thought it herself. And she wasn't certain if that was a good thing or not, except that it certainly felt right in this situation. There was no easy way to stop this. They would have to ride it through.

How long could the battle last, anyway?

David always returned to Huntress.

There was no escaping that legacy—remembering the battles, recalling the men and women who had fallen in that drive to end the Clan invasion in the only way the enemy understood: force, a devastating application of military power.

He could never forget, and the memory kept a stranglehold on David's dreams and many of his waking moments as well. Today, walking a long path around Radcliffe's massive parade grounds, he ducked his head away from the cutting spring wind and tried to shake free of the haunting images. Tried, and failed.

The hardest moment of that final battle had come right after he had picked his *Devastator* up from the ground, standing over the weapon-scorched ruin of the Clan *Black Hawk* and Vahn's gutted *Bushwacker*. The *Masakari*, having just put an end to Vahn's young life and promising military career, had half-risen from the ground and was now turning its attention back toward David.

"Someone get one of these Clanners off me!" Brevet-Hauptmann Polsan shouted suddenly. His voice held a ragged edge, but no longer the near-hysteria of moments before when the enemy rush came at him. He held the left flank on his own now that Vahn was down. Still wielding the *Nightsky*'s hatchet-arm as a club, Polsan's *Caesar* stood between a *Daishi* and a *Kingfisher* in a valiant but suicidal attempt to prevent their advance. Likewise, Kennedy's *Berserker* had its hands full on the right against a second *Gladiator* and a *Vulture*. She never once called for help, but she needed it almost as much.

One or the other. Whose life would he save?

It was a decision David, busy with the *Masakari*, hadn't been prepared to make until a pair of lithe forms jetted back into the fight on streamers of superheated plasma. The paired *Stealth*s he had earlier sent into the no-man's-land of the valley had somehow survived the initial onslaught and now came winging back with a vengeance. They fell on the crippled *Masakari* like wolves on a wounded bear, lasers tearing away armor, and short-range missiles grinding like claws rending flesh. From the backfield, Sergeant Isaak's *Enfield* broke to the left, supporting Polsan.

So many things could go wrong in a single second on the battlefield. An enemy could jump into your six, bringing weapons to bear against your back. A lucky shot could smash through a 'Mech's face shield, robbing you of an ally. Reinforcements could field against you. Air strikes, artillery, and simple accidents; the only thing there was never time for was hesitation.

But David's choice was really no choice at all. Kennedy was a more experienced warrior in a heavier BattleMech. The Smoke Jaguar *Masakari* was possibly the deadliest design left on the field, but it was tactically limited by a crippled leg and beset by two mobile scout 'Mechs. Trusting his people to hold, he wrenched his control sticks to the left, dragging his targeting reticle to the edge of the screen and reaching out to the side as he pivoted toward Polsan's position right behind Isaak.

Polsan's seventy-ton *Caesar* was miraculously standing up to the *Daishi*, thirty tons its senior and armed for blistering salvoes. Firing combinations of torso-mounted gauss rifle and right-arm PPC, the *Caesar* suffered under a savage counterstrike but held its feet long enough to wail in with the *Nightsky* hatchet-arm.

Isaak did not fare as well, getting off only a single shot from his LB-X autocannon before the *Kingfisher*'s pulse laser stabbed a flurry of jeweled darts into and through the medium 'Mech's chest. David actually saw a few emerald bolts melt through the back armor in passing, and then the fusion reactor burst free of the magnetic bottle that held it in check. Golden fire erupted in a scathing gout that ate up through the neck and seeped out through shoulder and hip joints. It bled plasma into the surrounding air, a halo of destructive force that sideswiped the *Kingfisher* before the *Enfield* exploded into the assault 'Mech's face.

The flare all but blinded David for a few seconds, the seasoned MechWarrior allowing his instinctive feel for the *Devastator* to keep him on his feet. Reaching out through the shadowed cockpit, David toggled for gauss and particle cannon and then drifted his targeting crosshairs over where he believed the *Kingfisher* to be.

He blinked his vision clear seconds before firing on empty air.

The *Kingfisher* had been unable to stand up under the fusion release, falling back to the ground shaken but quickly recovering. David wouldn't give it a chance. Already sucking blistering air into his lungs, he forgot his heat scale and added medium lasers to the barrage. Drifting his crosshairs down to the struggling *Kingfisher*, he shot off a point-blank salvo of everything he had left to give.

The reactor spiked off the scale as the energy draw demanded incredible amounts of power. Both particle projection cannon ate into the Clan machine's right side in azure cascades of raw energy that melted and blasted away nearly all of its protective armor. His first gauss slug smashed into the left leg. His second, lagging a half-second behind as a cross-feed mechanism pulled ammunition from the opposite bin, cracked the sternum open to actually reveal the spinning high-velocity metal of the gyroscope.

Still it was not enough, until the trio of medium lasers stabbed out ruby daggers. One found the *Kingfisher*'s exposed heart, cutting into the gyroscope even as the Clan 'Mech managed to return fire from the ground with half its laser-based arsenal. One large pulse laser worried away the last fragments of David's chest armor while a medium-grade laser splashed emerald fire over the *Devastator*'s forward shield. Some of that energy washed through the broken ferroglass, a flash of scalding heat that singed David's hair and burned the right side of his head and upper arm, perhaps two centimeters away from blinding him in the right eye. Half again as much power, and he'd have been dead.

Now, staring out over the bleak emptiness of the tarmac in Radcliffe, David reached into his coat and grabbed hold of his medal with a trembling hand. The cool metal star filled his palm, points digging into soft flesh as he squeezed it hard enough to draw a few spots of blood. Valor—which translated to the grace of a few joules of energy, a thumbnail's breadth in distance, and a number of lives spent on his behalf. And a legacy of pain that he didn't seem able to leave behind. He could do his job— was doing his job, here on Kathil—but when would he finally leave Huntress behind?

How long could one battle last in his memory?

15

Hall of Nobles
District City, Kathil
Capellan March, Federated Commonwealth
22 November 3062

Kommandant Eván Greene had thought before that the grand corridors in District City's Hall of Nobles could accommodate BattleMechs—that even the largest assault 'Mech would look at home patrolling the massive edifice. He'd been right.

The kommandant was hurrying down the corridor, late for the Eighth's command-level meeting. But in order to get there, he had to pass the ninety-five-ton *Nightstar* standing post at a junction where two of the titanic halls met. The vaulted ceilings stretched another four meters above the eleven-meter war machine, making it look as if it belonged in this oversized monument. With its widespread arms, the *Nightstar* obviously required care to maneuver along the balcony-studded hallways, but standing at rest with its back to the corner, it simply stretched one arm down each corridor. Every few minutes it shifted on the turret-style waist, the electric whine of actuators reminding the passing nobles that they were still under the Eighth RCT's "protection."

But a lance of BattleMechs had not been enough for General Weintaub. The general had worried that the militia might stage some kind of raid on the Hall of Nobles ever since he had subdued Duke VanLees. Gone were the guards in their ceremonial livery, which had been little more than another decorative feature of the Hall. Now Katzbalger infantry filled the alcoves and stood post in every other balcony, armed with static-defense PPC or autocannon turrets.

Overkill, in Eván's opinion, one that grew stronger with each passing minute. Even in his uniform, the MechWarrior had been required to present identification at three different checkpoints. Arriving late at the meeting was not a good way to begin his promotion to General Fallon's personal staff. He still commanded his battalion—no one would take that away from him—but had accepted additional duty as her aide-de-camp. And he knew the unspoken rules. She would help further his career, and in return could claim credit for his successes. Fallon was not short on ambition herself.

Eván eased open the heavy door and slipped unobtrusively inside the conference room. As late as he was, the meeting had yet to start. The upper brass mingled around the long mahogany table, while the braver junior officers hung on at their fringes. Most of the staffers kept their distance unless invited. He spotted Fallon on the far side of the room, deep in a private conversation with General Weintraub.

"Damned silly waste of time," a flame-haired admiral groused as he walked past Eván. Short and wiry, he moved with a swagger that belied his physical size. He paused long enough to forcibly shut the door, all but wrenching the handle from Eván's hand. "Army has no sense of how to keep a schedule."

Eván looked around, hoping the man was speaking to someone else, and caught Fallon's amused glance at his dilemma. Unable to find a convenient scapegoat, he asked, "Are you addressing me, Admiral?"

The gamecock admiral looked him over as if sizing up a raw cadet. His lips curled down at the Federated Commonwealth emblem displayed on the breast of Eván's uniform. The spacer wore an old-style Lyran uniform with appropriate mailed-fist crest. "You'll do," he said. "You and the others who can't seem to read a simple chronometer."

Eván smiled. He had no trouble picturing the admiral bullying his way past the checkpoints. "Operational security sometimes takes precedence over punctuality," he said formally.

The admiral's eyes narrowed dangerously. "On a taut-run command, you can have both," he snapped.

"Of course you can, Admiral Kerr," Karen Fallon agreed, inserting herself into the budding confrontation with a placatory smile already in place. "And good morning, Eván."

Her brilliant blue eyes, always alert, lit on his face for half a second. A warning? Or just natural caution? Eván managed a half-bow to his superior without taking his attention off the feisty admiral.

"Your man, General?" he asked, but his tone was civil with someone of equal rank.

"Yes, he's mine." Fallon's tone was possessive, as was the hand she laid on Eván's arm. "Admiral, may I steal my aide away for a moment? We have a few items to discuss before Mitchell calls us to the table."

Kerr shrugged, his pale eyes already scanning the room for a new victim. He traded nods with Fallon and then crossed between her and Eván, intent on someone by the window.

"I saw you slip in. Somehow I knew you'd end up butting heads with the admiral. Never shy about speaking up, are you?" She didn't wait for an answer. "What do you think of him?"

"Of Admiral Kerr?" Eván watched the man interrupt another conversation, hands on hips and chin thrust belligerently forward. "I wouldn't want to turn my back on him. He reminds me of a Chervun devil."

Fallon frowned slightly, but her eyes remained alight with interest. "I'm not familiar with that."

"It's an animal from my home planet. Psychopathic little beasts that will attack pretty much anything that moves, even at five times their size. Dangerous."

She glanced at Kerr. "An apt description," she admitted. "But his loyalty to the Archon-Princess is unquestioned. Even fanatical, one might say."

"Do we really need someone like that on our side?" Eván asked, concerned. The situation on Kathil was tense enough without introducing a zealot into the mix.

Fallon's blue eyes glinted at him. "Someone that fanatic, we do," she replied, and said no more.

Eván ran a hand over his hair, smoothed it back from his sharp widow's peak, and checked his watch. "I thought the meeting began promptly at seven?"

"We're still missing a few late arrivals. Price's men are being a bit . . . enthusiastic." She began a casual stroll about the long room, with Eván falling in beside her.

"That's one word for it," Eván agreed. "Stifling is another. And add inconsequential."

"Inconsequential." Fallon rolled the word off her tongue, as if savoring it. "Why would you say that?"

Eván shrugged. "I doubt any attempt will be made against the Hall of Nobles. Tearing apart Kathil's greatest monument in a firefight isn't going to win the militia friends among the nobility. And the simple truth is, they've realized that VanLees is not as important to their cause as they thought—not since George Hasek's address four days ago effectively ruined the Duke's credibility. And damaged ours too, by the way."

"How do you mean?"

Eván remembered the address very well—had committed it to memory as an example of achieving a military victory without firing a shot. Hasek, with his father's imposing height and lion's mane of dark hair, had appeared on trivid screens across the planet, wearing the uniform of the old Federated Suns. He had stated flatly that, with Mitchell Weintraub holding the capital and threatening the VanLees family, the duke was acting under duress. He commented that such tactics were more in keeping with House Liao or Kurita, not at all appropriate for a Davion or a Steiner. A nice trick, tying in the Archon-Princess through her much-vaunted Steiner heritage.

"I think our position was stronger when we were standing up against VanLees and Hasek both," Eván said. "Trying to control the Duke like some puppet cheapens our position. It makes it look like we have to fight for legitimacy. I would've thought the Archon's tacit approval was enough."

Fallon stopped and studied him long and hard. Eván tugged at one corner of his moustache, bearing up under the intense scrutiny with a feigned nonchalance. He'd deliberately steered the conversation in this direction, hoping to provoke a reaction from his new benefactor. Testing his limitations.

"You don't feel a bit to blame yourself, do you, for bringing in the Duke's family?" she asked pointedly.

"No more so than the person who ordered me to do so." Which had been General Fallon. "Or General Weintraub, who's the one holding them over VanLees' head."

In truth, though, it did bother Eván—though not for the reason Fallon suggested. These blackmail tactics did nothing for anyone. Eván wanted BattleMechs on the move, standup battles and decisive victories like the one he'd claimed over David McCarthy at Daytin. Strange, that. Eván had carried the day, but it was McCarthy who wound up with a promotion, just because his superior officer had been killed in the opening skirmish with Wendt's command. Some people had all the breaks.

Finally, the general shrugged the issue aside. "Just so long as you put it a touch more diplomatically when anyone else is around. I'm not here to act as your shield, Eván." She smiled thin and hard, implying that just the opposite was true. "And we aren't here today to worry about Petyr VanLees. We're here to decide what to do about the Capellan Dragoons."

Finally, Eván thought but did not say aloud. It had been a month since the duke had informed them of the Dragoons' impending arrival, but since then the issue had faded into the background in the face of the ongoing hostilities between the Eighth and the CMM. The arrival of another hostile BattleMech regiment in just two weeks had taken on fresh significance, however, because the Eighth had failed to bring the militia firmly to heel. The Eighth could hope to defeat either the militia or the Dragoons, but both?

"They'll land in Radcliffe," he said. "It's the only secure site they have. It will be harder, but I think we can keep them bottled up down there along with the militia."

"They're also doing a good job of keeping us bottled up inside District City, don't forget. We can't move far afield without worrying they'll storm into here with their entire force." She caught his gaze and held it. "It would be better if they didn't land at all."

From her tone, this was clearly a test. Eván's quick mind raced, sorting the pieces of the puzzle. His eye fell on Admiral Kerr, still fencing with his latest victim, and then he had it. "The *Robert Davion*," he said. Fallon nodded.

The plan was obvious, once Fallon had pointed it out to him, and Eván considered its implications. If Kerr could gain control of the *Robert Davion*, he could intercept Hasek's First Capellan Dragoons and leave them nothing but free hydrogen and a few melted scraps of DropShip armor. Having a WarShip on their side would alter the odds enormously. And they could even justify taking it over—after all, hadn't Katrina sent them here to protect the shipyards? Wasn't it their duty to prevent the *R. Davion* from falling into the hands of Victor's rebellious supporters?

And yet Eván felt an undeniable twinge of disappointment. Destroying the Dragoons before they even made planetfall on Kathil made strategic sense, but it lacked the intensity and honor of a good standup fight, 'Mech against 'Mech.

"Can't say I'd feel sorry for them," he said cautiously. "Though I think you know I'd rather see them on the ground, where we could meet them on the field."

"I know. You'd like nothing more than to send Hasek's Dragoons back to New Syrtis with a bloody nose. A true Hero of Kathil, right?" He shrugged, unsettled that she had seen through him so quickly. "What if I told you that I had a way to place the ball back in your court?" she asked. "Maybe Admiral Kerr will blow the Dragoons out of the sky. Maybe not. In any case, it will take him several days to make his preparations and assemble a skeleton crew that can run the ship. In the meantime, I have a backup plan that would at least get you back out into the field, and maybe put you in a position to bring the Dragoons down yourself. One man in the spotlight, taking on an entire regiment. It's been done before."

Into the field and against the Dragoons? That was what Eván wanted, all right, but what did it do for her? He knew better than to think her offer was selfless. Could Fallon be making a play for leadership of the Eighth RCT? Or did she have even larger political aspirations? Her obvious satisfaction promised Eván that she had something planned to beat the Dragoons cold—something big, and ripe with opportunity. For now, he would just have to go along. He'd made his bed, and now he would have to lie in it.

"You say it's been done before, and successfully?" he asked.

"It has. And it helped spark the career of one of the Inner Sphere's greatest military leaders."

He was hooked now. She was playing him, and doing an excellent job. He admitted his defeat with an impatient nod. "Yes?" he prompted.

"Eván, how would you like to walk in the footsteps of Morgan Hasek-Davion?"

16

David studied the rough sketch of Muran's eastern seaboard that Tara Michaels had drawn on the large dry-erase board. 'Mech-shaped magnets studded the colorful drawing, showing estimated positions for elements of the Eighth RCT and the matching spread of militia forces. A *Spider* magnet denoted light lances, *Enforcer*s for medium, *Caeser*s for heavy, and *Victor*s for assault-weight lances. Most of the Katzbalger 'Mechs were clustered around or were pushing down from District City, protecting the capital as if it possessed some strategic advantage other than political legitimacy. The militia continued to occupy Radcliffe and several nearby cities, though their hold on some were obviously beginning to slip.

"What about the township of Kelso?" he asked, circling an area on the board and smudging red marker onto his fingers in the process.

Tara leafed through a pile of maps, freshly printed that morning with more accurate data than she had slapped onto the board. Locating Kelso, she studied it and shook her head. "We could roll through there fairly easily. The Eighth has only two lances of green MechWarriors on station, supported by a company of armor. No aerospace support." She continued to scan the map. "But there's no advantage to controlling that area. Kelso is a dead-end community."

David slapped his palms against the sides of his legs in frustration. "Then why is the Eighth there?"

Tara pulled free the map she was studying and held it out to David. "It's across the Howell River from Woodland," she said, as if that explained it.

A quick glance at the map refreshed David's memory. "The Second NAIS Cadre. Right." In the past few days, the training cadre had moved elements in close to the edge of the spreading battle between the Eighth RCT and militia forces. They had yet to commit to support for either side, and their close proximity made everyone a bit nervous.

Especially General Sampreis, who was working hard to snare the Second into the militia. The unit was only a training cadre, but it was one of the most elite in the NAIS, and that meant neither side could leave it out of their calculations. Every day increased the worries that the Second might opt to side with the Katzbalger. At that point, the CMM would have little to no chance of holding out until the Capellan Dragoons got here.

But that was a problem for the old man, he decided, pushing the worry aside. Right now his task was to break the steady war of attrition the Eighth was waging against the militia. He exhaled noisily, feeling the pressure. Most of the militia was counting the hours until the Dragoons arrived in two weeks, but if he didn't come up with some kind of plan to cripple the RCT's offensive capabilities, there wouldn't be anything left to greet them. He had to meet with General Sampreis in thirty minutes and present his recommendations, and right now he had nothing to offer. Time was running out.

"So where does that leave us?" he asked.

Tara stretched, easing tired muscles, and dropped the map she was examining on the table. "It leaves the militia with no good targets south of District City. Not that I can find," she said. "It leaves us with red eyes from staring at maps all morning and me, at least, skipping lunch. Let's grab a bite, David. Take a break. Attack this again after."

David glanced up from the map he held, unsure whether he was reading too much into her tone. There had been something in her voice, something hesitant, and personal. It was more than simply calling him by his first name—as part of his planning staff, she'd earned the right to do so in private. But looking into her chocolate-brown eyes, he could detect the same tentative question she had implied—a hint of possible interest.

"After?" he asked.

"After a rest," she said. "Come back fresh?"

There was no mistaking her implication this time, but there was still that hesitancy—as if Tara wasn't certain herself what she hoped his answer would be.

She was certainly beautiful, and David could still recall the way her voice had electrified him at their first meeting, deep and husky. She had been interested in him too, he thought. But nothing had ever sparked between them. In fact, after that first connection, David had felt her drifting further away as he busied himself with other concerns, and other people. Amanda Black, for instance.

Meanwhile, Tara was growing into her own. She was developing into one of his best lance commanders, destined for her own company when a billet opened up in the TO&E. They worked well together and enjoyed each other's company. David looked at her for a moment, considering the possibilities.

Then he said, "No," hesitant at first, then growing stronger. "No, I don't think so." He was answering her unspoken questions as much as her obvious ones. "I have a meeting with General Sampreis in thirty minutes. You go on ahead."

Tara nodded and turned toward the door. She paused for only a second. "It's okay?"

David knew what she was actually asking. *We're okay?* He was getting so he could read the minds of most of his warriors, especially those from his original company command. It was a sign that he felt easier with them, and they with him. "It's fine," he told her with a smile.

His growing rapport with his soldiers didn't displace the weight of responsibility stooping his shoulders, but it did shift the load to a more bearable position. Now if he could only figure out how those soldiers could survive.

He paused suddenly, staring at the map Tara had dropped on the table before leaving. It showed District City, surrounded by the Eighth's heavy fortifications, extending even out to the suburbs in some places. Maybe, just maybe. The inklings of a plan began to stir in his mind . . .

David could feel the desperation hanging over General Sampreis' office like the haze of cigar smoke that churned around the slowly rotating ceiling fan. There was no brave posturing here, not among the top MechWarrior officers. Sampreis tried to hide his concern behind a mask of confidence, but then he was the general; he had to make some kind of attempt at nonchalance even among his senior staff.

But that façade crumbled when David announced his intended target as soon as he walked in the room.

"You want to hit District City?" General Sampreis said incredulously, nonetheless waving David to an empty chair between the commanders of First and Third 'Mech battalions. "Weren't you one of the people arguing against any attempt to challenge Weintraub for D.C., that it didn't hold any real strategic value?" Sampreis glanced at the holopic of him with Morgan Hasek-Davion on his desk. "Personally, I think we should have stormed in there to bring out Duke VanLees and his family. Leaving Kathil's ruling noble in the hands of that arrogant son of Amaris doesn't sit well with me at all."

Of course not, for someone with as many political aspirations as military ones. Though the Eighth had occupied District City early on, the general had continued to stall and work for a diplomatic victory. But once Duke Van-Lees had been seized, all Sampreis could think of was the loss of his local political backing. Never mind that George Hasek himself had excused Duke Petyr's actions to the populace and backed the militia's authority on Kathil. The general couldn't help assigning a high priority to rescuing the duke.

But except for a slight public relations boost, the operation would be a useless gesture. Nobles did not fight wars. They were good for starting them, and occasionally for ending them, though in this case George Hasek was their best chance for that. Once the fighting began, David believed, it was better to ignore the nobility whenever possible.

"I don't actually want to attack District City," David explained, "but close enough as to make little difference. One of my planning staff, Tara Michaels, clued me to the fact that there are no solid targets of opportunity south of District City right now. And with their shifting forces, we can't predict where the Eighth might leave an opening for a counter-thrust. So that got me to thinking. According to our intelligence, the garrison force in and around District City has remained fairly stable, to the point where I think we can predict its movements. If we hit at the right time, I believe we can force a window of thirty, maybe even sixty minutes before they could respond."

"Sixty minutes?" Lieutenant Colonel Marsha Yori, the new senior battalion commander, frowned and exhaled a stream of cigar smoke toward the ceiling. Her voice left no question about her opinion. These people wanted a plan that offered salvation. David had a plan—apparently the only one in the room—but at first glance it seemed useless. "What can we hope to accomplish in sixty minutes?"

David unrolled the map he'd brought with him, laying it out over Sampreis' desk. "We cripple the Kay Bume munitions plant," he said easily. "It's located here in Stihl, a suburb on the southeast edge of D.C.—mostly industrial yards and low-rent commercial properties. Except for the odd patrol, their initial defense will have to come from the spaceport, here." David stabbed a finger onto the gray expanse located on District City's eastern border, north of Stihl.

"What about the city defenders?" Major Karl Tarsk asked. "They've got to have a full battalion of 'Mechs and armor spread through the city. They could respond much faster."

"Closer to two," David agreed. "But their first thought will be to protect the DMC and Hall of Nobles."

"One munitions plant?" Tarsk persisted skeptically. "A slight tactical advantage only. Their stockpiles have to equal at least a week's output from the Kay Bume facilities. What can you hope to accomplish?"

"Missiles," Yori answered, beginning to see what David had in mind. She looked at Sampreis. "That plant is the only facility under control of the Eighth RCT that produces missiles. The other three on Kathil are under our control or that of the Second NAIS."

She looked at David and obviously read his surprise that she had caught on so quickly. She tapped her head with one forefinger. "Six years attached to the logistics corps, guarding factories and supply channels. I watch for the patterns, too. But I missed this one." She shook her head. "I've seen the same reports as Major McCarthy. The Eighth has been spending missiles very freely. Quite a few of their best 'Mech designs—*Salamander*s, *Rakshasa*s, *Orion*s—depend on LRMs for their main offensive capability. Take away their ability to renew their stockpiles, and you'll see a drastic reduction in offensive maneuvers."

Sampreis nodded thoughtfully. "Hitting so close to home might also convince them to pull back and give us some breathing room until the Dragoons make planetfall." He looked back to David, set his cigar in the tray and left it there. "How do you plan to approach the city? They paint you on sensors early, and you'll be swarmed by RCT support forces."

"We'll use a DropShip to set us right on the outskirts of Stihl and stand ready to pull us out of there once we've accomplished our mission. We'll need a heavy fighter escort on the way home."

Sampreis leaned back into his chair, his face showing a sudden disillusionment. "You'll need it on the way back, on the way in, *and* while you're on the ground. Not to mention the warning DropShip activity will give the Eighth. DropShips are not known for subtle approaches, Major."

"I'm counting on that, General. The DropShip will make a line straight for Ostin, on the coast. The Eighth might even scramble their ready-alert fighters and move them toward Ostin, which would be even better. Then we detour here"—David leaned forward to draw a line across the map, shifting through a yellow-highlighted area to end on the southeastern quarter of District City—"into Stihl."

Yori tapped the highlighted area. "That's a no-fly zone, Major. The Aston-McKinney geothermal plant is located in there, and the air overhead is laced with microwave power transmissions to the space yards and other satellite collectors. Your team would be fried to cinders."

"Except that Aston-McKinney is not a geosynchronous-uplink station."

Yori frowned. "Meaning?"

David was back on his home turf now. Quite literally—his early years on Kathil, and his legacy as a Uhlan, gave him a better handle on local history than any of the other officers. "Some geothermal plants beam their energy back into space to dock facilities held in geosynchornous orbit—matching rotations so they are always over the same spot on the planet," he explained. "That means they don't have to track between horizons. Some plants switch between facilities and orbital relay stations on varying orbits, so they have the capability to swing their transmissions all over the atmosphere.

"Aston-McKinney is an older plant, and a cross between the two. They switch between a selection of restricted-orbit facilities, filling in the occasional downtime for another geothermal station. Every week or so they hit a spot of dead air where they aren't required, so they power down for a day of maintenance. That dead air time comes in two days and creates a temporary access route for our operation."

David had them. The plan was rough, but pretty good considering he'd come up with it in thirty minutes or so. Over the next two days, all the officers would take their shot at breaking it wide open or—failing that—refining it to cover every contingency. But for now, it was the only thing on the table, and it was just audacious enough to win approval. Sampreis polled the other officers silently and added his own answering nod to Tarsk's.

Colonel Yori responded last. "Good luck, Major. And here's hoping you don't need it." She leaned forward to study the map again. "Risky, but our backs are to the wall." She waved her cigar over the no-fly zone. "If even one person out there is on the ball and flips the switch to light that microwave station back up . . ." She trailed off, tapping some dead ashes off her cigar, which fluttered down over the highlighted area.

"There won't be much of you left to hit the ground."

17

Kay Bume Munitions Plant
Stihl, Kathil
Capellan March, Federated Commonwealth
24 November 3062

"Intermittent contact. I'm guessing we have a 'Mech lance trying to flank us through Stihl. We're pulling back on the left." The note of apology in Amanda Black's voice was quite clear.

David registered the report, mentally acknowledging it but with no time to advise. He had larger problems of his own. Violent tremors shook his *Devastator* as a storm of twelve-centimeter autocannon slugs savaged the armor protecting its chest and arms. Tipped in depleted uranium, the slugs' extra mass converted directly to armor-penetrating power. Shards of Durallex plating rained to the ground. A handful of the hot metal breached a flaw in the armor where two plates had been improperly welded, ramming a fist deep into the *Devastator*'s chest and cracking the physical shielding that helped contain the tremendous heat output of the fusion reactor.

Already straining under the power spike from repeated weapons barrages, the 'Mech's heat sinks were overwhelmed by the additional raw heat. One burst under the strain, sending a geyser of greenish coolant through ruptured lines, eventually flashing into steam. What could not be dissipated bled upward, radiating through the deck and the *Devastator*'s air circulation system.

The wall of heat slammed through the cockpit with near-physical force, flash-drying the sweat beaded on David's skin to a salty residue. He held his breath for a few critical seconds and then exhaled slowly to convince his lungs that a fresh draw of air was only seconds away. The cityscape swam before his eyes, his vision blurring as heatstroke threatened, but his life-support system continued to pump liters of fresh coolant through the meters of tubes threaded into his cooling vest. The endothermic system kept his core body temperature at a safe level— barely. It was low enough that he could sweat out the difference and keep his wits about him.

"Too long," David whispered to himself as he fought for control of his BattleMech. He glanced at the countdown he had set on his chronometer. Ten minutes until forced recall. The battle to reach the Kay Bume munitions plant was taking far too long.

This assault had seemed like a much better idea when he'd thought of it two days ago. That was before a few outlying storage facilities went up in earth-shaking explosions, throwing a few ill-prepared 'Mechs to the ground, though everyone was now back on their feet and in fighting order. Black smoke billowed into the air, raining ash and soot down onto the nearby industrial areas. The two companies of David's battalion had initially spread themselves out in a wide V-shaped formation, covering the wide expanse of open ground that separated the munitions facility from the other industrial sites. The wings of David's line reached out farther every minute to envelop the munitions plant and its primary warehouse.

And its heavily augmented company of hard-line defenders, who pushed back with everything they were worth, buying time for reinforcements to arrive.

"Damn Sampreis anyway." Saying the words felt good, though David was careful to keep his voice to a whisper so the voice-activated mic at his throat would not broadcast the curse.

With several regiments of supporting forces at the militia's disposal, David had requested a full company of Manticores or even Goblins, which could form a solid defensive line while his BattleMechs concentrated on flanking maneuvers to contain the RCT position. Instead, General Sampreis had forced on David a demi-company of Centipede scout cars to guard David's flanks and a few VTOL craft to support infantry actions. Two companies of 'Mechs, the general had argued, would be more than enough to put down the predicted company of defenders. And the heavier armor was better saved to garrison important cities south of D.C. The RCT was moving along several spearheads, and David's raid already had a margin of two to one.

Except that the munitions plant had surprised David's assault force with a company of Typhoon urban assault vehicles, each mounting a large-bore autocannon, and a separate lance of LRM carriers that could throw out a net of three-score missiles per carrier—per salvo. These, plus a company of 'Mechs, had brought down a serious load of hurt on David's people in short order. Three of the general's vaunted Centipedes were now burning piles of junk, and two of David's 'Mechs were walking skeletons after tangling with the Typhoons. He had already sent them back to the DropShip, cursing their loss. This battle was being fought for meters, and every wasted minute brought reinforcements that much closer to the beleaguered munitions plant.

It was a pair of Typhoons that nearly brought David down as well. Concentrating on an enemy *Chameleon*, forcing it back between the low-slung munitions warehouse and the production plant, David had missed the approach of the UAVs from the backfield. Missed them, until a storm of lethal metal carved into his 'Mech, rocking it back on its heels and nearly sending him toppling to the ground.

Now the UAVs rolled forward as a pair, splitting up to pass along either flank of the retreating *Chameleon* and then closing back together as they reached a bottleneck formed by two drainage ditches. The Typhoons moved along on the independent drive of six armor-segmented wheels. Designed with low ground clearance, they were hardly off-road vehicles. Forced into close proximity, the two UAVs and the *Chameleon* presented David with an opportunity to strike back hard, opening up the middle of the enemy line.

Nine minutes. It was the best chance he was likely to get. Pinning the *Chameleon*'s outline with his crosshairs, David waited for even a partial lock from his heat-addled targeting system. "Someone better jump on those Typhoons, or your commander is walking home," he said into his comm system.

As his gauss rifles reached out to smash the *Chameleon*'s left side into ruin, one of the Typhoons cut loose with another long stream from its autocannon that barely missed the *Devastator*'s wraparound cockpit. David saw the gray haze of bullets slice over his BattleMech's shoulder, neatly shearing off his shoulder-mounted spotlight. Not that he'd need it, with Kathil's brilliant sun commanding a crystal-blue sky.

David readied himself for the savage attack of the second UAV, only to see its turret swing away from him, distracted by an onrushing shadow. His first thought was of his *Kestrels*, currently holding high cover over the field, ready to bring in the demolition teams to finish off the production plant. Except that the shadow passing over the ground was far too ungainly.

Then a pair of armored feet swung down into view, blurred by the plasma jets keeping Corporal Smith's customized *Cestus* aloft. The BattleMech came down directly on top of one of the Typhoons in a maneuver known among MechWarriors a "Death From Above." Sixty-five tons of metal slammed into the UAV's turret and left-rear quarter. One of the turret-mounted SRM launchers broke away under the impact, and the armor protecting the Typhoon's side buckled inward.

Corporal Smith managed to keep his machine upright as he glanced off the UAV and came down hard on the ground next to his victim. The wounded Typhoon still had its teeth, though, and it drilled several kilograms of armor-piercing slugs into the *Cestus*' left side. Armor peeled back to expose myomer musculature, actuators, and engine shielding. David couldn't tell what kind of damage Smith had taken, though it looked bad enough. The 'Mech fell to one knee and onto its left hand in an attempt to keep its balance. Then, without waiting to regain equilibrium, Smith triggered his custom-installed jump jets again and rocketed away from the deadly UAV just as heavy fire from Tara's lance came in to exploit the Typhoon's flank wound.

Laserfire and the cerulean energy from at least two PPCs poured directly into the UAV's fragile interior. The ammunition magazines blew first, tearing the turret completely off the vehicle and hurling the ruined equipment into the side of the second Typhoon. Then the fusion engine blossomed golden fire beneath the UAV in an explosion that tossed the bulk of the vehicle through the air like some discarded giant's toy, smashing through the roof and down onto one wall of the warehouse. David waited for a sympathetic explosion in the warehouse to clear a major portion of the battlefield, and half of his command along with it. Fortunately, the warehouse structure itself absorbed most of the force and protected the munitions stockpile.

The same could not be said of Smith's *Cestus*. Caught in mid-jump, the force of the explosion tumbled the Battle-Mech's gyro and kicked its feet out to one side. The *Cestus* drove forward on plasma jets, well over the warehouse before it reached the top of its arc, and came down on the hard-packed ground in a mechanoid belly-flop. David winced; that kind of fall could snap your neck or rupture an organ where the restraining harness hammered you back into your seat. At the very least Smith was looking at myriad bruises and wrenched muscles.

But not unconsciousness, apparently. A long second after the final bounce, David heard Smith's voice very distinctly over the comm system.

"Ow."

David moved forward on four-meter-long strides, growing more anxious with every second that ticked past. Tara's lance flanked him on the right, and beyond her, Captain Gerst's company began to curl back to support the line's shift. Holding his fire, sweating his heat curve back down into the yellow band, David spent a few of his precious seconds taking stock of his portion of the battle. One Typhoon destroyed. The other . . . He smiled to himself. The other was on its side, grinding around in an arc as its wheels dug partially into the ground, trying to right itself.

"Contact confirmed," Amanda Black called out, her voice charged with excitement. "It's a reinforcement lance, all right. We have them pinned behind some kind of co-generation power plant, eight o'clock relative to the munitions factory. I'm thinking we don't want to let them coordinate with whatever defenders you have left over there."

Six minutes and change, and now a new threat was opening up on the far left flank of the militia line. Amanda would hold—she had to. Meanwhile, the clock was pushing David to make something happen, and sooner rather than later.

David toggled for active weapons again, eyeing his heat indicators and hoping he'd let his equipment cool long enough. The *Chameleon* was limping back toward the munitions plant, past Smith's fallen *Cestus*, which had yet to show any sign of recovering. Another 'Mech, one of the newer *JagerMech III* designs, also fell back from its hiding place behind the production plant, ceding control of the area to David's command.

Neither enemy warrior would be allowed off so easily.

Cycling his gauss rifles and PPCs together, David finished off the *Chameleon* with one well-placed salvo. A gauss slug took the left leg clean off at the hip joint, while both PPCs cut through ruined armor to melt the gyroscope into slag. The *Chameleon* fell backward, a brief flash of fire licking around its head as the MechWarrior inside abandoned his machine rather than ride it to the ground. The ejection seat arced up and out on a tongue of fire, spreading a parafoil at the top of its arc to glide the warrior to safety.

The *JagerMech* was already taking spotty fire from Tara and one of her lancemates, but it might have held together long enough to bring off a retreat if not for Smith. Having played dead long enough, he levered his *Cestus* up on one arm to bring most of its weapons back into play. An arm-mounted large laser stabbed a lance of emerald light into the crotch of the nearby *JagerMech*, followed by a gauss slug that smashed up farther into the *Jag*'s abdomen. One of David's sensors detected the beginning of a reactor spike, the kind that usually prefaced a complete overload, which was abruptly cut off as emergency dampening fields banked the fusion reactor into dormant mode. It saved the 'Mech for another day, but the *JagerMech* was lost to this fight.

Tara was the first to comment. "Hardly sporting, Richard. I think a ref would call that a foul."

Smith worked his *Cestus* back to shaky feet. "He should have worn a cup."

All across the wide expanse of open ground, the Eighth RCT defenders fell back as a resurgent militia force pressed its advantage. A few Typhoons valiantly held their ground, thinking to make a static line behind which the defenders could regroup, but concentrated fire from Gerst's people made short work of that hasty plan. Enemy armor and 'Mechs alike fell farther afield. One large group of faster machines paused and then, led by a *Nightsky*, dodged south for the protection of nearby buildings.

South, toward David's weakened left flank.

*Kestrel*s were dropping out of the air behind the cover of the munitions plant, spilling the militia's infantry sweep teams and demolitions experts to the ground. They would need a few minutes to plant their charges, and then the entire force could withdraw to the waiting DropShip, where the facility could be blown apart by remote. Time enough still. With the main objective met, David pulled his lance toward Amanda's position. As it turned out, he was seconds too late.

"Jumpers! Watch your six for . . ."

"Damn! They're all over us . . ."

". . . coming out of the commerce district . . ."

"Evade," Amanda ordered, her command circuit over-riding the other transmissions. "Fall back!"

When things went to hell in a battle, they went quickly. In the time it took David to round the corner of the munitions plant, his left flank was engulfed in turmoil. Amanda's lance was caught in some kind of pincer movement. David guessed that the units pinning her were the lance she had reported earlier and the larger group of 'Mechs he had watched flee south. Tending to his top priority, he ordered the demolition teams to continue. "Gerst, you take Pachenko and hold things together," he added. "Tara, with me."

The slowest machine on the field, David's *Devastator* could never reach Amanda's beleaguered lance in time. And though he didn't order it, no one in the hastily assembled rescue team waited on their commander. Tara's *Enforcer* ran past him at its top speed of eighty-six kilometers per hour, and maybe pushing a klick or two above that. Sergeant Nichols, in her new *Lynx*, was not far behind. Even Smith's *Cestus*, limping along after its wild, ungraceful ride, managed to pull past the *Devastator* before David had covered a hundred meters.

He cleared the last corner of the production plant just in time to see the new, hard-pitched battle spill over into the nearby commercial sector. On his HUD, colored icons winked off as he lost tracking, the signals hidden in the shadow of the taller buildings. And not just the red triangles of enemy machines—quite a few green lights were fading as well.

"Amanda, report!" he snapped.

Tara had come upon the scene seconds earlier and had seen more. "She dodged behind that co-gen plant for cover with two of her lance, chased by at least eight enemy 'Mechs. Her fourth man is down. He's not getting back up." A slight pause, her normally husky voice flat with suppressed emotion. "Ever."

David could see the fallen *Quickdraw*, Corporal Barnes' last ride. Half of the 'Mech's head was missing, lasers having carved into and through the cockpit area before Barnes had a chance to eject. Two enemy BattleMechs lay on the ground nearby, including the *Nightsky* he'd noted earlier. Raising his eyes to the cityscape, tracking the skyline, David watched as a *Falconer* rose on jets of plasma over a building three blocks into Stihl. A few other jumping machines he had no time to ID also speared upward on jets before dropping back down into cover—driving his lost warriors farther from rescue.

"Damn it, Amanda, no," he whispered to his empty cockpit. "Not into the city."

18

Kearny-Fuchida Yare Industries
Kathil
Capellan March, Federated Commonwealth
24 November 3062

Kearny-Fuchida Yare Industries, one of Kathil's largest geothermal plants, providing energy for the southeastern seaboard as well as beaming power to shipyard space stations in orbit, was not an easy target. Not even when defended by the green warriors of the Second NAIS Cadre, who had refused to abandon the area and fought with determination to save the township and the facility. Eván would have preferred a full company, at the least. With his full battalion, there would not even have been a fight.

But Leftenant General Fallon had claimed that the RCT operations schedule did not allow for anything more than two lances and some light air support, challenging Eván to get the job done with the tools available to him. And he would—if for no other reason than to spite her for suggesting he couldn't. His two lances against the trainees' single lance and eight Po tanks. He'd deliver KF Yare to Fallon, and then he would hear more of her plans to stop the Capellan Dragoons, as she'd promised.

With his *Cerberus* anchoring the maneuver, Eván wheeled Pack lance to the north, at a right angle to their previous march on KF Yare. On the other side of the open fields, Hunt lance held firm and created the anvil on which his lance would smash the Second. The trainees had been holding a line between the actual township of Yare and the geothermal plant and broadcasting station just outside town. That was a lot of ground to cover. Now the cadets faced two flanking maneuvers with a hollow core, opening up several possibilities for their response.

They chose poorly.

The Second NAIS Cadre was good—there was no denying that, but they didn't have Eván's experience. The medium lance had fallen for the deceptive split in Eván's line, thinking to use its better mobility to wedge apart the RCT forces and hold the breach open until the slightly slower armored cavalry could join them.

It might have worked, too, if Eván hadn't called in his air strike of Yellow Jacket VTOL gunboats. Unlike the thwarted VTOL strike against McCarthy's command the week before, this one went off without a hitch. Strafing runs by three two-craft elements of VTOLs pounded the double lance of Po heavy tanks, the Yellow Jackets' gauss rifles hammering armor to pieces and sending their heavy, nickel-ferrous slugs smashing into the tanks' cramped interior.

A quadruped *Barghest*, the newest 'Mech assigned to Eván's command, leapt in at the kommandant's orders to help split the cadre's lines, isolating the Po heavy tanks in their duel against the faster VTOL craft while the bulk of Eván's two lances pincered the MechWarrior trainees.

His trap sprung, Eván now relied on his assault 'Mech's impressive speed to grab the enemy by the neck and force their submission. Running forward with the *Cerberus'* wide-legged gait, he barged into the middle of the trainee formation, his gauss rifles delivering their 'Mech-stopping power and his bank of medium pulse lasers spitting ruby fire. His first barrage burnt armor from the left side of a green-painted *Stealth*, stripping it away so that one of his following gauss slugs could crush the gyro inside. Its balance destroyed, the *Stealth* dropped to the ground like some massive metal marionette with its strings suddenly cut. His second barrage into the downed 'Mech's back ensured that it would remain out of the fight.

Beleaguered from two sides and with an assault 'Mech loose in their cramped formation, the overwhelmed trainees broke. An *Enforcer* tried to jump out of the trap, only to be slammed back into the ground by three converging PPCs and a wall of missiles. The *Hermes II* attempted to break around Eván's *Cerberus* and link back up with the Po tanks, and was easy meat for the *Barghest's* terrifying Disintegrator LB-X twelve-centimeter autocannon. The remaining *Hatchetman* spun around, titanium-edged hatchet upraised for a lethal downward stroke.

But then it found itself staring into the wide bore of the *Cerberus'* left-arm gauss rifle.

The cadre MechWarrior hesitated, and that probably saved his life. Eván punched for a general frequency, preset into one of his comm system toggles. "Stand down," he warned the other warrior, shifting his arm to better put the gauss rifle barrel directly over the *Hatchetman's* forward shield. He waited until his sensors detected a loss of the *Hatchetman's* active targeting system and then an emergency power-down.

"Smartest thing you've done today," Eván said, and finally allowed himself to relax while assessing his victory.

Eight Po tanks disabled or destroyed. Three 'Mechs disabled, one captured. He'd lost a single VTOL gunboat, and a *Lynx* in Hunt lance had taken fairly heavy damage. All in all, it was a rousing success—and one accomplished without Xander Barajas, whom Eván had left behind to oversee the DMC patrols that the leftenant had originally volunteered for. Despite any minor misgivings over Fallon's mysterious plan to attack the plant, he couldn't deny the thrill of a job well done. This was his victory, and his alone.

"Either shoot that *Hatchetman* or secure it, Eván. I'm not waiting for you."

Fallon! Eván glanced at his heads up display, spotting the trio of new icons the computer had painted over the HUD. Vehicles—no, more VTOLs—tagged with the codes for a Warrior-H8 attack helicopter flanked by infantry-carrying *Kestrels*.

"General," Evan said by way of cautious greeting. "What are you doing here?" He managed to keep most of his resentment out of his voice.

"Following up on my investment," she said. "Your action was most impressive, Kommandant. It will figure well into my report to General Weintraub."

The Warrior-H8 banked hard over the field, coming to hover off the *Cerberus'* right shoulder while the *Kestrel*s continued on to drop infantry forces at the front of Yare Industries. The H8 copter settled to the ground nearby. "Now I suggest you slip into something a bit more formal for the tour of our new facility."

"Of course, everyone knows the popular story," the harried plant manager said, escorting his visitors into the command center of KF Yare Industries.

Karen Fallon had been careful not to show much in the way of approval since meeting the manager—even during their tour of the broadcast station with its immense dish sitting atop the geothermal plant. As the manager opened the final doors, though, it was hard not to let slip some small sign of the impression the room made. It was like the command bridge of a JumpShip, only a dozen—a hundred!—times larger, and backlit by hundreds of monitors and banks of status lights. Such a sight was alien in the Inner Sphere—so much advanced technology prominently displayed inside a single room. And these people worked among such treasures every day.

A small army of technicians and engineers swarmed through the cavernous room. Each went about their duties with one eye nervously kept on the two dozen armed soldiers who commanded the center from strategic points, such as corners and computer banks that could also serve as bulwarks. The workers all knew that Paul Allison—their plant manager and ultimate boss—was in the room. Allison was only one small step down from the Vebber family, which owned a majority of the company. They also knew that Allison was no longer calling the shots.

KF Yare was under new management. Karen Fallon put the employees and the Vebber family out of her mind. This wasn't the first time in Kathil's history that KF Yare had been co-opted for military use. They would obey orders. Her orders.

"The story?" Fallon prompted.

Allison nodded reluctantly. "The story. Of how Morgan

Hasek-Davion arrived on Kathil and took command of this facility in an effort to destroy a Capellan invasion force," he said. "He wanted to destroy the Liao DropShips before they had a chance to land. And he got one of them, knocking a full company of Death Commandos out of the skies. There were no survivors."

Eván Greene, who was escorting Karen along with a small infantry bodyguard, looked a little out of place in coolant vest and shorts and the standard combat boots. He hadn't bothered to change into a formal uniform, likely intending it as some small protest over her arrival. Now, though, caught up in the history of this place and finally seeing the nucleus of her plans to stop the Dragoons, he could not refrain from asking, "You said that's the popular story. Are you implying there is a private one beyond that?"

"Oh, yes," Allison said. "That story's been handed down among employees for thirty years now. It's grown a bit in the telling, but everyone knows the important points." Allison seemed eager to talk, as if it relaxed him. "Old man Vebber initially refused to target an incoming DropShip, regardless of whether it was Liao. He changed his mind after Hasek-Davion . . ." He trailed off, as if realizing this was probably not the kind of story he wanted to tell a military force that had just seized KF Yare.

Karen did not miss his gaffe. "After he *what*, Mr. Allison?"

"Well, Morgan Hasek-Davion pulled his sidearm, General. Accounts differ, but they say he held it to the old man's head, ready to pull the trigger. Then a few others volunteered to do it, and Vebber saw that it was pointless to hold out." He spoke in a rush, as if trying to emphasize the story's insignificance. "He retired not long after."

The general looked at Allison with a glint in her eye. "I trust such theatrics will be unnecessary in your case?"

Allison nodded with feigned enthusiasm, though his worried brown eyes told a different story—mainly that he would rather be anywhere else but at Yare Industries today. Perhaps he was contemplating early retirement as well. "We're about to be invaded by the Capellans?" he asked, sounding almost hopeful.

Perhaps he preferred that to the alternative. Karen guessed he was a closet loyalist of Prince Victor and more beholden to George Hasek than Katrina Steiner-Davion. As they toured the command center, she made a mental note to assign a military liaison to Paul Allison. The man bore watching.

"I remember reading that they only intercepted one DropShip, and at a low altitude," Eván said. "So did someone make a mistake?"

"No, no mistake." Allison shrugged, reminding them that it had been long before his time. "The Tau Ceti Rangers came in behind the Death Commando, who fell toward Kathil on a high-G burn and were harder to track. So that made it difficult. But from my understanding, Hasek-Davion's order to hit them came late. No one is quite sure why." Another shrug. "Maybe he just wanted to see it himself."

"But you could hit a DropShip farther out?" Karen pinned Allison beneath her unblinking gaze. "How far out?"

"The dock working on the *Robert Davion* is about as far out as anything in orbit, sitting out at a Lagrange point. If you wrote the Archon's name on the side of the War-Ship, I could dot all the I's and cross the T's." He paused and smiled hesitantly. "Not that I would ever . . . ever hope . . . to have to fire on the *R. Davion*."

Karen gave him no indication one way or the other. "And you would do that from here? From this room?"

Allison pointed to one of the central consoles, around which three men labored with only about half of their attention focused on their duties. From where her party stood, Karen could see the console front and the red out-line of a DropShip limned in the upper corner like a kill marker on a war machine.

"That aims the energy broadcast station," he said in a resigned voice. "Give me a target, and we'll bring it down."

She smiled. "Perhaps you'd better show me to my new office, Mr. Allison, so we can discuss our operation."

Eván sighed in what he probably thought was silent exasperation, but Fallon caught it. Eván surely had no lingering doubts that she was here to take over the operation, but he should have expected that. It was part of their arrangement, after all. Karen Fallon was not going to let an opportunity slip by her, any more than he was. If anyone was going to walk in the shoes of Morgan Hasek-Davion on Kathil, regardless of what she'd told Eván, it would be her.

And when the First Capellan Dragoons arrived, they would find her waiting.

19

The ground shook, cracking windows and terrifying the people abroad in the streets. Smoke billowed skyward to the north, and chunks of ferrocrete rained down over Stihl's commercial sector. A few pieces pinged and gouged the side of Xander Barajas' *Falconer*. He knew the ammunitions plant was gone. Part of him railed against the loss, at the militia victory, as he touched off his jump jets and drove his 'Mech skyward. But there was a more insistent voice that pushed aside such concerns—overrode the failure in the face of a stronger lure.

The hunt was on.

Xander landed his *Falconer* atop a warehouse, stalking along the edge of the flat roof. He kicked aside the oscillating vents, crushing them as easily as an aluminum can. A low concrete wall that surrounded the roof cracked and crumbled where the 'Mech brushed against it, the bipedal machine's foot sometimes hanging a half-meter over the edge. In the streets below, people ran for the relative safety of stores and eateries. Vehicles slammed into each other in their haste, snarling the traffic. Xander laughed, finding some joy in their fear, but throttled his amusement as his HUD warned of a threat.

At the far intersection, an *Enfield* painted the green and red of the Kathil CMM turned down the avenue Xander guarded. The MechWarrior obviously saw the *Falconer* against the skyline; it abruptly reversed its course to disappear around a large hardware store. Laserfire and a spread of short-range missiles chased it through the intersection, followed a few seconds later by two RCT Battle-Mechs in such a hurry they nearly collided fighting for the lead position.

Xander let them go. The *Enfield* was really a poor challenge for his *Falconer*. With his gauss rifle and extended-range PPC—even leaving his four medium-class lasers toggled out—Xander would have torn the *Enfield* apart without much difficulty. No, he would leave it to the others.

He wanted the *Bushwacker*, the one that had held his lance off for several precious seconds, preventing him from reinforcing the Kay Bume plant. Only when he had moved his entire lance into position and was able to jump three of his four 'Mechs over the militia force had he broken their line. But it had been too late.

It was bad enough that Kommandant Greene had assigned him to remain in District City while Greene went off on some crucial mission for General Fallon. Now, a hard-fought battle was taking place, and over a rather important facility such as a munitions plant, and he arrived too late to claim victory. Someone was going to pay for that.

And this MechWarrior was a quarry worth the hunt. Though the *Bushwacker* had yet to stand and return heavy fire, for a ground-bound 'Mech it was making good time through the suburbs. Triggering jump jets, leaping his *Falconer* from one rooftop to the next, Xander tried to hold the pattern in his mind. West, south, south, west . . . If he was right, the *Bushwacker* would make an appearance one street over, still angling south-southwest. His instincts said the 'Mech would eventually turn back to the east, hoping to regroup with its now-distant comrades. Xander smiled to himself. Not if he found it first.

In the lethal hide-and-seek of combat among city streets, battles were won and lost in the seconds that an enemy was visible down a side street or racing through an intersection. That was one of the reasons Barajas preferred the rooftops—at least until he located his prey. Which he did at the next street over, right where he'd predicted.

Sensors rang out warning alarms as the *Bushwacker* ran into the intersection, paused to carefully turn the ninety-degree corner without crashing its widespread arms through a nearby building, and then throttled back up to speed. Too late, it registered the *Falconer*'s presence. Xander stabbed down on the thumb trigger, catching the other 'Mech just over the left knee with his gauss rifle. His particle cannon directed a cascade of focused energy toward the shoulder on the same side, but the *Bushwacker*'s low profile ducked the shot. Instead, the azure whip blasted through the brick facing on a nearby store. A cerulean backwash blew out the plate-glass front window and the store entrance, showering glass shards over the street and the civilians running for cover.

The other MechWarrior was left with several tough choices of how to handle the rooftop predator, finally turning into Xander's attack to try and run beneath him, where the *Falconer*'s weapons might not be able to strike. Barajas saw it coming, spotting the shift of actuators at the hips which were the telltale sign of a change in direction. He quickly dropped down to the street, crushing a parked vehicle and setting off its alarm system to wail impotently. He impatiently shook the car roof off his foot and stepped into the street to block the *Bushwacker*'s path.

Point-blank and personal was the way Xander liked it. His medium lasers, cooling until now, stabbed short arrows of ruby energy into the *Bushwacker* as it stopped short, bringing its arms up. But it was too slow. Xander was already toggling for his main weapons as they cycled back to ready. He cursed as his particle cannon missed high and wide again, scoring along a row of apartments offering housing over the commercial district. His gauss rifle managed to gouge a new wound over the *Bushwacker*'s chest, the silver slug rebounding to ricochet through another storefront.

His fingers stabbed at the toggles that fast-cycled his weapons. As the heat in his cockpit jumped several degrees, raising sweat along his brow and bare upper arms,

Xander tensed for the return barrage. "Come on. Come on! What do you got?" he snarled at the *Bushwacker*.

And then he watched in amazement as it backed away. Slowly at first, as if unsure whether to fight or run. Then it angled back into the intersection and throttled up for a stab at the cross street, its choice made.

"No! Fight me, damn you!" Xander slammed his throttle forward to the physical stop, angling for the edge of the intersection and stabbing down on his trigger as gauss and medium lasers finally cycled free. The lasers peppered the militia 'Mech and part of the corner as well, scouring armor and brick and sending small molten beads of metal flying. The gauss hit just behind the *Bushwacker*, skipping up off the street to ricochet down the avenue. The *Bushwacker* vanished from sight, but for seconds only, as Xander chased it into the intersection and planted his 'Mech's right foot for a hard, ninety-degree pivot.

Seventy-five tons of upright metal, balanced precariously by a gyroscope and a neural feedback system, accelerated forward at better than sixty kilometers per hour. That was a danger when running along city streets: even the diamond-rough tread on a BattleMech's foot couldn't grip the pavement well. Xander felt his planted foot slip and skid a few meters, hyperextending the *Falconer*'s hip joint. Then his left foot caught behind him, anchoring him into a left-hand spin as the *Falconer* was claimed by the none-too-gentle hand of gravity.

Sparks showered as his shoulder and left knee glanced off the pavement in a series of ungainly bounces. His right foot speared through a delivery truck left abandoned on the corner, its side panels catching in the ankle joint and pinning the leg in place. The force of the fall threw Xander against his harness, teeth grinding together in fury and eyes clenched against the disconcerting loss of equilibrium. Then he opened his eyes, staring out through the *Falconer*'s shield and down the cross street he had been aiming for.

He was just in time to see the *Bushwacker* make the next corner and again disappear from sight.

Xander saw red with fury as he kicked his foot out of the delivery van and worked his arms beneath him to lever the *Falconer* back to its feet. Not about to chase along the *Bushwacker*'s path and risk another fall at the next intersection, he chose the straightest path between the two 'Mechs: into and through the corner building. A paint store, he saw through the curtain of falling bricks and mortar dust, gallons of bright colors splashing into the air as his behemoth stride shattered displays and hurled cans high into the air to bounce off walls and ceilings. Bright yellow paint splashed over his forward shield, staining a large area of the ferroglass. Not enough to stop him, though.

It was never enough to stop him.

Back at the Kay Bume facility, Amanda had known a moment's fear when the retreating defenders linked up with their reinforcement lance. There were too many enemy machines in close quarters, where the Eighth RCT preferred to fight, and not enough time for McCarthy to lend her support.

Watching Barnes' *Quickdraw* fall victim to the *Falconer* had pushed her to desperate measures. She had been leery of cityscapes ever since her simulator duel with McCarthy, but seeking the protection of the streets had been the only way to save the rest of her lance. Calling Sergeants Geriene and Benjamin after her, she raced to put distance between themselves and the Katzbalger BattleMechs. They split up in the streets of Stihl, trying to draw the enemy in several different directions and hoping that each would find a way to link back up with the command. Sergeant Benjamin had—Amanda caught a piece of his transmission as he found McCarthy, but she lost tracking again as she slipped into the communications shadow of another large building.

Now her fear had returned—not for her lance, but for the residents of Stihl. As she'd anticipated, her run through the city was costing innocent lives—people she had sworn to protect as a member of Kathil's militia force. But that oath apparently did not bind the MechWarrior who piloted the *Falconer*.

For a moment, as she caught a glimpse of its fall on her rear-video monitor, she had hoped to shake the seventy-five-ton nightmare from her back. If she could find a parking garage, or maybe a warehouse—anywhere without heavy traffic—she might go to ground temporarily and then make her way back toward the industrial district. Toward the DropShip, and her only path of retreat.

Then, on the monitor, she saw the explosion of bricks and plaster rain into the street behind her. The *Falconer* kicked its way free of the building, its upper body coated in gray dust and its legs covered with wild splashes of color.

Caught short of the intersection, Amanda could only keep running forward or dodge through a building herself. But these buildings weren't constructed of polygonal graphics burned onto the phosphorous screens of a simulator. There would be no simulated cost in materials and lives. These were valued in thousands of real C-bills and the immeasurable cost of Kathil lives.

As she was slowing into the turn four strides short of the next cross street, the *Falconer*'s gauss rifle caught her in the back. Cracking her armor case like a fragile shell, the nickel-ferrous slug smashed through titanium support struts and worried deep into her left side. The status indicator for her torso-mounted machine gun winked red, warning her that the heavy projectile had destroyed perhaps the least critical piece of equipment she had.

The *Falconer* fired again, its PPC biting low at her right ankle, blasting apart the actuator and fusing the joint like some massive arc-welder. The *Bushwacker* stumbled and only Amanda's quick use of her giant arms let her keep her balance and save her from a fall.

The damage was done, however. The ruined ankle cut her speed enough that the *Falconer* would have no trouble catching her. She might gain the next corner, but then what? Have the Katzbalger warrior run through another building to catch her? How many lives was she willing to sacrifice?

Easing back on her throttle, Amanda walked her *Bushwacker* down to an easy limp and then to a complete stop. A second gauss rifle slug caught her left arm as she turned to face her enemy. The shot snapped the 'Mech's limb back and wrenched the shoulder socket, but did little more than smash through the last of its armor protection this time. The particle cannon glanced off her right flank, runneling some armor to the street but spending most of its strength on a nearby Avanti sports car. The vehicle erupted into a red-orange fireball, the flames licking at nearby buildings.

Amanda stood still, her wide-shouldered 'Mech squared off against the approaching *Falconer*, which had throttled down into a cautious walk. Her crosshairs pinned the enemy machine dead center, framing the gyro casing that depended from the main body. The reticule burned the hard golden color of a good sensor reading, the whistling tone alerting her to a solid missile lock.

Still she couldn't fire.

What kind of damage could one missed shot cause? And what would a reactor overload do in the middle of a city? It didn't bear thinking about. Amanda had run her course, given her people their chance to escape. Now she settled back into her seat, hands falling away from the control sticks as she waited for the end. A dark shadow crossed over her as a cloud hid the sun. The *Falconer* came to a full stop, preparing to fire. It was over.

Then the first missile barrage rained down on the *Falconer*, straight into the blast pockmarks in its shoulders and upper body and ringing a few warheads off the side of its head as well. The scattered net of missiles also fell over nearby vehicles, punching through their roofs and filling the interiors with destructive fire. More nicked the corners of buildings or impacted directly on rooftops, spreading the damage over several hundred square meters.

"Where. . . ?" Amanda glanced around, checking her HUD and auxiliary screens. No friendly units nearby. Nothing her sensors could read. Then she remembered the dark cloud that had passed over the sun, on what had been a beautiful Kathil day. With her ferroglass shield bubbling up over the top of the cockpit, she barely had to crane the *Bushwacker* toward the sky to look up herself and see it.

Unless they had been designated as a target, sensors rarely painted DropShips on the HUD. They were too big.

The militia's massive *Overlord* hung over the city like a gray, thirty-story skyscraper suddenly gifted with flight. From its side-mounted launchers, the DropShip sent out another net of missiles. All they had to do was aim straight down.

The *Falconer* stood up under the second barrage, though heavy damage to its right shoulder left the arm hanging useless at its side. With a long, seemingly calm look skyward, it turned and plunged back into the hole it had already smashed through the building, escaping under the cover of the cityscape.

Amanda watched it go, her muscles trembling with pent-up emotion. She didn't know how to feel about her rescue, or her decision to take to the city, or her choice to become a MechWarrior in the first place. And that was the hardest admission she'd ever faced. Tears brimmed in her eyes. She was tired and afraid, and sick to the bone of watching her world being torn apart.

And in the isolation of her cockpit, where no one could hear and nobody would know, Sergeant Major Amanda Black wept.

DropShip Masse Noir
Yare, Kathil
Capellan March, Federated Commonwealth
28 November 3062

Eván lay in bed with the pillow bunched up under his shoulders, propping himself into a half-sitting position. Hands clasped behind his head, he stared around Karen Fallon's stateroom. Fallon had called for the *Masse Noir*—the Black Hammer—after securing the area, moving her personal DropShip in to loom over the small township of Yare like a physical warning. It was better than sleeping in his 'Mech cockpit or risking the locals' hostility by taking a room in Yare, he decided. The DropShip's red "night lights" barely provided enough illumination to pick out details, though they certainly would prevent him from killing himself during an alert by falling down a flight of stairs or braining his head on a low-mounted cabinet.

Not that he would have such worries in here. Karen's stateroom was furnished with Spartan taste, very much in keeping with her personality. Bare metal bulkheads stood over a vinyl-tiled floor littered with yesterday's clothing. There was one closet—locked—and a desk covered in maps and reports. The one thing it did have was room, a precious commodity aboard DropShips. Fallon at least knew how to use her rank to effect.

"You're not sleeping," she said, rolling over to lay her head on his bare chest. It was statement, accusation, and question, all rolled into one.

"No," he said, tilting his head to look down into her dark hair. What was going on inside her mind? Calculating the best way to use this night together for her advantage, most likely. He had not expected her carefully phrased invitation in the wake of their successful "liberation" of the plant, but he had not thought to refuse. Fallon was a beautiful woman, in addition to being a very useful one.

Outside the room, someone shuffled down the passage: another senior officer heading off to sleep, no doubt. Fallon raised her head slightly, waiting until she was certain the person had moved past. She kissed Eván's chest. "What are you thinking about, then?"

All sorts of things, from McCarthy's devastating strike at District City to the relative quiet that had enveloped Yare and the KF Yare Industries facility in the few days following the battle. Fallon had joyfully described Weintraub's failure to safeguard the munitions supply as if the logistics problems the explosion had created meant nothing to her beyond serving to further emphasize her own success. While Eván dealt with memos complaining about the munitions shortage, she continued to rein him in and secure a power base independent of Mitchell Weintraub. Eván was beyond caring about her plans to destroy the First Capellan Dragoons using the Yare Industries energy broadcast station, especially now that he was just the "hired gun" on the project. There was little left to do here that might win him any chance at recognition and further advancement, and a sneak attack on a ship he would never even see was not his idea of a glorious victory.

"Wondering why I'm here," he said at last.

"I invited you," Fallon said, her tone less playful than it had been earlier. "You said yes."

Eván shrugged. "Wondering why you asked me, then."

"I wanted to see if you ever dropped your guard," she said matter-of-factly, not even pretending at feelings. "I can see now that you don't."

Eván recalled his thoughts of a week back, about lying

in the bed he'd made. He laughed silently. How true that had become.

"What's funny?" Fallon asked. She trailed a fingernail over his ribs, counting them through his skin. "It better not be me."

"No," Eván said, sobering, "Not you. Kathil. Kathil's funny. It conspires against me. It strangles my victories and make my oddest thoughts come true." He was drifting a bit, speaking without thinking about what he was saying, and that was not a habit to encourage. Eván shook himself more fully awake.

"You've been thinking about McCarthy again," Fallon accused. "His raid against the munitions factory was inspired planning."

Eván remained quiet. Without firing a shot in either of their directions, McCarthy had hurt them seriously.

"Are you worried that it overshadowed our play down here in Yare?" she asked.

"I'm thinking that I've had enough of his 'Hero of Kathil' routine," Eván spat out, transferring his frustration with Fallon safely over to McCarthy. "Damn Barajas for not bringing him down when he had the chance." Venting some of his rage calmed Eván enough to think clearly again. He didn't really wish Xander that opportunity—hurt McCarthy, maybe, draw him out. But Eván wanted to be the one to stop the militia hero dead in his tracks. Then all of McCarthy's victories would become his as well. He said as much to Karen.

"Then kill him," she said simply.

"I'll leave tomorrow."

"But I want you here," she said. "At Yare. I can't afford to have you haring off when every second might count. This facility is mine, and I don't want the militia or Second NAIS Cadre moving back in to take it away."

Eván exhaled noisily. "You just suggested I kill him. I can't do that."

She sat up, curling her feet beneath her and staring down at his relaxed form. The dim lighting smoothed her curves into hints of flesh and shadow. "I didn't say to 'do' both. You merely have to *accomplish* both. Send Barajas. Your wolf will make a fine attack dog. He has to be

smarting over his failure to stop McCarthy, the same way
you worry about McCarthy's star outshining yours."

It wasn't the same, sending someone else in your
place—at least not to Eván. But then what kind of advice
could he expect from someone who was content with destroying the Capellan Dragoons by remote rather than
meeting them on the battlefield? And other than disobeying Fallon by leaving, Eván's only choice seemed to
be to send Barajas or find a way to lure McCarthy to him
here. He sensed Fallon's tension in the way she stared at
him unblinking, her eyes hollow pits in the red light, waiting for him to show some disloyalty.

"I'll give Barajas his orders in the morning," he said,
and watched the wariness bleed away from her body as
it settled comfortably back against his. She nipped him
hard on the shoulder, and Eván bent his head to hers,
finding her greedy lips.

He *would* set Leftenant Barajas after McCarthy, but not
to kill him. He would send him to hurt McCarthy, to draw
him out onto the battlefield where Eván could finally take
his shot. If Xander failed, then maybe Eván could find
a way to convince Fallon of the need to bring the man
down personally.

And Eván knew exactly how to lure McCarthy out.
Striking directly at him was useless—he was safely en-
sconced within his battalion. But just a few hours inland
was a place with no 'Mechs to defend it—a place whose
destruction would wound McCarthy deeply, perhaps even
mortally. A few words in Xander's ear would point him
in the right direction, and Eván would wait for McCarthy's rage and grief to bring the man to him.

In the meantime, he would play the part Fallon demanded of him and watch her all the more closely, ready
to stand for himself as necessary. Part of their arrangement was that she would help him find opportunities to
advance his career, and those were coming. As the fighting on Kathil continued, they couldn't help but come.
Postponing his final confrontation with McCarthy was
giving up the short game with an eye toward the long
game.

And Eván was beginning to look long down the road
indeed.

*   *   *

If Admiral Paulsen thought Kerr's bringing up three shuttles from the surface of Kathil was strange, nothing was said. Kerr knew that nothing would be said, not over comms, and not between two old space hands, even if one did come up through the Lyran Alliance military and the other through the Federated Commonwealth. There was always that unwritten law of instant acceptance among spacefarers. Working in the deadliest environment known to man, such implied trust was necessary.

In more ordinary times, at least.

The *Robert Davion*'s small hangar bay had been repressurized and a small review committee drawn up to welcome their new XO. They stood along the upper catwalk, hands and feet hooked beneath low rails to anchor themselves in the null gravity. A WarShip had grav decks and, like a DropShip, could create artificial gravity by remaining under thrust. But in space dock, that wasn't possible. Whatever wasn't fastened down floated off.

Kerr smiled thinly as he noted several officers who'd made changes to the Commonwealth uniform to more exactly reflect their ties to the old Federated Suns. Not the captain of the WarShip—an admiral should be above such things—but several officers. It confirmed Kerr's suspicion that he was needed here. The Archon was worried about her WarShip commanders, the very reason she'd arranged the posting of Lyran officers to the Commonwealth vessels. Any final reservations that might have pricked his conscience evaporated like water boiling out into space. Without his presence, the ship might even be turned against the Archon-Princess, and that was something he could not allow to happen.

A bosun's mate stood by the ladder that led down from the shuttle's hatch, both his feet strapped to the deck, leaving his hands free. In his left hand was a portable mic that patched him into the ship's all-hands 1MC circuit. With an antique whistle cupped in his right palm, he trilled off the four-note call to attention.

"Executive Officer, arriving," he announced formally. Another bosun, somewhere back in the ship's depths, pressed the button that chimed five bells in acknowledgment of Kerr's rank.

Hatches were being cracked on the other two shuttles as Admiral Paulsen glided with practiced efficiency along the railing to shake Kerr's hand. The admiral was a large man, the very image of an ancient fighting sea-captain, with a leathery face, callused hands, and sharp, storm-gray eyes that were made for sextant and spyglass.

Kerr hated the man instantly. No doubt someone had identified him while he was a lieutenant, squared away and commanding, and branded him a future admiral. Now here he was, skippering possibly the greatest piece of martial technology the Commonwealth had produced in centuries.

For about another thirty seconds.

"Admiral Kerr, welcome aboard," Paulsen said. "I hadn't expected you for at least another two weeks. We're operating on a skeleton crew so we have no formal welcome-aboard ceremony in place, but once we have a full complement, I expect something can be arranged."

"That's all right," Kerr said easily. "I've already made all the arrangements we need."

Barely had he spoken when a team of Katzbalger special infantry began dropping from the just-opened hatches of the other shuttles. Though not standard marines, they had some zero-G training and knew enough to rely on their magnetic-soled boots to ground them on the deck. No one reacted quickly enough to protest until nearly a dozen armed guards had taken up firing stances in the hangar. Then a leftenant shouted, "Call in an alarm, you fool!"

But the only man present with comm capability—the bosun—already had four laser rifles pointed at his midsection. Kerr held out his hand, and the man surrendered the mic to the admiral.

"What the hell are you doing, man?" Paulsen fumed, caught between outrage and shock at seeing his billion C-bill ship pirated out from under him. "What's the meaning of this?"

Kerr stared up at him, resenting the man's advantage in height. "Sorry it had to be this way, Admiral Paulsen," he lied, "but this is a change of command. By the authority of Duke Petyr VanLees and his duly appointed representative General Mitchell Weintraub, I am taking command of this vessel."

"I won't stand for this!" the admiral snapped.

Four riflemen tensed, eyes sharp over their sights. Kerr held up a hand, stalling their reaction. His voice took on a harsher edge. "I will only tell you this once, sir, and after that you may argue with a firing squad. You and your officers will stand down, and, by the Unfinished Book, I mean now! You are to be transported to Kathil's Hall of Nobles, where you may make any protest you wish to the duke's representative. If you resist, you and your officers will be shot."

Admiral Paulsen wisely calmed down for the sake of his subordinate officers, but not without a serious internal struggle that Kerr could read on his transparent expression. Anyone could tell the battle was a lost cause, the bay swarming with infantry and not a single weapon among his officers. They might get an alarm out—Kerr saw that idea flit briefly through the other man's eyes—but as more infantry spread out from the shuttles, Paulsen clearly decided that whatever small marine force he had aboard would stand no chance. He nodded once, curtly, defeated.

Kerr gestured to his infantry and began pointing out all those with uniforms reflecting an allegiance to the old Federated Suns. Then he addressed those remaining. "If any of you have misgivings about serving under me as captain and acting in the best interests of Archon-Princess Katrina Steiner-Davion, you should stand aside now."

If Kerr had hoped to cow the rest into obedience by invoking the Archon's authority, he had only partial success. Another three officers volunteered to join their companions aboard the shuttles for a return trip to Kathil.

"You can't take command with a skeleton crew and no officer corps," Paulsen exclaimed.

"I have a crew," Kerr said, careful not to let his reservations show as the technicians, navigators, gunners, and other rates that Weintraub had located for him finally began to offload from the shuttles. Promoted from DropShip crews or called as volunteers from D.C.'s retired Navy cadre, they would be adequate, if not ideal. They waited to one side for orders to move into the ship and

begin work. "Don't worry about my problems, Admiral."
Then he turned to one of the infantry seniors. "Sergeant,"
he called out, "escort this man off my ship."

His ship.

That felt good.

21

CMM Staging Grounds
Radcliffe, Kathil
Capellan March, Federated Commonwealth
29 November 3062

David knew instinctively that the knock at his door could bode no good—especially since someone had taken the trouble to seek him out in his private quarters. The military followed many oversimplified rules and procedures, and one of them seemed to be that good news could always wait until morning. It was the bad news that you had to share immediately.

David had heard his share of bad news and then some in recent days. Despite the destruction of the munitions plant, the shortages were not having as drastic an effect as he'd hoped. Yes, they were causing the RCT some problems, but not enough to reverse their advance and drive them back toward D.C. And just as his battalion was destroying the plant, the Katzbalger had moved even farther inland, striking at Yare, of all places. That had secured them an important power center, forcing Radcliffe and many cities southeast of them to divert to an alternate facility. More important, though, it showed that the Eighth was strong enough to take on both the militia and the Second NAIS.

Forcing himself away from his work table, David

crossed the floor in quick strides. Steeling himself for a new setback, he opened the door in one crisp motion. Amanda Black was waiting in the hall, wearing full dress uniform complete with half cape and leggings, though at first glance something seemed to be missing. She stood at rigid attention. Her brown hair was clipped back tightly from her temples, accenting the martial look.

Proud and beautiful, and very much alone. That had been one of David's first impressions of Amanda Black, and it was even truer now. But a new fragility haunted her eyes. It was a look he'd never seen before but that he recognized instantly. It was the same expression that so often stared back at him from mirrors.

"Sergeant Major Black to see the Major," she said in a determinedly formal voice.

David nodded a cautious greeting and glanced over her uniform once again, catching what had bothered him earlier. Although formally dressed, Amanda was not wearing her rowless spurs—a tradition in the old Federated Suns army, reminding MechWarriors of the ancient cavalry days. Leaving them off, and making a request for a formal interview, could only mean one thing.

As if reading his mind, Amanda reached into her pocket, pulled out the spurs and offered them to David. She was here to resign.

"Perhaps you'd better step inside, Amanda," he said, ignoring her outstretched hand. He stepped back inside, leaving room for her to pass. He shut the door behind them.

David watched her practiced gaze sweep over the tightly made bed and closed lockers, linger briefly over his desk where small noteputer and stack of papers betrayed the work he'd brought home, and then stop cold at the table with the open bottle of brandy sitting in plain sight.

"I was about to indulge in an early drink," he admitted.

"It's a bad habit to fall into, drinking alone," she said after a moment. "If you don't mind my saying so, Major."

David had to agree. It wasn't about to stop him, but he did agree. "If that was an offer to join me, Amanda, I'll find another glass."

She nodded hesitantly, and David procured a second

glass from a small cupboard, then poured a dollop of the purple beverage into each glass. He inhaled on first sip, taking the heady scent deep into his sinuses. An exciting taste, dry without losing its flavor. It had traveled well.

His senior sergeant was still standing. "Come on, Amanda. Takes the edge off, I promise."

Amanda moved a few careful steps closer, searching her commander's face. "Takes the edge off what?"

"Us," he said.

She tossed her spurs onto the table next to the bottle, the metal ringing against the glass, then accepted the drink. If she had been expecting a local Kathil beverage, the first taste quickly disabused her. She swallowed wrong and coughed. "That's good," she said, when she had recovered.

David hooked a chair out from the table and motioned for her to sit across from him. "New Syrtis stock. Kathil makes some excellent wines, but a good brandy is hard to find here. They don't distill it correctly."

Her next sip was more careful, turning into a long draught once she had the brandy's measure. Setting the glass back on the table, she accepted the chair David had offered, pulling it around to face him. Their knees were almost touching, and when she leaned forward David smelled the brandy on her breath.

"I'm through," she said, nodding at the spurs.

David leaned back into the chair. This wasn't what he had wanted for Amanda. Even during those first difficult weeks of taking command, he had recognized her worth. Losing what was potentially his best warrior hurt deep, hurt where he hadn't felt pain since Huntress, and that surprised him a little. But her resignation did not. Amanda wasn't the first since the war for Kathil had begun. She wouldn't be the last.

"I know," he finally said. "I've wondered about that since your showdown in Stihl. You damn near let the *Falconer* take you apart."

"I couldn't fire," she said, staring into her glass. "All I could do was run, and then not even that. I froze."

"I froze once," David admitted before he could think better of it. "On Huntress. It wasn't much more than a heartbeat, a split second to evaluate the situation. I tell myself that some nights. On other nights, most nights, I still hear their calls."

"Whose calls?" she asked softly.

"Polsan. Kennedy. Fletcher and MacDougal. Isaak. We were the last. Everyone was calling out challenges and asking for help. When Kennedy went silent, I knew she only had seconds left. I had to decide between two lives, and I hesitated. I knew I should turn one way or the other, but instead I fought my own battle and avoided the larger responsibility."

"So what happened?"

"Fletcher and MacDougal jumped their *Stealth*s in to take my opponent—mine and Isaak's. It goaded me to action. But the delay cost a fine hauptmann, Kennedy, her left arm when a *Vulture* sliced lasers into her cockpit. Isaak died a few seconds later. For the rest of the battle I fought like a machine, with no thoughts to slow down my reactions. But for a moment, I froze. It was easier than choosing."

Amanda nodded. "It was easier to surrender than worry about what that *Falconer* would destroy next."

If her will to fight was gone, he knew better than to push her to continue, no matter how much they needed her. David leaned forward, took her hand and gave it a reassuring squeeze.

"It's a fine line," he said. "Deciding to give yourself up, but knowing that will leave a MechWarrior like that *Falconer* loose in District City. It's the same thing we do when we decide if an operation is worth the potential losses. Military triage."

Her smile was forced. "And what did General Sampreis think of our operation?"

David jerked his chin back over his shoulder at the paperwork strewn over his desk. "He thinks the attack against the munitions plant came off fairly well, all things considered. It slowed the RCT, though their push into Yare shows they aren't rolling back as we'd like them to. General Sampreis rated the loss of Sergeant Deveroux and three 'Mechs destroyed as 'acceptable' casualties. We destroyed the munitions plant, the stockpiles, and better than two hundred tons of enemy 'Mechs and armor, and salvaged two machines over the ones we lost."

"Is it that easy to decide?" Amanda asked, her voice nearly a whisper.

He released her hand and poured them both another long splash. "It is for some. Others work at it. A few never make it through the rougher parts. Most everyone has their limits." Amend that. "Everyone."

"And Huntress helped you prepare for this?"

"Nothing could help you prepare for this. You deal with it or you don't." Or you fight it the rest of your life, he thought. The one thing you don't do is banish the memories.

"I can't do it." She managed a startled laugh. "I never thought I'd hear myself say that, but I can't. Not when it's my world. Damn it, David, I never liked Weintraub or most of his martinets, but I did have some friends in the Eighth RCT. People do that, you know, make friends inside other units that are supposed to be your allies. And now I'm supposed to turn around and kill them?"

He didn't miss her use of his first name. And he didn't mind, either. "How are they? Have you heard?"

Pain flashed across her face. "Sergeant Rastling I don't know about," she admitted. "Sergeant Yeats was one of the men Weintraub had shot for desertion."

There really wasn't anything to say to that. He'd heard about the desertions from Sampreis, who was prepared to take similar measures if forced to. You had to keep your army in line. The commander in David recognized the truth behind that. MechWarriors could resign from combat duty, but they couldn't be allowed to completely turn their back on the military. If Amanda wanted to resign as a MechWarrior, he wouldn't stop her, but he would have to find another way for her to serve.

Amanda exhaled a long, drawn-out sigh. Her eyes sought out his and held them. The brandy was having its effect on them both, easing their discomfort and lowering their guard. "How did all this get started, David?"

He shrugged. "The right conditions and the wrong word said? How does any war start?" He sipped at his brandy. "One of my older brothers is an engineer. Before I left for the academy, he explained warfare to me in a way I've never forgotten. He said humanity is a closed system. No matter how far we spread out among the stars, we're still confined by boundaries. And when you put pressure on a closed system, it affects the flashpoint—the lowest temperature at which it will ignite. Usually it takes a definite spark, but under enough pressure, all it really takes is some heat."

"Pressure and heat." Amanda smiled sadly. "Yes, we've had those."

David nodded. "Katherine Steiner-Davion put the pressure on when she took the throne. Prince Victor supplied the heat when he returned home from Clan space. He didn't mean to, but he can't ignore the situation much longer. It's been back-building since then, filtering down through George Hasek and the other nobility to the lowest level. To us. And we provided the spark."

"So will the arrival of the First Capellan Dragoons lower the pressure, or increase it?"

"If the Dragoons hold to the schedule forwarded by Field Marshall Hasek, they should be arriving in another week. We'll find out then. Or, more likely, a few days before that."

Amanda's hand edged out along the table, took David's and held it. "*You'll* find out then. And you'll do fine. Look what you've already accomplished here on Kathil, David."

Her touch was warm. Why did women always seem to have a higher temperature than men? He squeezed her hand in what he hoped was a reassuring manner.

"I'm sorry to lose you, Amanda. You're good. Maybe one of my best. And despite how you feel now, you were progressing nicely." He wondered if he could have uttered any platitudes more banal. He stood, uncomfortable with the entire situation but unable to release her hand. Some of her earlier uncertainty had vanished, and in its place was a resurgent desire. Or maybe he was reading into her too much of his own feelings. He tugged lightly on her hand, helping her stand. "But if you're sure . . ."

That was a question he would never finish, as Amanda stepped forward into his embrace. Her lips trembled on his, and for a moment David forgot to breathe. He broke away first, wanting to be certain that this was really what they both wanted. Amanda looked almost as surprised as he felt. But David could sense the chemistry between them that he'd never felt between himself and Tara Michaels.

The attraction had been there from the first day, though their natural antagonism had hidden it.

And it might have stayed hidden, if not for one moment of vulnerability between two frightened people.

"I've never kissed a sergeant before," he said, not meaning to make light of the situation but trying to tell Amanda that he wanted it.

The desire in her eyes gave him his answer. "Shut up," she said and pulled David back to her.

That was all it really took sometimes.

Pressure, and heat.

Maybe things would work out, after all.

22

FCWS Robert Davion
McKenna Shipyards, Over Kathil
Capellan March, Federated Commonwealth
29 November 3062

Old sailing masters, the ones who had challenged Terra's oceans in previous millennia, had required an unobstructed view: the wind in their face, the taste of salt on their lips, and total command of the horizon. In battle this became even more crucial, giving the ship's captain a platform from which he could monitor his enemy and command his vessel.

As ocean ships grew in size and power, eventually becoming the templates for the first space-faring vessels, that open-bridge mindset remained. A command center technically able to run the entire vessel might be buried within the ship's bowels, but command routinely stayed on the upper decks, where incredible ferroglass shields opened up on the spacescape. How many battles had been lost for exactly this reason, when a chance collision or a lucky missile strike opened the bridge to hard vacuum and the captain was lost?

Not on the *Robert Davion,* though, or any other ship of the New Avalon class. Their command bridges were nestled far below decks, shielding them from almost anything but a special forces boarding party—and even a boarding party would have to work their way through a dozen levels before they could do any damage to the ship's nerve center. Large video screens, able to shift camera angles or zoom in and out, replaced the limited viewfield of ferroglass shields. A holographic tank fed by three different sensor systems could simulate any battle in three dimensions, an old technology only recently brought back to life by the new Avalon Institute of Science. And although most ship functions were still handled by remote stations, there wasn't one critical system that could not be handled almost as well by slaving it to one of the command center's many computer consoles.

Kerr liked that—liked being able to take full command of the *R. Davion*, its power in the hands of men under his direct control.

Of course, most of the ship was under his de facto control as the infantry guarded critical systems and watched over the crew's shoulders. Their orders were to shoot anyone committing a mutinous act, a command that had already been carried out once when a junior-level engineer tried to sabotage the WarShip's fusion drive. Although critically short-staffed, Kerr had left open his offer for anyone to join the Davion-lovers traveling back to Kathil. That was all the leniency he had been prepared to offer.

And now that the time was upon them, that window was closed.

"Light her off, Mr. Tremmar," he said. It would be one of his last orders given on a dead ship.

The *R. Davion*'s new engineering officer passed the commands along to the rearward stations, which fired up the main fusion drives and efficiently switched from ground-supplied microwave power to the WarShip's electrical network. Then the raw power of those fusion reactors was harnessed and fed back through the exhaust ports, creating thrust that began to inch the massive vessel out from its cage of catwalks and support stations.

Leftenant Myers, filling in for the usual enlisted-grade radioman, smiled as he reported, "No challenge from the auxiliary vessels. No one has even passed the word that our drives are lit."

Kerr eased out of his chair as the power of the main drives made themselves felt. Artificial gravity of about one-fifth standard pulled everyone toward the bridge's floor. It gradually built up to point-three G, where it would stay until they had cleared the shipyards. "They'll figure it out soon enough," he said. "Weapons, stand by."

For twenty hours now, the battle-ready DropShips and shipyard facilities that usually safeguarded the *R. Davion* had squabbled about the legitimacy of Kerr's actions. Never mind that Duke VanLees and General Weintraub backed him up—the admiral was the one on trial over the comm system. Not a few captains were branding him a mutineer or a Lyran pirate, though just as many had hailed the move as a strong measure to support the Archon-Princess.

The trouble was that no one on either side was sure what to do. Two smaller vessels had resorted to laserfire and an exchange of missiles. At point-blank range—as space battles went, anyway—each ship seriously damaged the other before a few of their larger companions intervened and enforced a fragile peace.

But it was a "peace" in which scathing arguments were still passed back and forth in an attempt to out-honor each other, calling on loyalties to Prince Victor and Archon Katrina and some going back even to their parents—Melissa and old Hanse. Kerr had held his temper and his silence—though barely—tallying up who was against him and who was for, and who would blow with the prevailing winds.

Of course, the *Robert Davion* could generate one hell of a breeze on its own.

Myers laughed suddenly and threw a switch that spliced his general comm feed into the captain's public address system.

"—the hell! She's underway!"

"I never thought—"

"That burn must reach back three hundred meters if it's—"

"—coming about, can anyone—"

"Beautiful."

Beautiful. Kerr could well imagine. He had done nothing but eat, sleep, and breathe the *Robert Davion* for months. He'd run the simulations, watching as the eight-hundred-meter WarShip ran maneuvers through asteroid belts, over moons, and in programmed battles. Seeing better than seven hundred thousand tons move with such majestic grace would leave its mark on any spacer.

"By the Unfinished Book, not on my watch!"

The transmission snapped Kerr from his brief reverie. There was no mistaking the hostile intent that laced that voice, not even through the static of distant transmission. Not that such a response was entirely a surprise to him— no matter how suicidal it was for a pilot of any of these ships to go up against a WarShip, he had known that someone would inevitably try.

"Leftenant, track that transmission if you can," he snapped. "Tactical, watch for any radical maneuvers." He stared at the darkened holotank. "Why don't I have the tank lit up yet?"

Chief Deborah Watson, who was pulling double duty on sensors and tactical feed, stammered under the admiral's glare. "Sir, we can't charge up the tank until we're clear of the docking structure. The space-dock cage moving so close by is confusing the sensors."

Kerr glared daggers at Watson and barked out, "Get me aft-camera and sensor feeds on the viewers!" He launched himself from his chair, flying four meters in the low gravity before catching himself on a rail. He half-walked, half-pulled himself to the main screen. "Any captain worth his command would never attack from the nose or side," he muttered, mostly to himself. The nose lacked any critical systems, and the main sensor package was backed up by redundant features around the *R. Davion*'s midline. And coming on broadside to a WarShip was tantamount to suicide. "He'll go for the engines."

"There!" he said, stabbing a finger at a drive flame that slid across the screen. It was lost for a moment behind a shipyard catwalk, and when it reappeared, it was spitting lightning into the dark reaches of space. At least one of Kerr's supporters was challenging the threatening DropShip.

"We have it." Watson gave a high thumbs-up. "*Excalibur* Class—it has to be the *Guardian*. Retrofitted with a single naval-grade PPC. I know the commander—she's a strong supporter of Prince Victor."

"She's a fly to be swatted," Kerr said, rounding on the petty officer manning his weapons console. The mid-grade enlisted man had been the best available; Kerr would have preferred an officer, but all those with solid experience had taken the shuttle back to Kathil. "Olsen! Charge our aft fifty-fives. Put both lasers into her bow."

The hawk-faced petty officer looked up in alarm. Maybe it had all seemed like a big game, being the biggest bully on the block. But now things were becoming deadly, and moving fast. Maybe too fast. "Admiral? You mean across her bow?"

Kerr had already decided how best to handle the first real challenge to his authority, and it didn't include warning shots—or having his every order questioned. "I said what I meant, weapons!" he shouted. "Don't waste any more time and don't pass the order back. You're slaved into the weapons net, and this is an easy shot. Put both these naval-grade lasers into that *Excalibur*, and do it now!"

There would be no further delays on his bridge.

On the screen, Kerr watched as a pair of brilliant emerald lances stabbed out at the *Guardian*, which was just swinging full into the *R. Davion*'s aft. The DropShip, massive by most standards, was a gray splotch against the hard, dark backdrop of space. It might reach an eighth of the WarShip's size, with less than one-fiftieth the mass.

"Magnify," Kerr ordered. Then to Petty Officer Olsen. "Again—hit it again."

The picture changed in time for the admiral to see the shafts of destructive energy stabbing deep into the guts of the spheroid DropShip. The *Guardian* bled molten armor and atmosphere into space and began to tumble. It might be armed to ward off fighters or threaten another DropShip, but it could never stand up to a WarShip's guns.

The comm chatter had faded to a soft background static as the enormity of Kerr's action sank into each captain. If they had wondered about his willingness to pit the WarShip against any of them, that question had been answered.

"By the Prince," a feminine voice whispered over the comm. She could obviously think of nothing else to say. "By the Prince."

Kerr smiled. As good an oath as any to leave in the

middle of his doubters. Now to burn it in permanently. "Hit it again!"

Olsen looked over, his expression near fright. "Admiral, she's spinning off on her—"

"Again!" His left hand slashed the air in the recalcitrant petty officer's direction.

This time the lasers silenced the *Guardian*'s drive flare, leaving it with no way to stop itself. It would tumble on until it hit Kathil's atmosphere or was torn apart by one of the microwave power transmissions.

Tremmar held up a hand, counting down on his fingers. "Two . . . one . . . and we're clear of spacedock."

Kerr stabbed a finger at another senior petty officer, who was filling in for a vacant officer position. "Helm, bring us around toward Kathil. Mind the no-fly zones and park us in a transpolar orbit." They would wait there, a spider hovering over its web, for the Dragoons' arrival. As much as he would prefer hunting through the dark of space for the inbound DropShips, the odds were too great that they might slip by him. But they would all have to come to Kathil sooner or later.

He paused, knowing he had forgotten something. Oh, yes. "Olsen, you are relieved. Get off my bridge." The petty officer was fortunate—the next person to challenge his orders might find himself ejected out an airlock.

"There's an *Octopus* heading out after the *Guardian* on a high burn," Watson informed the admiral, naming a utility tug with its variety of manipulator arms. It would get the *Excalibur* under control.

"Ignore them," Kerr said dismissively. He'd proved that such ships could never stand against the *Robert Davion*. If the others became a problem despite the *Guardian*'s example, he would deal with them just as easily. But he would prefer to save his attention for worthier prey.

The First Capellan Dragoons would not arrive in anything much more threatening, but Kerr expected their deaths to be vastly more satisfying.

Judgment Under Fire

War is the continuation of politics by other means. It can [therefore] be said that politics is war without bloodshed while war is politics with bloodshed.

—Chairman Mao Tse-Tung, 1938
On Protracted War

23

Coming home to his family's farm in his *Devastator* wasn't exactly the way David had planned to return. Swaying with the assault machine's lumbering stride, riding nine-plus meters over the ground, he crested a small ridge ahead of the Manticores escorting his trio of 'Mechs. He already knew what to expect. Fly-overs by *Corsair* aerospace fighters and the two Kestrel VTOLs hovering nearby had warned him. But seeing it for himself made a deep chasm open up inside him.

The Eighth RCT's assault had left little standing. Some fields smoldered where laserfire had been turned against the crops, intentionally scorching them down to bare earth. Others were simply torn up by the passing of Battle-Mechs and armored vehicles, and recon infantry released by the VTOLs were working to clear vibrabomb mines they had found buried in some areas.

A chill sweat dampened David's brow as he surveyed what was left of his parents' house—what had been a grand, two-story home for a large, happy family. A few studs and one water-supply pipe was all that was left standing. The pipe sprayed a jet of water straight up, the stream fanning out to rain down over the ruins.

The house had been leveled—systematically torn down, crushed, and the pieces kicked around so that very little was recognizable. Personal vehicles had also been mashed flat, though David could still recognize the yellow Grand Spirit Wagoneer belonging to his sister Pauline. His heart sank further. How many of his family members had been here? Would there be anyone left to rescue?

The latter question had plagued him ever since General Sampreis had brought him word of the raid, pulling David out of a planning session with his officers on ways to counter RCT advances inland. The general, probably thinking he was being kind, had broken it to him slow and easy—but that was the worst way to deliver such news.

"Vorhaven?" David had asked, stunned. No major RCT movement had been predicted that far inland. "You mean the Katzbalger has fought their way through Vorhaven?"

The general shook his head. "No fighting. And not exactly through Vorhaven. Just your parents' farm, David. I'm afraid this looks like a strike aimed at you. Just you."

Just David. And his father and mother. His sister. Her kids. No, this wasn't just about David. He might have been the cause of it, someone trying to target him through his family, but it would forever change dozens of lives.

"David, I'm so sorry," Tara Michaels said over the comm system. Her *Enforcer* had stumbled to a halt and now picked up the pace to regain her commander's flank. Though newly promoted to captain and responsible for half of David's command, she'd exercised her right to accompany her commander. She'd left the bulk of her people with Captain Gerst, bringing along only Richard Smith. Two good choices, usually, for morale and moral support. Now, though, she was silent, as if unable to find anything more to say.

Corporal Smith, as usual, was not at a loss for words. "Damn, Major. Someone had a big hate on for you. Who would do this?" There could be no doubt that it was a personal attack—the McCarthy farmland was the only area destroyed around Vorhaven.

"I don't know," David said mechanically. He saw the old ironwood oak standing nearby, a tire still hanging from a massive lower branch by a length of rope. He felt better that the attacking force had left at least that much standing, and just as quickly realized that he must be in a major shock for such a minor consideration to have so great an impact. "I don't know," he said again, "but I'll find out."

"Do you . . ." Tara paused, obviously considering, and decided to push ahead. "Do you think anyone escaped this?"

"If they made the shelter in time." But no infantry had reported survivors. In fact, no infantry seemed to be working near the house at all. He frowned and shifted comm frequencies. "Major McCarthy to ground command. Leftenant Reed, why is there no one working over the ruins of the house?"

"Major, we checked it with listening gear. I'm sorry, sir. No one's alive in that ruin, or we would have dug them out. We would have heard even the faintest heartbeat." The man's voice was flat; he was no doubt as affected as the rest of them by such wanton destruction aimed at civilians.

But a thrill of hope ran through David. "Could you hear it through two meters of ferrocrete? Did you check the shelter?"

All homes inland of Muran's southeastern coastlands had some kind of storm cellar or shelter. In the high summer days, when the farm belt was hammered by dry windstorms and occasionally force-four tornadoes, such precautions were necessary. But the infantry officer and his men were not from the inland area, and David had neglected to mention it in his preoccupation.

With the *Devastator* and the *Enforcer* lacking hand actuators, Smith's *Cestus* was the best candidate for clearing away the wreckage. He could grab large handfuls of broken lumber and scoop up piles of plasterboard and the shake siding. Smith burrowed down through the tangle that filled the cellar, throwing it aside while David, abandoning his *Devastator*, paced anxiously at the front of a gathered crowd of infantry, neighbors, rescue volunteers, and other family members who had finally arrived from Vorhaven.

The *Cestus* straightened up and moved back. David ran

forward, followed by his relatives and Leftenant Reed, while the majority of the infantry held back the others. Peering down into the cleared portion of the cellar, David saw that the iron door leading into the shelter had been smashed inward. It wouldn't open easily.

He leapt down, taking the three-meter drop on all fours and then shoving his way through the debris to the wall of smashed ferrocrete and rebar. A large crack looked like it might run deep enough to reach into the shelter. "Dad, Mom, Pauline!" he shouted. "Anyone in there?"

A faint voice answered back. "We're here, and everyone's fine." His father's voice. David must have sounded panic-stricken. Or maybe his father was trying to calm the others trapped in the shelter with him. Either way, Jason McCarthy sounded no more concerned than if he was asking David for a hand up. "Could you get that door yanked out? We're kind of tired of the dark in here."

It took a little while to find a length of chain long enough and strong enough that it wouldn't snap as Smith's *Cestus* took it in hand and pulled the door and several large chunks of ferrocrete free. The reunion didn't wait to reach the surface, the McCarthy family swapping hugs and tears in the midst of their former cellar. Jason McCarthy took it all in stride, his face remaining calm until he finally climbed up the pile of debris to see what was left of the family home.

"Jumped-up, good-for-naught, chicken-scratch sons of Liao," he yelled at the sky, his bellow loud enough to be heard over the cheers from the crowd and the carrying-on of the rest of the family. He looked back down and smiled with an effort as his storm-blue gaze swept over David and the rest of his family. "Hell with 'em," he said mildly. "I always wanted a bigger home anyway."

David had to practically force his father into going with the others to the Vorhaven hospital. The elder McCarthy wanted to stay and recover anything he could of the family possessions. The house was destroyed, but some of the things that had helped make it a home—pictures, quilts, mementos; the small items David's mother would care for—might be salvageable. David finally persuaded him to leave by promising that he and his brothers would handle the search.

He also pointed out that the more infantry it took to escort his father to the hospital, the fewer would be left behind to help sort through the debris.

Twilight was darkening Kathil's sky to a pale gray by the time David uncovered one of the large albums his parents had put together, filled with photos and holograms and other memorabilia. A 'Mech had stepped on it, the tread shredding the album cover and creasing it down the middle, but most of the material inside could be saved.

"I hear everyone's all right," a voice said from behind, startling him.

It was a familiar voice, but David couldn't place it at once. He turned, and at first he thought the man standing behind him in the dim light was a member of the militia infantry he had yet to become acquainted with. Then he noticed the slight variations that placed it as a Commonwealth uniform, not the old Federated Suns. It was close, though—close enough that a confident man might walk right past the militia infantry, most of who were currently occupied sorting through debris. He recognized the rawboned face and dark mustache now, the salt-and-pepper hair smoothed back from a high forehead. He had last seen the man at the reception for his award—the kommandant escorting General Fallon.

Greene . . . Evan Greene.

Launching himself at the other man, dropping the album so he could knot his fist in Greene's uniform, David slammed him back into the broken wall of the cellar.

"Everyone's alive. Far from all right," he snarled, pulling Greene forward and slamming him back again. "Witnesses tell us a *Falconer* did this. A *Falconer* leading a lance remarkably similar to the one we encountered in Daytin and in Stihl. Go on. Tell me this wasn't you!"

Greene winced as David ground him back into the rough wall, but he did not resist. "It wasn't me, McCarthy," he said, his voice low and even. "It was my man, yes, and I did give him orders to draw you out." He glanced around at the destruction, a haunted look clouding his eyes. "But I never authorized this kind of violence against civilians. I told him to send you a message—that's all."

"And if you had known what he had planned?"

To his credit, the kommandant gave the question serious consideration. "I don't know," he said slowly. "I've agreed to things I never thought I would have in the past few weeks. But I'd like to think I would have found a less bloodthirsty means of creating my opportunity."

Somehow, reluctantly, David believed him. Maybe it was Greene's matter-of-factness. No apology. No real remorse, even. Just a blunt appraisal of what he'd intended and what had happened.

"An officer is responsible for the conduct of all subordinate officers appointed below him," David quoted from military regs, "and the actions of enlisted personnel given over to his command." He glanced up at the waiting infantry who, attracted by the commotion, had lined up along the rim of the cellar, two of them holding rifles at the ready should Greene try anything rash. David shoved him against the wall again, rapping his head against the ferrocrete. "Tell me why I shouldn't turn you over to them right now."

Greene shook his head to clear it. "Because you want what I have to offer. Information on Yare."

David remembered that the RCT had pushed into Yare, taking it from the Second NAIS, a little more than a week ago. "That's nothing I can't get by having Leftenant Reed up there beat it out of you," he lied. After today such tactics might sound tempting, but he doubted he could actually see them through. Greene was too confident, though, and David wanted to shake him up. "What makes you think I'll just let you walk?"

"Xander Barajas," Greene said. "The man in the *Falconer*. He's my insurance." He smiled wickedly. "You take me out of action, I guarantee he'll be promoted in my absence. The man is a wolf in MechWarrior's gear, McCarthy. Want to see what Barajas can do with a company? Or even a battalion? He'd probably start with leveling Vorhaven, and move on from there."

Damn the man! This decision reminded David too much of his recent conversation with Amanda Black—having to weigh both sides of a losing proposition. After a long pause, he released the other officer and stepped back. He found Leftenant Reed waiting at the edge to the basement and waved away the infantry support. Reed reluctantly began to pull his men back.

"I don't strike deals with the enemy, Greene," David said icily. "If you have intel for me, say what you came to say and get out of here before I turn you over for military arrest."

Eván Greene straightened up to his full height and brushed off his uniform. "If you had any idea what I risked by coming here, maybe you'd be a bit more receptive," he complained. "General Fallon would not understand."

"Fair enough," David said. "I don't understand your coming here, either."

"Are you blind?" Greene asked in amazement. "Fallon and I are the ones holding Yare."

"I didn't know where you're stationed."

"I'm sure your general knows. He's just watching Mitchell Weintraub too closely to care. That's a mistake. In fact, Sampreis should be very concerned about what Karen Fallon and I have been up to."

David could see that his counterpart was walking a fine line in implying what his superior was up to without directly betraying her. "Why?" he asked, tired of the games and hoping a direct question would yield better results.

"You know the First Capellan Dragoons are in-system?"

"I know. Six days until planetfall," he lied.

Another of those crafty smiles. "Five, actually, but nice try."

"All right, five then," David conceded. "And we know you've taken control of the *Robert Davion*. And, yes, we're worried about orbital bombardment. Some people are fleeing Radcliffe in case Kerr has simply decided on the Turtle Bay approach." Turtle Bay was the city that Clan Smoke Jaguar had eradicated from space during the Clan invasion.

"It's been considered," Greene admitted. "The tactical-level strikes only. The trouble is, the *R. Davion* isn't fully crewed. Still, I wouldn't try forming up for any large maneuvers. Admiral Kerr just might decide to test his luck."

"So Kerr is waiting to destroy the Dragoons as they run in-system," David said slowly, beginning to fit the pieces together. He wasn't really surprised. "What does that have to do with Yare?"

"Ah, there's Karen Fallon's back-up plans to consider. Just in case the Dragoons somehow slip by the *R. Davion*. Another lesson drawn from history."

David was exhausted, physically and emotionally, and in no mood for more games. He grabbed Greene's sleeve. "So what are they?" he demanded. Then, as Greene remained stubbornly silent, he began to put it together for himself. Yare. Dragoons. History. If you took the *Robert Davion* out of the equation . . . No!

"What are they, Eván?" he asked in a stifled voice.

"Maybe you should talk to your general. You were a Uhlan. You'll figure it out." Greene shook himself free of David's grip, walked over to a tumbled section of the wall and climbed out of the cellar.

David followed only as far as the bottom edge of the pile. "Greene, why did you come out here? Why warn me?"

Standing on the ground, staring down at his rival, Eván Greene crossed his arms imperiously. "I can't stop Kerr and I can't stop Fallon. Why would I want to, really? We're winning this war.

"But you're a fair target, and a high-profile one at that. All I've ever wanted was the chance to stand out in battle. You're going to give that to me. Nothing personal, you understand. But if I can't take the time to hunt you down in the field, then I have to make sure you'll find me.

"And if the lives of the First Capellan Dragoons hang in the balance—well, so much the better," he said. "For me, anyway."

24

CMM Staging Grounds
Radcliffe, Kathil
Capellan March, Federated Commonwealth
4 December 3062

David walked into the planning session late, easing the door closed behind him and nodding his apologies as he moved toward the side of the table on which Tara Michaels sat. His arrival prompted a few whispers among the junior officers sitting along the walls of the room on folding chairs. Most of the senior officers either nodded back or offered him tight smiles of sympathy. Colonel Yori showed no reaction. Karl Tarsk tapped his brow in a quick salute.

General Sampreis had paused in his briefing and looked temporarily at a loss for words. An unfamiliar leftenant general stood next to him, with Sampreis' left hand on her right shoulder. He pulled his hand back and rubbed his palms together briskly. "Major. It's good to see you." He paused, seemingly unsure how to best handle a private matter in such a public setting. "We weren't expecting you back for another day."

"Is everything all right?" Yori asked, her eyes searching.

"My family is fine," he said. "A little shaken still, but they're strong people." His lips quirked up in a hesitant grin. "My father threw me out this morning. Told me to get my . . . well, to get back to work. With your permission, General.''

David wasn't going to be left out of the planning just because Sampreis wanted to milk more out of David's status as a hero of Kathil—that was the main reason Sampreis had granted him three days of leave to stay with his parents. The sooner he left Vorhaven, the sooner the news hounds would leave his family alone.

Yori surreptitiously caught the general's eye, giving him an unobtrusive nod. Sampreis smiled a politician's smile. ''Welcome back, Mr. McCarthy. Please join us.'' He nodded toward David's usual seat, and Tara started to rise. David waved her back down.

''Tara has been sitting in for me for two days now,'' he said. ''I'm sure she's doing a fine job. I don't want to disrupt anything, so I'll backseat her and try to catch up.''

He grabbed an empty folding chair and set it up against the wall behind his new captain. Tara turned to give him a very subtle shake of her head, her soft brown eyes radiating a peculiar blend of caution and excitement. David could see there had been new developments while he'd been gone, and not all of them positive. That figured. It was the chief reason he had returned a day early, despite assurances that there would be no major activity for at least another forty-eight hours. Something was up, and he wanted to be around when it happened.

''All right, then,'' Sampreis said, retaking control of the meeting. He looked over at the new officer. ''I was just introducing Leftenant-General Helen Sanderson, of the Second NAIS Training Cadre. They've been bumping heads with the Katzbalger, but have been trying to maintain a low profile since the clash at Yare. The last time a training cadre involved itself in this kind of political struggle was on the planet of Northwind, and you all know how that turned out.''

David remembered. Five years before, the mercenary Northwind Highlanders had split over loyalty to either Katherine or Victor, and local nobles had tried to enforce the Prince's will with military force. The Second NAIS had been used to reinforce renegade members of the Highlanders. Eventually the Highlanders ended up severing their political ties to the Steiner-Davions, though they remained under contract to the family. FedCom units, the NAIS cadre included, received an "unofficial" reprimand—meaning that it wouldn't go on record, but everyone knew the Prince's displeasure.

"Their decision to stay neutral ended when I communicated our belief, based on intelligence gathered by Major McCarthy, that the Eighth RCT will try to use Kearny-Fuchida Yare Industries' energy broadcast station against the inbound First Capellan Dragoons," Sampreis continued.

General Sanderson nodded. "I'm sorry that we were the ones who gave up that facility to Weintraub's forces. Or, more accurately, to General Karen Fallon's command. We've kept Yare under surveillance, though, and we know that she is still using the local township as a base of operations. She grounded her personal DropShip, the *Masse Noir*, right between the town and the control facilities. It won't be easy evicting them," she said, retaking her seat.

"Why Yare?" Tarsk asked. "Why would General Fallon risk antagonizing the Second NAIS by seizing the power station at Yare when there are at least three broadcast stations already in their zone of influence?"

The general allowed Marsha Yori to field that question. "Fallon's personal ambitions aside, there is one tactical consideration," she said. "The Yare Industries broadcast station is one of the best suited for tracking and destroying an incoming target. Not every facility can track their microwave beam from horizon to horizon. Yare, though, was built to take on additional capacity as necessary, and has an impressive one hundred-sixty-degree arc across the top and the full three-sixty around. That can punch quite a hole in the atmosphere."

The militia's infantry general, General Lars-Erik Gennady, leaned forward. "You mentioned personal ambitions?"

Yori nodded. "Major McCarthy?"

David rubbed at the side of his neck, taking a moment to organize his thoughts. Sampreis and Yori knew that the information had come from Eván Greene—a highly suspect source. But the logic of David's arguments had swayed them toward believing the kommandant. He would try to reason it out for Gennady as well.

"It's a part of Uhlan history," he explained. "In the Fourth Succession War, in 3029, House Liao targeted the geothermal station network to bring a halt to JumpShip production. Yare is the location of Morgan Hasek-Davion's valiant stand against the Liao Death Commandos and the Fourth Tau Ceti Rangers. He was the one who came up with the plan to use the broadcast station against an incoming DropShip. And he did it, destroying a *Union*-class vessel and its entire company of Death Commando warriors."

He exhaled sharply, hoping he could make this next part clear. "By returning to Yare, Karen Fallon accomplishes two things. First, she borrows against that legend, and she can use it to vindicate her own ruthless action against the Dragoons. And if we move against her, that same stigma works against us."

Gennady frowned. "How do you mean?"

"We're going to be attacking Yare against a Federated Commonwealth occupation force," David explained. "Don't you see the role we'll be cast in?" He smiled sadly. "If we're successful in stopping Fallon, we do so only by completing what the Death Commandos failed at thirty years ago." Of course, if the militia was successful, Fallon wouldn't get the opportunity to cast them as anything. The militia would have to attack and lose for her strategy to work, at which point the public-relations problem would most likely be moot. David was willing to take that chance.

Still, no one around the room liked the notion. People shifted uneasily and tugged at their collars. "And the second thing?" Yori asked.

"The second point is that there is obviously a measure of fame attached to the history," David said. "I believe she's after the ego boost as well. When you want to make a big splash, you need a very big rock."

"That's a pretty tough argument to beat," Major Tarsk agreed. "The situations are just similar enough. Except that Morgan Hasek-Davion was operating in a time of declared war, on orders from Hanse Davion to protect

Kathil at all costs. The war effort truly did hang in the balance. In my mind, that has to make the difference."

Most everyone nodded at least casual agreement to that. Except David. "I see a greater difference, Karl," he said.

"And that is?"

David searched for the right words before answering. "Morgan Hasek-Davion actually regretted that he ever had to commit such an act. He was never proud of it. I don't see that kind of reluctance in General Fallon."

Why such an observation would elicit sharp frowns of displeasure from General Sampreis and Colonel Yori, David wasn't certain. Sampreis looked almost insulted. Yori simply uneasy. They weren't happy with his comment. Not at all.

"We don't intend to let matters progress that far," the general assured everyone. "We can't do a lot about the WarShip in our present capacity, so we will concentrate on the ground threat until it is eliminated. The plan is to take the facility back from Karen Fallon and her forces and, only if necessary, destroy Yare Industries' broadcast station. We proceed as outlined. That's all for now." General Sampreis nodded a general dismissal. "David?" he called out. "I'd like you to remain, please."

General Sampreis held back Colonel Yori and General Gennady, waiting while the others slowly exited the room. Tara started to get up as well, but David rested his hands on her shoulders, urging her to stay seated. She had been too critical in the past few days to divorce her from the planning process now. If this meeting was about something else, then Sampreis could dismiss her personally.

He didn't, and David took a seat next to her. If Tara had felt at all nervous sitting in for David among the top brass, it had either worn off or she was very good at hiding it. In fact, when Sampreis and Yori seemed reluctant to begin, Tara opened the discussion herself.

"The timetable's been pushed back," she told her commander. "We hit Yare in three days, not two."

"Three days?" David looked to the general. "Sir, that's the day the First Dragoons are set to arrive."

Sampreis stood behind his chair, hands clenched on the backrest as he stared down at his subordinate officers.

"Can't be helped, Major. With the addition of Leftenant General Sanderson and her people, we need time to coordinate. Also, with the boost in manpower, we're organizing a second strike force."

Tara's glance in his direction told David that this was the new development that had her worried. "Splitting our forces?" he asked. "Isn't Yare a bit too important for that?" That was one of the first decisions they had made after David's encounter with Greene—to suspend all other activities until Yare was neutralized. The Dragoons would detect the WarShip threat and take measures to evade it, but there was no way for them to warn the inbound regiment about the broadcast station. Not with the *Robert Davion*'s ability to scramble comm channels from the planet into space. They hadn't been able to get a message through since November 28, when Kerr had seized control of the WarShip.

"It's more important than you know at the moment, Major," Sampreis said, his tone hard. "But along with ensuring the safe arrival of the First Capellan Dragoons, I want to clear up any confusion surrounding their chain of command."

It didn't take David long to unravel that idea, and he knew he didn't cover his surprise well. "Duke VanLees? You plan to hit District City?"

"Not to occupy," Yori put in. "It's a rescue mission, David. We pull out Petyr VanLees and his family, and we regain the moral high ground."

"If anyone actually believes the duke's recent condemnations of us, they'll think he's changed his mind only because now we control his family," David protested. "It's a no-win situation, Colonel, General."

Sampreis looked unconvinced. "Major, we've been over this, and we believe it's a sound plan," he said, emphasizing David's rank. "And that's before we even take into account what the Dragoons will make of VanLees' position. They were sold back into his family's service, after all. If he's still seen as publicly supporting the Eighth . . ."

David could feel he was battling an uphill argument. "Marshal Hasek had already relieved the Duke of his authority over the Dragoons. They're his unit again."

"And we're all supposed to be under the command of

the Archon-Princess," the general reminded him quietly. "Look where we are now, Major. I don't want to risk losing the Dragoons to a political play after paying such a heavy price to get them here."

The finality in Sampreis' tone brooked no further argument. "Yes, sir," he said. "May I ask how this affects my battalion?"

Tara provided the details. "The 'Mech battalion is being brought up to full strength, thanks to some transfers from the Second NAIS Cadre. Less air cover, though, since we're throwing a screen of fighters up to shepherd the Dragoons' arrival and try to get a warning through to them. And aerospace fighters only, no VTOLs—those go with the general to D.C. Better armor support, also courtesy of the Second."

"Infantry?" David asked, glancing at General Gennady.

"We do get some powered-armor infantry from the cadet force," Tara admitted. "The rest, except for General Gennady's auxiliary command, has been pulled."

Not good. All in all, it weakened the assault on Yare, making the need to destroy the broadcast station rather than capture it intact more likely. Duke VanLees had better be worth the price David's command was about to pay.

"My forces will hit District City an hour after you engage General Fallon at Yare," Sampreis told him. "We're hoping that your action will also function as a diversionary attack, pulling additional defenders away from the city long enough for us to effect the rescue." The general took a stab at a smile of camaraderie. "You'll have our backs on this one, David. Given your record, I can't think of a better man to have in that position."

If Sampreis had wanted to bolster David's spirits, reminding him of Huntress—even obliquely—was not the way to accomplish the task. The familiar weight of memory settled over him like a funeral shroud. "What about General Gennady's auxiliary force?" he asked, his concern about the mission coloring his voice. "Is it under my authority?"

"No," Gennady said. "Mine. I'll personally lead the raid on Yare Industries. While you engage the garrison, we go in to secure the broadcast station and control facility."

"General Gennady, no offense, sir, but Yare is going to

be a very large target on our heads-up displays," David warned. "If we can't put down the defenders in time—and it's sounding more likely every minute that we won't—the last place you'll want your men is inside that control facility."

Tara's warning look came too late as General Sampreis pinned David with his most commanding gaze. "The destruction of Yare is our final option, Major, not our first. In the meantime, you will do everything in your power to give General Gennady and his men every possible minute inside the facility, so they can accomplish their mission."

A different mission from his? What was more important than preventing Yare Industries from being used to destroy the inbound Dragoons? But then a weight like cold steel settled into his stomach. What did Karen Fallon already have planned for Yare? "You can't be serious."

"Major McCarthy, I don't expect you to agree," Colonel Yori answered. "But you will carry out your orders. This was not a decision we arrived at lightly, or one we are proud of undertaking. But the fact remains that the WarShip threatens to unbalance our entire position on Kathil.

"If we can, we intend to capture Yare and use it to knock the *Robert Davion* right out of the sky."

CMM Staging Grounds
Radcliffe, Kathil
Capellan March, Federated Commonwealth
7 December 3062

The 'Mech bay that served David's personal company felt charged with energy and anticipation as the late morning hours rolled on toward a noon launch schedule. Techs swarmed over the BattleMechs, making late-minute checks and packing ammunition bins to the last missile or auto-cannon round. One team worked to weld new armor over a small flaw they'd discovered on a *Stealth*. In small knots scattered over the floor, MechWarriors stood discussing the day's coming battle, dressed only in cooling vests and shorts, ready for the sweatboxes their cockpits would become. Several of them jumped in to help the technicians perform the final preps on their 'Mechs. The bay smelled of hot metal, the light oil used to grease myomer muscles, and the gunpowder scent of munitions.

David paced a long path that took him past each lance, intent on reviewing the entire company. Tara Michaels walked alongside him, in her capacity as acting company commander. He'd already done the same inspection for the rest of his battalion, including the new additions from the Second NAIS Cadre, watching them board two of the three *Union* DropShips that would take them to Yare. His company would take the third; the armor and infantry had their own *Seeker*-class ship. Some aerospace fighters had already left to support the militia-friendly DropShips around the *Robert Davion*, and the rest would launch from the base here.

David listened to Tara's status report with only half his attention, automatically checking off her salient points as he began to focus on the many conflicts that would be decided today. Whether they could take KF Yare Industries away from Karen Fallon and Eván Greene. The safety of the First Capellan Dragoons, which any hour now would face down the newest Federated Commonwealth WarShip. Or, if they managed to slip by, they would have to run the gauntlet against KF Yare's microwave broadcast beam. And then there was General Sampreis' raid against District City, hoping to spirit Duke VanLees and his family to safety, and the alternate plan to direct Yare's broadcast beam at the *Robert Davion* itself.

A critical day—very likely a pivotal one in the battle for Kathil. And much of that weight had settled on the shoulders of David and his warriors, some of whom would not be coming back today. How many this time? Images from Huntress rose unbidden to mind. A *Scarabus*, its cockpit cored out by golden flame, Isaak's *Enfield*, struck down in an instant. A *Berserker*: Elise Kennedy, the warrior he had turned away from in those final moments, being torn apart by two Clan OmniMechs.

David imagined being forced to choose again—to name three people he could lose from his company. It was an impossible task, though it underscored his responsibility of bringing back every one of them.

If there had to be someone who didn't come back, it might as well be him.

Corporal Smith sauntered over, his slouch more pronounced than ever and a lazy smile pasted over his face, as seemingly unconcerned about this mission as any routine patrol. He waved at a couple of the newer MechWarriors, and David saw some of their tension bleed away as they returned the salute. The man was unorthodox, irrepressible and undisciplined. But he did get results.

"Excuse me, sir," Tara said, excusing herself. "Richard was checking on our DropShip."

David nodded. "Go ahead, Tara. If there's a problem, let me know. Otherwise, start loading them up."

He watched her walk over to the corporal, noting absentmindedly the familiar ease with which Smith fell in at her side, at once comfortable and attentive. But if that thought was leading somewhere, it got sidetracked as Amanda Black approached—geared up for a 'Mech cockpit in combat boots, shorts, and her cooling vest. When he'd left her this morning, she'd said nothing about changing her mind and accompanying them, and he hadn't asked.

"Amanda," he said neutrally, avoiding the use of her rank until she made an issue of it.

Which she did immediately. "Major, I'm formally requesting reactivation." She glanced down at her battle dress. "As if that wasn't apparent. Sir."

David tried to sort out his feelings from his command instincts. Today was going to be brutal—easily as hard as the battle they'd fought in Stihl. He couldn't afford a warrior who might fall apart on him. It was all he could do to guarantee his own performance.

"You think you're up for it?" he asked finally.

"I really don't know," she admitted. "I've been wrestling with it ever since you came back early from Vorhaven. After you left this morning, I felt cold. I didn't want to be left behind."

"Not good enough," he said, shaking his head. "And I've already moved people up to fill your old position, Amanda. They've worked hard, and right now they're confident. I can't go demoting people right before a major battle."

"I'm not asking you to. But you do have a hole in your command I could fill." Amanda glanced over at her *Bushwacker*, racked in at the back of the bay, where it would remain while the rest of the battalion went out on the operation. "Just let me be a MechWarrior, David. If I don't go, I'll never be sure whether I gave up on myself too soon."

Better too soon than too late, David thought, his bitterness welling up. Better than dragging down others with you. But then he stopped as he absorbed the meaning of Amanda's words. Had he given up on himself too soon?

Huntress had plagued him for well over a year, the deaths of his people grinding down on him every day. But everyone had known going into that rearguard action that the losses would be high. None of them had expected to make it back. And if David truly believed it was better not to hang on to the end, what was he trying to prove by staying in uniform? That he was still a MechWarrior? That he could still command? But that had never been in doubt, except within himself. After several weeks of fighting in a hard-pitched campaign, it was time to put those doubts to rest.

If he was going to have that chance, he had no right to deny Amanda.

"Captain Michaels," he called to Tara, "move Cadet Driscoll back into Sergeant Major Moriad's lance. Sergeant Major Black will be rounding out our team."

Tara tossed him an enthusiastic salute. "Gladly, sir! Full company!" She moved off to comply, pulling Smith along in her wake.

David realized then that Tara and Smith had been holding hands. He felt a light twinge of jealousy, but his budding relationship with Amanda had doused the last remnants of his interest in Tara. Things worked out, it seemed.

And that was as good a thought as any to take into battle with him.

Admiral Jonathan Kerr watched the bedlam playing out on the bridge's large viewscreens with something akin to amused exasperation. The several hundred square klicks of space surrounding the *Robert Davion* were alive with a dozen sparring DropShips and several flights of aerospace fighters, locked into a deadly dance backed occasionally by a flurry of weapons fire.

And through it all the WarShip powered by in majestic might, untouched and unchallenged. After the object lesson Kerr had made of the *Guardian*, no other captain dared risk even an accidental clash with the admiral.

The space battle had been touched off around noon— Kathil local time, as reckoned off District City—by the arrival of fightercraft from the planet below. Militia-sponsored *Corsairs* and *Lucifers*, mostly, pouncing first on an assault-class DropShip with avowed loyalty to General Weintraub. Hoping to restore order quickly, Kerr had ordered two of the fighters destroyed, burned to cinders by heavy laser salvos.

Instead, that had sparked a massive free-for-all as some DropShips launched fighters and moved in to protect the militia craft while others retaliated against them. Soon everyone was involved, except for Kerr and the *Robert Davion*. His WarShip was the only vessel that could track the entire battle, following every last missile launch and fighter run. But very seldom could he identify a solid target. Some captains were solidly behind the Archon, while others were for Duke VanLees. Many more were acting purely in self-defense, or were simply trying to restore order among the flotilla of ships nominally charged with the protection of the *R. Davion*.

The space battle had been going on for two hours now, and Kerr had received word of a major engagement about to take place on the planet as well. It would ebb, the larger conflict breaking into a few isolated pockets of hostile action, and then surge back into full bloom as one of those smaller rivalries bled over into full-scale combat. At first he had tried to offer some protection to captains who had declared for the Archon, until two such vessels squared off against each other over some other insult, real or imagined. At that point he washed his hands of the affair. So long as they remained clear of his WarShip, Kerr would let them tangle amongst themselves as he waited for a more worthy target . . .

The First Capellan Dragoons!

Chief Watson sounded the alarm as she quickly fed long-range sensor feeds into the holotank. The scale of the holographic battle shrank until the DropShips were coin-sized splotches of color and aerospace fighters only pinpoints of darting light. Farther out, at the edge of the tank, a new cluster of red icons burned inward toward Kathil. The four larger spheres would be the main transports for 'Mechs and heavy armor. The two smaller DropShips carried supporting forces. A swarm of protective lights hovered out in front—their screen of aerospace fighters.

Kerr smiled, returned to his chair, and strapped himself

in tight. Gripping the armrests with rawboned hands, he had eyes for nothing but the new arrivals.

"And here they come," he murmured to no one in particular.

Kommandant Evån Greene was hearing scattered reports from his battalion scouts as they picked up intermittent contacts heading down from the northern foothills. This was it. David McCarthy had come—as he'd hoped, as he'd planned—and Evån would finally get the fight he'd been looking for. BattleMechs clashing in glorious combat, deciding the fate of the Dragoons, was much more heroic than stabbing out of the dark at an unseen target. The risk of defying Fallon had paid off—providing the Katzbalger carried this day. Only the smallest of doubts niggled away at the back of his mind that they might not—that drawing the militia's attention might have been a mistake.

Too late to worry about that now.

He checked his lines, which were holding in a wide, V-shaped formation facing north, between the KF Yare plant and the approaching hostiles. His own company held the middle, where the fighting would be fiercest. The township of Yare itself anchored his rear right corner. His lighter, more mobile forces spread out and forward in long-reaching wings. Evån had sent forward a double lance of light armor to support the left wing and prevent the militia from attempting a flanking maneuver and establishing themselves in the township. BattleMechs weren't exactly stealthy, but some of them were fast. He wiped his sweaty palms dry on the ballistic cloth of his cooling vest, brought up his active targeting sensors, and checked once again that all of the *Cerberus'* weapons were cycled clear and ready to fire.

"General on the field!" a voice declared over his comm system. It sounded like Sergeant Case, a MechWarrior in Xander's lance—not that it mattered who had spotted Fallon first. He shifted the *Cerberus* around to face back toward the shortest approach from the *Masse Noire* to Yare and caught a visual as the general's HA1-O *Hauptmann* cleared a final stand of trees and paraded into Greene's defensive line.

"Paraded" was certainly the word. The Inner Sphere-designed OmniMech was one of the newest designs made available to the Eighth RCT, and Fallon added a swagger to its walk that left no doubt of her mastery over its controls. The masculine design of the 'Mech somehow suited her. The ninety-five-ton machine had been crafted to give it a manly presence, right down to the bulked-up arms and legs and the extended-range small laser that protruded from its lower face like some improbable cigar.

It moved with the slow, ponderous step of an assault 'Mech, and it could back up Fallon's obvious confidence with an impressive array of weaponry. Each arm ended in a combination pair of large- and medium-pulse lasers. Two Streak-equipped missile systems extended her ammunition to great effect, firing only if she required an unbreakable target lock. And riding over the right shoulder was the knockout punch—a Disintegrator twelve-centimeter-bore autocannon.

Eván switched over from his battalion's general frequency to a private line with Fallon. "Welcome, General," he said, wondering if his insincerity had given him away. "Passing through on your way to Yare Industries?"

"Defending my investment," she snapped back, short to the point of hostility. "David McCarthy has proved himself too able a commander to take lightly. So I have graciously decided to lend you my command experience."

There was no way Eván wanted to share command over what was to be his greatest victory, though he doubted Fallon was really talking about sharing. "Perhaps you would consider taking on the position of an independent warrior, General Fallon," he suggested hopefully. "My people will perform better without the confusion of dual command."

Fallon's voice dripped with false camaraderie. "Don't worry, Eván. I'm doing you a favor. Tell me you don't want the freedom to go head-to-head against David McCarthy."

If Fallon was really doing Eván a favor out of generosity, it would be her first. She was too much an opportunist not to always put herself first. In that regard, at least, she and Eván understood each other. And, unfortunately, there was no arguing with a general.

Or time to do so, even if he wanted to try.

Sensors wailed cautionary alarms at him as they locked onto enemy targets that showed briefly between the rolling hills north of Yare. Still outside his weapons range, but closing rapidly. Two companies at least—three, more likely, and he would have to watch for the more elusive armor support. The militia forces were lost from visual sight among the forest blanketing the hills all the way back to the far ridge to the north, behind which they had no doubt left their DropShips for fear of the Yare energy broadcast facility. That wouldn't be the only thing they would have to fear before the day was out.

Eván toggled his comm back to a general frequency and ordered flanking forces ahead on the left and right. "Heads up, Third Batt," he said.

"Here they come."

26

With one eye pasted to the chronometer, counting the minutes as the militia force rolled deeper into the afternoon and ever closer to the First Capellan Dragoons' final deadline, David McCarthy stalled his own advance for the fifth time this afternoon. He throttled the *Devastator* into a backpedaling walk, trying to pull Kommandant Greene's defensive line out of position. Long-range laser fire splashed around him, scorching the pale yellow-green grass and bursting a few trees as the water inside flashed to steam and sought release. The amber lance of an extended-range laser painted his torso with a molten red stripe, carving away armor that spattered to the ground in large, fiery droplets.

It did no good. Eván Greene obviously knew how to use a defensive position, anchoring his backfield with the township of Yare, and keeping his line from rushing forward. An RCT lance edged out past the others to David's left, but refrained from an all-out charge. A *Falconer* was in the lead, and David remembered the lance from the Howell River and the Kay Bume munitions factory. From

Amanda's tentative starts and faster retreats, she'd recognized the lance as well.

"We've stalled the advance on the western flank, as ordered," Dylan Pachenko reported over the comm system, sounding flustered but nowhere near panicked. "Sir, we're catching holy vengeance over here from their VTOLs."

And that was the way this battle was going. David strafed the Eighth RCT with his aerospace fighters, and Greene countered with two lances of VTOLs running high-risk but damaging paths among his weaker lances. Seven of his 'Mechs were down, and nearly twice as many armored vehicles, none of which could stand up to so much firepower. Enemy casualties weren't running nearly as high—maybe a lance of 'Mechs.

And David's drive had stalled again, wasting precious time as the Dragoons burned in toward Kathil and Fallon's crews at KF Yare prepared to pick off whatever the *Robert Davion* missed. Captain Gerst had needed one of Tara's lances to help push back the RCT to the west, but that had weakened the militia's middle. David's third company, under command of Cadet-Captain Thomas, late of the Second NAIS Training Cadre, was running into difficulty on the eastern flank trying to break through into Yare. The medium-heavy mix had come up against a heavy defensive line augmented by Pegasus hovertanks. They were going nowhere.

"Everyone hold position," David ordered. His left-arm gauss rifle spoke first, and then the right, alternating their heavy, high-velocity payloads. One found Eván Greene's *Cerberus*, gouging a good scar over its left arm. The other machine shrugged it off and angled obliquely to the left. It almost looked as if the *Cerberus* was intentionally blocking the advance of a *Hauptmann* OmniMech. That had to be General Fallon's machine, the way Eván was protecting it. Those two assault 'Mechs fronted a solid line that would cost David dearly to breach.

He knew it had been a gamble, marching his battalion columns abreast down the wide, sloping valley toward the township of Yare and then widening out to a box formation. Kommandant Greene's flanking forces were pressing in from the east and west, and with the Katzbalger defensive line, they formed three sides to a larger box that threatened to surround David's battalion. Only the infantry were immune to that pressing danger. Gennady's men still hung farther back, waiting to push closer to Yare Industries. David had deployed the power-armor infantry of the Second Cadre on a long, sabre-cut strategy meant to flank the Eighth RCT. Moving stealthily, they were finally coming up on a position David might be able to exploit. That was one of the two surprises he'd readied for the enemy.

From the middle of the militia's formation, the armor assets David had brought along continued to snipe at the RCT line from the protection of their larger battlefield cousins. Goblin support vehicles and Drillson heavy hovercraft gave David a solid backfield, ready to catch any breakthrough from the sides. They also hid his second surprise, which David would spring on the RCT if he could engineer the opportunity.

"Dylan, I want you to press forward hard," he ordered. "Give Captain Gerst some relief by drawing fire." That was a hard order for a scout lance, but David was out of options. He remembered the last time he'd sent a scout lance into the middle of a heavy firefight. Sergeant Denning's *Scarabus* had lasted all of ten seconds on Huntress. Denning hadn't lasted much longer than that. He remembered, but ruthlessly shouldered the memory aside. "Press forward for a moment, then fall back. And I mean turn and run the hell out of there."

"That will leave a hole in Gerst's line," Pachenko protested.

David had to turn his attention to the controls as a hail of autocannon fire sparked new gouges across his left shoulder and right knee. The *Devastator* would have lost its footing if David hadn't used his arms to balance out the hundred-ton machine. "I'm counting on it," he told Pachenko.

He then swapped long-range fire with both the *Cerberus* and the *Hauptmann*, buying Pachenko thirty seconds to make a nuisance of himself on the western flank. Tara eased forward, trying to draw fire away from her commander, and drew a pair of *Quickdraw*s instead. The *Falconer* paced several steps forward again, its pilot obviously impatient to engage the enemy.

"Amanda, take up some of that heat. Angle wider left." That placed her right where she undoubtedly didn't want to be, squared off with the *Falconer*. But if the other MechWarrior—Barajas, Eván had named him—turned with his entire lance toward Tara, he could scrap her *Enforcer* in a matter of minutes.

"Everyone else, leapfrog forward by pairs," he ordered. "Pay for the real estate as you advance." It would hurt, but if Dylan's gambit on the left flank was to pay off, it had to look like David's main drive was forward, into the middle of the RCT line.

The *Hauptmann* seemed to sense what was happening and moved up to better challenge David's *Devastator*. The range was long for its assault-class autocannon, but the OmniMech's heavy armor could stand up to incredible punishment while continuing to fire its extended-range lasers at David's war machine. One amber lance splashed armor off his left shoulder. A later attack did the same against his left leg. With his feet planted in a near-unshakable stance, David weathered the assault and paid Fallon back with interest as both of his gauss slugs took her high in the chest. His energy cannon missed wide, instead catching an unlucky *Caesar* moving across the RCT's backfield.

This was all taking way too long. From their late start this morning to the slow, cautious way both sides had edged into full-scale battle, minutes were becoming precious. How close were the First Capellan Dragoons to Kathil? An hour? Less? The smart thing to do would be to go after the broadcast station dish with his aerospace fighters. If he couldn't do anything about the *Robert Davion*, at least he could eliminate the secondary threat. Except that David was under orders to keep the station intact until the last possible moment. General Gennady's men were still waiting for their chance. But if they waited until the dish started tracking on the inbound DropShips, it would be too late to prevent a catastrophe.

Drifting his crosshairs over the *Cerberus*' broad silhouette, David toggled for his particle projection cannon but just one gauss rifle, concerned with his ammunition reserves. One of the PPCs whipped azure energy across the legs of the other assault machine, while the gauss smashed armor from the *Cerberus'* chest into shards and razor-sharp splinters.

It also drove the *Cerberus* back about two steps, a move echoed in two lances that were helping to hold the RCT middle line. Only the *Hauptmann* and the *Falconer* remained in the foreground, intent on targeting David and Amanda, respectively. The *Quickdraws* that had gone after Tara had started to fall back as well, but now one throttled back into a forward walk to support his lance leader, firing on Amanda's position.

"Major, Amanda isn't looking too steady," Tara warned David on their private channel.

Amanda's *Bushwacker* had faltered in its advance, but she was still holding up under the savage fire, and David had no time to worry about her. She would survive. She'd do it because she had to—David couldn't take the time to coddle her back into combat. Instead, he readied his last-ditch order for a hard drive forward, but left the words unsaid when his western flank crumbled, as he'd known it eventually would.

"Major," Leftenant Pachenko's voice crackled over the comm system, "we're in full retreat. I lost Sergeant Campbell. Clean ejection." Losing a 'Mech hurt David's force, but at least his man was alive. It was a small favor, but one David would gladly take.

On his HUD, David watched as icons shifted around to show his western flank stall, waver and begin to fall back. Risking a quick glance out the right-hand ferroglass shield of his wrap-around cockpit, he saw an increased flurry of laserfire stab into his formation.

"They're pouring through!" Captain Gerst shouted, not bothering to hide his concern. "If they get behind us and hold a strong line—"

"Cavalry lances, plug that hole," David ordered his armor, not waiting for Gerst's full report. "Richard, hold them off our backs." Corporal Smith's *Cestus* turned back to the west, ready to challenge any RCT MechWarriors who made it past the armor. "Now, Cavalry, open the box!"

It was a desperate throw of the dice, and everyone knew it. MechWarriors relied largely on their sensors in large-scale battles, saving visual tracking for their chosen target. But sensors needed more than a blip on the magnetic resonance scope to identify a specific design. The computers relied on detecting the active sensors of an enemy and profiling the armor silhouette. And that kind of detection system could be subverted—could be fooled.

His Drillsons led the stopgap measure, skating out ahead on their fans to delay the RCT's breakthrough on the west. The Katzbalger was ready for them, as a lance each of Cavalry and Yellow Jacket VTOL gunships cruised in to rain heavy fire on the Drillsons. One burst open as a magazine ruptured, filling its crew quarters with devastating fire and flipping the craft end over end. Faced with the Katzbalger assault, the Drillsons broke apart, allowing two lances of RCT 'Mechs to slam into the front of the Goblin line.

Only there were more than Goblins in that line. Hidden within the armored cavalry units of the NAIS Cadre, invisible to enemy sensors, a lance of Challenger X Main Battle Tanks had left targeting systems powered down in the hope of taking the RCT forces unaware. At ninety tons, the MBT's had a knock-down power equivalent to many assault 'Mechs, if not quite the mobility or armor protection. They each sported a gauss rifle, LB-variant ten-centimeter autocannon, and an Artemis-equipped long-range missile launcher for long-reaching firepower, switching to Streak SRMs and medium pulse lasers at closer ranges.

Now, held in reserve for so long, they unleashed their full fury in devastating barrages on the Katzbalger advance. Concentrating two MBTs to a single 'Mech, the cadets pounded on a *Talon* and a *Chameleon* with incredible results. Both 'Mechs went down under the Challenger's guns, pounded into submission as armor rained to the ground in a sparkling shower.

The Yellow Jacket VTOLs had already sped off to follow the retreating Drillsons, and though the Cavalry copters tried to regroup and distract the MBTs, the assault-grade tanks shrugged aside the missile salvoes laid down by the VTOLs and fired another barrage of their own into the downed RCT BattleMechs. A lance of Goblins managed to add their lasers to the growing firestorm, keeping it up until both cockpits blew outward on explosive charges, the Katzbalger MechWarriors spreading parafoils over the battlefield and gliding out of danger.

With their breakthrough blunted so effectively, and their morale no doubt taking serious hurt from the appearance of the Main Battle Tanks, the surviving elements of the RCT push turned back against Captain Gerst's line in hopes of fighting their way free. With armored tanks at their backs and VTOLs spreading fire everywhere, the entire western flank fell into chaotic shambles, with Gerst and his men fighting like savage wolves. One 'Mech fell, and then another. Icons winked out on David's heads-up display, militia and RCT both.

Never one to avoid any action, Richard Smith fired off his *Cestus'* jets, sailing over one fallen militia BattleMech to come in hard at the rear of the trapped RCT elements. Approving, David readied a full shift in his lines, planning to throw his main drive toward the east, but was forced to stop and trade another salvo with the *Hauptmann* as General Fallon pressed forward yet again.

The delay in David's orders to advance saved several lives. Dirt and grass geysered up around the legs of Amanda's *Bushwacker* as she fought her way forward, still under David's orders to advance on the angle. Then another detonation shook the field as Tara's *Enfield* stumbled under a similar explosion of earth.

Minefield.

Lifting another page from Morgan Hasek-Davion's earlier defense of Yare, the RCT had seeded the valley with vibrabombs—or possibly the LRM-delivered Thunder munitions. Not heavily, for sure, or Greene would never be able to take advantage of any militia retreat. But the RCT warriors would know where the safe paths lay, while David's people could only guess. In fact, there was no telling how far into the minefield they'd already progressed.

"She's shaky!" Tara called out—not worried for her own 'Mech, though. Amanda was stumbling backward, holding the *Bushwacker* up by sheer force of will. Its left leg was stripped down almost to the titanium skeleton, and at least half its foot was missing. She righted herself and pulled back sharply from the enemy line. "David, she's going to rabbit!"

"Hold ground, hold ground!" David shouted, throttling

down to a halt, a sitting target where Greene and Fallon could concentrate their fire. He could not let himself worry about Amanda; he had to concern himself with his command as a whole. "Angel Lance? Where are those Corsairs? We need a strafing run along the RCT line, and we need it now!"

But the strafing run, when it came, fell not on the Eighth RCT but on David's forward-most BattleMechs, a pair of ninety-ton Chippewas winging overhead to stab down with lasers and missiles. A few infernos burst in the open ground, raising instant firestorms that bled soot into the clear sky. David's *Devastator* rocked under twoscore missiles, the warheads gouging and pitting his armor and nearly throwing him over backward.

"David, she's running!" Tara cried.

Amanda's *Bushwacker* had turned for the western field, the safest route despite the chaos there, with Greene and Fallon pressing forward and a minefield stretching before the militia. Her *Bushwacker* moved in halting steps at first and then throttled up into a full run for the flank.

David had just opened his mouth for a new order when the second flight of Chippewas streaked over the field, raining fire.

No one touches the *Bushwacker*. Was that such a hard order to understand?

Xander Barajas had made it very clear to his lance that the *Bushwacker* was his. He had failed to reach the Stihl munitions plant in time, and his kill had been denied to him by the timely arrival of that DropShip. Now he would be the one to bring it down. The paired *Quickdraw*s were supposed to concentrate on the *Enforcer*. Sergeant Haden's *Lynx* was free to choose any other target except the *Bushwacker*.

He would have achieved his kill long ago except for the other MechWarrior's timid approach and Eván Greene's orders for Xander to hold his position coming every two minutes. The MechWarrior snarled his frustration, silently cursing his commander and the other warrior and Yare itself for taking priority over his own vengeance. Even when one of his *Quickdraw*s fell, brought down by the guns of a militia *Enforcer*, Xander was denied the chance to exact retribution and ordered to hold his place.

Then the RCT's left wing collapsed inward to mire itself in McCarthy's neatly played trap. Barajas couldn't help taking some satisfaction from his commander's failure, and in doing so slipped the leash set on him by the chain of command. He stalked forward, flanked by Sergeant Case's *Quickdraw*, intent on putting an end to that coward of a MechWarrior once and for all as the *Bushwacker* hit the edge of the minefield. It stumbled and shook under the explosion, barely recovering. An easy kill.

Until it decided to run.

Again.

Xander howled in fury and turned his *Falconer* to parallel her course west. He would cut her off and then cut her to pieces. Shoving his throttle forward to its physical limit, he pivoted into a right-oblique path that would take him safely through the Thunder-delivered minefield.

And then he had to veer off as Sergeant Case cut in front of him, angling for that same path while spitting out long-range missiles like there was no shortage, trying to claim range on the *Bushwacker* with his bank of medium lasers.

Xander Barajas would not tolerate such an insult. Not this time. His order had been clear, and Case was disobeying. Xander wrenched at his controls, pulled his targeting reticle over the back of Case's *Quickdraw*, and stabbed down on his triggers.

It had been a dare he had used to liven things up on patrols—and a threat to keep his people in line when they needed it. It was a dark source of amusement. Now that game had turned into something much more dangerous: betrayal.

His particle cannon and gauss punched in through the back of Case's *Quickdraw*, burning through or smashing aside the weaker rear armor. One of his medium lasers burrowed in among that wreckage, cutting at the *Quickdraw*'s gyroscopic stabilizer. The BattleMech took one more shaky step forward, its leg swinging wide of any stable stride. Twisting its right leg beneath sixty tons of unbalanced metal, myomer and munitions, the *Quickdraw* pitched forward and slammed into the ground.

And Xander raced past, hitting his maximum speed of eighty-five kilometers per hour as the fusion spike pulled out of his reactor by the energy draw radiated intense heat into his cockpit. He basked in that warmth, and chased off after his vengeance, leaving his man, and his command, far behind.

As Fallon's *Hauptmann* finally managed to crowd in front of him, Eván throttled back with disgust written all over his face. Having seen fit to ace him out of his command in this battle, she wasn't even going to leave him his fight with David McCarthy. If anyone was going to claim the mantle of glory around Yare, it would be Karen Fallon.

Except that with her single-minded focus on McCarthy, Fallon had let the reins of command slip from her grasp. The flanking force Eván had sent northwest reported a breakthrough followed by the surprise of McCarthy's masterfully hidden Challenger Xs, and finally the retreat into which his forces were pushed. Intent on trading shots with the *Devastator*, Fallon paid no attention to the chaos her western flank had slipped into.

Then Leftenant Barajas fired on one of his own men and abandoned his lance, throwing Eván's eastern line into disarray. Fallon did nothing, immortal in her *Hauptmann* and still trading salvoes with McCarthy. Fed up with her, Eván fell back out of line, leaving Fallon's position exposed. With any luck, McCarthy's people would rid him of that albatross, and he could resume his forward push.

Not willing to rely in that luck, however, Eván called in the Chippewa aerospace fighters he'd held in reserve just out of detection range, for just such an emergency. Their double pass left the CMM's forward line rocking under the assault, stalled and worried but, unfortunately, not as confused as he'd hoped. And judging by the babble of voices over his comm system, his soldiers were in nearly as much turmoil as their enemy.

"They're pulling back. No, right."

"He's after Leftenant Barajas . . ."

"No, the entire line—"

"Barajas attacked Case first. Did he turncoat?"

The militia's entire line was shifting west now. In effect, the militia major was rotating his entire formation ninety degrees, their forward line now holding the flank against the Eighth RCT. Their armor unit took point along with the previously disrupted 'Mech forces on McCarthy's right, while the militia's eastern forces took rear guard. It would net them an easy push out of the box Eván had so carefully created and gain them a few kilometers toward KF Yare Industries, though the Katzbalger could still intercept and push them back.

Hurling two gauss slugs at McCarthy, Eván knew a second of satisfaction as both took the *Devastator* in its right side—one at the hip and the other just below the shoulder. Then he fell back farther from the front line, trying to regain the threads of his earlier assault plan and hold them in his mind. He had to pick up the pieces, and quickly, to counter this latest maneuver, since Fallon was showing no interest in commanding the battle.

McCarthy's return fire washed the energy of his twin PPCs into the *Cerberus'* left arm, blasting away armor under a scourge of manmade lightning and fusing the lower arm actuator into a mess of ruined metal. Grinding his teeth together, Eván broke away from the battle and picked up Xander's lance. Sergeant Case was just getting to his feet, the *Quickdraw* shaky but mobile.

"Stalker Lance, with me," he ordered before shifting over to a command-wide frequency. "Eastern flank, do not pursue. Fall back into Yare. Everyone else swing west. Swing west and contain. Do not engage heavily at this time. Regroup, regroup, regroup."

He waited for Fallon to countermand the orders and was faintly surprised when she did not. In fact, she too began to fall back, swapping one last blast of her lasers for McCarthy's PPCs and a gauss slug that spanged off her left knee, snapping the limb straight and obviously crushing the actuator. Her *Hauptmann* limped back until it was even with Eván's *Cerberus*, as if guarding the rearward line with him.

It was just one clash, not the battle, that McCarthy had won. This was merely a shift of arms to a new front. Eván would have liked to put down the militia with one decisive blow, but a drawn-out victory would taste just as sweet in the end. He would give Fallon the time she needed to use the Yare broadcast station, bringing down the First Capellan Dragoons in a final grand gesture of defiance, and then Eván would carry the rest of the day for himself.

The harder the battle, the greater the eventual reward. And this time, he would not allow Fallon to rob him of it. Not without a fight.

Kearny-Fuchida Yare Industries
Yare, Kathil
Capellan March, Federated Commonwealth
7 December 3062

Karen Fallon paced her *Hauptmann* OmniMech along
what had been the Eighth RCT's western flank and was
now the forefront of the battle. She gave ground slowly,
falling back toward the township of Yare, but making the
Kathil militia pay for every meter she gave up. Better yet,
making David McCarthy pay, as her large lasers carved
yet more armor from his already savaged left leg.

A blast of furnace-hot air circulated through the cockpit
as waste heat from her Omni's fusion-reactor power spike
invaded the life support's air-recirc system. She took shallow breaths, waiting for the temperatures to fall again as
her 'Mech's heat sinks worked to compensate. Sweat stood
out on her brow, trickling down her face and dripping off
her neurohelmet's chin strap. The sweat ran more freely
on her bare arms and legs, though the neoleather skin of
her control stick grips wicked it away to keep her hands
from slipping.

An *Enforcer* hammered at her with a heavy-bore autocannon, the slugs chewing across her 'Mech's chest but
not doing enough damage to threaten her. McCarthy's
Devastator was a bigger concern, though he carefully re-

stricted his firing patterns to a single gauss rifle and one particle projection cannon at a time, the better to conserve ammunition and manage the *Devastator*'s heat curve. The PPC scoured armor off her right arm, enough that another solid hit could eliminate half her long-range weaponry

Karen twisted the *Hauptmann* along its turret-style waist, rotating its right arm behind her, the better to protect it. She walked backward another ten paces, drawing a new forward line on which the nearby Katzbalger 'Mechs formed.

Despite Kommandant Greene's micromanagement, Karen Fallon felt that her battle was proceeding fairly well. McCarthy's springing the Main Battle Tanks on the RCT had proved fairly effective, but the overall strategic picture certainly leaned in her favor still. And now Eván Greene was haring off on his own again, desperate to run every facet of Yare's defense, leaving her to bring down David McCarthy, a right Greene had claimed as his sole privilege. She would have been willing to share that victory with him.

Oh, well—his loss.

Karen had learned years before that there was no need to attend to every little detail on the battlefield. You might save one more life or you might make the wrong call when your subordinate officers could manage on their own. She had tried to help Greene by accepting some of the command responsibility. But when she leant him her supporting firepower, he took that as an opportunity to reclaim full command of the battalion. He was now organizing the bulk of the command west of Yare, trying to avoid a fight through the township.

Well, let him! Fallon would take McCarthy apart and claim the credit for stopping the Capellan Dragoons. Then she would retake command of the battalion for the mop-up and claim her due. Eván simply did not understand the bigger picture. His success would always be a portion of hers. Only when you divorced yourself from your upper command, as she had in moving away from District City to take charge at Yare, could you make a truly independent stand. That's what she was doing. Making an independent stand. Let Mitchell Weintraub play his political games. In the meantime, Karen would go out and win victories for the Archon.

The comm speakers built into her neurohelmet crackled. "Leftenant General Fallon, this is the Yare Command Post. We've heard from General Weintraub. Admiral Kerr has engaged the Dragoons."

Damn. Karen fell back a step from the line and passed quick orders for her fellow 'Mechs to fall back slowly to Eván's position. She and the tattered 'Mechs of Eván's original lance moved for the township border, seeking a brief respite. A few intermittent sensor blips on her HUD suggested that another one or two RCT units might already be inside the township partially hidden by the buildings.

"Engaged?" she asked. "Or destroyed?"

"Engaged. Admiral Kerr has so far been successful in keeping most of the Dragoons away from Kathil, though one damaged DropShip made a landing in Thespia. But he has yet to destroy any of them."

"Then why haven't you done something about it?" she asked sharply. The landing in Thespia couldn't be helped—if it had circled around at extreme range and come in below the horizon, there was no way Yare could have targeted it. But she refused to believe every Dragoon DropShip was making runs outside her targeting zone. "You said we were tracking the *Robert Davion* and all nearby DropShips." She sniped at McCarthy, who was at the extreme edge of her weapons range, and missed.

A new voice came over the comm system. The plant manager, Paul Allison, was agitated. "G-General," he stammered. "This is not targeting software we're dealing with here. We take sensor feeds from the satellite net, and our computers extrapolate most courses based on known orbits and the transmitted course deviations from any vessel running close to a no-fly zone."

"What happened to your promises of crossing all the T's and dotting all the I's, Allison?"

"General, the *Robert Davion* is a rather large target. DropShips are another matter. Right now there's a chaotic mess boiling over Kathil, some kind of huge naval battle between the support ships. You point at a target, and I could destroy it, but our computers can't sort out a particular vessel and identify it with any degree of accuracy, especially a cluster of DropShips running highly evasive maneuvers through that chaos."

Karen had moved her *Hauptmann* into the township proper, her jaw set as she listened to Allison try to explain why he couldn't give her what she wanted. She didn't care about the reasons. She wanted it done. A hot flush burned at the back of her neck.

But any rebuke she might have delivered was diverted as a new panicked voice jumped in on the conversation. "Ambush! Elementals! Get them off me, get them off!"

As incongruous as it would be for Clan powered-armor infantry to be stalking the battlefields on Kathil, the MechWarrior's warning rattled Karen for an instant. Elementals were terrifying in large numbers—the armor-clad infantry could take direct hits from 'Mech scale weaponry, then jump onto the BattleMech and begin ripping armor plating off with their mechanical claws. Her HUD suddenly swarmed with the red threat icons for such troops throughout the township, several moving rapidly in on her position.

Selecting for her large lasers in a rush to defend herself, Fallon sliced through two power-armor suits before realizing the mistake her man had made. These weren't Elementals, but Cavaliers—the Inner Sphere equivalent originally developed by House Davion. With weaker armor and lighter arms, they were no cause for panic, but they were still not a threat to take lightly.

McCarthy! While all attention remained focused on the valley battle, he had infiltrated powered armor into the township in a second trap for Karen's people. What a waste to have him fighting against her.

The lancemate who had called out the initial warning, in a *Penetrator*, was covered in the armored infantry. They set in with claws and small lasers, ripping and cutting at the seventy-five-ton 'Mech like fire ants swarming a preying mantis. Cursing herself for her moment of panic, Karen walked her *Hauptmann* over to the struggling 'Mech and pushed it over onto its back. Its gyroscopic stabilizer helped roll it immediately back to its front, ready to stand again, but it had left several broken bodies on the cracked ferrocrete road.

"Stop, drop and roll, you idiot!" she barked at him.

It was an ages-old command for putting out a fire to one's clothing; MechWarriors had co-opted the phrase to remind them of a basic thrashing attack. By lying on the ground—crushing those infantry caught between the tonnage of a 'Mech and the unyielding earth—a 'Mech could kick its legs and thrash about with its arms and generally make itself a lethal hazard for any infantry, augmented by power armor or not. The *Penetrator* finally put that tactic to good use, clearing off all but the most stubborn Cavaliers, which Karen had to pick off carefully with her medium lasers.

But the infantry unit was not without its victories. What had been a perfectly good *Caesar* now lay in ruin on the street, its left leg separated from the body by explosive charges and the remains of its gyro raining out of a large wound in the 'Mech's back. The infantry leapt from rooftops and among alleyways, making for difficult targets as they sought to come at the *Hauptmann* from its blind spots. Her sensors detected at least two of the furious battlesuits already clinging to her lower legs.

"Out of the city," Karen ordered, making a quick decision. "Abandon Yare." She throttled into a backward walk as the *Penetrator* regained its feet and matched her retreat. They aided each other in shooting a few Cavaliers off their backs. "All units, this is General Fallon. Yare is infested with armored infantry, though not—I repeat, not!—Elementals." No doubt these were elements of the Second NAIS Cadre. "Fall back on Kommandant Greene's position. Avoid Yare, but watch that we keep the power armor pinned inside."

Another small victory for McCarthy, but this one was easily contained. In the close streets of Yare, the infantry held a slight advantage. But if they ventured into the open fields surrounding the township, they would become little more than target practice. The Yare Industries energy broadcast station and control facilities were all located well outside the township anyway. Which reminded her . . .

"Allison!" she growled, switching back to her line to the Yare Industries command post. "Allison, you said we are tracking the *Robert Davion*. Does that mean you have its location fixed at least?"

"Ye-es. Yes, General. The WarShip gives us a fairly obvious sensor profile. Like the shipyards and several major factory stations in high—"

"My point," Fallon said, cutting him off, "is that you can tell the difference between the WarShip and any DropShips?"

"Of course." A slight pause, and then, "General, I can't—"

"You can and you will," Fallon snapped as she led a quick march toward Eván Greene's new defensive line to the west. Whether Kerr knew it or not—wanted it or not—he was about to receive assistance from the ground. She smiled grimly, imagining the flustered look on the admiral's face as her contingency plan began claiming victories.

"Yare Command Post—Major Simmons!—get that man to the console," Fallon ordered. "Everything up there but that WarShip is expendable. You will begin selecting targets at once, weeding through them until you find those damned Dragoons! I don't care if you sweep the skies clean of every satellite, fighter, DropShip, and space station.

"This ends now!"

On one of the *Robert Davion*'s main bridge viewscreens, a fireball of orange and red roiled as an exploding fusion drive ate through a DropShip, consuming all the air in one large flash and gutting the vessel. The explosion winked out just as quickly, leaving only a charred hulk drifting against the black backdrop of space.

Distracted from the holographic tank by the explosion, Kerr spun his chair around to face chief Deborah Watson. "Was that a Dragoon DropShip?"

Watson shook her head, her short-cropped hair bouncing lightly in the uncertain gravity. The main drive cycled between full thrust and station-keeping acceleration, turning on attitude thrusters as necessary to prevent a Dragoon DropShip from approaching Kathil. "No, sir. A Mule spacedock barge."

Kerr snarled his annoyance. "I don't give a damn about barges and fightercraft. Or any DropShips but the Dra-

:oons'. Get me a solid firing solution, damn you." He threw himself back into his seat and glared at Leftenant Myers, who continued to monitor all communications. "Pass the word—I want our infantry forces posted at the weapon bays. I don't believe these men are really trying."

Since dismissing Petty Officer Olsen, Kerr had been forced to rely on the remote stations to target and fire all weapons. So far a brace of naval-grade particle cannon had scourged one of the Dragoons' auxiliary DropShips into a dead hulk, but one of the larger DropShips had evaded him to come down over the island continent of Thespia. That would not be allowed to happen again.

Watson was not so quickly distracted. "Admiral, that wasn't from one of our volleys. Sensors detected a swing in one of the energy beams from Kathil—from Yare Industries. It stabbed upright through this area, though it's supposed to be a free-fly zone."

Ground fire to support a naval operation? Kerr had heard of stranger things in his day, but not many. Though it did ring a bell. That upstart officer from the Uhlans, on his way to take post with the militia. McCarthy. He had talked about it.

Kerr glanced at his forward screen. "So someone down there thinks he's Morgan Hasek-Davion." Weintraub? His face clouded. He really should have been told about such plans.

Filing the general's oversight until later, he returned his attention to the live video. Kathil hung large in the forward screen, the yellow-green orb taking up most of the screen. With the edge of its atmosphere only a few hundred kilometers off, Helm sweated bullets every time a major course correction pushed them closer to that invisible boundary that separated space from planet.

"Another one," Watson said, voice mechanical as she reported the death of another DropShip. "The *Manxkatze*." A ship the *R. Davion* had earlier tried to protect, its captain a solid supporter of Katrina Streiner-Davion.

Was a solid supporter, Kerr amended, furious with the ground station for interfering. "Well, if it's to be a race for the Dragoons, we'll oblige," he said grimly. "Comm! Send a message down to Yare and to General Weintraub specifically, warning him off. If I lose one more captain who's committed to the Archon, or if just one of those microwave transmissions came within a kilometer of this WarShip, we'll teach Yare Industries something about space-to-ground accuracy." In the meantime, they would try to beat the probing microwave beams to the real prize. He had to show both sides what a WarShip could do.

Kerr pinpointed the vessels in his holotank that he thought might be evasive Dragoons. Two were making wild stabs toward the planet, one planning to slingshot around to the far side and come in dark. By splitting their paths, they almost guaranteed at least one ship would make it.

Not on his watch. "Weapons, order our Barracuda missile stations to intercept that running ship, designated D-2 Bravo," he said. "If they can't hit the damn thing, they'd better be able to scare it off that run. Helm, take us lower."

Petty Officer Erikson glanced nervously at the acting engineer, Hauptmann Tremmar, and then asked, "Lower, Admiral?"

"Lower, you little fool. Lower! Get us over Muran and in the way of that first DropShip, or it'll be your ass. Weapons! Prepare starboard bays for a full broadside. I don't want to miss this one."

The bridge crew fell to work, and Kathil grew larger yet. It crept into the holographic tank as a solid wall, at that scale no curve showing on the surface. The *Robert Davion* skated closer to the edge of its operating room, leaving behind the battle save for the approach of the Dragoon vessel and one other large icon racing in from around the backside of the planet.

"Contact," Watson called out a second after Kerr noticed it himself. "Bearing one-seven-niner, mark fifteen. On an intercept course."

Kerr frowned. "The Dragoon DropShip we missed earlier? It can't possibly be making an attack run against us!" Even an assault-class DropShip was hardly a threat unless it got within point-blank range. And even then, the *R. Davion* could crush it without suffering more than superficial damage.

"No, Admiral." Watson pulled up a blurry, long-range visual. It looked like a double sphere, complete with two drive flames. "Sir, it's the *Guardian*," she said, naming the DropShip Kerr had disabled on taking the WarShip out from spacedock. "She's been recovered and is under tow by that Octopus that set off after her."

A few days' time to intercept, bring the *Guardian* into a stable flight path, and return her to Kathil orbit while working to fix her engines. Not bad, Kerr decided, even for Davion-lovers, and promptly dismissed them as his attention returned to the Dragoons.

"Both drives are operational, though her flight mechanics suggest that the Octo is doing all the course changes," Watson persisted, typing rapidly on he keyboard. "I'll redesignate them D-7 and D-8. We have to assume they're still pro-militia."

Kerr waved his hand at the image. "I said to ignore the auxiliary vessels. So they rescued the *Guardian*. If they have to tow her back into the fight, she can't be too threatening. Concentrate on your task, Chief Watson, and get me that Dragoon DropShip! Don't worry about the others. They'll veer away.

"If not," Kerr said with a savage smile that didn't come close to touching his eyes, "I'll be obliged to pay them my respects a second time."

28

Kearny-Fuchida Yare Industries
Yare, Kathil
Capellan March, Federated Commonwealth
7 December 3062

Listening to his lance self-destruct had almost turned Xander Barajas from his hunt of the *Bushwacker*. Almost. Then Eván Greene had rallied Xander's men, and Xander knew there was no going back. He railed inwardly at the situation he'd gotten himself into and now had to see through to the end. He's turned his back on the RCT for the sake of his vengeance.

That was all he had left, and he planned to make the *Bushwacker* pay.

Twice now the militia warrior had run from Xander, denying him the kill. He felt personally insulted that such a coward had managed to lay claim to the title of Mech-Warrior. Somehow he'd expected more from the local militia—a better performance, more of a challenge. It was their world, after all.

He glimpsed gray metal between the trees as the *Bushwacker* poked its forward-thrust cockpit and barrel-appendage arms from the yellow-green canopy of a stand of stunted maple. Xander sneered his contempt as his sensors wailed the alarm of a missile lock. Twin flights of long-range missiles speared outward from the trees, trailing gray contrails as they arced across the distance to rain over the ground separating the two 'Mechs. At the same time a large laser stabbed an emerald lance into Xander's side, melting away armor and digging into his endosteel skeleton but with no lasting effect.

A coward the other MechWarrior might be, but Xander couldn't deny the *Bushwacker*'s strength or the warrior's ability to wield it with quick and devastating results. The 'Mech was like a cornered animal, growing all the more dangerous the closer it came to death. The manmade lightning of his left-arm PPC whipped at the *Bushwacker*, the energy twisting back on itself as it snaked over the ground to burn into the other 'Mech's flank.

Xander was sure the *Bushwacker* would run again. Like any good hunter, he recognized the patterns of his prey. He throttled forward for the chase, moving onto the scarred ground, torn up seconds earlier by the *Bushwacker*'s LRM rounds.

But he hadn't taken more than a step when he was rocked back against his seat as the LRM-delivered Thunder minefield blasted apart the ground underfoot, dirt and scorched grass geysering up against the *Falconer*'s shield. The *Bushwacker* broke clear of the trees, its LRM launchers now delivering real warheads that hammered along Xander's shoulders and upper body. The laser-autocannon pairing worried more armor off his chest and legs.

Was the *Bushwacker* finally about to deliver a real fight? Xander rode the impact of his enemy's fire, balancing himself by thrusting the *Falconer*'s arms forward. He spent one of his last few gauss slugs, the silvery blur ringing against the other 'Mech's chest as his PPC and four medium lasers spat lethal energy that washed over the *Bushwacker* in a violent cascade of blue-white twists and gem-colored darts. He would break the militia MechWarrior this time. The *Bushwacker* would fall, or it would run.

In fact, it did neither.

As another light minefield of Thunder munitions exploded under Xander's feet, the *Bushwacker* struck with everything at its disposal. Missiles rang hard against his right side, two warheads exploding against the *Falconer*'s head and leaving Xander's ears ringing. The autocannon dug into his right knee, hammering his upper leg actuator to shreds and introducing a violent tremble into an already shaky step. The laser melted away another half-ton of armor, further unbalancing him.

Gravity, Xander had learned in Stihl, was a very unforgiving enemy. He fought through one awkward step, and another. Then his damaged leg wrenched around beneath him, thrusting the *Falconer*'s torso forward past any hope of retaining its balance. He lowered his arms in an attempt to break his fall, digging the end of his gauss rifle barrel into the soft ground before folding seventy-five tons of metal over it.

The casing was twisted and crushed, ruining the launching rail, ammunition feed, and energy coils. The coils' stored energy washed out in an unregulated release, feeding back through the power system and then washing a charge of raw energy up through his neurocircuitry. His teeth clamped shut on his lower lip as pain lanced through his head, and his back arched with the sharp-edged fire up his spine.

Xander clung fiercely to consciousness, tensing for the final, bone-rattling impact against the ground, then fighting immediately to get back up on his feet. Missile fire continued to hammer at him, and the *Bushwacker*'s ten-centimeter autocannon spat a seemingly never-ending stream of bullets. Tipped in depleted-uranium, those bullets managed to crack his engine casing and chip away at the fusion reactor's shielding.

Waste heat washed through his 'Mech, adding to the power spike from the reactor on Xander's earlier barrage. A new alarm threatened an emergency engine shutdown. Xander clawed at the override, then jammed his throttle to its physical stop, centering his rage on the *Bushwacker*, which stood not three hundred meters distant.

It would break. Break and run—or die.

He thrust his arms out in front of him, spitting lightning from the barrel of his autocannon and then dry-firing his damaged gauss rifle, never noticing that it failed to deliver one of his remaining nickel-ferrous slugs. He also fired his bank of lasers into the *Bushwacker*'s chest and arms, the sapphire beams melting armor even as they raised the power draw on the *Falconer*'s fusion reactor to dangerous levels. His heat crept past tolerable levels, and breathing felt like he was taking hot coals into his lungs. Xander ignored it in favor of the sweet taste of vengeance. He smashed down on the override again. And again.

And again.

Amanda Black still didn't know exactly what had made her turn away from the fighting, away from the militia line of battle. Maybe she would never know.

She remembered sweating, both from the rising heat level in her cockpit and from the merciless onslaught raving the armor on the front and flanks of her *Bushwacker*. She felt a flash of hope as David sprung his trap against the Katzbalger advance, but it evaporated instantly as her 'Mech entered the minefield. Jostled against her harness, fighting to remain on her feet, she was sure the militia would never make it across.

Amanda knew what the Thunders could do to a 'Mech. She had employed them herself. Trying to cross such a field would cost the militia more than it could afford to pay. Their advance would be stalled, and they would never reach KF Yare.

Then the RCT aerospace fighters barraged their lines with missiles and laserfire, and all Amanda could think of was finding a way out. She let instinct turn her away, dragging her westward as she fled through the chaotic fighting. She couldn't be sure whether she was retreating or leading a charge.

David had already ordered the shift in his line, moving everyone along her path, before he tried to contact her. "Amanda, where away?" he called over the commline.

Where was straight through the heavy fighting that embroiled their right flank. Captain Gerst was gaining the upper hand, but his ranks were thinning. She raced past two downed militia 'Mechs, one of them Dylan Pachenko's *Stealth*.

"Running hard, David," she said. She knew the *Falconer* was in pursuit. She was counting on it. They two had unfinished business, and drawing an enemy commander far out of line could only help her unit. "Swinging southwest."

David was her lover, but she trusted him to give her a commander's advice. Pull back? Push forward? Hold? He apparently trusted her as well. "Good luck," he said simply, leaving her free to pursue her own course.

And that had brought them to this battlefield. As near as Amanda could tell, her battalion was fighting less than a half kilometer away, just on the other side of a ridgeline that hid the Yare Valley from her current location, where she had decided to put an end to her questions, one way or another.

The hard buffeting that shook her 'Mech as the *Falconer* returned fire rattled her teeth together painfully and dug the straps of her harness into her shoulders. Knocking him down had been no surprising feat. Her opponent had underestimated her from the start. She knew that as surely as she knew that he wouldn't stay down.

Three hundred meters. The *Falconer* levered itself back to its feet, throttled up into a run and came straight for her, autocannon and lasers flaring brilliant and damaging. Just like it had in Stihl. She managed to carve a red-rimmed weal across its chest with her laser, quickly it began to cool and darken at the edges.

One hundred-eighty.

Dark smoke wisped out of the joints and burst seams on the *Falconer,* its heat levels climbing into critical. Flame licked out of one wound. A grayish-green burst of coolant sprayed out through one hip joint as a heat sink ruptured under stress. Amanda toggled off her log-range missiles, the *Falconer* now within their minimum targeting range. Her laser and autocannon slashed open its chest, sloughing away armor to reveal the bright glow of a fusion reactor beginning to leak, eating through physical restraints as well.

Ninety . . . eighty . . . seventy . . . The *Falconer's* flurry of lasers bit hard into her *Bushwacker's* left arm, slicing into the autocannon and destroying its ammunition feed. Another sapphire bolt splashed across her forward shield, the flash half-blinding her. Amanda nearly pulled away then, her crosshairs drifting wide as she considered for a fraction of a second whether to break away.

But running would mean deciding to leave a Mech-Warrior like that free, a man with total disregard for the people he was supposed to protect. The people she had vowed to protect. She remembered watching the *Falconer* crash through buildings, kicking aside cars in the street—doing whatever it took to get his kill.

Never again. She wasn't going to leave this man to run roughshod over hers or any other world. Reaching forward with both barrel-like arms, she punched several dozen rounds from her autocannon straight into the *Falconer's* forward faceshield while her laser splashed across the open torso.

At fifty meters, the reactor shielding burst outward in a rain of molten metal chased by a gout of golden fire. The stream scorched across the front of her own 'Mech, slicing through armor and melting a gouge in the ferroglass shield protecting her cockpit. Then the *Falconer* simply ceased to be—its arms and legs cartwheeling through the air as the reactor expanded to consume the body of the once-humanoid war machine. The force of the explosion toppled the *Bushwacker* over backward, like being shoved in the chest by a giant hand. The 'Mech slammed against the ground, and Amanda thought her spine was going through her rib cage.

The pain washed away slowly, until finally she could open her eyes without wincing into Kathil's blue sky. Drained, she didn't expend the effort to silence a few last alarms.

"Never again," she whispered.

Her wireframe damage schematic showed that the *Bushwacker* had lost most of its armor as well as its right arm, and had thrown its gyro slightly off balance. It was nothing life-threatening, nothing some time in the 'Mech bay couldn't fix. If she made it back.

There would be no more running, not with a damaged gyro, but she could still stand and walk her 'Mech back to the fight. It wasn't over. "So what are you waiting for?" she asked herself, quietly enough that it did not activate her internal mic. "Get up, Amanda."

It was a simple maneuver. Flex the elbow. Roll the 'Mech onto its chest. Use one arm to lever it onto one side and then get its feet beneath her.

She continued to stare at the empty sky, unmoving.

"Get up," she whispered.

29

Kearny-Fuchida Yare Industries
Yare, Kathil
Capellan March, Federated Commonwealth
7 December 3062

This was the Eighth RCT's final stand. David knew that.

Half a kilometer past the township of Yare, having finally pushed the Eighth RCT back from the surveillance and control facilities for Kearny-Fuchida Yare Industries, his battalion hit a wall they could not force.

The Eighth had anchored their line between Fallon's grounded *Masse Noir* and the geothermal plant and broadcast station. Sitting over the ferrocrete bunker that housed the underground geothermal plant, the station's massive broadcast dish loomed over the RCT's backfield. An engineering marvel, the station was nearly as big as Fallon's DropShip. A network of titanium struts supported the dish, and a massive configuration of gears and actuators could turn the antenna by hundredths of a degree as it swung between the horizons.

No longer giving ground but turning to hit back hard as they were able, the Katzbalger made their presence felt with hard-hitting barrages of missiles and laserfire. PPC fire arced their lightning storms over the field, while gauss rifles and autocannon hammered back and forth, littering the yellow-green sward with shards and scraps of armor.

A few 'Mechs covered in blazing gel fought on as the Cavalry VTOLs continued to strike—but more often missed—with their Inferno missile rounds. Large patches of grass and landscaped shrubs blazed unnaturally, drifting a greasy smoke up into what had been a beautiful Kathil sky.

David pushed the *Devastator* up a small, grassy knoll. Stepping over the body of one fallen 'Mech, he landed on the severed arm of another. It rolled under his foot, throwing a jog into his gyro before his one hundred tons crushed the limb and planted his foot solidly back on the ground. He tilted forward, staring out his ferroglass shield at the corpses of two ruined BattleMechs. One displayed the crest of the Federated Suns, the other of the Federated Commonwealth. Supposedly the same state. The same army.

Not any longer.

He reached the top of the knoll, planting his feet in a widespread stance as Karen Fallon's *Hauptmann* Omni-Mech continued to track him. An amber lance cored into his left side, cutting through supporting skeleton but fortunately finding no critical components. He returned fire automatically, while an auxiliary monitor showed him General Gennady's infantry force flanking the defensive line and storming into KF Yare behind the fighting. They immediately reported heavy resistance as Katzbalger infantry crews set up static defenses in the halls and stairways. As much as it pained him to give up his supporting forces, David passed the order for the power-armor infantry to regroup around the side of the control facility and support Gennady.

But the general was too late. It was all too late.

The broadcast dish had already shifted its track three times in the past thirty minutes, most likely cutting apart the arriving Dragoons. Now it was shifting again—not that he could tell by watching the dish; it was so immense that shifts of decimal points were lost to the eye. But movement among the gears—that David could see.

And there was very little he could do about it. The cost of his earlier advances was making itself felt as first one and then another militia BattleMech finally succumbed to the merciless pounding being dished out by the Katz-

balger RCT. Dylan Pachenko had never made it past the
Yare township, the head of his *Stealth* carved out by a
particle projection cannon. Captain Gerst had died when
his reactor blew through the magnetic shielding and evis-
cerated his *Dragon Fire*, and Cadet-Captain Thomas was
sidelined with a destroyed gyroscope.

Of his senior officers, only Tara and a young leftenant
were left, struggling to help David lead two abridged
companies of battered 'Mechs and MechWarriors. They
essayed another push forward, and again the RCT re-
pulsed them. David remembered a similar battle from the
other side, the desperation that could drive defenders to
hold in the face of overwhelming odds. And here, with
the forces fairly well matched, the destruction took its toll
on both sides with ever-increasing severity. Sampreis' raid
against District City—however well or poorly it might be
going—might well have doomed David's chance for a victory here. One more company of BattleMechs, he thought,
would have cinched it for the militia force. Or a line of
armor—even some dependable aerospace.

But the militia's *Corsair*s were down, swatted out of the
air by the much heavier *Chippewa*s. One remaining assault
fighter continued its strafing runs against David's people,
though the RCT's final two Yellow Jackets posed a much
larger problem as they danced around the Challenger X
Main Battle Tanks and threatened to put an end to the
vehicles. But the MBTs continued to roll forward up to
the last minute, spearheading a drive by the remaining
armor units to split the Katzbalger line.

David also pushed his *Devastator* against the RCT line.
Tara Michaels had fallen slightly behind, her *Enforcer*
nursing a frozen hip joint and damaged leg actuator. It
was Corporal Smith's *Cestus* that now kept pace with the
battalion's leading assault 'Mech, lending his quartet of
lasers and gauss rifle to the *Devastator*'s twin gauss and
PPC combinations.

David angled their attack toward the geothermal-plant
broadcast station, away from the devastating barrage Fallon's DropShip laid down against any militia 'Mech foolish enough to challenge its side of the field. His heat scale
climbed through the yellow band and deep into the red
as continued use of his energy cannon overworked the

Devastator's fusion reactor. His breath came in fits and gasps, his lungs burning, but he refused to back away. He would break through or fall trying.

The latter possibility was looking more likely with each passing minute. General Fallon guarded the station as if it held the holy grail, striking with deadly accuracy as her lasers continued to slice away armor from David's arms, chest, and legs. Greene's *Cerberus* patrolled off to her side, trading salvoes with Smith and occasionally finding a good angle to smash a gauss slug into the *Devastator's* side as well.

With the two RCT assault machines holding this end of the field, nothing short of a suicidal blitz would break their line. It was over, despite everything David had done to stop it.

Despite everything he had done. Familiar words. Despite everything he had done, his command had been unable to hold back the Clan advance on Huntress. Despite everything he had done, his rearguard action to protect the Uhlans had cost the lives of five fine MechWarriors, some of the best he'd ever served with, and ended the active careers of four others.

Sergeant Isaak had been crushed in his cockpit as the *Kingfisher* righted itself and walked over him to get to David, the scream picked up by his voice-activated mic mercifully cut short. That scream still rang in David's ears. Hauptmann Kennedy, pitting her *Berserker* against two OmniMechs, never once called out, knowing David had no time for her. Polsan's *Caesar*, still wielding the *Nightsky's* hatchet arm as a club, stood up to the monstrous *Daishi*. Fletcher and MacDougal, their *Stealths* falling on the wounded *Masakari*, bought mere seconds for David. And only three of them walked away from that battle. Only three.

But you won on Huntress. Amanda's words, echoing through his mind. *Is that why you're still afraid? Because you never got to finish that fight?*

Despite everything he had done.

No, David chastised himself, dragging his mind back into the present, not everything. Not yet.

But the cost was going to run high—again.

A gauss slug blurred across his ferroglass shield, a silvery arrow that came within meters of ending his plans. It smashed into his left shoulder instead, rocking the *Devastator* back on its heels. David bent forward, using his own sense of equilibrium to feed the 'Mech's gyro and hold it on its feet. According to his damage schematic, the nickel-ferrous slug had lodged in the joint, limiting any wide rotation of his *Devastator*'s arm. Not a large worry—his target wouldn't be hard to hit.

"Cavalry units, stand ready at flank speed," he ordered. "On my order, drive forward and break that line however you can. MBTs, hold the break. Drillsons spread into the right flank, Goblins the left." That would put the Drillsons under the *Masse Noir*'s guns, but with the superior speed of the hovercraft, they might evade the heavier fire. It was the best chance he could give the armored vehicles—better than the 'Mech forces would get.

"Third Batt, you will disengage on my mark. Repeat, disengage. Turn on my position and make your best speed for KF Yare. Your target is the base of the antenna dish. We're bringing it down. Don't stop for lancemates. Ignore the Katzbalger 'Mechs. General Gennady," he said. "Pull your infantry back."

Sampreis might have David's command for this, but if David was going to be damned, he'd do it fighting on his own terms. If there was a chance to save the incoming Capellan Dragoons, he'd take it. There was nothing they could do about the *Robert Davion*—they would never break past the RCT in time to take control of the antenna dish—but the militia could at least prevent the death of any more DropShips. And the last thing David wanted for his command was to live with the idea that they had paid such a terrible price, and failed.

Despite everything they could have done.

David triggered off one last barrage, targeted on Fallon's *Hauptmann*. "Now," he said.

Fighting the combined loss of two tons of armor and the raw impact of the *Devastator*'s twin gauss slugs, Karen Fallon rocked her control sticks back and forth to help balance out the struggling *Hauptmann*. Caution and warning lights fired off like ornaments on a Christmas tree, flashing for attention as alarms rang out deafening blasts.

What had been eighteen and a half tons of armor was more memory than material now, with most of the Battle-Mech's chest laid bare and her right arm attached by little more than a battered titanium humerus and some my-omer. The reactor shielding was breached, the heat sink ruptured, a reactor shutdown in progress. Fallon smashed a fist down on the override, risking ammunition explo-sions or even a critical reactor failure, but not about to be left powered down and helpless on this field.

She continued checking off damaged equipment. Guardian ECM suite destroyed. Medium pulse laser de-stroyed. Damn—autocannon feeding mechanism de-stroyed! Her Mech-killer weapon, hoarded for any final charge McCarthy might try, was effectively useless now, the ammunition she carried for it no better than a fused bomb, waiting to be lit off by one stray round into the magazine. She toggled for an ammunition dump, ejecting two and a half tons of twelve-centimeter ordnance out the rear ports, where it rained impotently over the ground.

Battlefield maintenance duties occupied her for all of three seconds, but it was long enough for McCarthy to move out of her forward shield. She twisted her 'Mech at the waist, leaning into the turn and tensing for the impact as her enemy came back into view and twin cascades of azure energy sparked and twisted out from the *Devasta-tor's* PPCs.

Passing wide and high, they struck at the KF Yare broadcast station.

One dug a molten furrow into the ferrocrete bunker, as likely to penetrate the geothermal station as a knife carv-ing on a DropShip's armor. The other, however, sliced into the titanium network of struts and girders that helped hold the massive dish aloft. And it wasn't alone. Two flights of long-range missiles pitted and pocked the struc-ture while a half-dozen jeweled laser beams lanced around or through other supports.

All across the enemy line, BattleMechs were turning aside from their duels to charge the broadcast station. One lance . . . two. A company! Still more! Fallon pinned an *Enforcer* under her sights as it leapt into the air, rocketing forward on jump jets with autocannon trained on the an-tenna. Twin lances of energy stabbed into its right leg, cutting the limb free while the 'Mech was in mid-flight and tumbling the jumping 'Mech off to the side.

No! She would not allow this. Not when she didn't know if her plan had brought down even one of the inbound Dragoons. Not while she commanded Evan's battalion. "Pull south—fall back!" she ordered. "Keep between them and the broadcast station. Hit them now and hit them hard!"

Yanking her throttle into full reverse, she walked her *Hauptmann* back into the shadow of the titanic dish, lasers scouring the militia line as it continued to advance. A *Penetrator* and an *Orion* paced her, the ad hoc lance she'd formed on the last regroup. Evan's *Cerberus*, holding closer to the line's center, was also not too far away and could move quickly. Between them, they had the firepower to tear apart the militia line. McCarthy had made his first— and last—critical mistake.

And Karen Fallon knew how to exploit a person's mistakes.

Evan Greene ducked reflexively as a rogue flight of long-range missiles hammered in at him. His overhead antimissile system, its ammunition long spent, took the brunt of the damage and protected his cockpit as the *Cerberus* stumbled into the clear.

His sensors flashed only a cautionary light that they detected hostile 'Mechs nearby—no warning alarms of missile locks. Smiling at his good fortune, Evan took an extra second to line up a long-range gauss shot that smashed into the shoulder of David McCarthy's *Devastator*. He wasn't about to forget the enemy commander.

Then the militia line shifted. Like a card player reading the body language "tells" of his adversaries, Evan sensed the shift before the more obvious change of direction threw the remnants of his battalion into confusion. The *Devastator*, drawing lines of azure energy between its cannon and the antenna dish. The *Cestus*—the same one that had shielded McCarthy from many of Evan's attacks— shifting its path toward the broadcast station, followed by a jumping *Enforcer* and a hard-racing *Nightsky*.

Fallon was a solid five seconds behind him on reading the move but the first to issue a command, ordering the

Katzbalger MechWarriors to fall back and protect the station. Eván wanted to shout his exasperation. Now was the time to order a counterthrust into the flank of the militia. If he had been a second faster . . .

But there was no countermanding the general's order now. It would only confuse his people more, and they were already reeling from the several "changes in command" and the general policy of trading ground for time rather than hitting back with their entire strength. It was the bane of the RCT, it seemed, lacking the cohesive nature of the militia—the strength that allowed the enemy to work so well together and keep coming. Xander, Eván, Fallon—when had any of them ever truly worked together?

But if it was normally a weakness, right now it might be a strength, leaving open for Eván one final opportunity. While the majority of his command reacted blindly to the general's orders, he paced the militia's lead elements and tried to angle in for a head-to-head with David McCarthy. Bring down the enemy commander, and the drive might falter. If not, Eván would at least be in the midst of the militia, where he could wreak incredible damage. He wouldn't be caught cowering against the walls of the geothermal plant, trying to form one last defensive line.

Eván Greene was on the attack!

Stalking his *Cerberus* forward, he ran an intercept course with McCarthy's *Devastator*. The battalion officer continued to ignore him. Eván reached out with his gauss rifles, spending two of his last eight nickel-ferrous slugs. One slammed into each arm, spoiling McCarthy's aim and wrenching the left arm back, where it froze in place. Eván selected for a single shot, tying in his medium lasers as they came within range, but this time the *Cestus* was back, moving into the way and taking the devastating assault itself.

Neither militia 'Mech bothered to return fire, a situation that began to anger Eván Greene. "Fight me, McCarthy," he muttered. "Fight me, damn you."

He throttled the *Cerberus* up to its full speed of sixty kilometers per hour, racing along parallel to the militia movement, trying to get in front of it as he closed with Fallon's position. The antenna dish rose before him, towering better than twenty stories high over its base on the low, ferrocrete bunker. Eván spared it hardly a thought, noticing only that it blocked Kathil's bright sun as he stepped into its shadow and cut in sharply, planning to come up against McCarthy at point-blank range.

Until twin emerald lances slashed over his head and chest, burning through armor and into the interior of the *Cerberus*. The assault machine shook as if poleaxed, tossing Eván against his seat restraints. The acrid smell of ionized air and scorched metal reached him, the near-miss against his cockpit breaching nearby armor and filling the tight confines with a sooty gray smoke.

The *Cestus*, its aim no longer on the broadcast dish, landed in front of Eván on jets of fiery plasma. He hadn't figured on McCarthy's lancemate meeting his charge, and had ignored the 'Mech's approach until it was almost too late. Now, in a knee-jerk reaction, he stabbed down on both main triggers, hitting the *Cestus* with every weapon at his disposal. Gauss slugs mashed into and through the right torso, caving in one ammunition bin and hopefully robbing the *Cestus* of its remaining gauss ammunition. Eván's lasers worried armor into molten streams and puddles all over the other machine, costing it at least a solid ton of protection.

Still, the *Cestus* stood up under the attack, bobbling only slightly as it fired back with a pair each of large- and medium-scale lasers. Emerald fire sliced his arm at the elbow, and the gauss rifle dropped uselessly to the ground. Eván stumbled a step back, again surprised by the ferocity of the assault.

He throttled into a backward walk, still a hundred meters in front of Fallon's lance and with plenty of room to fall back. He dropped his targeting reticle over the *Cestus'* outline and lit into the other 'Mech with his remaining gauss gun and lasers as the crosshairs burned from red to the gold of a solid lock. Fallon had always horned into Eván's challenges, and Xander Barajas had attacked McCarthy's family rather than take on the major directly. Generals Weintraub and Sampreis were equally devious, hiding behind whichever political leader was convenient at the time. Did no one fight his own battles but him?

Then a groan of stressed metal echoed over the field

and turned into a tortured shriek that grated on Eván like
fingernails across a slate. The shadows in which he stood
lengthened, shook, expanded. He twisted the *Cerberus* on
its turret-style waist, turning to glance up at the broadcast
antenna, unbelieving at first.

Unbelieving, until he saw the massive dish actually
move.

Several thousand tons of metal, even when suspended
on a huge network of supports and gearing, did not move
without a tremendous effort. But there were few forces
more persuasive than gravity. Supports, weakened by the
constant barrage of militia firepower, buckled and twisted,
the dish swinging backward and down toward the battlefield. It fell over the bunker building that housed the geothermal plant, crushing one wall before rolling on its
rounded back toward the ground.

Eván Greene was no longer watching—he did not need
to see the dish land on Karen Fallon's *Hauptmann* or the
remaining 'Mechs in his old command lance to know that
they were almost certainly dead. He shoved his throttle
forward, reversing his direction and gambling on his assault 'Mech's better-than-average speed. The *Cestus* that
had knocked Eván back from his charge was airborne,
rocketing up, over, and behind the *Devastator*. In fact, all
of the militia BattleMechs were retreating to the *Devastator*'s backfield as McCarthy's assault machine remained
rooted in place—waiting for his people.

McCarthy's stubbornness in standing firm promised
them safety as they fled past his position, an assurance
that he wouldn't sacrifice one of them to save himself. It
reminded Eván of Karen Fallon's comment that directing
the victory was just as glorious as firing the final shot
yourself. And as the network of twisted, stress-fractured
girders collapsed over him in a final, shrieking cacophony
of tortured metal, knocking the *Cerberus* forward, Eván's
last action in his 'Mech was to reach for his ejection
controls.

He did so with the knowledge that David McCarthy,
without destroying either 'Mech personally, had defeated
both General Fallon and himself.

30

FCWS Robert Davion
Near Orbit, Kathil
Capellan March, Federated Commonwealth
7 December 3062

Six different DropShips were now making a run for Kathil, vessels friendly to the militia trying to cover the First Capellan Dragoons as the regiment made its final stab at the planet. The *Robert Davion* tracked them, painting the ships into the holographic tank and trailing their paths of flight out behind them. If they converged on Kathil in their current pattern, they would hit the atmosphere at six different points, only one of which fell close to the WarShip's location. A seventh also looked like it would pass fairly close, the track of the returning *Guardian* and its Octopus escort, but that one Kerr could ignore.

He bared his teeth and gripped his chair's armrests so tightly that his arm muscles quivered. At best he might be able to smash two of the inbound DropShips. At worst, he would spread his efforts too thin and fail to cripple either. Just then, Kerr would have offered up the Archon to her brother Victor for a full crew and maybe a decent screen of fightercraft to herd the enemy into his killing zones.

But he didn't have either, and Kerr didn't intend to allow the *Robert Davion*'s first battle to come to a lackluster end. The vessel tracking closest to his WarShip was a Dragoon DropShip—an *Overlord*, carrying a full battalion of the BattleMech regiment. They would be his target. His prey.

His victory.

"Admiral, we've lost readings on the Yare microwave broadcast beam," Chief Watson reported. "It's gone silent."

Kerr grunted acknowledgment, staring hard at the holotank. So Yare was finally leaving the battle to him—so much the better. The indiscriminate energy broadcasts had done some damage to the vessels supporting the militia, but in the end it could only rob the *Robert Davion* of her due glory.

"Lower!" he yelled at the helmsman. Petty Officer Erikson was sweating profusely, trying to nudge the large WarShip up against Kathil's atmosphere. It was a dangerous maneuver for such a large vessel. At the relative speeds between planet and WarShip, and its angle of approach, hitting the atmosphere would be akin to flying an aerospace fighter into the side of a space station. The station's armor might give, but you wouldn't recognize what was left of the fighter.

Admiral Kerr stared at the holotank, watching as the Dragoon *Overlord* attempted to change course. The track of light trailing after it warped ever so slightly, a change verified when Chief Watson read out its slight shift in velocity.

It would not be enough, though. The Dragoons' momentum was too great; they were coming into Kathil on a hard burn, pulling at least three gravities of deceleration. Momentum allowed you to turn only so far, and the *Overlord*'s impetus committed it to a narrow range of approach angles. They might push themselves several klicks one way or the other, but the *Robert Davion*'s reach spanned hundreds of kilometers when one took into account the intercept capability of its naval-class Killer Whale and Barracuda missiles.

"They can't do it," he said, his voice confident. In his mind he quickly replotted the *Overlord*'s maximum deflection and the reach of his WarShip. "They can't escape our range."

"No," Deborah Watson confirmed. "They can't."

"Stand by, missile bays," Kerr ordered. "Plot intercept paths and wait for my order to fire." He was seconds away from an overpowering strike. Kerr would reduce a full third of the Dragoons to free hydrogen in space, and then he would link up with Weintraub and find ways to support the general's war with tactical bombardment. Very soon now, the Archon-Princess would once again have undisputed control over Kathil.

"Change in secondary target path," Watson called out, her voice shifting from a confident edge to confusion and then to alarm. "Ad—admiral! The *Guardian* is shifting track!"

Of course it was. A wounded DropShip, even an old *Excalibur*-class refitted as an assault ship, was not about to trade broadsides with a state-of-the-art WarShip. Why would Watson sound so worried? Kerr glanced at the track of the *Guardian* and the space tug, saw the line bend . . .

Inward, toward the *R. Davion!*

"Detachment!" Watson called out as she punched the two vessels over to a main viewscreen. The *Excalibur* continued on its own drive flare, set on a ballistic course as Kathil's gravity worked to bend it around toward the WarShip. The Octopus rolled over ninety degrees, its own drive straining to push the tug away from the destruction-bound assault ship.

"Damn their intrusion!" Kerr shouted. To the enlisted man manning weapons, he ordered, "All starboard batteries, track that bastard Liao of a DropShip captain and pay her my kindest respects. Cut that vessel open and spill her guts to space!" The enlisted man began to relay the order.

"Why isn't she tracking us?" Watson asked no one in particular. "No active sensors at all; it's like she's a dead ship. Like . . . there's no one aboard." Her face twisted in horror. "Admiral! I think they mean . . . I think they mean to . . ." She couldn't seem to get it out.

Kerr read her meaning in her voice, though, and he watched in growing alarm as the *Guardian*'s track slowly came around to point unerringly at the large icon that was the Federated Commonwealth WarShip *Robert Davion*. Watson slowly stood, eyes riveted on the main screen

where the *Guardian* was steadily growing larger. "Oh . . .
my . . . God . . ."

"Fire!" Kerr screamed at his weapons man. "All guns,
full broadside! Fire, damn you all, fire!"

It was the admiral's last command, given on what was
effectively a dead ship.

The *Robert Davion*'s naval-grade lasers speared out brilliant
shafts of light, drilling into the nose of the *Excalibur*-class
DropShip. A pair of hastily launched Barracuda missiles
managed to clip the side of the *Guardian*. Banks of particle
projection cannon and waves of regular missiles followed
them in, hammering at the large DropShip in a last-ditch
attempt to turn it from its course. Fragments and molten
globules of armor swirled out from the critical wounds,
and what little atmosphere remained to the *Guardian*
burned in quick flashes before being dissipated to
vacuum.

And through that cloud of debris, the *Guardian* plowed
onward. As Admiral Jonathan Kerr had noted earlier, the
impetus of a space-borne vessel was not something that
could be shifted lightly.

The weapons discharge did slow the *Guardian* by a
small fraction and pushed it aside by perhaps half a degree. Over greater distances, that tiny change could result
in kilometers of difference. In fact, left to itself, it would
have eventually caught the edge of Kathil's atmosphere,
ripping the vessel apart and scattering it into a debris
field.

Would have, except that the *Robert Davion* stood in its
way.

Sixteen thousand tons of DropShip under a near-
constant acceleration of one standard gravity over several
hours built up a formidable amount of kinetic energy—
enough to instantly obliterate both vessels in a perfect environment. Such was not the case here, as the *Guardian*
rammed the *R. Davion* amidships and nowhere near
square on.

Even a glancing blow, however, imparted enough energy to shear away a full third of the *Guardian* and snap
the back of the eight-hundred-meter WarShip. The *Robert
Davion* actually folded slightly as the DropShip smashed

into and through its spine. The engineering section, containing its massive fusion drive, twisted twelve degrees off the regular axis of the WarShip; it would be the first part of the *R. Davion* to strike Kathil's atmosphere, thirty seconds later.

The *Guardian*, its drive flare finally extinguished for good, deflected off the atmosphere, the impact all but crushing the gutted hulk before it spun off into the dark, cold embrace of Kathil's solar system. The *Robert Davion*'s death was nowhere near as quiet. Its drive section now dragging in the atmosphere, the WarShip shuddered and pulled around so violently that a new rent opened in the forward third of the vessel—the structure fracturing as it was subjected to stresses it was never meant to bear. And as the entire ship fell into Kathil's atmosphere, tumbling, the unshielded armor glowing red and trailing out behind in a fiery tail, the WarShip finally broke into three large pieces.

The nose of the vessel dove down at the steepest angle, the heat melting its armor into white-hot slag. What was left by the time it hit the planet struck Kathil's ocean far southeast of the continent of Thespia. Its impact flash-boiled millions of gallons of seawater into steam and raised a fifty-meter tidal wave that swept around the world. By the time it hit Thespia, fortunately, most of its power had been lost, and it amounted to a single rogue wave only three meters high—enough to inundate the streets of two coastal cities, but the loss of life was minimal.

Not so lucky were the small townships of midwestern Muran, a timber-producing territory. Thousands of acres of forestland and the buildings of one village were flattened by the shock wave as the crumpled drive section flashed by and then buried itself in the heart of the Ironback Mountains. The quakes that resulted caused even more destruction and woke up Mount Daffyd. The eruption of the dormant volcano spilled lava over more timberland and, though too far from the local townships to threaten them directly, rained heavy ash over them for days and prompted the abandonment of two smaller villages.

That left only the middle section of the once-mighty

Robert Davion, the section that had contained Admiral Kerr's command bridge. All commands now silenced forever, the ruined section tumbled through the upper atmosphere longer than the others, shedding a wide debris field. Its bulk finally plummeted to Kathil and struck in the deserts of Thespia, far from any inhabited area and eventually forgotten. As to its detritus, some of it would remain scattered in a permanent orbit over Kathil, a hazard to satellites and small craft. The rest fell out of the sky over the next several months in a brilliant display of shooting stars that children wished upon.

Progeny

CMM Staging Ground
Radcliffe, Kathil
Capellan March, Federated Commonwealth
10 December 3062

The two infantrymen, dressed in field camouflage and with their rifles held at port arms, looked very much out of place in the white, antiseptic environment of the militia's on-base hospital. In a place of healing and rest, such military alertness would always stand out.

Eván Greene left his own escort at the door, and nodded at the two guards, noting their confused frowns as he went in. They had their orders to let him pass, though they obviously also had their doubts. Fair enough, Eván decided—he had yet to put his own reservations to rest.

Karen Fallon lay in the room's only bed, one leg up in traction and her chest so heavily taped she might as well have been in a body cast. She glared at him, her brilliant blue eyes drawn into cat-like slits. The fact that she had survived the broadcast dish rolling over her assault 'Mech, crushing it into an unrecognizable mass, should not have surprised him. Fallon was a survivor. She always seemed to have a way out.

"What are you doing here, Eván?" she said tightly.

He produced a scraggly bouquet of flowers, purchased on his way through the lobby. Their light scent barely made a dent in the room's disinfectant smell. "I wanted to check on you, Karen." Not "General." She noticed the informality and frowned daggers at him. He shrugged. "McCarthy owed me that much."

"Traitor," she spat.

Eván feigned a wounded look and tossed the flowers onto the foot of her bed. She looked much smaller and more fragile than she had in the field. This was the woman he had hoped would elevate his career? When it came to choices, he had made a poor one in following Karen Fallon.

"You'd have a hard time convincing a military court of that," he said, glancing back at the door. "And I don't see you getting that chance anytime soon. You're about as dangerous as a newborn kitten, and they already have your door double-guarded."

Fallon curled her lip in disgust at his choice of comparisons. "You're working for McCarthy," she accused him, as if that said it all.

No, he wasn't—though maybe he should have been. Eván remembered the clarity of his sudden realization that he and Fallon had conspired to let McCarthy beat them in Yare—by not working together, by each looking after himself, while McCarthy worked with his entire unit to carry the day. Eván had never worried about his own unit. Not really. If he had, perhaps he would have curbed Xander Barajas. Perhaps he would not have abandoned his people so willingly to Fallon's schemes in Yare.

Yes, he remembered that moment of clarity and fear as he smashed down on the ejection controls, the cockpit of his *Cerberus* splitting open with the explosive charges and his command chair rocketing up on a brief tongue of flame. He had felt the rush of heavy wind as the broadcast dish collapsed behind him, crushing his 'Mech into scrap. One support had nearly impaled him as it rebounded from the ground, spearing halfway through the back of his chair as it deployed the parafoil and glided him safely over the destruction.

And over the *Devastator*, which had held its ground in the face of the collapsing structure. By Eván's estimate, the dish had buried itself into the ground not fifty meters from McCarthy's feet. McCarthy never made any move to retreat.

"I'm working for myself," Eván finally admitted. "As I always have. And right now that does mean cooperating with our victors. Better than spending my time pacing a ten-meter-square cell. And I hear things. Like how the battles are progressing, for instance."

She so obviously wanted to ask, and fought with herself for several long seconds before giving in. "So what about the Dragoons? Did they make it down?"

"Most of them," Eván told her. "They lost an auxiliary DropShip with armor support and weapon stockpiles—the WarShip got that before it hit the atmosphere. You took out three DropShips but missed the main prize." He shook his head. "The Dragoons bit into the Katzbalger like the dogs of war unleashed. From what I'm hearing, we've suffered three reversals in the past few days."

"Even with Duke VanLees condemning them for joining the militia?" she asked in surprise.

"Weintraub lost Duke VanLees. While we were fighting at Yare, General Sampreis raided District City. I understand the fighting knocked a few corners off the Hall of Nobles. VanLees is here in Radcliffe now, though the general still holds the Duke's family hostage against his good behavior. Sampreis failed to bring them all out."

A spark of fire returned to Fallon's blue eyes. "That will be enough to keep VanLees in line, then. And Mitchell will rally the RCT. We can hold District City at least long enough to get reinforcements."

"Maybe," Eván said. "But the militia can summon more forces too. They're not about to fold, Karen. Get used to that idea. And no matter who comes out on top, you'd better be ready to stand trial for your actions at Yare. I doubt General Weintaub or the Archon wants anything to do with that disaster." He leaned in. "The difference is, Morgan Hasek-Davion didn't lose."

He watched Fallon's face collapse as she came to the realization that her failure at Yare had opened her to prosecution. The winners write the history, and he was right: she was no Morgan Hasek-Davion.

"Eván," she called out, stopping him as he turned toward the door. "Is that all you came here for? Truly?

You could have let me find out the news from someone else.''

"I could have," he said. "But we both know, General, that I prefer to do things myself." He smiled thinly. "This was just one more opportunity."

Huntress' morning fog had dissipated, seemingly burned from the air by the intense wash of energies playing out over the battlefield. The ground smoldered where weapons had gouged into formerly pristine earth. The metal corpses of fallen BattleMechs stretched out under the first hint of sun.

The *Kingfisher* spat a flurry of ruby darts from its pulse lasers, runneling the last of David's armor to the ground and digging deep into his left side. The destructive energy fused together the barrels of his particle projection cannon and laser and then cut deeper to destroy their focusing lenses as well. David came back with everything left to him, knowing he could not stand up under another barrage like that one. His gauss rifles delivered his last two nickel-ferrous slugs into the *Kingfisher*'s chest.

He knew it wasn't enough.

The *Kingfisher* kept on its feet, savaged to the point of ruin but determined to bring its enemy down with it. David glanced once at his ejection controls before bracing himself for the next salvo, waiting for his own weapons to cycle. He mashed down his triggers, hoping at least one weapon might fire before the OmniMech tore him apart.

Seeing the short flight of missiles scream past him to corkscrew into the *Kingfisher*, it took David several long heartbeats to remember that his *Devastator* did not carry missiles at all. The realization came just as his own weapons cycled free and he wrenched his crosshairs over the Omni's outline . . .

"Only to watch it tumble backward. Its reactor didn't let go, but I saw that telltale flash and knew it was a near thing. The emergency dampening fields came down just in time."

David could picture those final moments clearly as he recounted them to the remnants of his battalion. He'd forced a backward step out of his nearly ruined *Devastator* and turned to see Sergeant Fletcher's *Stealth* stagger over from the dead *Masakari,* wisps of gray smoke wreathing its missile launcher. Darker, oily smoke piled above Mac-Dougal's *Stealth*—he and Hauptmann Kennedy had been the Uhlans' last casualties of the day. Polsan had miraculously survived his point-blank meeting with the *Daishi,* and the three of them could now begin the task of looking for survivors.

"We found only a few," David said, his eyes distant as he regarded the battlefield of Huntress in his mind. "Four of ours, three of theirs. The Jaguars had disconnected their ejection features. The ones who lived did so despite their best efforts to die fighting."

The briefing room lay still, silent. Tara Michaels held hands with Corporal Smith, the slight breach in military etiquette ignored as everyone paid homage to the sacrifice of the Uhlans, trying to understand the legacy of Huntress. That legacy belonged to them, now—McCarthy's Marauders.

Amanda Black had already heard the story, privately, and was studying the others along with David. Though she had taken herself permanently off the active combat roster, she remained in charge of unit training and most personnel matters. In that she worked closely with Tara, who had been promoted to battalion exec.

I'll never be sure whether I gave up on myself too soon. David remembered Amanda's words before the fight at Yare. Now she knew.

And so did he.

In that agonizing time, between Huntress and Kathil, David had questioned himself to the point of almost believing he had, letting the guilt of his survival chip away at his confidence and self-esteem. But the memories of Huntress had bothered him less and less as the fighting between the militia and the Eighth RCT came to a head. In the command ceremony for his medal of valor, David had finally allowed himself to begin grieving for the fallen. And as he grew closer to his unit here on Kathil, they had begun to replace the empty billets in his mind. Many of them had been lost as well, but the fight wasn't over yet.

David hadn't given up. Nor was he about to, with the Capellan Dragoons on station helping the Kathil CMM roll back many of the Eighth RCT's advances. They could hold on now, and maybe eventually push the Katzbalger off Kathil entirely.

They weren't through fighting—not yet. But David still had hope that calmer heads might prevail.

The trivid viewer washed to life in a haze of blurred color and soft lines, snapping to a crisp image of the ComStar crest. The hovovid, delivered only an hour before by HPG, was now playing all across Kathil on every station. There had been a number of rumors, but no one could say for certain what they were about to hear. Some people thought it might be the Archon's public condemnation of George Hasek. Others hoped for better news.

They hoped in vain.

The ComStar crest faded to black, to be replaced by the sword-and-sun insignia of the old Federated Suns. The digital picture segued into an actual flag stretched across a wall, backing a podium. The national colors were edged in black, a sign of mourning, and Prince Victor Steiner-Davion stood at the podium, hands gripping either side as he stared straight into the eyes of the viewer. He wore the full military dress of the Armed Forces of the Federated Suns, a uniform last worn—officially—during the rule of his father. Conspicuously absent was almost every decoration, award, or ribbon to which he was entitled. Only the rank badge of field marshal and the crest of the Suns graced the uniform.

"Good citizens of the Federated Commonwealth," he began. "I regret many things. I regret that the Commonwealth has failed, destroying my parents' dream for a grand union. I regret that I ever found it necessary to leave you in order to put an end to the Clan invasion." His voice tightened, edged in resolve. "I regret that my sister, Katherine, has a hunger for power that continues to demand destruction, bloodshed, and lives.

"Those are my regrets," he said, "yet still I had hope. I wanted peace for you all. That is why I stepped aside and accepted a post with ComStar. This is why I left Katherine on the throne. But any hope for peace died with my brother Arthur, killed two days ago in what can only be described as a vicious terrorist attack."

Victor paused, his military bearing almost slipping for an instant, but he composed himself again quickly. "Arthur was a soldier," he continued. "A good man. And he was learning to become a leader of men, women, and worlds. For that, someone believed he had to die.

"Arthur's murder underscores the fighting already taking place on worlds such as Kathil, Nanking, and Kentares. His ghost reminds me"—a hint of anger and pain animated Victor's face—"that I have allowed a power-mad ruler to sit on the throne. Someone who strikes with violence against her own family. Someone who betrays the trust put in us by the citizens of both Commonwealth states. His ghost points to people who want freedom, liberty, justice. And it points to the necessity of resuming my rightful responsibilities.

"I can no longer abandon my duty. The problems plaguing us have been ignored too long. Now we must live with the results. We must take measure of the differences that continue to divide my sister from me and my people from each other. Yes, I have regrets. And my deepest regret is that no other course is left for us.

"Nothing," he said heavily, "but war."

Bushwacker

Hauptmann

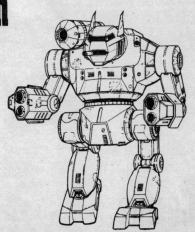

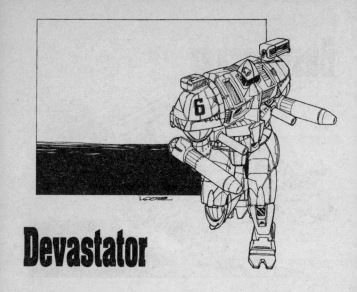

Devastator

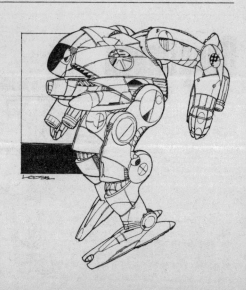

Cestus

Cerberus

Falconer

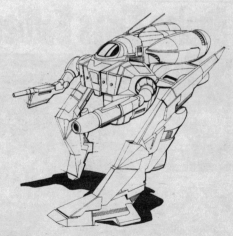

Challenger X MBT

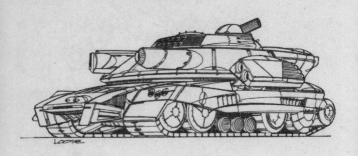

Avalon Class Battlecruiser

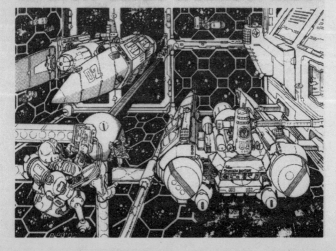

About the Author

Loren L. Coleman lives in the Pacific Northwest state of Washington with his wife, three children, and a trio of Siamese cats.

Coleman began writing fiction in high school, but it wasn't until his final year in the United States Navy that he began it as a serious career. Since that time he has published short fiction, on-line chapter serials, and nine novels. Much of his work to date has been set in the BattleTech® universe, where he chronicles the political machinations and military conquests of the thirty-first century. He has also worked for computer game companies on such projects as *MechWarrior 4* and *MechCommander*.

Flashpoint is Coleman's sixth novel in the BattleTech® series. His others include *Double-Blind, Binding Force, Threads of Ambition, Killing Fields,* and *Illusions of Victory*. He has also written novels for the Vor™ series and the Crimson Skies™ series based on the Microsoft computer game.

PENGUIN PUTNAM INC.
Online

Your Internet gateway to a virtual environment with
hundreds of entertaining and enlightening books
from Penguin Putnam Inc.

*While you're there, get the latest buzz on
the best authors and books around—*

Tom Clancy, Patricia Cornwell, W.E.B. Griffin,
Nora Roberts, William Gibson, Robin Cook,
Brian Jacques, Catherine Coulter, Stephen King,
Ken Follett, Terry McMillan, and many more!

**Penguin Putnam Online is located at
http://www.penguinputnam.com**

PENGUIN PUTNAM NEWS

Every month you'll get an inside look at our upcom-
ing books and new features on our site. This is an
ongoing effort to provide you with the most
up-to-date information about
our books and authors.

Subscribe to Penguin Putnam News at
http://www.penguinputnam.com/newsletters